NEWBORN PINK

MIDLAND TALES BOOK 1

SHAWN WAYNE LANGHANS

This yarn is dedicated to my good friend Brad Jones who spoke to the ghosts in his grandfather's cabin and left this world long before any of us were ready. I remember trying to explain the plot of this story as I was writing it two weeks before you passed away. I really miss you bud, but I know your parents miss you more than I can ever fathom. So, this novel is also dedicated to you Tammy, and to you as well Jeff. I'm sorry for the cruel things I said, Mr. Jones.

This one is also dedicated to all of my grandparents, living and dead, and all of your grandparents too!

PART 1

———

"When people are ready to, they change. They never do it before then, and sometimes they die before they get around to it. You can't make them change if they don't want to, just like when they do want to, you can't stop them."
— Andy Warhol

THE TALKING HEADS

And What They Said

"Good morning, Midland! We're here with some good news for all you out there that are sick of this dreary rainfall-"

"Tesla stocks are on the rise again since the multi-billion-dollar merger with Ama-"

"In local news the Midland Robins have won the state playoffs-"

"From farm to table might be an outdated saying in the near future what with the rise of the lab-grown meat industry. We're with Pea Tree Farms spokesman, Arnold Workman who is here to talk about the launch of their newest product-"

"Hey there Midland, it's Primo Perry here at Perry's Primo BMW with some exciting news for you!"

"-study shows that the radiation could be coming from the Chumquah fields, however these reports are disputed by the tribe-"

"-and KGVT News will be back after these brief messages from our sponsors, Pea Tree Farms-"

The bartender, having heard enough of the same-old same-old, turned the flatscreen television off, and awaited his nightly patrons. While he put away the last of the pint glasses, the door chimed with the entry of two friends. First came the dentist, then appeared the weatherman, and not long after that the prior shared with the latter a story about a man.

A very loveable, albeit very ugly man.

ITS STARTS IN A DENTAL ENGINE

And Ends In A Field Of Meat

The man in white poked across his mouth, and the patient swallowed. "No doc, not there," he tried to say, but with the various metal tools in his mouth, the statement came out without consonants. "Ohh ocgh, odd 'ere."

"Can you open just a little wider? Just a little bit more."

The dentist seemed to be asking Paulie to dislocate his jaw. "I'm not as young as I used to be," he wanted to joke, knowing that were he to attempt to say that he'd likely spray the dentist with saliva and only be able to pronounce the vowels. Instead, he stretched his mouth open, feeling that same painful click he'd been experiencing every time he yawned. A squishy pop, not unlike pressing down on the base of your thumb with your opposite hand's pointer finger and other thumb.

"Quap," his temporomandibular joint said, quietly, while he accidentally gleeked his spittle on the dentist's face shield.

"Okay, now hold that. Hold. Right there is perfect," he said, ignoring the saliva sliding down the clear plastic separating

Paulie Galamb and his dentist. Paulie tried hard to focus on the spit itself, and not the mole under the dentist's left eye. It looked like a tiny inverted square tear or maybe the state of Indiana, painted freckle brown. He was not sure.

Thoughts of Indiana left his mind when the dentist poked something soft, something spongy. Something that was most certainly not made of tooth. Something certainly not wanting to be poked or prodded. Paulie made this clear by yelping under his breath and coughing the dentist's hands from his mouth. For a moment, Paulie thought he heard the dentist whispering into his mouth, but he was not sure.

"Well, it's not an infected pocket. In fact, there's hardly a pocket at all. Mostly just the fresh regards of future scar tissue," the dentist reassured him, placing one tool down and grabbing another. Paulie half-glanced at the metal tool in his hand and couldn't help but imagine it as some kind of double-sided fish-hook with a pen-sized metal rod between each stabbing implement. Was this the Gracey Curette or the Curved Sickle Scaler?

He only knew these names because before his visit he wanted something to distract him while this man fooled around in his mouth-hole or lack thereof. Earlier in the week he had borrowed a trivia book that only captured his attention when he flipped to a page about the various odd names of dental equipment. There he took it upon himself to learn the names of the tools of his mouth-hole doctor's trade.

With one hand, the dentist stuffed the mouth mirror back in the deep-far-down area where his wisdom tooth used to sleep undisturbed for forty years before some unexpected pocket of pus formed and inflated and forced this man to pluck the sneaky bonus bones from his jaw. The infection had pushed on the slumbering wisdom tooth, which pushed on his molars, on his canines and incisors. For forty years, his teeth had been good enough for television, but after this muck-up, he was considering orthodontic assistance. Right now, he was considering pushing away the doctor, and leaving this place, but he knew the pain would only follow him home.

"However, I am also seeing no signs of scarring or tissue damage, which only concerns me," he said, putting emphasis on the word 'damage' by poking him somewhere in the back half of his throat with the Curette or the Scaler, "because I am also not seeing any evidence that there ever was a wisdom tooth here."

With his mouth once again dentist free, Paulie used it to form words with both consonants and vowels used in unison. "Well, that doesn't make a lick of sense."

"You're not wrong, Mr. Galamb. As I recall, I was the one that plucked that pesky poker out of you less than two weeks earlier."

Paulie remembered. It had been less than two weeks. Nine days by his count. It was high on his list of his most painful experiences ever experienced in his forty-seven years of life. Worse than the double-clavicle break of sophomore year. Worse than his first and second hernia. Worse even, than his divorce five years earlier. For him anyway. He imagined Toni was doing just fine wherever she was in Central City at this point.

But the pain of having that damn tooth pulled nine days ago was not as bad as having his catheter being removed by his angry father when he was seventeen, after Paulie had drunkenly crashed his dad's Volkswagen into his dad's wood-working shop.

"Yeah, don't remind me. After that, I called about the dry socket a few days later but that disappeared after four days. But then the swelling just never went down. I mean, how long does it usually take for this to heal?"

"Mr. Galamb, perhaps I haven't made myself clear. I am

not seeing any signs that I pulled a tooth from your mouth. No scar tissue, no hole."

"Then why am I feeling the same pressure still? I can feel it when I yawn, when I chew, when I swallow."

Not that he had been chewing much lately. In nine days since he had his bastard wisdom tooth removed his diet had mostly consisted of blended meals. Swallowing had grown so painful that he had taken to eating like a duck, by staring up at a lightbulb while he poured the liquid meals down his gullet, trying to not choke and his spray his liquid food about while he did it.

It had been greatly affecting his work, his livelihood, as a food product tester.

Try to imagine testing a revolutionary new lab-grown meat product that had to be blended into a liquidy pulp just so you could judge it by its flavor and imagine the look on your boss's face when he has to tell the lab-coats that the results were non-conclusive because you gagged on the slurry when you tried to swallow it. Sue Ellen, his supervisor, having to send him home because he couldn't do his job.

Imagine the embarrassment you'd experience if your boss refused to allow you back to work until you saw a dentist again. Or a specialist. Whatever it would take to get those tastebuds back to tip-top shape.

Not that his pain affected his taste buds, no, he could still taste his pain.

The doctor put the back of his blue-gloved hand to Paulie's forehead, "Well, you don't seem to have a fever," Do dentists use thermometers? "But I do believe the back of your jaw is quite swollen. I'm not sure if it's your lymph nodes, no, too far back, or if maybe it's a keloid. Most likely that," he said without an air of certainty.

"What's a keloid, doc?"

The doctor set his tools down on the tray, with Paulie being able to name the obvious Tartar Scraper next to the Dental Pick and Probe, next to the Mouth Mirror. Though he was still unsure whether that last one was a Gracey Curette or the Curved Sickle Scaler. The doctor turned his back on Paulie, took his face shield off, and changed his cloth mask underneath it.

"A keloid is, hm, essentially an angry piece of scar tissue. However, the lump over the area where your wisdom tooth had been pulled doesn't look like your typical keloid. It's, how do I say, larger than I am comfortable with. Normally I would expect to see a convex indentation or a slight divot. At the very least, I would expect to see the stitch marks."

"But?"

"But here, I see nothing. And instead of convex, I am seeing concave. I see no evidence of stitches, no scars, just a mass," said the dentist, grabbing a prescription pad and a pen from his pocket.

"A mass?" Paulie asked, while the dentist scrawled out something on the pad of paper.

"I believe it to be a tumor, Mr. Galamb. However I am afraid that this is not my area of expertise. An X-ray from me may confirm my suspicions, but beyond that I am of little help for you further. I am going to recommend you to a specialist, just to be sure."

"What kind of specialist, Doctor?" Paulie asked, while staring at the freckle of Indiana under the dentist's left eye.

"I think it best for you to see Dr. Fejes. He's my wives' oncologist. I think you should see him about this mass in your throat. Could be nothing. Could be benign. You never know until you get it checked out," he said, handing Paulie a slip of paper. On the paper was the name, 'Doctor Joseph Fejes, Oncologist' followed by a phone number. Elsewhere on the paper was the phrase, 'Medical Prescription Form' and the letters 'RX' in the corner.

"Oncologist," Paulie said solemnly. "That's the cancer doctor right."

The dentist used his foot to press the pedal on the dental engine, raising Paulie from the dead like some kind of ugly Frankenstein's monster. "I'm afraid so. Now I don't mean to worry you, Mr. Galamb, I just think you should see Dr. Fejes as a precaution. Could be nothing. Could just be a pesky keloid. Yes, I'm sure that's all it is. I mean, I'm not sure. You should go see this man at your earliest convenience."

When Paulie sat up, he felt and heard his stomach gurgle, which the dentist heard as well. Paulie tried to hide his discomfort, but it was wildly apparent. You can't hide the Indiana birthmark any more than you can hide the fear in the face of a man who was just told "Maybe it's cancer?" Nor can you hide the hunger of a growling belly from a man who just had his hands down your mouth.

In lieu of the gurgles heard, the dentist stuck his hand in his pocket and plucked out a tiny red lollipop. He held his hand out to Paulie who was busy putting his jacket on.

"No thank you, doc."

"I insist. It's a red one. Red ones are my very favorite flavor. It'll cheer you up. Always works for me. I eat one of these every time I feel glum, and let me tell you in my line of work, that happens fairly often," the dentist said, smiling. It seemed disingenuous. Paulie couldn't help but appreciate how perfect this man's teeth were, any more than he couldn't help but glance at the freckled state of Indiana one last time before he left. Paulie reluctantly took the lollipop and made for the exit.

"Oh, one more thing, doctor," Paulie said, wanting to ask the dentist why he found himself so sad so often, but he realized he had no place. Instead, he asked about the metal things the dentist had put in his mouth.

"Yes?"

"That last tool," Paulie said, pointing at the small aluminum tray, "Was that a Gracey Curette or the Curved Sickle Scaler?"

The dentist gazed down at the tray of tools and used one gloved finger to stir them. As he swirled his finger around the sharp tools, moving them about in no particular order, he said "I really don't know anymore, Mr. Galamb."

Paulie quietly left without a farewell, while the dentist continued to move his single finger through the tray of metal dental tools, longingly. The dentist, he stared until he knew not what he was looking at. I'm afraid that if you look at a thing long enough, it loses all of its meaning. Semantic satiation in the physical sense. When the door closed behind him, the dentist pulled out three red lollies, hastily unwrapped them, and bit down hard on the lot of them with his dentures.

* * *

Later that night the dentist would stop by the Ol' Watering Hole for a drink or two or three with his good friend Tom. Tom Hedasky you probably knew from the ten o'clock news as Tornado Tom, a nickname earned by risking his life filming a twister back in his early days as a meteorologist. Together Tornado Tom and the dentist would probably not reflect on their dormitory days spent together nor the age difference between them nor would they talk about teeth or tornados.

Instead, they complained about their lives wasted, and their professions that most others hated. Nobody appreciated Tom for lying to them in front of a green screen, and nobody ever truly wanted to be lying in the dentist's chair, while they lied about how much they flossed their teeth and gums.

Here, they sat together as old friends here in mutual understanding of one another's self-loathing. These two men, they understood their roles in society. To be needed, but also that meant to be hated. Their professions were the crosses that they chose to bear.

The difference here was that the dentist was just getting off work, whereas the weatherman was due for work in an hour's time. The dentist peered at his reflection in the amber beer mirror below him, looking past the State of Indiana, and thought of his last patient.

"Tom, today I worked on the ugliest man I ever saw again. A real doozy of a face. It's haunting me right now."

"Oh yeah? Tell me about him," Tornado Tom said, looking at his own handsome face in his own amber beer. With the two of them staring at themselves, the dentist told the story of Paulie Galamb.

"He was a very honest man. That much can be said. He was among the very few to tell me he hasn't flossed since college, and Tom, let me tell you, I believed him." Thinking back to the stinking breath that no cloth mask or face shield could cover.

Somehow the dentist told details of this man that he had no right to know. Of where he lived, of how he lived, and that which lived inside him. Patiently the meteorologist listened while the dentist spun his yarn.

"You got a moment, Hedasky? Can I bend your ear for a moment?"

You got a moment, reader?

WE-STORE STORAGE

And Those Who Remain

Paulie was one of three legal residents at the We-Store Storage Units because he had been grandfathered in, so to speak. After so many years of living here it was only recently starting to feel off-putting. When he first bought the condo here six years ago, he had done so in an attempt to save his marriage, to give his wife just a little more space. A year after that purchase, his wife left him and then We-Store moved in. The storage company had offered everybody in the condominium complex a sizeable sum to get up and go, and almost everybody did.

Everybody except Paulie, Niles, and Edith. Normally, the company wouldn't allow three people to hold up the construction of a large multi-block storage complex, but their three condos were at the end of the giant structure and could be left standing without the company losing too much ground. We-Store still had to pay them out for the inconvenience of turning the rest of the condominium complex into a gated storage facility. The only catch for the three condo-owners was an agreement that they would rent a storage unit each. These rentals were conveniently located under their condos, in the area that had formerly been their individual garage ports.

Every morning Paulie left for work he would walk through the long twisting streets big enough for one vehicle to drive down, surrounded by a few hundred padlocked garage doors with no discernable difference between any of them other than the number above the door. He did not drive motor vehicles for no real reason, other than maybe he didn't deem it necessary here in this small town.

In this Midland, just about everyone either drove their own gas-guzzling car or sold all-electric vehicles at their respective places of employ. But for Paulie, a two-mile hike in mostly moderate weather each day did wonders for his awkwardly pear-shaped body.

After so many years, he had this labyrinth memorized. He could navigate himself through the We-Store Storage Unit's maze with his eyes closed if he wanted to.

And he sometimes did walk blindly through the maze to prove to himself that he could, assuming there were no customers present. Right now, he was busy juggling three-wheeled trash bins with two hands, awkwardly pulling them towards his home and the homes of his two neighbors, so he didn't allow himself the added challenge of doing this with closed eyes.

Occasionally he'd see someone putting boxes into their own storage unit or pulling boxes out and loading them in their cars. Pieces of furniture, mattresses, always coming and going. Every night he returned, he'd float through the dimly lit semi-streets once more, only this time the only souls that passed through here was his gruff one-legged neighbor Niles, the elderly Edith, and the occasional minimum wage security guard. I think his name is Ken or Kyle or Cal, but he's not important yet. Not until the end.

At the end of this labyrinth of two stories of garage doors you'd find the three homes at the end of the block. All three homes were located on the second story, with the first floor having been converted into storage units. Their former garage ports that they now paid a monthly fee to store their belongings in instead of owning outright.

Paulie didn't mind losing his tiny garage port, but Niles did. "That was my man-cave," Niles had argued a few years earlier. "It was all I had!" It was a pointless argument, Paulie knew, because technically We-Store had paid off their mortgages on the grounds that they paid full price for two storage units every month. One of those storage units being their old garages, and the other being an imaginary one where their homes currently sat. All and all, Paulie found it much more desirable to pay several thousand dollars less every year just to have fewer neighbors.

Not that he had many problems with his neighbors before the conversion, as he typically kept to himself. Niles and Edith, his neighbors of six years to his north and south, had simply become constants in his home life. Niles would gripe, and Edith would dote. Niles was the kind of man who would rather die with his blue jeans on, one leg and all, and Edith was the kind of lady who would fall in love with a man like that in a prior lifetime.

As he got closer to the end of the gated facility, he heard Niles' 80's hair metal music from half a block away. If you could call it a block.

When he turned the last corner, he saw the third to last storage unit door wide open, with vape-smoke billowing out just as visible as the Metallica was audible.

Niles poked his head out, his bald head glistening like a

freshly waxed bowling ball and greeted Paulie by pointing at him and glaring down his finger as if it were a gun with sights. His typical greetings, mind you. Paulie just lifted his limp left hand in a loose wave as he made his way towards the staircase past the three storage units. He added a fake, nervous smile at the end, to feign friendliness.

Paulie saw that Niles was balancing on his "Monday Leg" as he had called it.

Niles was in his own world beyond that acknowledgement. Just an old biker listening to his music, throwing his darts at the back wall of his storage unit, mostly pricking the drywall with tiny needle marks instead of hitting the board itself. He had a light beer in hand, and his oversized vape cartridge sticking out of his T-shirt sleeve like some sort of technologically advanced greaser. He used to spend most of his time at the biker bars down in Chumquah Flats but that was before he lost his good leg. That, and the local watering hole didn't quite tickle his fancy.

With his peg-leg and his pirate-like drunken sway, you'd expect a parrot on his shoulder. Instead, there sat an oversized snail about the size of a soggy, squishy grapefruit, deflated, who seemed to be stretching its eyes towards the vapor cloud Niles was exhaling.

Paulie didn't know much about the man, but he knew he had the snail for longer than Paulie had owned his condo. Why, though, he did not know.

The overwhelming smell of the fruity fog tickled Paulie's nose as he strolled past his own closed garage door, with the number 102 above it. To himself and no one else, Paulie wondered if pet snails could grow addicted to nicotine like anything else. Surely if beagles and chimpanzees could, why not Niles' disgusting lil' companion?

Past that was Edith's garage door, the contents within he never knew nor hardly pondered as he went up the stairs. He walked by the closed-curtained windows of his elderly neighbor's apartment, the last on the block. Beyond her was the end of the line, with nothing but a fence. Past that, a water tower. Without saying hello to Edith, he continued towards the second to last apartment on the block. His own.

He'd lie if he ever told you he was happy here, but Paulie Galamb wasn't much of a liar.

He wasn't happy. He was complacent. He was reminded of this every time he entered his empty home, as his wife of five whole years had left him for the same reason they had first agreed to wed. The dust on the motivational posters that covered his otherwise bare walls had grown thick, layers of dead skin and Paulie-particulates stacked on themselves, and he found himself unmotivated to clean it off.

Inside his condominium of complacency, there were no photographs of himself, nor were there any mirrors. When he brushed his once perfect teeth, perfect before the bastard wisdom tooth muddled up his already unpleasant face, he did so without staring at his reflection. This was by design, as both Paulie and the former Toni Galamb both acknowledged that they were not pleasing to the eyes. When he dressed himself for work, when he worked, he did so without confirming his appearance in any mirror. As long as he saw his shoes were on the right feet, the buttons all buttoned correctly, he was content. Consistency being key to his complacency.

He pulled the red lollipop out and tossed it in the recycling bin next to the trash can next to his dining room table that had plastic flowers on it, caked in dust thicker than the dust on the poster with the kitten that reminded him to hang in there. "Hang in where?" he sometimes contemplated, with the voice in his head responding, "Here." Here in the condominium-turned-storage facility, next to the only people he dared call barely friends, next to the only neighbors he had left.

Paulie noticed that Niles had turned his music down, revealing that Edith had her television volume cranked up to previously compensate. The not-so-recently deceased Alex Trebek was in the other room telling three contestants whether or not their questions were the correct ones to his answers. A man named Anton stood behind one pedestal, Klaus behind another, and someone named Afro behind the third. They were important, of course, but not as important as the search for a new Trebek. This was after a year of failed guest hosts didn't attract the ratings television execs sought, so they just went back to old reruns of Trebek and his digital ghost. If I could bring him back, I would. I swear to you.

(Maybe in the next story, Hedasky.)

He wouldn't bother knocking on her door to let her know the volume was too loud, because she was likely too deaf to hear his knocks, or fast asleep herself. That, and occasionally he liked to pretend to play along with Alex and his three contestants. Paulie didn't own a television, so he got his Jeopardy fix through these thin walls.

It was here, sandwiched between Jeopardy and Metallica, where Paulie considered the piece of paper in his pocket. His little gift from the dentist he had only seen thrice before. He didn't consider the lollipop in the recycling bin, or his poor aim when he threw it there and not in the trash bin.

He read the chicken scratch scrawl of the dentist and said the word "Oncologist" out loud between the cacophony of noise to his north and south. He said it over and over again while pacing inside his mirrorless abode. "Oncologist." Paulie paced from end to end of his condo, from east to west. from the sliding glass door that went to a segmented porch in the back he never used, through the kitchenette, past the dining room-ish, and into the micro-living room. "Oncologist." From the barely audible Metallica of his northern neighbor to the overly loud Jeopardy of the old woman to his south. "On-call-oh-jist," Paulie said one final time before the semantic satiation stole the definition from his mental dictionary.

Absentmindedly he added, "What is the medical profession for someone who specializes in cancer?" to no one in particular. The voice of the ghost of Trebek affirmed this.

"This is a no-shoe house," his ex-wife used to say, and out of habit he barely obliged. Paulie kicked his shoes off in the middle of his living room and made his way toward his dueling mini fridges in the kitchenette. One sat on top of the faux marble countertop that ran along the north wall, and the other sat in a pocket under the cabinet where once upon a time a dishwasher formerly lived. The one above contained the man's neutral foods, his plain seltzer waters, his gruel.

These were the foods he'd usually eat and "prepare" for himself every morning, for every lunch, while he worked. Flavorless nothing, as plain as plain could be, so as to not spoil his palette while he tested various new foods at Pea Tree Farms. Plain rice, unseasoned quinoa, unbuttered grits, a slurry of nearly gelatinous briquettes of oatmeal, unflavored corn-cakes, et cetera. All prepared and packaged in sealed Ziploc bags by the wonderfully bored Edith Post. All she ever asked was for help taking her trash-bins to the curb on Sunday, and return them on Monday, which he had just done.

The other fridge contained the foods he purged on in secret when he was done working for the weekend. The floor fridge was filled with little cardboard trays with segregated portions of mashed potatoes with artificial frozen pads of butter on top, next to a tray of overly salted green beans, next to a slab of ground-beef-themed meatloaf covered in some form of brown gravy. TV dinners. His cheat meals.

If Pea Tree Farms was the company that was going to revolutionize the future of the food world, then these TV Dinners were the ones who had done it in the past. Banquet's Meat Loaf Platter, Stouffer's Salisbury Steak with Gravy, Hungry Man Select's Mac-And-Cheese Dinner. Where Pea Tree Farms was reinventing the meat industry, these former giants had long ago reinvented the meal.

Alongside the stack of frozen trays was a dozen or so different canned beverages, strange flavored generic soda's that the big corporations wouldn't touch. These sodas and individually packaged meals were courtesy of 'Meals On Wheels', who delivered these dishes and off-brand drinks to Nathaniel Niles on account of his disability. Niles would then give most of them away to Paulie on the same condition as Edith.

He just asked that Paulie took his trash-bins to the street as well.

With Niles missing a leg, and Edith nearing eighty, Paulie didn't mind the extra chore of juggling three trash-bins down the twisting corridors of the storage unit facility. A trip that took about fifteen minutes there and back, nearly a mile of narrow streets to mosey through, twice a week for free food was a good deal when he could enjoy it. Back before the bastard tooth emerged out of nowhere after forty-seven years of hibernation, ruining his teeth, and nearly costing him his job.

Paulie placed the piece of paper on the upper fridge, wedging it between his breakfast, lunch, and dinner meals and a small magnet that had the insignia of the company he worked for on it. A small yellow and red laboratory flask with a black and white hanging plant shooting out the top. In the center was a small fleur-de-lis made up of peapods in the middle of the flask, above the words "Pea Tree Farms". Next to his dentist's note were other important notes, such as the due dates of his library books, his neglected vitamins list, his receipts proving he had paid his taxes last year, a picture of his favorite space shuttle, as well as a list of emergency contact phone numbers that was only five bullet points long. Two of which were no longer in service.

The other fridge, his useless fridge filled with solid deliciousness that he could not currently consume and tasty beverages he could not enjoy without something savory coating his stomach beforehand, had very few items attached to the front of it. Not because Paulie lacked magnets, of which I assure you he had plenty, but because the front of the fridge was not magnetic. Instead, it had a fake wood-paneling look to it, with the paneling itself being made of some kind of cheap plastic to which magnets could not adhere.

As he used one foot to peel off the other foot's sock, he wondered what harm could come of calling this new doctor now. This unknown Dr. Fejes, the oncologist. Fear of change kept him from dialing the number on his landline phone next to his two mini-fridges. Among the very last landline phones in all of Midland. Paulie Galamb never answered his telephone this late in the evening, nor did he ever call out lest it was an absolute emergency. "The cancer or possibility of could wait until the morning," he thought as he peeled off the second sock between his big toe and next toe. The pointer toe?

Paulie balanced on one foot and tossed the sock towards the middle of his living room, roughly where he left his shoes. Then he switched feet and grabbed the first sock with his foot-turned-fist and tossed it towards the other.

Or as close as he could approximate for a three-hundred-pound man.

With his toes acting as tiny tastebuds, he stretched his bare feet on the awkward kitchenette carpet. From the top fridge, he grabbed one of the several half-pints of skim milk (that came from Niles and Meals on Wheels, but it was flavorless enough in itself to earn its place up here) as well as one of the quart bags filled with quinoa. He turned around and opened the microwave. Over the sink, now facing the south, he could hear Alex Trebek announcing the Daily Double while he poured the whole half-pint of milk into the Ziplock bag. Carefully he mostly resealed it, leaving a corner just barely ajar. Then he tossed the empty Tetra Pak into the left sink. He'd rinse it out later. In the sink between the discarded milk container and the microwave was a second sink that was filled with various plastic bags that he had meant to clean out earlier. He'd rinse those later as well.

Paulie placed the bag of grains and milk into the microwave, setting the time at one minute and fifteen seconds. He pressed start, and the bag spun in circles inside the box. While he waited between the dueling mini-fridges and the dueling sinks, between the dueling noises of his neighbors to his north and south, he spread his bare feet out on the unnecessarily carpeted kitchen. He stretched his feet open, then squeezed them shut like a kitten kneading on its mother. He looked down at his thick hands instead of his repulsive reflection in the glass surface of the microwave.

For a whole minute and fifteen seconds, Paulie stared at his hands until his vision blurred and repeated the word "Oncologist" until it lost all meaning. His stomach gurgled impatiently, and the tumor in his throat did it's best to mimic the gurgle. For a moment, Paulie thought he heard the second gurgle, but if he did, he did not pay heed to it.

The tumor in his throat had no interest in the wet milky quinoa his host was about to consume like a duck, but it understood the man's predicament even if it didn't understand the noises the man was making. "On-call-oh-jist. On-call-oh-jist." While the host muttered this, the tumor practiced it as well, in a whisper.

"Aaah-caah-oohh-jizz" it said while it waited hungrily in the pocket of Paulie's mouth, waiting to be fed.

BARSTOOL BANTER, PART ONE

What The Dentist Saw Within

At the Ol' Watering Hole, Tornado Tom snorted back his laughter in a phlegmy display of sarcastic disbelief, following that with a quaff of his beer and a quippy remark, "So you're saying this patient of yours has a talking tumor? I know a fib when I hear one the same way my grandad can tell if it's going to rain based on the aches in his knees."

"Is that where you get your weather reports then, Hedasky?" the dentist said with a smile, before adding, "Hear me out, Tom, for I wouldn't lie to you about this. Earlier today, I met the growth, and it changed me. While I stared at the small fleshy marble, I had realized that I had not lived my life to the fullest. A strange moment of clarity had overwhelmed me. I knew then I wanted to protect it."

"The growth in this man's mouth?"

"Yes. I mean, no, it is more than just a growth."

"What do you mean?" Tom asked, waving at the bartender who was busy flirting with a gaggle of out-of-towners. The bartender held up a single finger, as if to say, "Just a moment,"

"The growth, Tom, it's going to change the world. I don't know how to describe it, not yet. I knew I needed a second opinion, so I sent him to Dr. Fejes, a friend of mine from Duke University. Before I met you. Not because I thought it was cancerous, no, but because I knew Dr. Fejes would see this with the same curiosity I did. The same fascination."

"Well, did he?"

"Tom, this was a few hours ago. What Dr. Fejes does next isn't up to me. All I could do was set the ball in motion," the dentist said as he scratched the small brown birthmark under his eye. His own upside-down Indiana.

"You can lead a horse to the oncologist."

"The last thing I did before the hypnosis wore off, was whisper into Paulie's mouth."

"What did you whisper?"

"Simply one word. Parlay. I whispered it one time, but while I did that, I focused on the meaning of the word, so much so that I felt the meaning of the word slip out into obscurity. Then I took my hand and tools out from inside Paulie and was once again transfixed by his ugliness."

"You mentioned earlier that he was ugly."

"'The ugliest man I ever saw,' I believe my words were. He reminded me of Ron Howard's uglier, younger brother Clint, but only if Clint Howard had an uglier, younger brother than himself. His eyes were annoyingly far apart and sunken in, giving him the appearance of someone who was gaunt or underweight. Which was far from the truth, as he was teetering somewhere between obese and morbidly obese. Judging from the way his arm skin hung off his flab, I assure you at one point he was clearly much, much larger than he was now. He wasn't abnormally tall or short, but the way his gut had settled on his slightly-taller-than average frame made him appear more like a pear than a man. Now, I didn't see this man's downstairs business, but I could tell you he wasn't proud of what dangled between his legs."

"Oh yeah? How could you tell that?" Tom asked, clapping his still-empty beer on the bar top.

"The quickest way to a man's heart is through the stomach. And if that were true, then my domain is at the gates of that stomach. Just seeing his teeth, his gums, and my fleeting glimpses at his uvula, I can tell a lot about a man. Not much different than reading someone's palms or reading the secret details of the tea leaves. I could tell you he had never pleased his wife enough for their marriage to last based on the wisdom tooth I plucked out. I knew he had intestinal issues from the plaque growing on the inside of his incisors. I could tell his belly button was an innie, not an outie, by the subtle rotation of his canines. Hell, I would probably have guessed his birth year based on his lower molars alone had I not already known it from his medical charts."

"Fascinating," Tornado Tom said, in such an oblivious fashion that the dentist knew he had lost the meteorologist's attention. Tom didn't mean to lose focus, but he was now going on his third attempt to grab the bartender's eye in high hopes of getting one last beer. The dentist could see this, so he excused himself.

"Tom, I'll be right back. I've got to call my wife. You, uh, you should go talk to those girls if only to distract the barman long enough to get your last beer in. Let's reconvene here in, say, ten minutes?"

"Sounds good," he said in a daze, already levitating towards the other end of the bar with his empty pint glass in hand, propelled by his thirst for more beer, not by desire.

The dentist took out his phone and scrolled through his

contacts until he found his Joanie halfway down the list. He pressed the green symbol on his phone and waited for the dial-tone.

In the distance, he saw his friend strut up to the three girls, all of whom were obviously not from Midland or the surrounding area, yet still the lot of them recognized him as the man from the news. The charm of a second-rate local celebrity was hard to deny in a small town like this.

An automatic voice spoke to him, "The number you have dialed is not in service."

"Hello love," the dentist said. He was blushing now, though that may have just been the booze.

"Please hang up and try again," the automatic voice said, before the line went dead.

"Oh, I'm fine. I'm just here with Tom at the Ol' Watering Hole. My day? Oh boy, you won't believe the day I've had."

Begrudgingly the bartender was filling a pint glass full of amber ale for Tornado Tom, who was now the center of a selfie-circle with a handful of college girls. Elsewhere, Paulie Galamb was eating lukewarm quinoa cooked in milk like a duck. Nathaniel Niles was feeding his large pet snail. Edith was snoring loudly while the dead Trebek droned on.

Even more elsewhere, the real Alex Trebek was probably in Heaven.

THE DREAM SEQUENCE

Introducing The Main Players

Everybody goes to bed eventually. And whether or not you believe it, everybody dreams. Remembering these dreams upon waking is half the battle.

What does the dentist dream of when he rests his head in his office? He had a dream about his wife, and the day she revealed she had cancer. He'd wake up crying in the middle of the night, even though he would not remember his dream.

Tornado Tom, after his late-night weather report, goes home to his condo in the next city over called Central City, and dreams of golf courses even though he hates the sport. The vastness of perfectly manicured fields of green puts a smile on the meteorologist's face, who sleeps with a mask over his eyes to both keep the light out and for its anti-aging effects. He is a face on television, after all.

Edith Post? She relives her wonderful life, even the elements she's not ready to share with a stranger quite yet. The secret life of a lady nearing her eighties, and what she did in 1970's.

Nathaniel Niles dreams of Sweet Cherry Pie, which is what he had called his previous Harley Davidson. He dreams of riding his motorcycle, of crashing her, of holding his severed leg in his hand. Then these dreams are interspersed with memories of a rock concert he attended in his late teens with his long dead father.

Even his pet snail dreamt. Of fruits and large leaves, most likely.

Everybody dreams, even the people you haven't met yet. Such as Dr. Fejes, who had a nightmare about losing his practice again and again. Juan and his gang of runaways and dropouts had individual dreams about scoring beer and smokes and riding BMX bicycles and sometimes even of their homework. Even Doctor Koop and his corporate stooges have dreams but theirs are unimportant, and mostly capitalistic in their essence. Paulie's co-workers, the ones who are still alive, they dream. The security guards dream, the naked lady hoarder dreams, and yes, the growth, it dreams too.

But in time we'll get to them all. Right now, Paulie's dreams are the important ones. For now. Paulie, after his neighbor's television automatically turned off after an hour of inactivity and re-runs, he lay in his bed, tossing and turning, his stomach filled with milky quinoa growling for more sustenance than offered.

In his restless sleep, he does not dream of his potential cancer. No, instead he dreams of eating the perfect chicken nugget, savoring every micro-bite, analyzing its full flavor. Like a fast-food sommelier, he takes one bite and chews it thoroughly, rolling it around in his tongue. Morsels ground down by molars, juggled around by the sides of his tongue, so he can taste the perfectly salted breading, the almost-sweet tang of the ground chicken trying so hard to slip down his esophagus. If you could call it chicken. Not due to the way it was mechanically separated like a Slim Jim, but rather the way it was created. In a test tube, instead of from an egg, ending that age-old argument that distraught philosophers for centuries with a post-modern twist. What came first: the chicken or the egg?

Then his ex-wife Toni, clad in a nurse's scrub, holds out a small plastic cup and tells him, "Spit." So he does, like a good husband. Only when he goes to look at her, instead he sees his dentist.

"Spit," he said once more, but the confusion overpowers him into waking up. Alone.

Elsewhere, far away, his ex-wife still sleeps soundly. Somewhere in Central City, so far from Midland. What she dreams of is not known to me or you or Paulie Galamb, nor is she in his thoughts anymore.

Like the dentist, Paulie did not remember his dream from only moments before. Instead, all he can think about is the growth in his throat and the potentiality of it ending his life.

6

A WORLD WHERE BUGS COULD TALK

And What They Would Say

The voice on the other end of the phone was so heavily accented, Paulie had to stick a finger in his ear just to be sure he could hear it and only it.

"You have reach the office of Dr. Fejes. I regret that I could not make it to the phone right now, however, feel free to leave message with your name, number, and brief description of any issues you may be having. I intend on getting back to you as quickly as can, however if it is emergency, please hang up and dial nine-one-one. You can also schedule an appointment in person at my office," said the voice on the other end. Then the voice rattled off an address that Paulie recognized as being near his favorite bench in all of Midland, which was located in the center of his favorite strip mall in the county. The Midland Park Business Plaza.

Then the voice listed the office hours. Monday through Friday, 9:00 AM through 4:00 PM.

It was now early Tuesday morning. A whole ten hours had passed since the three-hundred-pound man drank his milky quinoa, following that with six or seven hours of light sleep and strange dreams. Eventually the northern music went to sleep along with the southern quiz show, as well as his respective neighbors. Since then he had consumed runny oatmeal, unsweetened, in the same way a duck would eat a hot-dog. Right now, Dr. Fejes should be at his office, though he was probably with a patient. Paulie decided he would spend the day meandering over to the Business Plaza and at the very least try and schedule an appointment with the oncologist.

He'd have to call his boss. But he also knew that his boss was the type of man that would most certainly cross reference the number he called from. Paulie's boss knew that Paulie himself did not own a cellphone, so he decided he would ask to call his boss from the doctor's office.

Having finished his sludge-for-breakfast, Paulie got dressed in his bathroom that still looked like a beachcomber had found all of their sandy treasures at an Ikea store. Which was mostly true, his ex-wife was the faux-beachcomber, and Ikea was the faux-beach, excluding the snail shells that his neighbor gifted them each time Slugger grew out of one.

Slugger was Niles' pet snail. Slugger was somehow older than Paulie's failed marriage lasted. He, nor Niles, nor myself understood how that was possible.

Paulie didn't care for the snail, nor slimy things in general, but he was grateful that his neighbor didn't have a loud dog. Metallica and Jeopardy he didn't mind, but the grating sound of a dog barking would drive him mad. There was something about an animal wailing and screaming that bothered Galamb; not knowing what they were saying, or what they were wailing and screaming about perturbed him to his core, and at this point in his life he avoided routes that involved loud, angry canines.

As he pulled his favorite sweater, a sweater he had since his early twenties that simply read "Harvard" in all capital letters, he tried to imagine a world where snails and slugs could bark. He pulled his blue jeans up and pulled his belt taut under his gut. He always loved the blue jeans and Harvard sweater combination. Something about representing an Ivy league school (that he had not attended) and the working man's pants was ironic to him, especially since he had little to no experience doing anything seriously laborious.

He grabbed the piece of paper the dentist had given him from the fridge, now with the address scrawled on the back, and headed out the front door. Paulie was stuck on barking snails and other bugs. Paulie was trying to imagine a fly screaming for its life while a large spider cackled maniacally. Paulie locked the door and laughed quietly when he thought about this made-up scenario where the fly pleaded for its life.

"Parlay!" Paulie demanded, pretending he was the imaginary bug in a world where bugs could talk. Though he had said the phrase quiet enough that his nearly deaf neighbor Edith, who was sitting on her rocking chair outside of her condo, couldn't hear him.

However, he had said it loud enough that he did not hear the voice of the growth in his throat attempting to repeat the phrase itself, "Pahh-layyy."

He walked past Edith, who was knitting or crocheting (he could never remember which was which) and told her to have a good day. She looked at him with a smile that he had grown accustomed to; it was the smile of lady who had not heard him correctly, so next would be her parroting it back, incorrectly.

"Did you say have a parfait?"

Paulie shook his head gently, unsure if she had heard him say "Parlay" or "Good day"

"No, no, Edie. I was just telling you to have a good day!" he said, followed by an involuntary hiccup, "Pahh-layyy"

Edith turned her smile away and went back to her yarn and needlework and responded absent-mindedly. "Must be a frog in your throat. Have a good day yourself, Paulie. There's going to be a party you know, and we're all invited. All of us! I hope you'll be there. Really, I do."

There were times when Paulie was unsure whether she was slipping or if there was truth to her babble. It was obvious that her mental acuity left something to be desired. However, in this case he knew what she was referencing. Slugger's birthday. Niles had been talking about it for a month and seeing as how he was currently out of work there was no avoiding it.

"You should bring Toni! She would love it."

He didn't mean to stop in his tracks, as it was purely involuntary, but sometimes hearing her name did just that. His ex-wife's name stung like a sliver in the nail bed of his favorite big toe.

But there was no need to present his upset to this little old lady. Like a toddler poking its mother with a red-hot curling iron, Edith didn't know any better. So, he found himself not quite lying when he told her, "We'll see," even though he knew there was no seeing. There would be no Toni. And that both saddened him and relieved him. The pain in his mouth was hot and constant, but the pain of his divorce seemed eternally lingering like a wet fart in a humid sweat lodge.

With Niles' apartment to his right, Paulie heard the whoosh of his neighbor's garage door fly open. Once again, he found himself forced into another human interaction he would have preferred to have avoided.

"Good morning, Niles. What are you getting into today?" he asked while his neighbor held the door open above his head with one arm, using his free arm to scratch his exposed hairy belly, as round as the bald head above it.

"Yeah, what's so good about this particular Tuesday morning, Paulie? What in these last few hours make it any better than yesterday or the day before?"

He wasn't wrong, he was just a dick.

Glancing down, Paulie immediately noticed he was wearing his "Typical Tuesday Leg", which unlike the very simple peg-leg prosthetic he wore yesterday, today you could see the plastic flesh of his faux leg poking out under his shorts. It would normally come off as quite passable to someone who didn't know Niles was missing the limb.

That is, of course, were it not for the crude drawings Niles had drawn on his prosthetic. "Tattoos" as he had called them. They weren't terrible drawings, but if they were real tattoos then they would be terrible ones at that.

"Well, we're still here for one." Looking away from Niles legs. Leg?

"It wasn't a rhetorical question, smart ass! I'll tell you what's so good about today. It's this boy's ninth birthday," Niles said, smiling widely, revealing his silver incisors, as he picked up the large snail from the plastic fold-out table that was centered in his so-called man-cave. Slugger the snail did not seem to mind being picked up.

From end to end, the slimy suction cup was nearly eight inches long. Its body was a gelatinous blue-to-gray gradient with a pair of two-inch-long eyeballs on poles jutting out from the area that must have been its head. There were no awe-inspiring patterns or markings on this here snail, but it's shell was a masterclass in pure visual machismo. At one point in

Niles' alone time, he had painted on this shell the logo of another 80's hair metal band. Some kind of long-haired ghoul whose face was either some kind of permanent grin or grimace. Iron Maiden, I think? From what Paulie could tell, the logo seemed to be meticulously painted on with different colored nail polishes.

"Oh, I didn't forget," Paulie said glumly.

"So, you still going to swing by tonight? Edie said she'd be there, said she'd bring some kind of cake for this little badass," he said, still holding the garage door over his head while the snail slowly crawled up his other arm, leaving behind a semi-translucent goo in its wake. Never once in Paulie's nearly five decades on this planet had he ever thought of a snail as a little badass.

He couldn't help but think that Niles was trying to flex his muscles by holding the garage door up, because that's typically the kind of guy this biker was. Always flexing when absolutely no flex was necessary.

He attempted to make an excuse in one final effort to get out of making an appearance tonight, preemptively knowing that would not be possible.

"I, uh, I have an appointment today, but I'll see where-"

"Oh yeah, doing what? What is so important that you get to just skip out on work all week and then ditch my boy on his special day?" Niles exclaimed, before letting go of the garage door, which stood its ground and did not budge an inch, it's springs having locked as soon it had opened fully. By design.

"I have to go see an oncologist. Since getting my wisdom tooth pulled, I've noticed a- well, my dentist noticed a growth in the back of my throat."

"Oh your dentist, ay? Is your dentist some kind of ent?"

(Paulie reflected on the word but did not know the context. He had read most of Tolkien's Lord of the Rings. What he had not read, he assumed Peter Jackson had filled in the blanks when Paulie had seen Jackson's extended edition trilogy. Back when movie theaters were still in style, back when he had a wife to take out on dates. Why Niles was asking if his dentist was a walking, talking tree man, Paulie knew not.)

"A what?"

"What's your dentists name? If this guy thinks he can just spot cancer from the largest hole in your face then maybe I should see about my leg?"

Was he talking about his missing leg or the leg he was balancing on? Was he implying he had or has leg cancer?

"Huh? My dentist's name? I never caught it."

"You let a man fool around in your mouth and you never caught his name. You're a strange one, Galamb. Anyways, cancer is for pussies. Go see your oncologist and tell him to his face that you aren't afraid of no stinkin' cancer. It'll set the tone if you know what I mean. Then after that, swing by here. Maybe bring some beer."

Paulie did not know what he meant but that was fine, because with that said, Niles began hobbling over to his dart board. Not before placing his suction-cupped friend back on the plastic table. Slugger immediately beelined it towards a fallen beer can that lay on its side in a tiny puddle of abandoned stale beer. As fast as a snail could beeline it anyways. Paulie took this as his cue to meander on.

"Oh, another thing, Paulie."

"Yeah?" the ugly man said, turning back towards his bald one-legged neighbor. "What is it?"

"You don't have to worry about getting Slugger a gift or anything. It ain't a big deal or anything. Good luck with the cancer. Fuck cancer."

"Okay Niles. Thanks. I'll see you a little later today."

Paulie took his leave as he heard the thuds of metal-tipped

darts hitting the dry wall. For a man that practiced throwing darts every day, he was terrible at it.

* * *

As he passed through the mostly quiet storage facility, he tried to imagine what an appropriate gift for a nine-year-old snail would be. A new shell? A stuffed animal? Some fruit? Because he knew now he couldn't show up to his neighbor's house without a gift tonight.

"Would I have to wrap it?" he thought to himself as he wandered away from Niles' man-cave through the twisting maze of storage units.

Halfway to the entrance of the lot knelt an older man who was rummaging through his own storage unit. He typically tried to not take note of the contents of other people's lockers as he walked past them, nor the people themselves, as it was never his business what people stored in their rented units, but this time he had to double take.

Upon first glance it seemed like there were dozens of naked women standing in the dimly lit storage unit, all with shocked faces plastered about them. Almost immediately, he recognized them all as some sort of hyper-realistic sex dolls. The man inside seemed to be searching for something in particular while he was on his hands and knees. As Paulie tried to sneak past, the man took notice and greeted him. "Beautiful ain't they!" Damn his wandering eyes, Paulie had been spotted.

"Uh, yeah, sure. What is it you're looking for down there?"

"I'm don't know yet, but I'm sure I will when I find it. Well, you have a good day now! I should get back to it!" said the man as he brushed aside scraps of paper and debris on the floor. What appeared to be a shiny plastic cucumber rolled away while he rummaged around.

"Good day, uh, to you too," Paulie said, his face having turned a bright red, while the meat in his throat parroted the noises he made.

"Oood aay, ooo doo" said the growth in his mouth, quiet enough that Paulie didn't notice.

7

A BIRD'S-EYE VIEW OF MIDLAND

Specifically This One

A weird man once said, "Land really is the best art." And I think that applies to all lands.

From the highlands to the swampy lowlands, this world of extremes has so much beauty to offer. Even if you wind up in this boring middle-of-nowhere Midland. That weird man also said he was a deeply superficial person, so I guess take it all at face value.

If you were to climb onto the nearest water tower, the big pink one just behind the We-Store Storage Units lot, you would be able to see everything this Midland had to offer and everything this Midland lacked. Atop the faded salmon-colored structure, at a hundred fifty feet up, you could see clear across the small city. Assuming the security guards at We-Store didn't catch you climbing it, of course. Not that they would really do much to stop you, anyways.

From the modest downtown plot a mile north with a dozen or so sort-of-skyscrapers, with only one being slightly taller than the water tower (the county courthouse, and it was only taller due to its radio tower and lightning rod) while the rest were significantly shorter. The second tallest building, just past the downtown stretch, belonged to Paulie's place of work, Pea Tree Farms. Though that building was far from farm-like. It was more mausoleum than farm. At eight stories tall, there were only windows on the first floor and the eighth. Just like the city's logo was plastered on the side of big pink water tower, Pea Tree Farms was plastered on the side of this large grey building, in addition to the beaker-logo with the fleur-di-le made of peas.

Surrounding that building was a vast expanse of parking lot, which seemed to be filled with cars and trucks of all shapes and sizes. In that modest downtown there was also a four-story building that contained a handful of medical offices, including Paulie's dentist's office. Whatever his name is.

But then again, that's what most of Midland looked like from up here atop the pink water tower. A random smattering of tall-enough buildings surrounded by a larger swath of parking lots. This was because most of Midland's business came from selling cars and or manufacturing them. It didn't have that Detroit vibe, where everybody got together after a fourteen-hour shift working in the different warehouses doing the same thing for different car companies. Ford plant workers drinking merrily with Chevrolet workers. No, because past the downtown stretch, past the courthouse and Pea Tree Farms building were the fields upon fields of factories, and for the most part, very few humans worked there. At this point in human history, the machines built the electric cars. The humans just sold them to each other.

Just past those factories, a little hard to see from this vantage point, is Midland High School, home of the Midland Robins. Past that, you could see nothing but miles of suburban sprawl: cookie cutter houses as far as the eye could see until the curvature of the earth hid them from view. Somewhere past that was the remains of the Chumquah tribe and the fields of windmills and solar panels, but that comes later.

From this vantage point, you'd see the top of the We-Store lot. If you didn't know any better, you'd swear you were looking down at a labyrinth. Lucky you, that you now know the way as well as Paulie Galamb. Surrounding the maze are large fences fitted with barbed wire. Just past the walled lot is an empty broken-up parking lot with a 'FOR LEASE' sign in front of it. In that empty plot you'd see the tiny tumble weeds of plastic bags and surgical masks rolling around listlessly. Years of abandonment had left the ground cracked as nature feebly tried to reclaim it. Asphalt spread wide enough for dandelions to take root and shoot out towards the sky. Most of the tar was covered in large swaths of moss. In the largest indentations long ago caused by semi-trucks too heavy for this lot grew tiny pockets of grass.

It's not important, just a reminder that nature still finds a way.

On the opposite side of the storage facility, there was the Midland Recreation Area, which mostly consisted of a covered gazebo, a basketball court, and a tennis court. Neither the basketball hoops nor the tennis court had nets anymore, teenagers having long ago stolen them, probably as some sort of Senior prank or something.

If you looked carefully, you might even see some teenagers harassing every passerby for spare cigarettes or arguing with the Hispanic worker who was maintaining the grounds around them. Do not fret, for they are friends.

If you wandered to the other side of the water tower, you could see the rest of this Midland, which wasn't much more than a series of fast-food establishments, freeways, and apartment complexes that never rose over two stories tall like the We-Store below the tower. The closest thing to nature you'd find on this side of the water tower was the large artificial retention pond that was christened "Midland Lake" by the previous mayor ten years prior. Maybe it was some sort of joke due to the pond's small size, or maybe it was an attempt to pull some tourism into the city, of which this Midland grossly lacked. There was a dog park surrounding the pond, but due to a recent poisonous algae bloom, both the pond and park were currently closed. Now it was just a green puddle that produced mosquitos and muskrats that Midland's stray cats sometimes chased around until they disappeared under the thick muck.

Not far from that pond, you could see the largest strip mall in the city. The Midland Business Plaza. All the big-name businesses had long since come and gone. No longer did the giants of the strip mall reside: Claires, Walgreens, Pay-Less, and PetSmart had long abandoned the city, leaving behind vacant or subdivided commercial spaces that collected dust. Between every vacant space was a smattering of smaller businesses that were either brand new or closing soon, it seemed. There was a joke at the local watering hole, where if you couldn't make it in car sales or fast-food, then you might as well try your hand at the Midland Business Plaza. If you failed at making that work, then this Midland probably wasn't for you and maybe you should find another Midland.

(I say this Midland, because the story here takes place in one of twenty-one similarly named towns or cities in the United States. This isn't the first Midland, nor the last, just another boring highway town in another fly-over state. The kind of place you stop for gas and go and forget about. There are no clever bumper stickers to commemorate your brief stay here, and the only hotel in town barely turns on its "No Vacancy" sign.)

Among the many businesses in the Midland Business Plaza is said watering hole. Midland's most famous pub, "The Ol' Watering Hole", was smack dab in the middle of the strip mall, right between the space that used to contain a Kohls, and the space formerly known as Dick's Sporting Goods. In that vacant spot next to the bar there used to be a mannequin in the window wearing hiking gear, advertising low-priced camping supplies. Now there was a sign advertising a used furniture outlet store "Coming in 2019!" however, the sign was covered in two or three-years' worth of dust at this point.

Wait, look down there!

If you squint, you can see the ugliest man the dentist had ever seen turning a corner just past the entrance of the We-Store Storage Units, making his way towards the Midland Business Plaza, just past the Arby's and the Subway. If you listen carefully, you can hear some teenagers mocking him. Harassing him, threatening him. Let's have a listen, shall we?

8

SMALL TOWN TEENAGERS

Harassing Small Town Adults

"Come on Mullet, maybe if we pound on this guy's face a bit he won't be so fuckin' ugly?" said the shortest of the four kids surrounding Paulie. He couldn't have been older than thirteen. Heck, the lot of them were probably all under eighteen.

"Fugly motherfucker," the looming teenager said while looking down at Paulie. Paulie could smell the obvious artificial compounds that made up the flavor profile on a Cheeto. The orange dust around the corners of the mullet-clad teen only concreting his nose's correct deduction.

"We'd be doing this Harvard-ass nerd a favor," said one of the two twins, though he was unsure which. Paulie could tell this was escalating quicker than he had hoped for, and though he did not want to use a Taser on a bunch of teens he very well would do that right now. Had he brought his Taser with him, anyways. Having forgotten it (because why would he need one so early on a Tuesday?) he attempted to de-escalate the situation to the best of his ability.

"Hold on, easy now. You asked me for a cigarette, I said I didn't smoke. You asked me for a beer, I said I didn't have one. And immediately after that you start insulting and threatening me? Boys, that's no way to treat a stranger. If you let me go, and you're still here in a half hour, I would gladly buy you a beer and cigarettes."

The mullet-sporting teenager aptly nicknamed Mullet turned to the shortest and obviously youngest teen, "Whaddya think, Stocks? Should we let 'em go?"

Paulie studied the short kid, who was wearing an oversized black polo with a red logo on it. Gamestop. He recognized it as one of the many companies that came and left the Midland Business Plaza, but he had never been inside. It was some kind of video game company, that much he knew. Maybe it was this teen's older sibling's former work-shirt or something, because there was no way he was legally allowed to have a job. The short kid noticed him staring at the logo on his polo.

"Oh, you like what you see, eh?" the kid said, pulling his shirt down to reveal a gold chain that he had probably stolen from his parents. There was no way these hoodlums had any real clout to their attitude. Even the tall teen named Mullet posed no real threat to Paulie, he just didn't want to deal with this today. "Too bad, old man. You can look but you can't touch."

"You tell him Stocks!" said one of the two twins, both wearing blue hooded sweatshirts. Once again, Paulie had no idea which one said it.

The kid named Stocks walked up to him, glaring up at Paulie's face in a strange attempt to intimidate the grown man. Paulie wasn't having it. He was en route to see a doctor about a growth in his throat, and now he had the peanut gallery gang harassing him for beer and smokes. "Well, I ain't saying this is a robbery, fatso, but it's starting to look like one."

Paulie was by no means a tough man, but after decades of abuse and bullying, he wasn't scared of a teenager throwing a punch or a few slanted insults his way. Really, he just wished he had brought his stun-gun.

"Listen kid, I don't have time for this."

Just as he said that the short kid moved out of the way then the tall lanky one was in his place. Mullet, with the Cheeto breath, was now holding on to the shoulder pads of his Harvard sweatshirt. "Now this is going to hurt, old man."

Paulie closed his eyes as Mullet pulled back his arm. The teen in front of him probably weighed a hundred pounds, stretched like Mozzarella to fit his six-foot frame. He wanted to say, "I doubt that very much," but instead a different voice came out, "Par... lay."

And where a punch should have landed, Paulie felt nothing.

"Parlay, he says? Okay, we'll parlay. Let him go, Mullet. Yo Billy, or Brian, one of you go fetch Juan, will ya?"

"On it!" said one of the two blue twins, and he ran off. Mullet let go of Paulie, who found himself sweating. Not because of the threat of physical violence. No, because he felt the hiccup in his throat croak out the word "Parlay". Not only did he hear it, but so did these bullies.

Billy or Brian, doesn't matter which, was already sprinting back toward the group. In the distance, Paulie could see an adult finally ambling towards them. From here, Paulie could tell he was some sort of park worker. Judging by the high-visibility-yellow he wore, he must have been a groundskeeper or landscaper.

But as the man got closer, Paulie realized he wasn't much of a man. Sure, he had all the makings of a man. A mustache, a hard hat, and a name tag, but really he was just an overgrown boy. As sure as that punch would have come had his throat not barked "Parlay", the man-child's name tag read "Juan". Brian or Billy was out of breath by the time he returned to the group. Juan, however, was taking his time. Dare I say he was walking at a snail's pace.

(Sorry Slugger.)

"Brian here says you wanted to parlay? Well, what are the terms of your surrender?" said the landscaper with the barely formed mustache. If Stocks was the youngest, then Juan here was clearly the oldest. At seventeen. Maybe eighteen.

"Uh, yeah. I offered these kids, er, young men beer and cigarettes in exchange for..."

The word was escaping him, only because it seemed so ridiculous. That, and he was worried if he didn't say it quick enough, the voice in the back of his head would betray him.

"...for passage."

Juan glanced back at the other four. Mullet, Stocks, Brian, and Billy. They quickly huddled and whispered amongst one another. When Juan turned around, he was grinning wildly like a child that just got away with murdering a stuffed animal, blaming it on the dog. Brian or Billy scratched at their downstairs, while Stocks rubbed his two palms together violently, mischievously.

"Okay, first off, what's your name, ugo?"

"It's uh, Paul. Paulie. You can call me Paulie." Did he really just give these little hoodlums his name? Get it together, man!

"Parlay Paulie? I like it. I like it. My name's Juan. I'm the leader of this crew. It seems you offended my two leading men here. Mullet, the brawn, and Stocks is my brains. Me, I'm the heart. And you know what they say about the heart, don'tcha?!"

("Absence makes the heart grow fonder?")

He shook his head.

"It's the strongest muscle on the whole body!"

Paulie knew this to be untrue, but he understood the

teenager's sentiment. The strongest muscles were arguably the masseter muscle and the tongue worked harder than the heart, but obviously it got more credit due to, well, keeping Paulie alive and all. He didn't bother pointing this out, because he knew his battle with these boys was nearly finished, and he wanted to end it on an upswing.

"Here's the deal, Parlay Paulie. When you come back this way, I want to see a brown paper bag under your arm. In that bag, I expect to find two forty-ounce beers, one pack of Marbs, and one Hustler magazine. I imagine I don't need to tell you what will happen if you show up empty handed."

"What is a physical beating, Alex?" he dared not say out loud, even though the correct answer would have been, "What is a mild attempt at a physical beating?"

Instead of arguing, he just shook his head and played nice.

"We got a deal, Juan. I won't come back without the stuff. I promise."

And just like that, Paulie knew he would be following through with this stupid fetch quest. Not because he felt intimidated, not really, but because he accidentally said he would do it. If there's anything you should know about this man, it's that he was an honest one. To a fault, some would say.

"Good, good. We'll be seeing you, Parlay Paulie. Now scram, old man!"

As Paulie began walking away, wondering if this is what it's like to negotiate with terrorists, he found himself bothered by one question. Even at the risk of physical violence, he turned around and asked the group, "Hey, why aren't you guys in school right now?"

The left-most Brian or Billy answered first, pulling his hood down, revealing the only difference between him and his twin. His left ear was pierced, where the other Billy or Brian had his right ear pierced. Naturally, with matching gold studs. "We're home schooled. By each other."

The other Brian or Billy, "Yeah, we teach each other, turn in our books, and get our marks. I teach history and social studies. Billy over here, he's our science tutor. Fuck high school!"

Stocks balled up his fist and popped his thumb out, jabbing it into his own chest, "I teach these fuckers mathematics. With a side of calculus and investment theory. And we do it right here, not in no broken ass school system."

"What about you, Juan? Are you also one of the teachers?"

"Me? I teach these fools life experience. Shit they'll need to know to find a job in this dying world. Survival skills, ya know. I teach ma boys how to survive the fuckin' end times. Gangsta shit."

"I can respect that," he said truthfully. His father had been a doomsday prepper to some extent, not that he would ever consider his father a "gangsta" or anything.

"You best, ugo. That, and I'm the only one here old enough to hold down a job. Some of us need to work to keep a roof over our heads. That, and I keep them in line just like I'll keep you in line if you don't bring us back the goods."

Paulie furrowed his brow and waved at the teenagers. He had a mission about him now. Buy these boys eighty ounces of beer, a package of cigarettes, and a skin mag. After he dealt with, you know, the potential cancer and all.

Instead of arguing, Paulie just wandered on. It wasn't until he heard the voice of Cheeto breath behind him shouting out, "Hey don't you want to know what I teach?"

"Not really," he thought, but the sad inner nice guy came forward anyways, "Yeah, what's that Mullet?"

"I teach these kids Shakespeare!"

Well, Mullet, these violent delights have violent ends.

Paulie continued through the park, under the shadow of

the pink water tower towards the Midland Business Plaza. He wondered how the day would have been different were he to have packed his Taser. What an interesting conversation that would have been at the oncologist's office! With the group of ne'er-do-wells behind him, he trotted on to see about scheduling an appointment with the oncologist once more.

With the shadow of the big pink water tower clear behind him, and the scum-covered pond-called-lake to his right, all that was ahead of him was a dozen or so big-name fast-food restaurants, half a dozen smaller chains, and a series of small businesses that were all likely to fail. Including the office of one Dr. Joseph Fejes. He fumbled in his pocket and found the slip of paper with the man's number and address and continued forth. Not before kicking aside a tumbleweed consisting of cheap plastic and one or two snot-encrusted surgical masks.

The tumbleweed didn't mind. It had nowhere to go, really. It was just here for the ride.

9

AN OTORHINOLARYNGOLOGIST

Is Not An Oncologist

On the corner of 5th and Main was the north-western most corner of the large strip mall. It was the second largest strip mall in the Tri-County area, and all of the advertisements for leasable space advertised it as such. It did not advertise that the largest strip mall was currently foreclosed and set to be demolished next spring, nor did the advertisements mention the extremely high turnover rate. I mean, why would they? Unless your business was selling cars or slinging cheap hamburgers, what were you even doing in Midland?

Past the "For Lease" sign was a bar that Paulie never cared for. Past that was another "For Lease" sign, then a convenience store with boarded up windows, then his destination. Beyond that, you guessed it, another "For Lease" sign. To his left were vacant store fronts that had been broken into judging by the finger paintings done on the insides of dusty windows. To his right were dozens of cars, which would normally seem impossible since there were only five or six open businesses in the entire Midland Business Plaza. Other than the convenience store ahead and the Super K at the end of the mall, it wouldn't seem like there should be so many matching fancy cars parked in this otherwise mostly empty parking lot.

Paulie knew why, though. He had heard from his co-worker Sue, she was a real gabber, that the owner of Perry's Primo BMW cut a deal with Bob Robbins, owner of the Midland Business Plaza. Sue said she'd heard Perry was advertising his luxury vehicles here on the grounds that he paid rent just like the other five or six tenants did. Just like the fast-food restaurants stationed at the exits and entrances of the plaza did. Just like Dr. Fejes, allegedly.

His thoughts of Sue reminded him of a time where everything seemed normal outside a bit of mostly manageable tooth pain only two weeks before. Hell, even yesterday he was just seeing a dentist about a lump in the area where his wisdom tooth had been. Now here he was, heading towards the cancer doctor's doorstep.

Which had a small laminated cheap sign taped to the back, to his surprise, did not read "Oncologist". Instead, it read 'Doctor Joseph Fejes, ENT'

Below that Paulie read out loud "Ear, Nose and Throat Specialist". Niles had not been referring to his dentist as a walking, talking tree man after all. Logically, this made sense.

What did not make sense was the contradictory statement claiming that walk-in's were not welcome. Appointment only. The voicemail earlier had stated otherwise. Paulie could see through the slightly frosted glass that the office appeared to be empty. Worse than the contradiction, was the fact that he did not see the word "Oncologist" anywhere on this door.

Just thinking of the word, he could almost hear it inside his neck trying to escape.

He opened the door and entered, welcomed by a door

chime that reminded him of Trebek's contestants buzzing in the right or wrong question to the gameshow host's questions. The air in here smelled faintly of, he couldn't put his finger on it, wrongness. The bristly hairs rose on his arm under his Harvard sweater as he approached the desk.

"Hello?" he asked the desk behind the plexiglass shield with nobody at its helm. No response. Paulie noticed another sign on the desk, this one handwritten, that gave the reader instructions were the desk vacant.

"Out to lunch, be back in fifteen. Feel free to call my cell-phone or come back later!"

There was no number listed below that, nor did Paulie have a cellphone to call the doctors even if a number was present. He looked at his watch and saw that it was only half past ten. If you asked him, he'd tell you that half past ten was too early to qualify for lunch, let alone brunch.

What to do, what to do.

Paulie sat in the meager waiting area and rummaged through the selection of magazines the office had to offer. The AutoTrader did nothing for him, nor did the dated copies of People magazine (Nobody cares about Brad Pitt and Jennifer Aniston drama a decade after their divorce, Dr. Fejes), and most of the remaining magazines were in some undecipherable foreign language. It wasn't quite Russian, but it followed no recognizable pattern that Paulie had ever seen. His final choice was an advertiser, something he hadn't seen since his youth when he used to throw newspapers at people's doorstep for a living decades earlier. Back when he was but an ugly teen.

Inside the newspaper were advertisements for most, if not all, the various car dealerships in town. Past that were dozens of real estate listings in this town and the towns surrounding Midland. Beyond that were people summarizing themselves in tiny paragraphs in hopes of someone calling them for a date.

The Tinder of yesteryear, Paulie thought. He couldn't imagine that anyone still posting these, or reading these, were any younger than fifty.

An age which he found himself rapidly approaching.

Past the personal ads was the Help Wanted section. In the age of the internet, Paulie had only ever read the Help Wanted section once with the intent of finding a job, and that was in the very tail end of the 1980's. The job he found from that advertiser thirty years earlier was the aforementioned newspaper delivery job.

In the bottom corner Paulie saw a very familiar logo that piqued his interest. Like the magnet on his fridge, printed on the newspaper was a cartoonish laboratory beaker with a fleur de lis in the center. In the middle of the fleur de lis was a small pea pod with four circles inside. Below that were the words, "PEA TREE FARMS", his place of work.

Very quickly, Paulie flipped the advertiser around and checked the date. It was from last week. For a moment, Paulie felt a twinge of fear and panic in his gut. Worse than the revelation that the painful pocket in his jaw was potentially a cancerous lump, but not as bad as his ex-wife announcing her departure.

Seeing the advertisement for "Sensory Panelist" under his place of employment's logo implied that either somebody else had been let go or quit, or that he himself may have been out a job. The description below that used an absurd amount of capital letters, and seemed to be written in code, but really that was just to weed out potential flakes from sending in their resumes. Sensory Panelist, as Paulie had long ago learned, was just a fancy way of saying 'Taste Tester'.

"Now Seeking Sensory Panelist for Radical New Lab-Grown Products!"

In the two weeks he had been out of work, he had not

thought his job was at risk. His job did pay for full dental and medical, so why would they fire him for utilizing the benefits they offered?

Paulie continued reading the responsibilities of the Sensory Panelist as he thought of his co-workers.

"The Individual will Interact with Fellow Sensory Panelists, the Panel Leader, the Sensory Technician and the Research Scientists responsible for leading Descriptive Analysis projects."

Maybe Sue Ellen had been fired. She was the panel leader, but also the most loose-lipped of the crew. However, she was a gabby grandma know-it-all whose mental facilities had seemed to rapidly deteriorate in the last few months.

"The Individual will Apply Appropriate Focus and Concentration on Tasting Responsibilities, engage in Discussion Regarding Sample Descriptions,"

Or maybe Doug, "Just Doug", a fellow sensory panelist, had intentionally fallen down a flight of stairs and sued his way to retirement, as he had often joked about before and after the sampling.

"The Ideal Candidate is Expected to have Excellent Tasting Skills (ability to discern Differences in Samples for Appearance, Taste, Texture); assessed via Taste Acuity Testing. The Candidate Must Achieve Successful Performance on Screening tests for Sensory Acuity."

Whatever that meant.

Perhaps Gordo Fierri, a nickname he earned for looking like an obese variation of the famous chef, had finally had enough of ingesting lab grown meat instead of the real deal?

"If You Meet The Below Qualifications please Contact Arnold Workman or Arrive in Person with Your Resume And Cover Letter at the front desk."

Lastly, Chris Wagner may have finally been institutionalized for his crazy doom-and-gloom conspiracies that he was always running his mouth about. Whether or not a single one was true, Paulie did not care.

There was no way of knowing who quit or who was fired, or whether or not he was fired during his sick leave. Whatever the case was, he knew he needed to call his work sooner than later. Paulie checked his watch and saw that it was closer to eleven o'clock.

The last two people he considered was the man behind the screen, Arnie, and the wizard behind the curtains, Doctor Koop. Arnie was only ever shown on the flat-screen televisions placed in each of their Sensory cubicles, and the mysterious Doctor Koop, the preferred moniker of his co-workers, was only ever mentioned in passing. Sue Ellen was the only co-worker who interacted with Workman, and Workman was the only person in their department that interacted with Koop.

He needed to call Pea Tree Farms. Paulie glanced to his right and saw vast grayness outside. There wasn't anybody living in the parking lot outside, just the cars and trucks outside the Plaza coming and going. Beyond that was the park where he could maybe, just barely make out the teenagers in the distance. He saw cars wrap around the two fast food restaurants like boa constrictors, but beyond that there were no pedestrians in sight. Paulie got up out of his seat, groaning while he did, and quickly paced toward the plexiglass shield again.

"Be back in fifteen minutes, my ass," he thought as he reached under the shield and grabbed the office phone. Paulie punched in his employer's phone number, having memorized it like every other number worth his attention. Instead of a dial tone, he heard a chime.

A chime that reminded him of Jeopardy contestants buzzing in the right or wrong questions. With the phone in hand and up against his ear, he turned around slowly and saw a diminutive old man standing in the doorway. He wore a thick overcoat, and in each hand was a brown paper bag. One labeled Subway, the other labeled Arby's.

"Who are you? And what are you doing in my office?"

Paulie slowly put the phone back on the receiver and introduced himself. "Hi, uh, I'm Paul. I tried to schedule an appointment-"

"I have no appointments today."

"Are you Dr. Fejes?"

"Yes, that is I. Again, I ask you what are you doing in my office?" the small man said. His Eastern European accent was as thick as paprika ground in a mortar and pestle.

"My dentist recommended me to you, though he said you were an oncologist."

"No, no, you are mistaken, that is my brother Gabor. I am otorhinolaryngologist."

His head spun, trying to decipher the eight syllables as he heard them churned out like chunky butter. Ow-tow-ray-now-leg-run-gah-luh-gist.

"Excuse me?"

"My brother, he is cancer doctor. Me, I am ear nose throat doctor. His office is in Central City. Not here. What is it you want?"

Paulie pulled the slip of paper out of his pocket and handed it to the man, who set his brown paper bags on the coffee table to receive it. Dr. Fejes pushed his glasses above his nose and squinted down at the small slip of paper.

"You say dentist send you? What dentist?"

"I never caught his name."

"You let man in your mouth, and you no catch his name. How foolish!"

"I'm sorry, I just, I didn't think it was necessary."

"Get out, I am to eat my lunch. Come back later with name or do not come back. If cancer doctor you seek, you seek my brother Gabor. Me, I eat lunch now, goodbye!"

The short man hurried over to Paulie and put his small hand on Paulie's back, escorting him toward the door. Paulie, feeling defeated, let the old man guide him. The door chimed once more, as he found himself outside again in the gray outdoors.

The musical door slammed shut behind him, and before he could turn around and plead his case, he heard the bolt lock shut. When he did face the doctor, the doctor was already walking away with his bags of food somewhere beyond the plexiglass shield.

Paulie felt like screaming, but he was never a man for commotion or excessive grabs for attention.

He wondered what his next course of action would be. Would he make the trek across town once more, just to retrieve the name of the man whose hands were in his mouth the day before or return home with his metaphorical tail tucked between his legs?

No, he couldn't go back the way he came without the teenager's beer, without his neighbor's beer, without a gift for his neighbor's snail. He was a man of his word after all. Sheepishly, with his head turned down, he made his way toward the convenience store two doors down.

10

ATTEMPTING BEER MATH

And The Conspiracy Theorist

This store was, at most, five feet wide. It seemed to run the length of the strip mall, about thirty feet deep, with a lone store clerk standing at the end of the hallway-shaped shop. From the entrance, Paulie could barely make the clerk out in this poorly lit store. He had to squint to confirm the man was smiling.

"Welcome to Mid-Market, buddy!" the clerk said enthusiastically, his voice bouncing off the drink coolers and snack shelves to Paulie's left and right. Paulie thought he recognized the voice but the acoustics in here may have been throwing him off. He flashed his palm as a loose wave hello as he started browsing the many refrigerators filled with beer and other bubbly beverages.

See, the problem here was this man barely ever drank beer, wine, liquor, or really any kind of intoxicant for that matter. He wasn't a total Prudish Peter, mind you. Paulie had gone to college and acted a fool like the rest of the boys in his circle, but after those days were done he left his boozing ways in his dormitory along with his virginity. He had probably had a total of ten, eleven, maybe twelve alcoholic beverages since his time spent at college. Roughly half of those were drunk at his wedding a lifetime ago.

It was easy to assume the rest of those beverages were drunk following his divorce.

The man just didn't know how to buy booze. He should have gotten a specific list from the teens. At least with Niles he had a visual memory to go off. The old biker always drank either Busch or Budweiser, referring to them as his Coke and Pepsi ("I don't mind either as long as you don't slip in that Wal-Mart brand generic piss schwill? I ain't no Coors or Keystone guy, you hear me?") but the teens only specified the amount the wanted. Eighty ounces of beer. Or specifically, two forty-ounce beers. A pack of Marbs. A Hustler magazine.

Though he had never smoked a cigarette in his life, his own mother had smoked Marlboro Lights before she gave them up for the gum. And truthfully, he had never paid for a porno-graphic magazine, because he was never really a sexual person. Even with his wife.

Okay, at this point he was a total Prudish Peter, but who are we to judge in this day and age.

He found himself staring dumbly at the vast wall of beers, wines, and tiny liquor bottles.

There were no forties, as he had heard them dubbed from his college days, upon this wall of liquid inebriation. There were twenty-twos, tall boys, four packs, six packs, half racks, cases, pints, fifths, and half gallons. There were bottles of wine, boxes of wine, jugs of wine and even tiny wine shooters. Hell, even the sodas and energy drinks came in every shape, size, and amount (though he thought the idea of a thirty-two-ounce Red Bull was probably lethal enough to kill a bear) but there wasn't a singular old-fashioned forty in this whole hallway.

Paulie could make do, he just had to crunch some numbers. Seeing as he wasn't the one drinking these beers, he didn't pay much attention to the percentages, just the ounces and the cost.

All of this math, the only purpose it served at this point was to distract him from his future. It seemed like he was careening hopelessly down a series of wrong turns on a roller coaster. His teeth had betrayed him, potentially costing him his career. His body was turning on him, which could cost him his life. Teenagers had threatened him into this menial task, and his dentist's recommendation was a useless old curmudgeon.

And worse yet, twice today he was made fun of for not knowing his dentist's name. Why the hell was that such a big deal? In fact, do me a favor real quick. Go grab a pen. I'll wait here.

Now write down the names of your last three dentists. Take as much time as you need.

1._____

2._____

3._____

In the time you took to think up three names, made up or not, Paulie managed the following possible combinations of beer to appease the four teens and their leader.

He could grab one twenty-five-ounce Hurricane Malt Liquor, one sixteen-ounce can of Sparks and two nineteen-point-five-ounce Red Hook Indian Pale Ales, coming up to a solid eighty ounces at $9.40, before taxes. Though it seemed like a good option, allowing a beer for each boy (the twins could share the Hurricane, he thought), it was also more than he was willing to spend when negotiating with teenage highwaymen.

His second option would be to grab two thirty-two-ounce Corona Extras and one sixteen-ounce Mikes Hard Lemonade for a total of $8.30 for forty ounces in all. He opted out of this because he didn't want to come off as presumptuous by buying a Mexican-themed beer for a young man named Juan.

The last option was just to get two forty-two-ounce Steel Reserve High Gravity Lagers for six dollars, even. It was the cheapest option, plus it was closest to the original order. Plus maybe the four extra ounces would earn him a little respect. Because that's what you need right now, Paulie. The respect of some delinquent teenagers.

Carefully he juggled the two large plastic bottles of beer that proudly advertised the fact that these bottles were shatter proof, placing one under each armpit. Then, without much thought, he grabbed a six pack of Budweiser and meandered to the end of the hallway toward the still-smiling store clerk. As he did, he ignored the growls and grumbles in his stomach that seemed to be echoing in his throat. "Uuhnngeee" came out of his mouth in the form of an awkward belch.

Approaching the clerk, whose smile was both beaming and jarring, he realized he did in fact recognize him.

"Hey there buddy, how are you today?"

"Chris?"

Upon saying the man's name, his smile quickly dissipated into a confused pucker.

"I'm sorry, do we know each other?"

Paulie almost second guessed his own memory for a moment, but here was a man whose face was not easily forgotten. Sue Ellen, the gossipy supervisor (The Sensory Panel Lead, as it were) always whispered ugly, demeaning things about the man at work. "He looks like a Pug. Except his teeth are worse than those awful little dogs if you could call them that."

Though it was true, she was no catch herself. Nor was

Paulie, but that never gave him the idea that he could be cruel like everyone typically was toward himself.

"It's me, Paulie. Paulie Galamb. We worked, er, I work at Pea Tree Farms. We worked in the same wing together. In Lab Grown Meals and Meats Replacements, remember?"

A faint glimmer of recognition had shown on Chris Wagner's asymmetric face, but then it faded into apologetic confusion once more.

"Oh. I'm not so sure about that. I had an accident, you see."

Chris lifted his hat, and just above his left eyebrow was a large red gash that had been sewn together with a dozen thick black stitches. It did not look infected, but it definitely did not help the man's impish demeanor.

"Doctors say I fell and hit my head and had what they call a braumatic train injury. I lost my last job, but worse, I don't remember my last job. You recognize me? Did you know me? Were we close buds?"

In the last few lines, he saw the confusion change into something strange. Though it was almost childish in sincerity, it creeped Paulie out to see his old co-worker's eyes widen as much as they did.

And he was now worried he'd hurt the man's feelings by being truthful.

"Not terribly close," he answered. The truth was Paulie always found his conspiracy theories ranging from repugnant to asinine or sometimes downright stupid. This was a man who believed the twin towers were actually vaporized by energy weapons. That lizard people controlled our government. That Tom Hanks bathed in the blood of babies. Worst, Chris was sometimes far too vocal on his awful beliefs about the Holocaust which I won't touch with a ten-foot pole. He didn't have to vocalize all this, especially to a man who didn't recognize him after a few weeks.

"But I believe that was kind of the company's intention. I don't think Pea Tree Farms wanted us to mingle much. They didn't want us to corrupt our data-"

He stopped himself when he saw that Chris was staring straight ahead, through Paulie. Chris' eyes had a seemingly glazed over appearance.

"Welcome to Mid-Market, buddy. Is it just these today?" Chris said, smiling at the beers under Paulie's arms and on the counter in front of him.

"Uh, hm, can I also get a pack of Marlboro Reds, and, uh, that copy of Hustler behind you?"

"Oh, it looks like someone's having a little party!" Chris said, still staring past Paulie. Without breaking his gaze, the man grabbed a pack of cigarettes from above the register, and one of the lewd magazines behind him.

He wanted to deny that these items were his, but how cliché would it seem. More importantly, did it matter?

Chris rang him up and Paulie paid with a twenty-dollar bill. As Paulie grabbed his brown paper bags of party favors and porn, Chris grabbed his wrist more firmly than Galamb was comfortable with.

His jovial nature was gone. Paulie met his eyes and saw that Chris was glaring at him, "You don't have to go back there. They can't make you go back there."

"What are you- let go of me!"

He almost dropped the bag of beer as the skin around Chris' hand, his skin, had gone white from the strength of his former co-worker's grip.

And then just like that, Chris let go.

"I'm sorry about that. I hit my head you see," he said, almost in a whisper. Paulie could see a thin line of blood had started flowing from the stitched-up gash above his eye, as thick as a piece of red yarn.

Paulie backed up a step, watching the blood flow into the clerk's eye before he turned around and hurried towards the door. As he left, he could hear Chris repeating himself once more, "Welcome to Mid-Market, buddy," before he accidentally slammed the door behind him.

Outside, he could hear his heartbeat pounding in his ears. He didn't realize he was holding the bag up against his chest tight enough that one of the beer cans had punctured through the paper. Paulie only snapped out of his trance when he heard a man to his right repeat the following word three times. In the form of a question, as per Jeopardy rules.

"Pigeon? Pigeon, pigeon?"

11

BY APPOINTMENT ONLY

Except For Right Now

Unease turned to confusion, but also momentary relief as the oncologist waved at Paulie, repeating the bird's name once more.

"Pigeon?"

"Excuse me?" he said, still festering on the strange interaction with his conspiracy theorist co-worker only seconds earlier. Former co-worker, apparently.

"Pali? Is your name Pali?"

"Yeah, though I don't go by that other than on paper. I prefer Paulie."

"Pali Galamb?" asked the short old man, clutching his wool overcoat with his small, wrinkled hands.

"Uh, yes, though I didn't give you my last name."

"I spoke with Seltzman. He said it was very important you should see me, that I should see you. Come, come. Quickly now."

Curious, Paulie obliged. He cradled his paper bag and

followed Dr. Fejes back into his office. His demeanor seemed wildly different from their interaction moments earlier. Entirely. He was ecstatic, excited, thrilled. For a second, he wondered who Seltzman was, but Dr. Fejes was quick to remedy that.

"I talked to your dentist. Seltzman. He told me he saw you yesterday. When you say dentist tell you to seek me, I realize I know very few dentists in this shithole town. So, I call, and he tell me about your problem. Follow me, I will inspect right now."

"What about your lunch?" Paulie asked, remembering the two separate bags of food he had come in with. When he was waiting here, trying to call his work.

"No time for lunch. Here, this way."

He followed the old man past the miniscule waiting area, into the plexiglass-shielded receptionist area. From there, Dr. Fejes led him into another room that looked like a cross between a masseuse's office and a prison cell. There was a single overhead light, a sink, a mirror, a toilet, a handful of mismatched knick-knacks, and what looked like a massage table. No windows. The table itself was covered in loose pieces of paper that seemed to range from receipts and patient files to magazine subscription cards and mostly finished crossword puzzles. The more Paulie thought about it, it seemed like this room had been a bathroom first, and then an examination room as an afterthought.

The aloofness of his dentist, allegedly named Seltzman, had seemed unprofessional and off-putting, but the general disarray and haphazard mess of this so-called office disturbed Paulie.

But then again, he thought, what would you expect out of an oncologist located in a strip-mall. Ahem, Otorhinolaryngologist

"Pali, I am Joseph Fejes. Ear nose throat doctor. Not oncologist. Seltzman, he is my friend and colleague. He tells me, 'You must see his growth. You must see his growth now!' so I will. Here, shake my hand," he said, offering Paulie his hand, "As practice, you should never let strangers into your mouth. See, now we are not strangers."

Paulie took his hand, who found himself impressed by the strength of the old man's grip. With his free hand, Dr. Fejes gestured towards the table.

"Shouldn't I get an X-ray?"

"What do I look like, a man made of gold? Do I look like I can afford these things? I am simple man, Galamb. Sit, you sit here."

Against his better judgement, once more, Paulie blindly obliged, sitting in the middle of the table. The old man walked to the sink, opened the hinged mirror, and retrieved a small cloth mask that he placed over his mouth. Then he quickly rinsed his hands in the water, a squirt of soap, and a splash of hand sanitizer before shaking his hands dry. Paulie watched in wonderment as the little man paced around the bathroom-turned-examination room at a speed that seemed unnatural for someone his age. With a swiftness, Dr. Fejes grabbed various instruments out of the seemingly random cabinets strewn about the room and placed them to Paulie's left and right. Lastly, he pulled out what looked like a toolbox from under the massage table, opened it, and fetched a small head lamp. Upon closer examination, Paulie saw that it was in fact a toolbox, as per the loose ball-peen hammer, tape measure, and various screwdrivers seen in the box.

Finally, he approached Paulie, placing the headlamp on his head, and said, "Okay, I am ready. I will touch you now, yes?"

"Uh-" he tried to offer an objection, but already the old man's two bare hands were on his throat. He wasn't sure if the man was giving him a gentle massage or about to strangle him. Judging by the handshake, Paulie recognized that he was very capable of either. He did his best to relax.

"Shouldn't you be wearing, I don't know, gloves or something?"

"No, I do not wear gloves. I am allergic to latex. Do not worry, my hands are clean. Open your mouth, no more questions."

His heavy accent must have had an air of hypnosis, because suddenly Paulie found his mouth wide open. And before he could object, Dr. Fejes had his bare pointer finger on Paulie's tongue. He could still taste the suds of soap bubbles past and a hint of alcohol from the hand sanitizer on the elderly man's finger. But past those awful tastes, he was catching hints of something else.

As the doctor shone the headlamp light into Galamb's mouth, illuminating the cavern where the growth lay hidden. Paulie could also taste the artificial horseradish flavor of Arby's "Horsey sauce", and even through the doctor's mask, he could smell the cheap deli meat of Subway.

Suddenly, Paulie gagged. It seemed like the old man was attempting to poke his uvula. "No doc, not there," he tried to say, but with the various metal tools in his mouth, it came out without the consonants. "Ohh ocgh, odd 'ere."

"Wider, Pali, I need you to open wider," he said, as Paulie winced with pain.

He tried his best not to do so, but the pain that had put him out of work following the removal of his treacherous wisdom tooth stabbed him in the jaw. As the electric sharp pain bit into his throat and jaw, it took great restraint to keep himself from instinctively biting down. Instead, he squeezed the fake plastic leather of the massage chair as if he were trying to tear through it. The pain was hot, fierce, and blinding.

He could taste blood now, which seemed impossible as only Dr. Fejes' fast-food fingers had been in his mouth, unlike the dentist and his Curved Sickle Scaler, a lifetime before when he thought he just had a dry pocket, or a tiny keloid. New words flashed before him, "Tumor", "Growth", and "Cancer" while the pain grew more intense.

He was going to scream; he could feel it trying to escape him. His knuckles had gone white as felt his fingernails puncture the pleather upholstery.

"Quap!" said his jaw, as a thin sprits of blood flew from under his tongue onto the cloth mask of the man in front of him.

It was seeing Dr. Fejes flinch when Paulie made an involuntary yelp from inside his mouth, but not his mouth, which forced him to shut his eyes tight enough to squeeze a tiny tear out of each one.

"My God," whispered the small doctor, pulling his hand out of Paulie's mouth. He could almost taste the doctor's breath. Salami, ham, mustard. When Dr. Fejes pulled away, it seemed like the pain had almost instantly vanished. Paulie got up and ran to the sink, and quickly spat into it.

There was more blood than he had expected. He wanted to curse at the old man, but his adrenaline kept him over the sink, huffing and puffing. Instead of berating the doctor, he turned the sink on, gargled a splash of water, and spewed out the pink blood-and-spit mixture back into the basin.

"Pali, I've never seen anything like this," the old man said, taking a seat on the massage table where Paulie had just been, sitting on the various tools he had lain next to Paulie but never used. When Paulie turned to him, he saw that the old man was holding his palms in front of his face, staring at them intently. "Never in my many, many years as ear-nose-throat doctor have I see this."

"Is it bad? Do you think it's cancer?"

"It's the most magnificent thing I have ever seen. And I believe you should make sure to not eat any more food. No lunch for you. No dinner tonight. No breakfast tomorrow. Do you understand, Pali?"

Paulie wiped the spittle off his chin, rubbing his jaw where the pain had just been, now non-existent, and answered the doctor truthfully, "No, Dr. Fejes, I do not understand. Is it cancer or is it not?"

"I am not sure, but I know one thing. You must return tomorrow. For surgery. I must remove the mass from you. This, it means you cannot eat lunch. Or dinner. Or breakfast. You may drink water, sure, I do not mind water. But no food. It will affect the anesthetic. I do not want you waking up during removal surgery, okay?"

Paulie felt faint as the bathroom-turned-office spun in circles around him.

Yesterday it was a toothache, then cancer, today it was unclear, and tomorrow it would be surgery.

This was happening too fast.

"Dr. Fejes, what time, uh, should I return?"

"Early. Say, ah, nine o'clock. Yes, nine should be fine," he said, as he brought his hands closer to his face. From behind the mask, which still had a small streak of blood, Paulie could see that the old man was wiggling his nose. Was he smelling his hands?

Paulie pulled his wallet out, and from there a tiny plastic card that a small caduceus on the corner, a symbol consisting of two red snakes winding around a winged staff. Below that, the card read "Midland Health" along with his identification number.

"Here, Dr. Fejes, here is my insurance card."

Instead of taking it, the man just shook his head. "No, no,

this will not be necessary. Just promise me you will not eat until after the surgery. Only water. No food."

Even as the smell of Arby's and Subway permeated off of the old man, causing his own stomach to grumble, he promised.

"Dr. Fejes, one last question."

"Fine, one last question, then you go. I must call assistant. I must prepare office for surgery," he said, bringing his hands closer to his face as he closed his eyes.

"Why did you say pigeon earlier?"

"I said Pigeon Pigeon. You, your name, it is like mine."

"What do you mean?"

"It is Hungarian. I know this because I am Hungarian. It is my mother's tongue and the tongue of my childhood."

(Paulie wanted to argue with him, as he was not Hungarian. He was gifted one of those DNA-swab kits that had been popular a few years back. The results revealed that he was a Scandinavian mutt, with an odd smattering of British Isles and a dash of Native American for good measure. But nary a single drop of Hungarian in his molecular make-up.)

"Pali, your first name. It is Hungarian for Pigeon or Dove."

"Uh."

"And Galamb, your father's name. It is other word for Pigeon. Your name, it means 'Pigeon Pigeon' and that is why I say this to you."

He had always wondered why his parents had named him Pali, and they had always told him they wanted to give him a unique name. Were they lying to him? Or was this strange old man who smelled like fast-food lying to him.

As Paulie turned to leave, Dr. Fejes finally rested his hands on his face, covering the majority of any visible skin not covered by his bloody mask or disheveled white hair. "What does your name stand for, Dr. Fejes?"

"It means 'stubborn'. Now you go. No food. Just go, will you? Just leave me. I have much work to do."

As the strings of fate pulled Paulie out of the office, Paulie considered his work. He had to call his work and let them know he would have to miss another day of work. To get a keloid or a tumor or a growth or whatever the tiny mass in his mouth was surgically removed. Another day lost from work. As he left the office, he was once again afraid of losing his job, or worse, losing his mind like the store clerk two doors down had.

The door chimed as he closed it, and very quickly he heard the door lock latch behind him. How quickly had the old man followed him out the door? When he turned around and saw the old man clutching a submarine sandwich, chewing it vigorously. Paulie, clutching his bag of beer, smokes, and porn, loudly asked, "Before I go, can I use your phone to call my work? To let them know I have surgery tomorrow."

Dr. Fejes did not open the door, instead he continued chewing his food without closing his mouth. He spit a chunk of brown-gray meat with some sort of yellowish-pink sauce slathered on it, onto the glass of his door when he asked Paulie, "Where it is you work?"

"Uh, Pea Tree Farms. On the other side of town. I am a taste tester there."

"No," the doctor said before he closed the blinds on the entrance once more.

For some reason, as the meat slowly slid down the glass Paulie realized that this particular chunk of meat had come from Arby's, as was the sauce. Horsey Sauce.

Did he really just go to two separate fast-food places just to make a Frankenstein super sandwich?

Yes. Yes he did. And if you peeked into his office, you would see that he was devouring it while Paulie Galamb's stomach grumbled hungrily.

12

SMARTPHONES AND PORN

And Permaculture

"So, Cobb and Birch's number one: nothing in nature grows forever, see? There is a constant cycle of decay and rebirth."

"You mean like reincarnation?" asked the shortest teenager, Stocks.

"In a sense, I suppose, but we're talking more literal here, more applicable. Number two should clear that up. Two states that the continuation of life depends on the maintenance of global biogeochemical cycles of the most gangster elements. Pop quiz bitches, what are those elements?"

Mullet raised his Cheeto-encrusted paw and blurted before he was called upon, "Oxygen, carbon, nitrogen, sulphur, and prosperous!"

Juan laughed, "Close enough. It's phosphorous. Write that shit down this time. Number three: The probability of extinction of populations or a species is greatest when the density is very high or very low. Both crowding and lacking too few individuals of a species may reach thresholds of extinction."

Instead of notebooks, the four boys used their thumbs to type out the wordy phrase their leader and current teacher spat at them. With lightning speed and horrendous abbreviations, they repeated Juan's teachings into their digital notebooks.

He'd say, "Four: the chance that a species has to survive and breed is dependent mostly on one or two factors in a complex web of relations of the organism to its environment."

And Billy or Brian would type, "4. Chc a sp. 2 surv. N brd. Is dpndt n ½ fctr in CMPX * of rltn of ORGNm 2 ENVRO"

Juan would read from his textbook, "Five: our ability to change the planet increases at a faster rate than our ability to foresee the damage done."

And Brian or Billy would paraphrase, "5. R abl-T 2 ¢ ERTH ↑ @a >>rt / R abl-T 2 4see the conseq." It's okay if you can't understand their abbreviated babble. It's more for them than you, anyways.

Only Mullet appreciated the dramatics of Juan closing his textbook before reading the sixth and final principle, as if to demonstrate he had it memorized, "Six. Living organisms are not only the means but ends, see? In addition to their instrumental value to humans and other livin', breathin' creatures, they have an intrinsic worth. Aw shit. Here he comes again."

The boys turned around on their park bench and saw Paulie in the distance.

"Okay, that's enough for now. Yo, Stocks, tell me this. What is the prime directive of permaculture?"

Stocks nervously glanced up, then quickly flicked his thumb upwards on his phone until he found the answer in his notes, "The only ethical decision is to take responsibility for our own existence and that of the next gen!"

"Very good. Mullet, what the fuck is the principle of cooperation?"

Mullet straightened his back out of the slouch he was in

and repeated his teacher's lessons verbatim, "Cooperation, not competition, is the very basis of future survival and of existing life forms!"

"Damn right. Billy, show me the life intervention principle! Brian, law of return!"

At the same time, the two of them spoke, overlapping each other to the point where it sounded like utter nonsense.

"In chaos lies unparalleled..." "Whatever we take, we must return..." "...opportunity for..." "or nature demands a return..." "...imposing creative order!" "...for every gift received!"

"You're missing one piece, Brian."

He rolled his eyes in thought and blurted the last chunk of sentence he had forgotten, "or the user must pay!"

"Class dismissed. My little badasses, you fuckers are most def going to survive the fuckin' end times. Now put your shit away, I don't want Parlay over here thinkin' we's a bunch of pasty nerds."

"Yeah, 'cause we'll kick a nerd's ass!" Mullet exclaimed, spitting out a small orange Cheeto to the ground, only to be caught by a hungry crow near his feet.

Paulie overheard the last line as he approached the group of five, who all seemed to be hiding their cellphones as he got closer. There was no way of them knowing he needed to use their phone, was there?

Also, if they all had smart phones, why did they need porno magazines?

"Hey guys, I got your beer. If you're still fixing to threaten me, just know I'm not in the mood."

"Why would we threaten you, Parlay?"

"Enough!" Paulie shouted, loud enough to startle the crow away at the boy's feet.

"It's Paulie. Not Parlay. Not Pali. Not Pigeon," he said in such an aggressive tone that even Juan stepped back. The group of kids may have outnumbered him, but at the end of the day, he was still a larger mass than the lot of them.

"Oh, excuse me, Paulie, I didn't know you grew a pair of cajones in the last hour. Fair enough, Paulie it is. You hear that boys? No more nicknames for Big Man over here."

"Got it boss." "Acknowledged." "Understood." "Word."

"So, you got the stuff, eh? Much obliged, friendo. What's the damage?"

"The damage?" Paulie asked.

"How much do we owe you?"

Paulie's shift in tone, which had both surprised him and the teens, had somehow earned him an inkling of respect and he wasn't unhappy with that. His brain quickly crunched the numbers, and his mouth spoke them out loud, "Uh, thirteen dollars, eighty cents. Thirteen is fine."

Without being told to, Stocks, the shortest and youngest of the group, plucked out a handful of crumpled bills from his deep pockets. He handed two of them to Juan, who handed them to Paulie.

"Here's fifteen. Keep the change. Pleasure doing business with you, Paulie."

Paulie took the money and folded the five and ten in half, placing them in his pocket.

"Before I go, do you mind if I use one of your phones. Please, it's an emergency."

Stocks pulled out his phone and used his thumb to unlock it, "No problem."

Galamb turned around to hide the fact he hardly knew how to use a smart phone, as he preferred phones with buttons instead of the smooth glass of the rectangle in his hand. Chubby clumsy fingers sometimes made this task more difficult than he cared to admit. He managed to dial the HR Department of Pea Tree Farms without revealing his own electronic ignorance while the boys rummaged through the brown paper bag. "Just make it quick, Paulie, I don't have unlimited minutes or anything," lied the boy though Paulie wouldn't have known better.

"I'll be quick, I just have to call my boss."

"Whatever. Boys, break's over," Juan said, cracking open one of the sixteen-ounce Budweisers while Paulie listened for the dial tone. Stocks stuffed the porno magazine into his backpack, and the twins grabbed the pack of cigarettes. Brian or Billy took one, handed another to the other twin, and a third one to Mullet who stained the end of his cigarette orange with Cheeto-dust.

"Hello, you've reached Pea Tree Farms. How may I direct your call?" said the voice on the other end of the smart phone.

"Hi, it's Paul. Paul Galamb. I need to speak with Arnie, er, Arnold. Mr. Arnold Workman. In Testing. Please and thank you."

"Just a moment."

The voice disappeared and was replaced with grainy jazz music. It was being put on hold that directed his attention to the crack and hiss of four more beers opening.

Wait.

Paulie turned around and saw that the five teenagers were all sipping from five-of-six Budweisers.

"Oh come on, I got you guys the forties, not the tall cans! Those were for- Oh never mind."

"Aw, hell no, we don't drink that Steel Reserve shit, we ain't fuckin' animals, Paulie. This piss beer will do us just fine, thank you. You almost done with my little man's phone or what?"

Paulie held up his pointer finger, silencing Juan once more, while a new voice responded in his ear.

"This is Workman. What's the word, Paul? You ready to come back to work?"

"Uh, I saw my dentist yesterday. He found a growth in my throat. A tumor. I just got back from, well, an ears-nose-throat specialist. He confirmed it." Paulie chose not to divulge that Fejes had done so by sticking his bare hands in his mouth.

There was a moment of quiet, punctuated by a bit of static between the boys smartphone and Arnolds. Arnie broke the silence by glumly asking, "Is it cancer?"

"The doctor said no, but he is having me go in for surgery tomorrow. I, uh, I don't know if I can make it back tom-"

Arnie Workman cut him off, "Paulie, you're one of our best panelists. Take the week off if you need, but that's all the time we can afford without you. You understand me?"

"I understand."

"I mean it, deal with the growth, rest, then come back. But be warned, Pea Tree can't go another week without you or without your position being filled. If you're not here Monday, then you might have to start considering other places of employment."

Paulie didn't want to ask about Chris Wagner, but he figured the ad in the paper was a hint at the seriousness of the situation. He, like Chris, could and would be replaced.

"Yes sir. I will be there Monday."

"Feel better Paulie. Get lots of rest," Arnie said, before hanging up. Paulie handed the phone back to Juan, thanking him as he did.

"No problemo. Now scram. You're interrupting class time. Thanks for the beer. Mullet, in one sentence, describe Entropy."

Mullet swallowed a large glug of beer, belched, and responded with, "Entropy is the measure of disorder and randomness!"

"Stocks, how does entropy apply to permaculture?"

The short boy answered while Paulie grabbed the mostly

torn paper bag with the two large plastic bottles in it, "The state of energy before and after a transformation requires chaos; there is chaos in growth just as there is entropy in decay."

"Very good. Just like the growth in Paulie, there is decay. Be well, Paulie. Good luck with your surgery. We'll be seeing you."

Paulie watched the five of them drink the wrong beers, as he made his way back toward his home, toward a birthday party for a nine-year-old snail.

13

A BADASS RECOGNIZES A BADASS

Sometimes Even He Will Blush

Very tediously, Niles combed in the dark brown sludge into his goatee, exercising great care to not let a speck of the stuff touch his skin. He had done so in the past when he first began dying the grays away, resulting in him having a few extra unwanted brown blemishes and birthmarks. Kind of like those temporary tattoos them hippie chicks at the county fair would dole out to children and lonesome old bikers like himself. Hannah? Hemmy? Henna? Whatever it was called, he didn't care for it, regardless of how cute them girls was. Tattoos was meant to be permanent, and any pussy-footin' around that permanence was, well, for pussies.

If you'll excuse his French.

He chuckled to himself, and carefully examined the edges of his goatee, making sure he didn't miss a spot or any wiry gray and whites. The border of his hair and skin was marked by a slick of Vaseline that prevented any of the dye from soaking into his face. Satisfied, he dropped his brush into the sink without washing the excess off, leaving a small splatter of brown goop on the off-white basin. Past stains dotted the inside of the sink from previous dye-jobs and past combs thrown just as recklessly. Niles wasn't much of a cleaner, and since We-Store tried to buy him and his two neighbors out, he couldn't really afford the cleaning lady anymore.

This was on account of him having to rent out the mandatory storage unit where his man-cave used to be, where his garage once was, where his baby girl used to sleep. Before he lost his cave, his garage, his girl, his license, and his leg. Now his disability checks, half of them go to We-Store, half goes to Meals on Wheels, half goes into his beer gut (his gas tank, as it were), and what little left he has left, that half goes toward his best friend.

Slugger.

Now you may be surprised that this fifty-eight-year-old badass had a soft spot for a squishy lil' thing like Slugger, but badasses recognize their own and always look after one another. Niles didn't have much left these days, but what he did have he held onto with pride.

Niles grabbed two large striped Navajo blankets from the closet next to the bathroom and hopped past his jukebox, past the large aquarium, over to the couch which wasn't in the best shape nor the worst. All the same, he figured for a party with company coming over, the stains could do with being a bit less visible. Like a tight-rope walker spreading his or her arms for balance, Niles opened one of the blankets and draped the thick wool cover over his sofa. He pulled the edges taught and pushed the sagging portions into the seats crevices as if he were making his bed in boot camp before he was given the boot from there some forty years back.

From behind him, his jukebox clicked over, automatically switching to the next record in queue. The Gabel Kuro, or

"Gabrielle" as Niles called her, was older than himself (Hell, the jukebox was older than Edith) but it still worked like a charm.

The first guitar riff "Bow-now-now-Now-now-now" tickled him pink.

"Get ready, Slugger, this one's for you!" Niles shouted excitedly, recognizing the riff as the start of one of his favorite songs. Slugger, unamused, crawled over to the large piece of crisp lettuce on the far side of its glass aquarium home, the Iron Maiden logo on proud display on the side of the snail's shell. As George Thorogood and the Destroyers began narrating the story of his birth, Slugger used his 25,000 teeth to start masticating the leaf under itself.

Niles grabbed his Typical Tuesday Leg and reattached it to his stump, caressing the tattoos hand-painted down the hard metal of what should have been his calf had it not been torn free several years back.

It was an event he didn't like to reflect on, so instead he let the music take hold of him while he begrudgingly cleaned his condo. He had no interest on remembering the day he lost his girl and his leg. The day he crashed Sweet Cherry Pie into the guard rail, killing her, still haunted him, but only when he slept. Luckily, the dope in his bong mostly kept him from remembering his dreams.

He focused on the lyrics. Slugger focused on the leaf. Niles didn't think back on the bad moments. Such as being ejected from his bike at fifty-five with no helmet, just his leathers. As he lay the second Navajo blanket over the coffee table, he did not think back to that day ten years earlier. Of him being in shock when he found his leg still caught in the mangled mess of crumpled metal and motorcycle. Of the meat and cartilage and blood stuck in the twisted remnants of his baby girl. Instead, he sang along with George.

"She could tell right away," he shouted, using his crutch as a broom to sweep abandoned beer cans under the coffee table in the center of the room. "That I was bad to the bone!"

It wasn't Slugger's fault, the accident that killed Sweet Cherry Pie, no. It was entirely his own. Niles could have simply not swerved out of the way. He could have just run-over the snail in the road, squished it flat and ended it quick. There'd be no pain, just a dark flash of black rubber over black asphalt with Slugger in between and it'd be over.

He'd still have his baby girl, his leg, but he wouldn't have the greatest friend a fifty-eight-year-old badass could ask for. Niles pulled various expired snack platters out from the fridge, courtesy of Meals-on-Wheels and placed them on the kitchen counter. Niles spaced the salami circles and various cheese squares evenly to give it the allure of fancy eating instead of dwelling on the anniversary of this new normal. The bald man with the freshly painted goatee smiled at his snail, who sat on its lettuce devouring it slowly, surely.

Niles never regretted saving Slugger's life, even at the loss of his leg and bike.

Because Niles knew Slugger was going to do something important someday. Because badasses like himself recognized other badasses. Because Niles knew he was bad to the bone. Bad to the bone.

B-b-b-b-Bad.

The antique juke box clicked over to the next track, but in the rare silence between songs Niles heard a faint knock at the door. Quickly, he hobbled over to the door, pushing aside any missed beer cans with his crutch. When he opened it, the badass blushed.

"Hello there, darling."

"Why, hello there Nathaniel."

Niles stepped aside and extended his arm out to help her

indoors. She took his hand, allowing him to guide her to the sofa. The seventy-eight-year-old slowly sank into the thick wool of the Navajo blanket as the former biker moseyed back towards the mess in the kitchen.

"Don't mind me, I just need to straighten up a little bit more, but can I get you anything? A snack? Water? Beer?"

"A kiss would do me just fine, Nathaniel."

Without much more than a second thought, Niles bent over, balancing himself on one crutch and his plastic leg with tattoos drawn on, and kissed Edith Post squarely on the mouth. Not everybody winds up kissing the wrong person good night. But more on that later, we've a villain to meet.

14

THE MEAT BEHIND THE CURTAINS

Spoiled Gray And Green

In the lobby of the drab monolithic office building that homed Pea Tree Farms, the sunlight was usually plentiful and inviting. "Come outside, play with me!" the front desk secretary sometimes pretended to hear as she stared at the sunbeams bouncing off of the off-white marble floors, happily blinding her as she spaced out and waited for the person to buzz in from outside, or the next phone to ring, or her next and last short break, or best of all, five o'clock so she could leave here for a whole twelve hours.

The sunlight that reflected off the large glass walls of the entire first floor, which shone into the otherwise bland lobby the secretary and two security guards quietly stood watch in, also served as a sort of timepiece. Other than the large slab of a desk where the secretary sat, there was little else but a door behind her that led to a small room filled with television screens and one security guard napping in front of them, and a hallway with four elevators each with four separate purposes.

They were labeled appropriate to their destinations. Administration, Testing, Research and Development, and Storage. To access these elevators, one needed a special card, and that special card only worked on one elevator each, lest your card was silver. That card, which only a dozen people had, got you anywhere in the building including a fifth and sixth area not labeled on the four elevators.

The other admins, they called those off-limit areas "Containment" and "Crematorium". Doctor Koop, he chose to call them home. If you weren't one of the twelve people with the silver key card, then you had no reason to believe this building consisted of anything but the aforementioned four sections. The existence of these two areas was surprisingly not often speculated on for a variety of reasons.

One was that communication between each department was not only discouraged, but a fire-able offense. Admins did not talk with R&D, the panelists did not talk with the handlers from Storage, nor did the janitors of one department dare talk to janitors of the next.

Another reason Containment and the Crematorium remained hidden was a bit more subtle. Other than this first floor and the last, there were no windows on the side of this large building. So, if one were to look up and try to speculate how many floors high this building was, they'd be hard pressed to guess the correct number. On paper, filed away at the county courthouse, Pea Tree Farms was listed as a six-story high rise. Interestingly, the tallest building in town was the courthouse, which was only ever so slightly taller than the Midland water tower. But in all actuality Pea Tree Farms was eight stories tall with two stories hidden below the basement, below the ground.

The final reason nobody knew about the sub-sub-basement prison and the top floor kiln, was because the knowledge of these places was guarded with the threats of death to any and all who would leak it.

The few that tried to spread word of what happens way below and far above the lobby, they've long passed through the hot end of the crematorium. And any that would dare report them missing or lost suffered similar fates.

So when somebody called the front desk secretary, she'd say "Hello, you've reached Pea Tree Farms. How may I direct your call?" and direct it accordingly she would. She didn't know who Paul Galamb was, but she knew Arnie as he was the department lead. She forwarded the call happily, hung up the phone, then went back to staring out the windowed lobby, praying for sunlight. Outside, the skies were gray, and without the bouncing beams of sunshine, time stood still. In between prayers, she simply waited for the next phone call, the next break, and for when it was finally time to go home.

Meanwhile, Arnie Workman was cussing behind closed doors five floors above the secretary, above the two security guards in the lobby, above the hundreds of scientists and researchers, below the corporate suits, below Doctor Koop.

With news of Galamb's continued absence, he'd have to use his special silver card and alert those in Administration. Worse yet, he would have to notify his boss.

Arnie looked at his reflection in the computer monitor and straightened his tie. He was a mostly handsome man that could have been in television had the universe allowed it. Instead, he guided an ever-shifting cast of typically obese men and women through a series of product tests, keeping tabs on their well-being and general health as Pea Tree Farms threw a thousand variations of the same product their way.

It was his job to make sure those who worked under him were kept happy, to ensure that those above him were also kept safe from the prying eyes of the local media. If one of his employees needed time off to deal with a mild sickness, flu, or illness, he'd happily give them the time off they needed. Liver issues, stomach issues, throat issues, you name it, just take the time off you need and come back when you can. If someone suddenly fell sick from a mysterious prion disease like Jakob-Creutzfeldt, then it was his job to allow them a long, paid vacation until the disorder ultimately rotted their brains away.

Because this happened more often than the company could ever publicly admit.

With Chris Wagner paid off and out of commission, he couldn't afford to lose a second employee. Galamb would be the third cancer case this quarter, the tenth this year, and potentially the thirty-second death that would not be reported on in any official means.

But still, Arnie would have to face the man upstairs. If you could still call him that.

He gathered his briefcase that carried nothing of import in it and left his office quickly. As he weaved through the maze of cubicles and ugly people, he tried to avoid contact with his lesser, but somehow Sue Ellen always found a way to get between him and his destination.

It wasn't just her faint smell of lavender and incense, which technically went against company policy of wearing any kind of cologne or perfume, but it was the way she talked to him like they were equals.

God, he hated her. He was one of the very few people that knew of the Crematoriums existence, and often he secretly wished she would fuck up enough to wind up inside it.

"Hey there Arnie, what's the good word today?"

Arnie loathed the fact that he recognized a kiss-ass from a mile away, as he was one himself. This old gabby-grandma had long ago purposely picked up on his mannerisms and parroted them back at him, as if to flatter him. It only annoyed him.

Almost as much as it did being called by his shortened first name instead of his surname. She may have been his elder, sure, but she was still very much his subordinate.

But he would not let his hatred show. He wore his customer service smile well, and with his smile feigned, he fed her bullshit.

"Oh, just have to talk to the people upstairs about Paulie."

"Is he alright? Is that tooth of his still giving him trouble?"

He winced in pain, and whether she noticed it or not was not important. He knew she knew that the panelists were to minimize communication, and her knowledge of his teeth problems was telling that she did not heed that rule. "I'm afraid so. He will be taking the rest of the week off. Any luck with the new applicants? It appears Mr. Wagner will not be returning after all as he chose to go in a different career direction after all," he said, skirting the subject.

"Oh well that's a shame. He was a nice young man, albeit a bit strange wouldn't you say?"

("No stranger than you, you old chatty-Kathy," he thought but did not say.)

Instead, he just chuckled and lied, "Yeah, but aren't we all a little strange here at Pea Tree Farms?"

"Ain't that the truth!" she said, laughing and playfully patting him on the back. For a moment, Arnie considered how easy it would be to break her arm. "But to answer your question, I just interviewed two young women who are excited to start as soon as Monday."

"Two? I thought you interviewed three women today?"

"Oh, why, yes, I did. However, the third girl walked out of the interview when I mentioned that the majority of the products we test here are meat-based products. She said she was a vegetarian before storming off, can you believe it?"

"Sue Ellen, you know the rules. You are not to advertise the products tested. Nor are you ever to disclose what we test to a mere applicant. Only after an applicant is fully hired, trained, and their paperwork signed are you to ever mention our products."

He grabbed her shoulder, and gave it a gentle squeeze, "You understand this, right?"

The old ladies chipper smile dissipated quickly as Arnie Workman squeezed harder. "Oh what harm can-" she said, until his grip on her caused her now to wince in pain. "I understand, Mr. Workman."

"I'm going to need you to call that young lady back, right now, and convince her to come back to sign an NDA. If she gives you trouble, find me. As for the other two applicants, see if you can convince them to start on Thursday. Offer them a sign-on bonus should they object. If they object further, then again, find me. I have to go now, Sue Ellen."

As he let go of her shoulder, she smiled at him once more before he rushed towards the elevator with his briefcase in hand. She'd be sure to call the three out-of-towners at her leisure, the young college-girls who were just here to make a quick bit of cash between semesters. The two that had taken the job would be easy to convince into starting earlier because Pea Tree was generous with their sign-on bonuses. The third girl, the vegetarian, she would be convinced too. Sue Ellen did have, after all, the gift of gab.

And Arnie Workman hated her for this. As he swiped his silver card in the elevator, a panel opened up and offered three more buttons than were usually present. He pressed the highest of the three, and up he went.

If there was a moment where Sue Ellen feared him, that fear was now coursing through himself. An employee should always maintain a healthy consternation and respect for their employer. Arnie would have preferred if that fear was turned up to eight or nine.

And to say Arnie Workman was afraid of Doctor Koop was an understatement. The man terrified him. As the elevator went above and beyond its expected path, Workman tried to steady his breath. When it arrived and opened at the top-most floor, Arnie did not look around at the bare black walls, instead he just followed the dim yellow lights on the floor. They reminded him of his youth when he would frequent movie theaters with his friends. Back when movie theaters were still popular. Back when he still had friends.

At the end of the hallway was a single door that was labeled "Boardroom", and when he stood before it, a small camera aimed itself at him. From a small speaker to the left of the door croaked an awful voice.

"Arnold Workman, what can I do for you?"

Arnie leaned into the speaker and pressed the small unlabeled button below it, held it down, and spoke nervously, "It's Paulie Galamb, sir, he, uh-"

He was cut off by a large buzz, and a click. Then suddenly the automated door opened. The smell was always the first thing to hit him, but only an instant before the blinding blue lights reached his eyes. The smell was an abhorrent blend of raw meat and damp fish, of ground pork and pulverized chicken. His eyes took a minute to adjust to the lights, not unlike those bright lights seen in a tanning salon, but when they did, he entered the room. In it was a large table, fifteen feet long, six feet across. There were six seats on each side, and a final one at the end of the table.

Where he sat, facing away from Arnie Workman. The man at the end of the table was staring out of the double-sided mirrors, staring at the fields of suburban sprawl and many car lots. If you were to look in from outside, you wouldn't see

Doctor Koop staring back, just the illusion of an empty, unused floor.

The ancient man spoke slowly and sternly, "What about Galamb, Mr. Workman?"

Just as slowly as he spoke, the hundred-thirteen-year-old man spun around in his seat.

Arnie Workman knew not to react, not visibly. Doctor Koop's square face, though pale and gaunt as it was, was accented by his remarkably edged beard-sans mustache. The same kind Lincoln would sport had he lived twice as long. The beard was as white as the bright fluorescent bulbs, if not brighter. What hair the supercentenarian had left atop his head was equally colorless, styled in a way that commanded a military-respect, as his attire had as well. His outfit looked like a cross between a high-ranking generals uniform and that of a scientist or doctor. A white formal lab-coat, with military medals neatly pinned over his heart.

His neatly kept beard and hair and uniform wasn't why Arnie purposely chose not to react. No, it was the writhing pink leeches of all shapes and sizes that writhed and wriggled all around the century-old man's visible flesh. One such leech was roughly the size of deflated baseball that pulsated on the ghostly-white skin of his neck. Another was expanding and contracting just above his thick rimmed glasses above his brow, no bigger than a golf-ball, as pink as raw liver.

When Doctor Koop spoke, he saw that inside his mouth, behind his yellow and brown teeth, there were hundreds of tiny fleshy growths inside, no bigger than grains of rice. Or maggots. They all moved around in a seemingly random fashion.

"He had a tooth removed not long ago. I gave him a few weeks off, as per your recommendation," Arnie said, trying to not pay attention to the thumb-sized chunk of meat crawling down the ancient man's long dead face.

"Yes. I recall," Doctor Koop said, with a single worm like mass slithering out of his mouth and into his nose. In the blue light, the pink leeches had an off-putting purple glow, just as much as his gray cataracted eyes seemed to shine brighter than the white of his skin and ghastly hair, like egg yolks gone rotten and then cracked into a porcelain plate.

"He called me today. He informed me of a growth in his throat."

Dr. C. Everett Koop jumped up, impossibly fast for a man his age, causing Arnie Workman to take a step back. As the skeletal man in military garb rose, pieces of flesh fell off of him. Not his flesh, but the tiny leeches. Maggots. Worms. Meat. As they did, they revealed the rainbows of infection hidden underneath where they were feeding.

The golf ball above his brow fell off as Doctor Koop contorted his face into an implausible display of anger, revealing a large yellow hole where his eyebrow should have been. Past that yellow hole was the sheen of his skull, outlined by a thin layer skin and muscle that was the color of spoiled beef.

As he barked at Arnie, the tiniest chunks of spittle and pink grains of rice flew out, landing on the boardroom table in front of him, "And what did you tell him!?"

"I, uh, I told him to take the week off."

Suddenly, Doctor Koop slammed his frail fists down onto the table, dislodging hundreds of tiny pieces of himself. They fell off, scurried about aimlessly, then hurried back towards him. From the other end of the room, Arnie nervously watched the man glare at the insect-like things crawl towards himself. They went onto the man's still balled fists and disappeared in the recesses of his sleeves. The only one that remained was the pink mass that had fallen off his face, above his glasses.

He had calmed himself down. Which meant that now Arnie could calm down as well.

"Come here, my boy," he said, grabbing the last meaty bit in his unclenched hand.

Obediently, automatically, he did as he was told, very careful to show no emotion as he came closer to the ancient man. They used to call him Surgeon General. The 13th Surgeon General. Now he was the leader of this company, the man behind the curtains.

Doctor C. Everett Koop was the only man with the gold ID card. The only man who had access to The PTM in Containment. The only man who had survived his own death nearly a decade earlier.

As he grew closer, the smell of rotting meat grew stronger. The stench was nearly making him gag, but he did not let that be seen. When he was within arm's reach of his employer, the man that was easily twice his age and then some lifted his arm to Arnie's mouth.

Then, without saying a word, he opened his palm. And Arnie knew. Inside he was screaming, but here in front of Doctor Koop, he was resilient, calm, and ready.

Doctor Koop grabbed the mass in his hand and placed it into Arnold Workman's mouth.

Try as he might, Arnie could not contain his fear any longer as the one hundred-thirteen-year-old man fed him the mass that had been eating the infection on his face. All he could do was chew and reject any urge to vomit up the gift that Koop was offering.

Painfully, he swallowed, and saw that the man in front of him was smiling with a mouth full of visibly cracked teeth.

"We'll keep an eye on him, Mr. Workman. Now leave me. I must think on this."

Arnie stood there for a moment, shaking, still struggling to swallow the last few bits of meat. Then, after the flavor subsided, he retreated towards the elevator door. Quickly, and with a feeling of pure elation in his belly.

When the doors closed behind him, he couldn't help but think how good he felt in this moment. He felt like running a marathon or fucking all night or climbing a mountain, not that there were any within a hundred miles.

Arnie felt like running up to Sue Ellen and hugging her, promoting her, hell, promoting everyone on his floor. A bonus for everybody!

He felt like a million bucks, felt like he could take on the whole world. The ecstasy flowing through him, he was convinced he could do anything. While the pink slug chewed to pieces slid down his esophagus, he felt like he could live forever.

But he knew this would pass, so instead of pressing the button on the elevator that would bring him back to Testing, he waited until his stomach acids melted the bits he was fed. He knew it was a quick process, much quicker than it would take to digest any other food, so he didn't dilly dally long.

And after a minute or two, he was back to his normal self. All that remained was the lingering stink of his breath that still smelled like raw beef. Once again, Arnie Workman adjusted his tie, and took his empty briefcase back down to his office.

15

A SNAIL'S EYEBALL STALKS

And Birthday Candles

"Never show up early to a party, but don't show up too late to be noticed" Toni used to say in the few times they went out together socially. Not that the couple was terribly anti-social, but after the last two pandemics things never really went back to the way things they were before. Everybody always spoke of "The Big One" in the same way Californian's feared the apocalyptic mega-quake, or the super volcano that'd blow up Yosemite. Except it wasn't a large-scale natural disaster people were afraid of, but the next virus that would indiscreetly kill whoever it got its grubby tendrils on. People were still afraid of people and the sicknesses they'd spread. It was evidenced by the tumble weeds of cloth masks and the garbage cans stuffed with mostly empty hand-sanitizer bottles, with dirty moist toilettes and squeeze bottles squeezed dry that formerly were filled with six ounces of hand-soap.

This never stopped Toni from pretending good party etiquette was necessary. She'd say, "Always bring a gift, even if they say you don't have to. Especially if they say you don't have to," even though they were just going to a company outing for his boss's boss's birthday. A man he'd never met, just some faceless CEO, who chose to anonymously go by only his last name's initial. Still, he was the one carrying a fancy electric wine opener he had been gifted from an aunt or cousin a year or two earlier.

That gift sat in the reception area with a handful of other gifts that were never opened, and the outing itself was hardly an attempt at a party. There was a minimal catering crew there, and the food was reheated slop that none of his fellow taste testers would touch. Himself included. A buffet of browns and green that Sue Ellen took one look at and raised her nose to the air. That Doug, "Just Doug", walked past three times in consideration only to hover around the portable soda fountain. Even Chris Wagner wouldn't touch the pizza the caterers kept under the red lamp hot hold, making no effort to keep the flies away. It had seemed like a strange prank, to offer barely edible looking food to a group of employees whose job it was to sample exquisite grade-A future food.

"And most importantly, never decline free food or drink if it's somebody else's party."

Though that party had taken place in the middle of October several years earlier, before the last two viruses rattled the world, Paulie never forgot his then-wife's advice.

It wouldn't be hard to be early or late when the party was on the other side of the shared wall between condominiums. The problem lay in her later two rules.

He still had no idea what to get a snail, or for the owner of a snail, even though he'd known Niles for several years now. "What do you get for a man that has everything?" he joked to himself while he freshened himself up in the mirrorless bathroom.

And he'd have to refuse all snacks and drinks offered due to the looming surgery.

This wouldn't be a problem typically, for a man of his stature he was typically able to deny his appetite, but the malicious combination of stress and pre-surgery jitters had him desperately wanting to raid his cheat fridge. The fridge filled with sugary off-brand soda-pops, TV dinners, and colorful Hostess cakes courtesy of Meals-on-Wheels.

But he was practicing restraint. Begrudgingly. Because he needed this surgery to go without a hitch, so he could go back to work, back to his routine, his most precious thing. No more new doctors, no more threatening teenagers, no lumps-in-throat. Paulie just wanted to go back to tasting revolutionary new foods, paying his bills, and listening to the typical cacophonic combo of Jeopardy and heavy metal while keeping to himself.

"Just one more day, and then the world will right itself," he thought to himself, unaware that this thought was ultimately a lie. Not that he intended on lying to himself, for he was an honest man.

Paulie glanced down at himself, and saw he was as prim and proper as he would get for the occasion. Still sporting his Harvard Sweater, he added to his attire a mostly matching maroon fedora. Fedora's were still cool, he imagined, and if they weren't he doubted Niles, Edith, or Slugger would complain. Then finally, he fetched one of the many sandy treasures from his faux-beach Ikea collection, making sure it had not originally come from Niles himself, and brought it to his kitchen. It was a small gray and greenish-blue starfish that he had chosen because in certain lights, it almost reminded him of the birthday snail's own color scheme.

Carefully, he wrapped the starfish in a page from last week's advertiser, where he saw once again an advertisement for his place of work. Instead of re-reading it, he skimmed over another headline that grabbed his attention.

"Do you live near the Midland Auto-Park? Do you live or work downtown near the Office district? Have you ever worked for Pea Tree Farms? If you or a loved one been diagnosed with Mesothelioma and any of the previous statements are also true, you may be entitled to financial compensation! Please contact us at LaVey Law Firm to see about your potential eligibility in joining us in this class action lawsuit!"

Immediately, Paulie recognized the address.

Because he had been there earlier today. Mostly. If it had still stood where it said it was, then Paulie had passed the location en route to see the strange old Dr. Fejes. However, this apparent law firm, if it ever existed, was no longer present in the Midland Business Plaza. It, like many others around it, was now another vacant storefront for lease.

Paulie wondered why business came and went so quickly in this town, but he had no one to wonder at, so he kept quiet, and finished wrapping the starfish. It wasn't pretty, but it'd do the trick. His ex-wife would be proud of him, re-gifting her décor. He himself never cared for the beach-themed bathroom, but it made her happy, and seeing pieces of it leaving his life made him happy now.

"Okay, you're ready. Go," said his head to his heart, the thought passing through his throat as well as down his spine. It carried him, one leg at a time, from the kitchenette through the living room and out the door, past the motivational poster reminders of his ex-wife.

Paulie held the two large plastic bottles of beer, now freshly chilled and recovered from the fridge under one arm with the paper-wrapped starfish inside as he left his condo. Before knocking on his neighbor's door, he touched the small hard marble behind/inside his left cheek, the lump that was threatening his livelihood and life, and spoke to it, "You've got one more day with me, bud, then you gotta go."

The growth, it wasn't aware it was being acknowledged, though maybe it felt it, maybe.

He knocked on the door, hearing the strangest music he had ever heard come from the condo of Nathaniel Niles. Stranger than alternative-rock or country, which he was known to secretly play late in the evenings, when he thought nobody was listening. Stranger yet than the one time Paulie heard Niles shower-singing the lyrics to "Gangster's Paradise" was the music coming from the other side of the door. Though he would never admit to his neighbor that he heard him doing so.

Nope. It was pop music. Some kind of psychedelic pop. Pan-flutes and drums, and electric basses made stranger by distortion pedals. Not quite Hendrix level rock, not quite Sonny and Cher level pop. The kind of music you'd expect from weirdos in tie-dye, from go-go-dancers in cages, from artists that introduced themselves as artists and not by their first names.

In Niles' own words, it was hippy shit. As jarring as it seemed, it was only temporary, because before the door opened in front of him the music was silenced.

Instead, he was greeted by his elderly neighbor to the south and the loud blaring honk of a plastic party noise maker that inflated towards him in an alarming fashion. Not something he expected out of the nearly eighty-year-old lady.

"You made it, Paulie! I'm so glad to see you here, today!" she said in her happy raspy voice. Her elation was just as jarring as the music that played before, as was her rosy cheeks. Had she been drinking? Did she usually drink?

"It's good to be here, Edith," he said, watching Niles hobble towards him from his jukebox. It had been almost half a year since the last time he had seen inside the former biker's abode. Remarkably, he noticed, this time it was clean.

"Galamb, I'm glad you could make it. I assume then that dentist-turned-doctor of yours was wrong about that cancer then?"

"Cancer? Oh my, Paulie why didn't you say anything?" said the tipsy old lady, holding her hand in front of her mouth.

"Well, no, the throat doc said it didn't look like a cancer that he had ever seen, but he wants me to go in for surgery, well, tomorrow."

"My goodness, so soon!" he thought he heard Edith say, only instead the words came from Niles' goatee, which seemed to be freshly painted since Paulie had seen him this morning.

"Uh yeah, so that means no cake for me, I'm afraid." ("That I so desperately crave right now")

"Yeah, last time I went in for surgery the doctor said no food or drink, but really all he meant was no food. In my experience, you can still get your drink on."

"Oh yeah?"

"Best believe it. A little beer won't affect the sleepy drugs. If anything they'll only make them more potent. Did you bring the beer?"

Also, do not listen to this biker. He is not a doctor, nor a man known for his sage advice.

Paulie nervously offered the bag of beers to Niles. He opened it, and in his face subtly contorted Paulie could tell he had made a mistake.

"Never look into a gift horse's mouth," his wife would say, "And if you do, don't be bothered by its breath."

That subtle contortion quickly changed to a large toothy smile. "My man! Let me grab some glasses for us to share these heavy hitters!" he said, pulling the two beers out, which sent the starfish-in-paper falling to the floor. "What's that?"

"It's just a little something for the birthday boy? Wait, is Slugger a boy?"

"How the fuck should I know? As far as I'm concerned, it don't matter. Slugger ain't defined by the dangles or woo-hoos under its tummy. Slugger is just a badass. Slugger is just Slugger. Though I've been known to call him a boy just 'cause I don't want weirdos getting the wrong idea, if you know what I mean."

He did not know what Niles meant.

Niles carried the beers to his kitchenette island, which was not unlike Paulie's own next door. The major difference being that unlike his well-kept counter that was clean and mostly empty, Niles' was covered in a platter of salami, crackers, cheeses, and empty beer cans. A lot of empty beer cans. There among the cans was the birthday badass in all its blue-green glory. Slugger seemed to be knocking the empty cans over with its eyeball stalks, then crawling over the small amber puddles that formed around the mouth.

"Your doctor mighta said no drink, but Paulie, tonight we are drinking and there ain't a thing you can say about it," Niles said as he placed the two forty-two-ounce bottles down. He picked up the snail, placed it on his shoulder, and grabbed three red plastic Solo cups from the cabinet under the island. Before Paulie could object, Niles had poured three foamy "glasses" full of Steel Reserve. One of three, noticeably less than the others. "Now be warned, Edith, this stuff is a bit stronger than last ones we were drinking so I only filled yours halfway."

Edith, who was usually very calm, turned around with a speed that baffled Paulie, who picked up the present that Niles had ignored, and she barked, "Then you best fill it up another half if you expect me to drink with you boys. I may be older than you two, but I can still drink you both under the table."

So, Niles did exactly that, then doled the two plastic cups to his only friends outside this home of his.

"Let us drink. To Slugger, and to your health, Paulie."

"To our health. And to Slugger!" Edith said, raising her solo cup.

"To health, and to the birthday badass. Hurrah!" Paulie declared, as he hesitantly brought the awful metallic smelling beer to his mouth. The growth inside, it opened itself to the strange new liquid and imbibed upon it curiously.

Niles had not told him that when the doctor told him no food or drink before his surgery, he had been sneaking hits of whiskey from his flask. That the doctor could smell his breath before they cut off the necrotic flesh that was rotting around his newly formed but barely healed stump some years ago.

Mostly, because Niles did not want to spoil this moment.

16

BARSTOOL BANTER, PART TWO

And What Would Follow

With the bathroom-turned-office now converted to its second form, a bathroom-turned-office-turned-operating room, Joseph Fejes was ready to lock up for the evening. He left his office, and took with him the uneaten remains of his Arby's/Subway monstrosity in a crumpled bag that he tossed into the trash-can that sat listlessly between the various abandoned establishments as he made his way towards Midland's most famous pub. There at the "Ol' Watering Hole", he was greeted by two colleagues.

One, like him, was freshly off of work, while the other was drinking before his shift.

Joseph was careful not to interrupt the dentist who seemed to be telling an unrelated story, "I'm telling you that since he was in college, he's probably had a total of ten, eleven, maybe twelve alcoholic beverages. About half of them were drunk at his wedding a lifetime ago."

"So what's your point," said the meteorologist. "He got all sorts of Tennessee-twisted off of one cup of beer?"

"Worse, he got 'white-girl wasted' off of one cup of high gravity malt liquor on an empty stomach."

Joseph Fejes could hardly contain his titter at seeing an otherwise respected dental surgeon use the phrase 'white-girl wasted', which had caused both the dentist and meteorologist to snap back into the narrative.

"Greetings, my friends," he said in his smoky paprika accent.

The man with the Indiana birthmark patted the smaller, frailer doctor on the back gently while the handsome man next to him demanded another beer from the bartender "Salutations, Joseph," the dentist said.

"Did you see him, Joe? Did you meet the ugly man that Seltzman here won't shut up about?"

Dr. Fejes thanked the bartender for the beer, and just as soon as the bartender turned around, Fejes downed half the glass in one large singular gulp. "Bartender, if you will, may I have one more, but with a splash of bitters in it. A heavy splash." Before swallowing the second half and letting loose a loud hearty Eastern-European belch out from within.

"Aye, I saw him. I saw it."

"The growth?"

"Yes, we have much to discuss. I'm going to need your help Seltzman. And yours too, Hedasky. Can you clear any appointments you might have? Any patients you can push forward a day? Hedasky, have you any hold-ups?"

Tom Hedasky laughed loud enough to alert the only other patrons in the bar. The out-of-towners from the night before, no longer enchanted by the allure of a local celebrity such as him, were celebrating their last night of the party life due to their newly gained employment at you-know-where! Well, two of the three girls anyways.

"What help do you need of me, Joe? I ain't no surgeon. Hell, I couldn't even perform CPR if I needed to."

Seltzman turned to Hedasky and patted him on the back, much more aggressively than he had with Dr. Fejes upon his arrival. "Oh bologna, I remember when you were taking those nursing classes back in college because you suddenly fell for Barb from Delta Phi. Whatever happened to her? Didn't you get the clap from her or something?"

It was hard to believe that with the visible age difference between the two men that they had been dorm-mates back in the early nineties.

"No, other way around. I gave her chlamydia. I should look her up some time," Tom wondered, "See how she's doing. Probably married, couple of rug-rats. Hell, she was feisty, she's probably divorced and remarried. God, I loved her."

Joseph Fejes, who had kept mostly quiet up 'til now, burst out calmly, but affirmatively, "Barbara Costello died of throat cancer in 2006. Leaving behind her first husband and, as you correctly assumed, her two children. Now if you two are done fraternizing, let me propose something to you two."

And with that, the small shrewish old man quaffed down his second beer in one proud glug.

17

MALT LIQUOR AND THE MASS

And His Early Drunken Exit

No, Seltzman wasn't kidding. Paulie Galamb was proper wasted. It took him a few attempts to get that first sip of Steel Reserve down, but with each sip the next went down easier than the last.

Though he was never actually a sommelier, he felt like he would definitely appreciate spitting this awful tasting grog out instead of swallowing it. The taste was somewhere between metal-coated bananas and fizzy stale carpet.

Which was to say, it tasted very unpleasant.

Before he made it halfway through his glass, each sip gave him that awful whiskey pucker one got from swallowing a shot of shitty bourbon. Paulie did not notice any visible distress from Edith or Niles as they drank their portions of the forty-two-ounce beer, but he just reasoned it was because they had already been drinking before he arrived. It wasn't until Paulie stopped making the whiskey pucker face after each sip that Niles noticed his neighbor's inebriation.

"How are ya feelin' boss? I can see you swayin' where you sit."

Paulie didn't hear any of that, so instead he answered the question he heard, "I like boring things. I just eat because I'm ugly and there is nothing else for me to do. I miss boring things and loving stuff," he said, slumping into himself. Even in his poor-posture, he still towered over Edith and Niles. Niles, who seemed to be painting something on a snail shell, while Edith was patting Paulie on the back in an attempt to rid him of his hiccups.

"That almost sounds like a quote from a man I knew a life time before. Don't put yourself down, Paulie, you're not ugly. You're just a different kind of handsome."

Every time Paulie hiccupped, he hiccupped twice, though the second hiccup seemed like a silly parody of the first. He tried to hide the hiccups by sipping from his red Solo cup, but he could not hide his melancholy. Niles could taste the sadness in the air, so he got up and changed the tempo of the room by filling it with a different album from his antique jukebox. When Dewey Bunnel started singing about a horse with no name, Niles went back to painting his shell with various colored nail polishes.

Paulie could not escape the cloud over his head, not that he was trying very hard. Usually, very few things struck his heart strings in such a way that he allowed the bad thoughts to take over. Among them was his divorce, a wound that had mostly scabbed over by this point even five years on, his lack of purpose, a wound kept fresh by his complacency in life, and a healthy fear of death.

That wound was bleeding. Rarely did he ever fear death. When he totaled his father's Volkswagen, driving it drunkenly into his dad's wood-working shop, he genuinely thought his father was going to kill him. And with good reason, as that crash very well could have cost Pappa Galamb not only his favorite car, but his livelihood. When Paulie woke up in the hospital decades earlier and saw his father fuming, he thought the man was going to strangle him right there and then. Instead, he just yanked out the hungover and battered teenager's catheter. Paulie probably would have preferred death, as opposed to clutching his bleeding member, spurting out little dribbles of dick blood.

No, his fear of death was new and fresh again, and to make matters worse he was teetering on incoherently drunk. He heard Edith singing along with the band America about the horse, but she seemed so far away. Death could take her first, or Niles, or even the snail lapping up beer foam from the empty plastic beer bottle, but it seemed obvious that Death was waiting for Paulie. That's why people got cancer, wasn't it? Because they were set to die soon.

Sure, the short old man he met today tried to persuade him it wasn't cancer, but then why would he summon him back a day later for an emergency surgery. There was something Dr. Fejes wasn't telling him. Hell, there seemed to be something the newly named dentist was holding back from him.

It didn't help his case that the tray of sweating cheeses and warm salami was eyeballing him from across Niles' townhome. Even the flies buzzing about the birthday platter were begging him to take a bite. What was it Seltzman, was it the Gracey Curette or the Curved Sickle Scaler? He thought he said it out loud, but instead the question came out wrong, "Gravy Corvette or the Curvey Sickly Scaly" and this elicited a giggle out of Edith who was in the middle of singing the chorus.

"Oh, go eat something honey, I feel like the alcohol is taking hold on your typically tuned senses. Tonight, you can afford to eat a bit, if not just to put something in your tummy."

He had misheard his elderly neighbor, and in his mishearing, he found himself internally ripping free the scab off his largest wound. Paulie, in his stupor, had heard, "Toni, you can afford to eat a bit."

A line spoken five years earlier, that would be remembered as the start of the penultimate chapter in their failing marriage. He saw Edith get up and mosey towards the platter, waving away the flies that buzzed about the salami, cheese, and crackers. Paulie finished his beer, and stood up fast enough that he felt light-headed, but he was drunk enough to not care. "I can't," was his response when she held the platter in front of him, only Paulie wasn't talking to Edith anymore, "I can't do this right now, Toni."

Edith smiled knowingly at the poor drunk man. There were times when Edith was unsure whether he was slipping or if there was more to his babble. "How is she, Paulie? How is Toni doing these days."

"No, no, parlay. Parlay is something different, Toni," he said, as he spilled the last of his beer all over his prized Harvard sweatshirt.

"Oh, party foul! Don't worry about it though, I'll call one of them Uber Lyft kids to pick us up some more-" But before Niles could finish his quip, Paulie was already out the door.

"Well shoot, he didn't get to watch Slugger blow out his birthday candles," Edith said, trying to make light of Paulie's sudden exit. Niles hobbled over to Edith, and grabbed the tray of food from her, and set it back on the counter where she had grabbed it from.

"That's okay. A snail's eyeball stalks and candles don't mix well together. Just like oil and water, and just like booze and Paulie. With him leaving, it's just the three of us. Will you dance with me, Edie?"

"Of course, Nathaniel."

And so they slow-danced while Dewey finished his song

about the nameless horse, and the flies returned to their bounty in the kitchenette. Edith, her seventy-eight-year-old arms interloped with his fifty-seven, she whispered, "He was only here for an hour if I'm not mistaken."

"Yeah, hour fifteen tops. He only had about a pint of beer to boot. Fucking lightweight."

"Language, mister!" she demanded as Niles crushed Paulie's abandoned solo cup with his fake leg.

"My apologies, dear."

18

MR. WING WARNED HIM

But The Boy Did Not Listen

Paulie did not mean to slam the door behind him, nor did he mean to leave so suddenly, but his random bout of thanato-phobia and obvious misanthropy had forced his hand and hurried his exit.

There were sides of yourself you showed to family, sides you showed to friends, to co-workers and neighbors, to strangers and to loved ones. Being a whingy baby at someone else's birthday was not the proper attire to wear to a party. This may not have been explicitly stated by his ex-wife, but then again why did his brain always go back to her for answers.

She wrote motivational posters. Bullshit catchphrases you'd find in hotel lobbies, in office cubicles, in fast-food restaurant bathrooms. That was all she did. She'd sit at her micro-desk in the kitchenette and stare out the window beyond the water tower and the vacant lots beyond We-Store, and just come up with tiny-tidbit solutions for everyday woes.

"Whaddya got-" interrupted by a hiccup (and a poorly

parroted 'hibbup') "-for cancer, Toni? What do ya say about a man, er, a me, with cancer?"

But she did not answer. Instead, he sat on the floor of his living room and stared at the cat on the wall, the cat that whose sole purpose in life was to remind one and all to just hang in there.

Paulie got up and glared at the cat. "Hang in there?" he asked the dainty kitten, "You want me to just hang in there. And just pretend er'things gonna be okay?"

Like his absent ex-wife, the cat poster did not respond.

So he grabbed the cat and tore it in one large diagonal swath, decapitating the kitten. Thankfully, there was no blood, as this fictional kitten was printed on the same paper you hold now.

With the piece of motivational poster dangling from his hands, he crumpled the cat into a large ball. "Hang in there?! Hang in here!" he yelled right before he stuffed the ball into his mouth.

As he chewed the poster, savoring its blandness, reminding him of quinoa slurry, of plain white rice, of textured vegetable protein without any artificial flavoring added. He tried to yell obscenities at what remain of the poster on his wall, of what had hung on there, but they came out in garbled slurs.

"Wah dun yew hehn in derr! Yew fuggin', uh, iddy!"

Right now, his anger, his sadness, his hunger was driving him, and it drove him to his fridge. He was sick of not tasting happiness. He was sick of boring blandness. Quickly and without clear thoughts about him, Paulie tore open his cheat-fridge and grabbed a cardboard tray containing an assortment of mini-meals kept separate by saran wrap and tiny dividers. Furiously he ripped the plastic off and took a paw full of the icy mush into his mouth.

"Gah amm it, Oni! Eye'd yew leebe me!" he said, choking on wadded up poster and frozen mashed potatoes.

Vigorously he chewed and tried to break down the poster and the mashed potatoes, but to no avail. Instead, he just focused on the flavors. He took a second handful of frozen corn from one of the other TV dinner trays and plopped into his mouth, losing bits of potato in the process. "Ee err opposed ta be togedder, Oni!"

It may have seemed like nonsense to you, but the growth inside him was learning so much about this man, who kept to himself, even from himself. The growth was absorbing the knowledge, the sadness, and the anger while the ugly man masticated the frozen food with no hopes of swallowing it.

"Gah amm it," he slurred once more, before spitting the food and paper into his sink, realizing he was committing his most personal sin. By eating this food, he was breaking a promise to a man he met today, but that didn't matter. It mattered to him that by eating this food, he was lying to Dr. Fejes.

Paulie Galamb was many things, but a liar, if he could help it, was not one of them.

"Goddamn it," he said once more, mouth now free of food. Just to be sure, he stuck his fingers in his throat, wiggling them until his esophagus set free the beer he drank into the sink with his slop.

For a moment, his fingers grazed across the mass growing in his mouth, and the mass appreciated it. It just wanted to be free. A desire shared by it and his host.

As Paulie spewed warm malt liquor into the kitchen sink, retching up his betrayal to Dr. Fejes, he thought he heard his voice say, "Hello Paulie," but clearly that was just a delusion brought upon by the beer that remained inside him.

Delirious and drunk, the man stumbled over to his couch,

took off his favorite sweater, and stared at the remains of the cat torn up on his wall.

All that remained was the lower half of a kitten, and the not-so-ominous phrase, "In There, Kitty" as he drifted off to dreams once more.

Meanwhile, still wide awake, the growth happily ate the food it had stored while Paulie had manically stuffed frozen food into his mouth. While Paulie slept, the growth grew.

19

THE HARVARD VOMIT SPLATTER

And Awful Body Shaming

The only thing he remembered from his dream was watching Niles dancing with a mannequin, a topless female dummy, which had a real human leg opposite his prosthetic. The strangeness of it lingered more than the fading visuals of his one-legged neighbor merrily cha-cha-cha'ing with a dusty store front display. Strange, because in the moments where reality came back to him, he remembered bits and pieces from the night before. He remembered seeing Niles smile and laugh and joke with Edith, and he saw her reciprocate those jokes with jokes of her own, matching his laughter as well.

In the many years he had been here, he had barely ever seen them interact.

Stranger yet than the lingering dream residue was the destruction and chaos about his typically orderly abode. Looking down upon himself he saw and smelled the puke that had splashed across his favorite sweater, which currently read HA---RD, only the punctuation was vomit instead of dash marks, including a stray kernel of corn that was glued upon the D. Beyond that, he saw a footprint in the carpet, shoeprints which were made more apparent by the added sheen of mashed potato, squished into fabric. Further exploration revealed that one of his shoes was still firmly planted on his foot, where the other one was on its side next to the shoe rack next to the door.

Worse was the torn poster. Not one he had cared for, but one he had owned long enough to render it a fixture of his home. I wouldn't say it tied the room together, but he might. From where he lay, he could see a thin sheet of dust barely hanging on to the poster that used to remind him to hang in there.

He remembered the sudden upset in his evening, where suddenly Edith was casually bringing up his ex-wife. Wasn't she? His memory was as foggy as it appeared outside, a dense whiteness where only blurred details could be made out. He remembered the awful taste of that awful beverage, and Niles' annoying music, and Edith calling him ugly or handsome.

Trying to dig at his headache for clearer memories was only exacerbating the hangover, so he gave up on remembering. Then, like so many others in his situation, he swore he would never drink again. Unlike most, he would actually follow through on this resolution.

He wondered what time it was, but in the four minutes he had been awake, he knew it wasn't long until-

"BRRIT BRRIT BRRIT BRRIT!" screamed the shrillest sound Paulie had ever heard from with the other room, the room he should have woken up in. As Paulie scrambled to turn off the alarm clock in his bedroom, he momentarily had a lapse in sanity. Against any sort of rational thought, Paulie instinctively threw the alarm clock out of his bedroom window. He heard a small crash outside in the vacant parking lot next beyond the barbed wire fence. Upon landing, the noise was silenced.

Having seen it happen a hundred times in the movies, he had always wanted to smash an alarm clock. As have I.

Realizing the time, Paulie dragged himself into the bathroom, and saw that it had remained relatively unchanged, minus one starfish that he had gifted to his neighbor's snail. Had Niles/Slugger opened that poorly packaged present? He did not remember, nor did he press his memory at this moment. Instead, he undressed, hanging up his HA---RD sweater on the hook, while dropping the rest of his clothing into a lump on the linoleum floor. Then, naked as the day he was born only five feet taller, and several hundred pounds heavier, he lifted his pear-shaped self awkwardly into the bathtub, and turned the water on.

Would you believe this monster doesn't wait for the water to heat up? He just stands under the icy cold until it warms up enough. He does this without making a peep, without a shiver, without a wince. He probably would excel at those polar plunge activities, where people stupidly decide to jump into nearly freezing lakes in the middle of winter, but Paulie wasn't much of an activity person. That, and nobody needs to see this man naked.

Now before we go any further, please understand it is not my intention of body shaming this individual. Beauty comes in many shapes and forms, but what is most important is one's own self-love and respect for the body they spend their time in. And as far as that was concerned, on a normal day, Paulie was complacent with his body. He had fluctuated in extreme weights so many times in his life that he was now used to the excess skin that hung off his still-large body, but that was what happened when you drop nearly half of your body weight in a year or two. By the end of his marriage, he almost weighed a cumbersome five-hundred pounds. Now, thanks to his routine of walking everywhere he could, he was down to an admirable three-hundred, and a lot of that was simply skin. He still had the flappy batwing underarm fat, and his stomach grossly resembled a rather gaping horizontal mouth in his muffin-top midsection, but he didn't mind it. Outside of the tumor, he was the healthiest he had been since before college.

And his happiness is all that matters to me. Sure, he didn't like the way his body hair grew in thick dark patches, he didn't care for the inconsistent male-pattern baldness, or that at forty-seven years old he had never been able to grow any semblance of a beard. Sure, he avoided looking in the mirrors since he started getting adult acne again, and because he didn't like the way his face was poorly organized.

And no, he wasn't happy with the length of his reproductive organs, but what male really is outside of the particularly well-endowed. But, having been mostly a non-sexual person, even in his marriage, it never ruined his day. If the word "asexual" or "ace" for short, had made its way to this Midland he might identify as such, but at the time of this reporting it had not.

My point is, you can point and laugh at how ugly this guy is if that makes you feel good about yourself, but I'd just compare you to those teenagers he dealt with the morning before. What are you, sixteen? Grow up. Paulie is happy with himself, and he's got thick skin. Thick, flappy, loose skin.

The only thing he didn't like about his body was this maybe-cancer-maybe-not growing in his throat. And after he sudsed his feet, his legs, his micropenis and furry butthole, his stomach, and his chest, he lathered up his soap and reached for his neck.

The shock he felt almost sent him out of the bathtub, but instead he fell against the wall between his apartment and

Niles' next door. On any other day, it would be enough to wake the former biker up and warrant a shout, but instead Niles just rolled over and rested his arm on the old naked woman in his bed.

The growth had grown. He hadn't noticed until just now, having been so distracted by the fog of his hangover and that quick lesson on body-shaming, but now he felt like screaming. Before he was able to feel it by gagging on his own tongue, rolling it back into the pocket where his pesky wisdom tooth had once been. Now, he realized he could feel it always pressing on his tongue, that he could feel it from outside his mouth. It felt like a numb pressure on his throat and jaw, but with his fingers he felt an egg-shaped lump that was solid to the touch. It had doubled in size from the night before.

This was it. This was cancer. He didn't know much about cancer, but he knew when it spread fast, that was that. He tried to remember the words he had seen on television back when he owned one with Toni. Metastasized. Bilateral. Incisional biopsy. Primary site. Spread to the bones and brain. Oncologist.

In his panicked state, he did not hear the egg in his throat repeat back to him, "On-call-oh-jist", but that was probably for the better right now.

He got out of the shower, suds and all, and scrubbed himself dry. Paulie abandoned his smelly-beer-soaked clothing and ran into his closet, throwing together a makeshift outfit that went against his usual attire. Unlike yesterday and every day before, he did not care if all the buttons were buttoned correctly. He was not content. Consistency was the key to his complacency, and right now that complacency was out the window with his busted alarm clock.

Paulie ran to his phone and quickly dialed the number he had learned yesterday, and it rang four times before he was greeted with Fejes' Uralic voice. But before Paulie could get a word in, he realized he had reached the doctors messaging machine once again.

"You've reached the office of Dr. Fejes. I regret that I could not make it to the phone right now, as I am very busy. Today, all appointments are canceled. Not that I had any. Except for you Pali. If you are calling, then you are wasting time. Get here. Get here now."

"God damn it," he thought, cradling the phone in one hand, his golf-ball sized tumor in the other. He slammed the phone down, and hurried out the door, not caring about the state of his condo, nor checking to make sure his shoes were on the right feet. This much, at least, he got correctly.

Outside, the world was quiet. A dense fog had come in from the east in the night. When he looked up behind him, he could not see the top of the water tower. Now it just looked like scaffolding that disappeared into the clouds. No neighbors were out; Edith wasn't crocheting or knitting, nor was Niles playing darts. This was fine. He didn't want to deal with his embarrassment any more than he wanted to deal with the larger-than-before mass in his mouth.

It was eerily quiet. Too quiet. He couldn't hear much in the ways of traffic. No security guards were waiting at the entrance to We-Store, nor did he run into the teenagers when he jogged through the park. When he got to the intersection that separated the park and the Midland Business Plaza, he only saw the glow of red lights turning green, but not once did he see a single car waiting, stopping, or going throughout the cross streets. He could smell the exhaust of cars all around him, the fog holding in place the stink of egg-farts and carbon dioxide, but there were almost none in sight.

The first car he saw was a rusty yellow Volkswagen waiting outside the Arby's drive thru. Not a classic Beetle like his father had, that Paulie had mangled, but the newer models that had come to popularity in the early oughts. He was pretty sure those were illegal these days but didn't care to dwell on it. Instead, he ran past the Volkswagen and weaved through the parking lot filled with Perry's Primo BMWs. Not once did he see another human being in the between here and there, Fejes' office and his home.

The first person he saw today was a reflection of himself in the glass of Dr. Fejes' office door. He saw the awkward pear-shaped man surrounded by the blank white fog surrounding him, he saw that his shirt was buttoned incorrectly, he saw a man he didn't hate, he could learn to love. But most importantly, he saw the lump in his throat, on his jaw, just past his cheek. The lump that meant to kill him.

20

FOUR MEN AND A LUMP

And Only Four Gloves Left

"My, how you've grown," were the first words to escape from Dr. Fejes, who was clad in white. Paulie was not amused. Paulie was sweating even though the foggy weather outside wasn't warm enough to warrant perspiration.

"It's grown, Doc."

Without warning, Dr. Fejes placed his clammy gloveless hands on Paulie's throat. "Two times in size, by my guess." Behind him, Paulie saw his dentist dragging a large green cylinder into the bathroom-turned-office. Next to the dentist, Paulie saw a man he recognized but could not place from where. Maybe a billboard or a bus stop advertisement? He couldn't be sure. "We operate soon. Should be no trouble."

No trouble? The growth had doubled in size, and the throat doctor was telling him it was no trouble. "Dr. Fejes, it's massive! In one night! Isn't this a cause for concern? I'm sorry, but I'm freaking out here."

"Hi "Freaking-out-here", I'm Doctor Joseph Fejes. You

understand, yes? I am doctor. You are patient. Do not bring that tone into my office. Here, come, come, meet my assistants."

Paulie followed the short old man into the bathroom-turned-office, that now looked surprisingly pristine and mostly empty. How he had preferred his apartment. His dentist, Seltzman, propped up the cylinder next to the massage table which was now covered in a white sheet and clear plastic. Seltzman was also wearing all white, only unlike Dr. Fejes, he was wearing blue latex gloves.

"Hello there again, Mr. Galamb. I see the mass has grown."

"So much for a keloid, right?"

"I was mistaken. I am sorry for that, but this is also why I sent you to see Dr. Fejes. He is a specialist, and will make quick work of the growth, I am sure."

"You said he was an oncologist. I remember."

"Memory is a funny thing. Now you are the one who is mistaken. Stress can do all sorts of strange things to one's memories. I would have sent you to his brother had I thought it was cancer."

Paulie wanted to argue, but he found himself questioning his memory. Three days ago seemed like a such a long time now. Or maybe it was just the hangover fogging his memories. He was not sure.

"Your name, Dr. Fejes said it was Seltzman?"

"Correct. Dr. Thomas Seltzman. And my good friend, associate, and currently fellow assistant here is also named Tom. Tom, meet Mr. Galamb."

The man that Seltzman labeled Tom turned and immediately reached out to shake Paulie's hand. Unthinking, he shook it. "Tornado Tom Hedasky at your service. Wow, these two weren't kidding when they mentioned how ug- er, how large the growth was."

"I know you from somewhere."

"Yeah, yeah, don't hate me, but you probably recognize me from KTVG. I'm the ten o'clock weatherman. I'd apologize in advance for this fog, but nobody saw this one coming. I just read my script and stand in front of a green screen."

It was Seltzman that interrupted his introduction next, "Tom, change your gloves. And don't shake hands with the patient. Its unclean."

Instead of responding to him loosely being called unclean, he asked Seltzman, "Why didn't you tell me your name?"

Seltzman looked away, hiding his eyes from Paulie's, though he could not hide the state of Indiana. When he spoke, he sounded distant. "Because you never asked, Paulie."

Paulie felt the hair on his neck rise when a set of hands landed on his shoulders from behind. It was Dr. Fejes' eastern European accent that calmed him down, "Okay, you sit here. Lay down. Relax. Wait, what is that smell?"

Before he could react, Paulie could smell the top half of Dr. Fejes' nose, as Fejes had his nose located a mere inch away from his mouth. His nose smelled like some kind of smoked bacon. For a split second, he wondered if it would taste as such, but the doctor's voice went from being oddly pleasant to terrifyingly accusatory.

"You ate food! I smell, what is it. Kukorica! And... smushed burgonya?"

"I, uh-"

"No I-uh, no excuse, no lies, Pigeon man. I smell potato. I smell corn. I smell alcoholic beverage. Pali, you drank alcohol?! Why would you do this to me?"

Paulie lowered his head, shamefully. "I'm sorry, it was my neighbor. He told me it was fine to drink alcohol before an operation, that he had done it before. I know I shouldn't have, but see, he was having a birthday party."

"This neighbor. Where does he practice?"

"What?"

"Your neighbor, he is like me. He is like Dr. Seltzman. He is doctor, yes?"

"Uh, no, he's retired. Or disabled. I'm not sure which."

Suddenly Paulie felt a sharp pain atop his already throbbing head. Dr. Fejes had whapped him with a curled-up newspaper. Where the hell did it come from, he wondered, and how the hell did the short old man hit with such a quickness?

"This is not good, Pali, no good at all, but maybe we will make this work. Yes, no, maybe, yes. We try. Assistant Tom, have you hooked up the anesthetic lines yet?"

"Uh, yeah, just about there."

"Okay, Assistant Seltzman, do you have the tools?"

"Check."

"Okay, Pali, or should I call you Liar-Liar man from now on, are you ready for operation?"

No. He was not. Nor was he a liar. Not usually. But having been labeled as such by the diminutive doctor, he spoke the first intentional lie he'd told in five years. "Yeah, I suppose I am. Get this thing out of me, doc."

So, they did just that.

21

TWO PEAS IN A POD

Til One Flew The Coop

The cavern opens and I see the man from yesterday. I see the man from the day before. These men, they've touched me before and I expect them to touch me again. I recognize them by their eyes, for their mouths are covered by a material I desire to feel, to taste. I want to rest myself on that color.

The faces, their curious eyes, are much more different when I am aware that I am the focal point of their expedition into my host. I see a man whose skin is textured like the one who lives near my host, wrinkled with age, who hides his eyes behind glass rectangles. I see another man with the visible discoloration on under his eye. A shape. A shape I know there is a name for I have heard it in my host's thoughts. I know him. I know them. I've met them before.

"Ihn-dee-ah-nah" I remind myself in thought and thought alone; I dare not say this out loud with the fear of their tools incoming. This is what comes next. I know this. The brightness beyond my host's exposed cavern is dimmed when the faces block out the white sun, until the faces retreat from sight and instead a large shape, a rounded triangle, nearly blocks my sight of the entrance. It is almost clear, but not enough to see through it. The word opaque comes to mind, but I am not sure of its meaning. There are many words like this, words I have heard but I do not know what they are. Such as scram, or gangsta, or pigeon, or entropy. They all taste so pleasant, like opaque or triangular.

I smell it before I feel it before I taste it. The smell is like nothing, and nothing is hard to describe in the absence of another sensation, but it is because I feel it I can identify it's smell. It is the smell of exhaustion, the smell of those moments in the middle of the night when my host shuts down, of sleep. The almost-clear opaque triangle, it is feeding my host this smell. I feel the motion of his communication as his voice booms past me with the aid of the other wet mass in here, the tongue.

"Ten... nine..."

He says, and I listen, and I repeat these words, or numbers as I've learned their name to be. "Dehn... nigh..."

I hear the voices as well, not his, and I smell their fumes. I understand the fumes, their purpose, and the intention of those voices. The voices want me to go to sleep but I am not tired.

"Eight... seven..." my host says, his tongue rolling over the stones more fluidly than usual. My friend, I can feel the weakness growing in the way it moves.

"Aye... she-ehn..." I can hear in his voice that he is drifting. This day cycle is not finished, so why should I sleep? I can feel that he is feeling the effects of the gas, and its nothing smell. His hold on my home goes slack, and I feel gravity pull myself down between his stones and his wet mass. There are words I've heard that come to me now as my home creaks and snaps.

"Quap" said my hosts temporomandibular joint as his jaw

goes slack, as my host sprays the inside of the triangle with a spritz of his liquid. I hear him feebly say more numbers, but they sound less like words now and more like thoughts.

"Siiihhh... fiiii"

He needs my help, I know this, so I complete the sequence for him. The rush of inhalation, of exhalation, seems quieter, calmer, distant.

"Six."

I experience what must be fear when I see the tongue give way and go limp, my only friend in this home inside of my host. I feel the weight of my host around me. Even when he sleeps, the tongue and I remain awake, except for now, something is different. I press on. I refuse the smell of nothing that puts my host to sleep. I speak the words, the numbers, the sequence.

"Five!"

There is another voice, another face, who appears as the triangular shape is quickly taken away, but I do not know him. His features consist of hard edges unlike the softness of these two men and of my host. He now is looking into the cavern, not at the stones or the tongue. The face is looking at me.

But I go on.

"Four!"

The face, it distorts itself into a strange shape I have not seen before. I want to taste that shape. I want to be that shape. I attempt to contort myself into the face's flavor, but I have done something wrong. I know this because the Hard-Edged face shrieks and leaves my cavern.

Quieter now, I continue, "Three." for I know of wrongness when there is wrongness exposed. The man with the discolored shape under his eye returns. The man with the Glass Rectangles and jagged skin, he looks at me, right at me. I can see the black circles in his eyes grow and shrink in focus. I know this word. So I say it.

"Pupil."

This causes the wrinkled face to retreat, but it does not shriek. Closer comes the face from two cycles before, with the shape under his eye. He asks a question, but it is not my place to answer.

Did it just speak?

Instead, I use my words. I declare to this face the name of his shape, "Indiana."

And like the first and second face before him, he retreats out of sight. For now, I am left alone with my friend the wet mass, and the stones that protect us, but this moment is brief.

Because in a matter of seconds, I see the hands come forth. I see that the hand, it holds the blade. I could hide, but I fear I've grown too large. I worry if I hide now and shield myself from the blade I will bring harm to my dear host.

I rock my mass out of my resting place, my pocket, and retreat atop the tongue. I feel the grit of my friend's foliate papillae, I taste the texture of his taste buds. I roll past the tops of his white stones and fall toward the tunnel down, but I am careful not to follow it deeper. I've seen what becomes of food that goes down there. The hand and blade attempt to prod the area where I just was, my warm pocket, but I have hidden myself. I taste my host's warm red as the exploratory knife cuts into my host.

I mimic the third voice and force myself to make a noise so loud it shakes the sleeping tongue. I scream. I shriek. I have never screamed before. I enjoy it. The hand retreats and takes the blade with it. I am not sure what is going to happen, but I know I cannot let harm come to him.

I say his name as best I can, "Paulie." in a desperate whisper.

Indiana reappears, staring at the small pool of red where I once was. It's gone. Then Indiana is gone once more. Hard-

Edged, the new voice, returns and points his hand at me, one finger, revealing me. It's over there. It moved. Glass-Rectangles shows himself. That's impossible.

I am not impossible.

I am my host, and he is me. We are one, but for as long as I am here inside him I will bring him harm, and I cannot do this. Because he is home, and I love him.

I reveal myself, pushing myself out of my hiding spot behind his sleeping tongue and pull myself over his stones and I roll toward the entrance of the cavern, the exit of his mouth. I stretch myself up to greet these faces, in their horror. I will sacrifice myself if it means they will spare my host. My Paulie.

If worms could scream, they would. I look at the three faces, I look at Indiana, I repeat to him the word he taught me. I repeat the word he whispered to me only I do not whisper it.

I scream it. I scream "Parlay!" until I cannot breathe. And even then I do not stop shrieking the word. I scream until their giant selves back away. Their faces, they're all distorted now. I am not afraid of them, their size. I stand my pink self at the edge of the cavern, and I scream. I scream for Paulie. I scream for me.

22

WAKE UP PAULIE GALAMB

Its Time For School

His ex-wife Toni was there, as was Niles. Edith too. He wasn't sure, but he thought he heard the voices of those awful boys, the teenagers from yesterday. Yesterday seemed so far away, so cloudy. Why the five teens, his neighbors and ex-wife were standing in the abandoned lot next door, he did not remember. In the distance he saw the water tower, only it was covered in moss, but the moss was wrong. From where he stood, the silhouette of the water tower behind We-Store was glistening red. Like wet meat, fat marbled steak covering the rusting metal support legs of the tower.

It wasn't just the tower. The whole complex was covered in pockets of different shades of meat. The entirety of his home, one of the last three condominiums in this side of Midland, was covered in pulsating moist beef, in jiggling pockets of raw chicken, writhing blankets made of pork flesh. It spread itself over the concrete, over the asphalt, and climbed high above the roofs of these three buildings. It spread upwards towards the heavens like a colony of ants crossing a vast expanse, using themselves as the building blocks of the bridge.

He turned and saw his neighbors holding hands. Niles and Edith Post. They were both covered in hundreds of small pink slugs, only they weren't snails. They were leeches, only they weren't. They were moving, eating, consuming, But Edith, Niles, they were smiling.

Paulie faced his ex-wife, herself equally covered in not-slugs-not-leeches. She was smiling too. She was holding his hand. Not in a way that denoted their love had rekindled. They held hands in the way one does when you can hear the whistle of a bomb falling from above you. Either way, it felt good to feel her, even if only for a moment.

The boys, behind him, they were also smiling, covered in their own tiny pink patties. He could hear the voices of his doctors. He couldn't see them, but he could hear them, and he was sure that they were smiling too. One last time, he glanced back at his home that was covered in one hundred thousand fleshy balls rolling over themselves, reaching upwards.

"Where are they going?" he heard himself say.

"I'm not sure yet. But we've got all the time in the world to wait and see," said his voice, but he himself did not say it. This second him, his other voice, was coming from his right hand, the one not holding Toni's. Paulie looked down at the growth at the end of his wrist, a writhing mass the color of his tongue, the size of liver.

"I should wake up now," Paulie said to the meat.

"I'll be there when you do," the meat said to Paulie.

In that moment, that half-second between consciousness and un, Paulie knew that it had a name, but before he could say it, this anesthetic dream faded to black. An iris slow wipe. Paulie transitioned from sleep to reality, leaving his neighbors, the teens, and his ex-wife behind. For now.

He found himself back in the backroom bathroom office of Dr. Fejes, with the weatherman washing his hands in the corner of the room.

Immediately, Paulie tongued the left side of his face. The growth was gone. Even though he still felt numb, he could taste the copper hints of his own blood. He could feel the coarseness of a stitch or two where his wisdom tooth had previously hid, where the growth had grown.

"Fejes, Seltzman, he's awake!" exclaimed Tom Hedasky as he dried his hands off on his baby-blue nurse scrubs.

Paulie's head felt heavier than usual, as if it were weighted or strapped down to the table. He was able to move it from side to side, but there seemed to be a lag. Perhaps it was just the drugs wearing off. Maybe he was still dreaming.

When Dr. Fejes and Seltzman returned, it very much seemed like he was still dreaming. First came the smaller man with the thick accent, Dr. Fejes. Behind him was the dentist with the pocket full of lollies, with the birthmark whose name he had only learned hours ago. Only Seltzman wasn't holding a red lollipop. He was holding a small wide-mouthed beaker.

The drugs were making him hallucinate, because as Seltzman approached, for a moment he was sure the dentist had a small, wet hairless gerbil in the beaker. It was newborn-pink in color, only as the two doctors came closer, Paulie saw that the gerbil had no face. It moved, pushing or pulling itself closer to the glass walls of the beaker.

"Mr. Galamb, I am not sure how to tell you this," said the dentist.

It wasn't a gerbil.

Paulie's head was spinning. This bathroom-turned-office seemed to have that effect on him. Maybe he wasn't ready to wake up. The small ball had tiny veins about it that he could see as it pressed itself up against the glass. The harder it pressed, Paulie could see pink turn to red and back to white again in a shifting transitionary gradient of flesh.

No, it wasn't a gerbil. It was the growth.

"There is not telling, Seltzman. Just show."

Paulie saw that the ball was now rolling up the side of the beaker. Little protrusions from the top hemisphere of meat seemed to be grabbing at the rim, trying to pull itself up. He began to feel lightheaded. Dizzy enough that if he were standing, he'd fall over.

"Show him? No, introduce him. It asked for the guy by name!" said the weatherman, who had turned away once more.

The dentist lowered the beaker in front of Paulie, so that the moist pink lump was only inches from his face. "As soon as you went under, Mr. Galamb, it uh, it spoke."

"Hello, Paulie," said the tumor, which pulsated as it spoke. The voice was not unlike his own, only fainter. Softer. Wetter. "I mean you no harm."

"Yes, just like that. It speaks," said the throat doctor.

"We've never seen anything like this," said the dentist.

"It's not natural. It's not right," said the weatherman.

"Hello, Parlay," said the patient, smiling.

23

THE PEA TREE MASS

Enter Stage Right

Arnie Workman was staring at himself in the reflective metal doors of the elevator as he rode it to the top. He straightened his tie while the elevator went up and up, courtesy of his silver key card. Past administration, in a floor known only as The Boardroom. Where men and women like him came to speak with the decrepit old man who claimed he was trying to save the world.

This was debatable, but Arnie Workman wasn't here to debate with Doctor Koop. Instead, this time he came to update the one hundred-thirteen-year-old man rather than upset him with bad news. This time, bearing better news, he was not as on edge as his visit to the top of the tower the day before. When it finally stopped, Arnie watched his reflection split in two as the elevator doors opened.

Arnie saw two men leaving the boardroom. He knew who they were but didn't bother acknowledging their existence outside of a nod. One of the two billionaires was holding his nose, the other was rubbing his eyes. Collectively the two men were worth four hundred billion, but all that money couldn't cure his baldness or prevent the stink from activating his gag reflex, nor could their billions help the other man's eyes adjust from the blinding blue lights of the boardroom.

He heard the bald man in the million-dollar suit complain about the stench, while the other quipped about the spryness of the ancient man in the next room over. Arnie hardly wondered why the two richest men in the world were visiting Doctor Koop, but he had a good idea of why they were here.

As Doctor Koop had often said, they weren't in the food business as it was widely thought. No, they were in the future business.

Their presence wasn't of any import to Arnie. Relaying his message to the boss was.

Arnold Workman walked through the dimly lit hallway, and as he got closer to the entrance of the boardroom the smell of raw meat and damp fish, of ground pork and pulverized chicken, grew stronger and thicker with each step forward. He'd never get used to it, but unlike the billionaires en route to the ground floor, he hid his disgust better.

He clicked the button outside of the door and spoke into the camera. "Doctor Koop, I've come with an update on Paulie Galamb."

Instead of a verbal response, a buzzer buzzed, a mechanism clicked, and the door swung open. The fluorescent blue lights attacked his eyes, but he maintained his composure as he entered the brightly lit room.

Across the fifteen-foot-long table the old man stood, wearing half of his uniform. Doctor Koop's white military style jacket was strewn across the end of the table. Koop himself was standing there with both of his hands splayed atop the black marble. The lights made the pink lumps that covered his shirt-less torso appear to glow. Arnie watched as one of the salmon-colored mass peeled itself off of the elderly man's wrinkled chest, revealing under it a bruised and discolored area of flesh. The mass fell to the table, rolled on itself, and reattached itself to Doctor Koop just above his navel. The noise that emanated from it upon its reattachment was not terribly unlike a cat purring, only wetter.

"Mr. Workman, what have you come here to tell me? Did Galamb survive his surgery?"

"He did, yes, at least as far as we can tell. I attempted to contact his dentist. A man by the name of Thomas Seltzman, but his office was closed. I then peeped through his call history and found that he had been in contact with another man, a doctor here in town by the name of Joseph Fejes. It turns out Fejes was the doctor that Paulie Galamb had seen yesterday. This was confirmed by my calling his office this afternoon, only to be met with a voicemail."

"In the voicemail, he mentions that all appointments were canceled for the day, but then he mentions 'Pali'. Upon further investigation, I found that he was in fact referring to Paulie Galamb. I drove to his office, only to find it closed. As an aside, I did check on Christopher Wagner, who we've placed in the employ of Bob Robbins, who owns the Midland Business Plaza, as well as the Mid-Market convenience store."

Doctor Koop lifted his face, and as he spoke, pink grains of rice fell out of his mouth, onto the backs of his hands. "Did he recognize you?"

"He did not. I did ask him if he knew anything of the whereabouts of the doctor who worked two doors down from his place of work."

"Very good. Did you manage to find this Dr. Fejes?"

"I believe so. Chris Wagner, though he had not met the man, said he had seen three men leave the office in the early evening. He said he saw them walk towards a nearby bar."

"He was smoking, wasn't he?"

"Excuse me?"

"Wagner, he was smoking cigarettes."

"I mean, I don't know if-"

"I can smell the smoke on you. And I know you would not dare smoke. You know how I feel about it."

Arnie felt his neck tighten. He swallowed hard, feeling his Adam's apple press against his necktie as he did. Yes, he knew of Koop's aversion to smoking. In his previous life, he had crusaded against tobacco and had sought to end its distribution in the United States. He had almost been successful had his old body had not failed him.

Moreover, Arnie was impressed that this senior was able to smell smoke over the stink of raw meat and poultry.

"He may have. I cannot be sure."

Doctor Koop snorted angrily, shaking free a small wet blob off the side of his head. The wet blob landed on his bare arm and rolled up his shoulder until it firmly squished itself into Koop's pale white skin. "Did you find Fejes at this bar?"

"I did. And to my surprise, I saw that he was also with Thomas Seltzman, and a third individual."

"Who was he? This third individual?"

"According to the bartender, he is a man named Thomas Hedasky. He apparently works for KTVG Media."

The old man slammed his fist down, atop a lump of rose-colored flesh the size of a small pork chop. The pork chop seemed unphased. "He works for the news?!"

Arnie straightened his back and tried to speak with confidence, but he couldn't keep a single bead of sweat from dropping down the side of his face. "He does. Though he is just the station's meteorologist. Not a very respected one, according to the bartender."

This reassurance did not calm down the old shirtless man,

covered in sores, bruises, and meat-colored slugs. Instead, it seemed to only agitate him further. This was obvious as the masses across his naked torso began to writhe and move about much faster, leaving a trail of wet ooze as they traveled randomly across his pale skin. They seemed to be feeding off the doctor's anger.

Or were they feeding off Arnie's fear, he wondered.

"Mr. Workman, I need to make something very clear. Word of this cannot, I repeat, cannot get out to the media. I don't want to hear about Paulie Galamb in the papers, on the news, on Facebook, Twitter, on whatever social media is hip with the kids these days."

"It's called Tik-"

"I don't care what it's called, I don't want to hear about Galamb in the media at all!"

"What will you have me do, Doctor Koop?"

"Later, I implore you to reach out to this Hedasky. Bring him to me. Directly to me. Stress that it is work related, that Pea Tree Farms needs the advice of a meteorologist. Find out his salary, then offer him triple the amount. Whatever it takes, just get him to me. And do so quickly."

"What about the others? Joseph Fejes, Seltzman?"

As maggots and chunks crawled around the shirtless man, Arnie's nose hairs burnt. The smell was growing more pungent as the masses writhed about his boss' body.

"I'll deal with them in time. As for Paulie, I think it best to keep a closer eye on him. You will visit him in the next few days. Convince him that he is to come back to work as soon as he is healthy, but in doing so, make mention of a promotion. Is there anybody we can, how do I say, replace?"

"Sue Ellen," Arnie blurted, "I feel like she has been, well, not following company protocol and is due for an early retirement."

"Is she the one the other board members refer to as 'The Talker'?"

"I cannot be certain, but it sure sounds like a valid descriptor of the woman," he said, trying to hide his pleasure in her upcoming discharge.

"Very good. We'll have someone in accounting draw up a generous severance package and arrange for her immediate removal. As soon as, of course, we make sure Paulie Galamb will accept it."

Arnie had wished worse for Sue Ellen. It wasn't difficult to make people disappear, as was evidenced by Chris Wagner and the lobotomy he received nine days earlier due to the conspiracies he was caught spouting off to his co-workers. Though most of them were harmless, or at their worst, tasteless and racist, he had stumbled upon a rumor of that which lay hidden in Containment. Worse offenders weren't so lucky and were typically gifted a one-way trip to the Crematorium just above Containment. Secretly, Arnie had wished that Sue Ellen had earned that trip herself.

But knowing she would be gone and out of his life was also fine enough.

"I'll get right on it, Doctor Koop. Immediately, if you see it fit."

"Not immediately. I want you to deal with this Hedasky first. Get him to me. Then we'll sort out 'The Talker' as it were, then with Paulie. But first, I want you to take a walk with me."

No. The fear in his belly was making its way up his esophagus. Trying to get a peek at what lay ahead.

"Come with me, Mr. Workman," he said, picking up his white military jacket from the table. As he did, every little bit of meat that had fallen off his exposed torso seemed to rapidly climb back onto him. From grains of repulsively red rice or tiny pink maggots to whole cuts of raw steak, they all retreated back to the ancient old man. All shapes, sizes, and shades of pink slug crawled back onto his skin, leaving behind traces of ooze on the black marble table, as he buttoned his jacket. The masses atop his face hid themselves on the inside of his collar until not a one was visible under his uniform.

As he walked towards Arnold Workman, the smell of red meat had grown stronger. It had a lightly bloody smell, almost metallic. He couldn't help but think Doctor Koop smelled like the way sucking on pennies tasted. The closer he got, the viler the smell grew. There were hints of ammonia, of soured eggs. Of meat gone bad.

Though the man seemed frail, he still towered over Workman. When he was within arm's reach, he placed his hand on the back of Arnie's neck. It was cold and slightly sticky, from when the man had slammed his hand on the chunk of flesh on the table, though the chunk did not seem to mind, now hidden somewhere on the inside of his jacket.

"We're going downstairs, Arnold."

No, please, no.

"I want you to see it."

God, no, please.

He would try to protest, but already he knew he was locked in a nearly hypnotic state. No magic, nor mystical force other than fear itself drove his feet forward while the old man's cold, cold hand barely rested atop the small of his nape.

Like a ventriloquist, Doctor Koop pushed Arnold Workman in front of him. From the violently bright blue fluorescents of the boardroom through the blackened hallways illuminated only by the dim guiding lights on the floor, he guided the man like a puppet. I'm sure if he squeezed the man's neck any harder, it would cause the terrified man to speak. Or scream.

Inside the elevator, Doctor Koop used his free hand to

reveal a dull metal card. If it had been cleaned, it might resemble gold, but at this point it was more of a rusty amber color. He swiped his card, then pressed two buttons simultaneously, and down and down they went.

Arnie focused only on himself. He did not let his eyes wander to the disturbing visage behind him, though he could feel the cataract-covered eyes burning holes into the back of his head. From his peripheral vision, he could see the rainbow stain of bruises and imperfections on the old mans hundred-year-old face, but he did not dare change his focus from himself.

He watched the numbers go down in order, five-four-three-two-one, but it did not stop at one. Instead, the elevator continued into the earth for another twenty seconds until finally it stopped. Once more, he watched his reflection rip itself in half. It was then he accidentally let his eyes drift, to see Dr. C. Everett Koop smiling behind him. Arnie could see one of the smaller growths crawl across his yellow and brown teeth.

He shook his head and looked ahead as the doors opened before him.

"Please, God, no, no, no," he thought, but God was not listening down here.

There were no labels down here, he knew. The smell of putrid death and decay hit him first as the stagnant air assaulted his nostrils. There was barely any light, but even from here he could make out its formless features.

On the ground was the same aisle lighting he had seen eight stories higher, that reminded him of movie theaters back when those were still in style. Back when he and his friends would sneak into a horror film on a Friday night.

The only difference here was the horror was not displayed on a giant screen, a trick of lights, cameras, and projections. Instead, the horror was shrieking in front of him.

The aisle-lights went on for a hundred feet until they disappeared under what Arnie could only describe as a living landfill of rotten meat and decaying flesh.

The Pea Tree Mass. It was an atrocity, a monstrous tumor-on-tumor-on-tumor a million times over. Every step closer felt like a violation to Arnie's very core. His mind was screaming obscenities, but his mouth did not allow them their escape.

Arnie tried to look away, but it was then that Doctor Koop had tightened his grip. Fear wasn't the only thing carrying Arnie anymore, no, Koop was actively pushing him forward. Try as he might, he could not resist. The smell of fetid human refuse, of mold and repugnance was so strong Arnold expected himself to lose his lunch any second now, and then he'd lose whatever else hid in his stomach. Yet somehow, he did not. Instead, his eyes adjusted to the near-total darkness, and he could make out two men between himself and the Pea Tree Mass.

The billionaires from earlier. They were stripping million-dollar suits off, unbuttoning their shirts and trousers, pulling their silk boxers down, revealing their billion-dollar butts and members to the mountain made of living meat.

"This is it, Elon," he heard one of them say, the bald man whose head shone even in the dim lights, "This will be the greatest revolution of modern agriculture. No. It's larger than that. This, this is the next step in human evolution."

But the other naked man said nothing, instead, he slowly walked towards the stinking abomination. Though Arnie could not be sure in this low light, he felt as if the rancid blob was reaching towards the nude billionaire. Arnie watched as the man disappeared into the foul mountain. The other man, the bald one, seemed to hesitate at first, but then like the first, he walked into the mass as well.

"Watch, Arnold."

As the second man was halfway inside the wet mass, Arnie

heard the muffled screams from within it. Though he had not heard the first man's voice clearly enough, he was sure that the shrieks were his. The bald man must have realized this, because for a moment he seemed to try and take a step back, but then he was violently sucked into into the Mass. His disappearance finalized by a disturbingly loud squelch. Blood oozed out of the base of the Pea Tree Mass, creeping slowly towards the abandoned million-dollar suits thrown on the floor. The screams continued for a moment as the Mass tore their skin from their muscle, their muscle from their bone. The Mass, it squished, stank, and pulsated and eventually it rumbled with what could only be described as a happy cat purring.

The men were gone, dissolved and absorbed. Maybe Doctor Koop was talking, but he couldn't hear his voice over the shrieks. It was then he realized he wasn't hearing the screams of billionaires inside the monster. They were his own.

INTERMISSION
BARSTOOL BANTER, PART THREE

And Their Opinions On It All

At the Ol' Watering Hole, Tom was leaning over his beer watching the condensation fall down the side while he chose not to drink it. Thomas was on his second beer. Joseph, his third. Tornado Tom just didn't have it in him to finish or start his drink.

"Oh come on, bud, the bloom is hardly off the peach here. Drink. To your health. To the slug. To Paulie and Parlay."

"Come on Seltzman, don't give it a name."

"Oh, and why shouldn't I? Everything deserves a name. There was a time when I didn't have a name and never have I felt so, I don't know, purposeless."

"A name does not give you power, Seltzman."

Joseph Fejes, the not-so-friendly neighborhood otorhinolaryngologist, chimed in after swallowing down half of his third beer. "You have your name; it is powerful name. Tornado Tom, they call you on the television. Do you not respect the power of tornado?"

Tom sighed, "They used to call me Tornado Tom. Now that name follows me places and leaves a wake of shame and guilt in its path. I know what they call me, I've seen Twitter."

("Twister was good movie," Joseph whispered in his glass half full, unheard by the others. Other than you, of course.)

"They call you a liar, I know. And almost everyone I meet; they always lie to me. We've had this conversation before. Too many times. Our conversations are often cyclical in nature."

"Yeah, and that's the way I've always liked it, Seltzman. Cyclical. Like a stationary bike that never goes anywhere. I miss that. Now, damn it, everything is different."

"Different can be good. Just like new is good. See, see, watch as I do," the eldest of the three said, finishing his third beer in a second gulp. "Bartender, please, for me can I have one fine glass of boxed wine."

From across the bar, the three men watched the bartender pull a dusty box of Franzia out from under the bar. He lifted another pint glass and pressed a small button on the side of the box releasing its murky contents into the cup. The bartender filled it halfway before passing it to the old doctor. Then the cardboard box containing the plastic bag full of wine was returned to its secret cellar under the bar mat, only to collect more dust.

"Now this wine, I know it has name. It is not Merlot. Not Cabernet Sauvignon. Not even fancy Malbec or Sangiovese. No, this variety, it is called "Chillable Red". I am not even sure you can call it wine," he said, holding the wine to his nose, gently swirling the contents, "But I know it is still called wine."

Joseph took a small sip, then loudly gargled it, attracting the attention of both the bartender, his friends, a suited man, and the out-of-towners. Then, to probably everyone's disgust, he spat out the sip into his empty beer glass.

"In another life, I was a painter, a father of three, a grandfather of ten. I collected antiques, and I drank wine from a box like this here."

"But even without a name, it still has the power. Giving it a name, it gives it more."

Joseph refrained from spitting any further, and the next time he sipped his wine, the onlookers stopped staring, and went back to their own stories. "Take for example this bartender. Describe him to me, Tornado Tom."

Tom sized the man up, who was serving the college girls mixed drinks that have probably never been made at this Ol' Watering Hole in the history of Midland, but he was doing it with the mastery of a man who knew his craft.

"I dunno, he's tall, handsome," ("More handsome than myself") "Probably in his early thirties. I can tell he definitely works out, and I'd guess he probably doubles as security, seeing as how this bar doesn't have a bouncer. Not that I've ever seen a reason for one. But this guy, he seems like he wants to come off as a tough guy to the men of this establishment, a sweetheart to the ladies. I bet he doesn't call his mother nearly as often as she wishes."

"Go on."

"Short hair, cropped in a style I mostly see teenagers wear, but he keeps it cleaned up enough that he doesn't seem like he's trying to hide his age. He seems like the type of guy that only lets women cut his hair, but he doesn't want her talking while she does it. I can see from his sort-of-visible wrinkles that he smiles a lot, probably due to his vocation. An unhappy bartender is about as attractive as a stripper crying unless you're at one of the biker bars on the edge of town. I imagine he doesn't like to smile, though. Not really."

Seltzman kept quiet while Joseph egged him on. "Tell me about his home life, what is he like outside of this job. What does he do for fun? Who does he like to make sex with? What are his passions, Tom?"

"I really can't say. He wears his mask well."

"Tell me, Tom Hedasky, what is his name."

"I, uh, have no idea."

Seltzman decided to speak up, having finished his second beer. "Bartender, one more if you don't mind." Shaking his empty glass at the nameless man. The bartender paused his conversation with the girls drinking their Strawberry Cosmos, their Bahama Mammas, their Whoozy-doodles and filled another pint glass full of beer. When he walked over with it, Joseph popped the question instead.

"Bartender, what is your name?"

"It's fuckin' Kyle, why?"

"I am just curious, patron. It is good. Now you have name. Now you have the power."

Fuckin' Kyle did not respond to that, just shook his head, and went back to his flirtation game.

"You see, Tom. This is why we name. Pali and Parlay. They deserve their names just like you or I or Fuckin' Kyle."

"I guess. But it still weirds me out. I mean, doesn't it freak you guys out a little?"

"I am afraid of things I understand. Things I don't, I study until I do. Like gingivitis or the cancer that took my wife."

"I am not afraid of Parlay. Though I do respect that it is a thing of power."

"A being of power, dare I say."

"Dare say it then. Respect it's power, Parlay's power and drink, Tornado Tom, because this night, it is only getting started."

And he did after a customary cheers between the three of them. Not a one of them noticed Arnie Workman staring at them from across the bar. Even the three girls paid no heed to him, nor did they know that he would become their boss for only a few days were things to stay cyclical in their nature. Before his death, before the fall, before the end.

But alas, the cycle breaks here, and as the weatherman said before, everything is different now. The moment that beer hits his lips starts the chain reaction that leads to everything else that happens next. Where entropy takes hold.

This is the point where the wagon wheel crumples on the path and the whole vehicle transforms into a toboggan, racing downhill towards some sort of gradual conclusion.

Which is really just a longwinded and pretentious way of saying buckle up, bronco.

Just outside this Ol' Watering Hole the sun is setting, and under the faithful watch of the water tower our hero tries to make conversation with a small, disembodied growth / our hero tries to make conversation with his ugly host.

PART 2

"The idea is not to live forever, but to create something that will."
— Andy Warhol

24

TAXOMY OF A TUMOR

And How To Comfort One

Woozy wasn't the right word, but it was the first word that came to mind as he walked back through the midday fog. Traffic had reestablished itself as the dominant species of Midland, and even pedestrians walked about the town again unlike the solitude Paulie had earlier this morning.

The world had a glow about it. A glow of normalcy returned. Like the way things had been before this morning. Back in the past, when his tumor lived inside him, or further back, when he didn't know he had a tumor. Or even further back again, back when he had a mouth full of teeth, a steady job, a regular consistent schedule.

Everything was seemingly back to normal for the world around him. Passersby ignoring others, unsmiling fast-food workers serving fast-food to frowning patrons, cars honking at one another, rebellious teenagers drinking in the park, a young landscaper weed-whipping empty beer cans into oblivion.

Paulie chose to walk on the other side of their turf today, to avoid any possible confrontation so soon after surgery.

Not that he nor his eclectic team of doctors would call the procedure a surgery. Or an operation. It was closer to coaxing a shy cat out from a tight space. Here kitty, kitty.

If everything was normal now, then why, Paulie wondered, was he carrying a piece of flesh, a piece of himself, that was currently asking him what 'Woozy' meant.

"It means dizzy, Parlay. It means I feel unwell. Sickly."

Paulie peeked down at the small undulating pink egg that sat or stood in the beaker Dr. Fejes had donated to him. There was no way of knowing whether or not the gelatinous meaty blob was looking at him, as neither Dr. Fejes nor Seltzman or the weatherman for that matter could find any eyes to speak of. When it spoke, it was a bit more obvious that there were hundreds of tiny holes that were barely visible, that opened and closed rapidly when it wanted to emit words or sounds. Words would come out of its mouth, causing it to visibly vibrate. There was no knowing what lay inside the growth without opening it up, nor knowing how the physiological make-up made sense or not, and Dr. Fejes was not one to cut up animals for the sake of finding out what's inside of them.

The weatherman, Tom Hedasky, had brought up a good point.

Was it an animal? As far as anyone could tell the definitive answer was a resounding no. Animals did not grow in people. Only people grew in people, and as per Paulie's biological makeup, it was not readily possible yet for people to grow in Paulie either. So it wasn't human, it wasn't an animal. Parlay here, it was something else.

"What is unwell-sickly, Paulie?"

Paulie watched the growth vibrate the question at him. He

gave the same answer to the growth he received from Dr. Fejes when he asked what the growth was, if not animal or human.

"I do not know. I don't have all of the answers right now."

The mass pulsed, a strange humming noise it seemed to make to fill the unsure silence. A light noise that had a faint vibrato to it. In reality, Parlay was mimicking Paulie's hiccups from the night before, but the man did not realize this. Instead, he carried the beaker that contained his cancer-not-cancer and carried on through the midafternoon haze.

For no particular reason, the fog decided it best to take its leave, as it migrated east towards Central City. Paulie and Parlay went west towards We-Store, towards home. Past the We-Store, Paulie's supervisor's supervisor was leaving the monolithic gray building, second tallest in all of Midland and heading towards the fog, towards the Midland Business Plaza. And at the We-Store residential section, Edith was returning home, and Niles was placing his friend Slugger in his aquarium, sharing it now with a dried-up starfish, courtesy of Paulie Galamb.

25

NILES, MEET PARLAY

Parlay, Meet Niles

Oh, that's right. His apartment was still destroyed. Remnants of a torn motivational poster, the scent of vomit still permeating, thawed frozen meal bits still scattered across the linoleum of his kitchen, attracting ants. He kicked his shoes off at the door and placed the beaker on the coffee table. Paulie began sorting his drunken destruction from the night before, in the opposite order that it had occurred.

He undid his sleeping arrangement in the living room floor, converting his makeshift bed of couch cushions back into the boring love seat he and Toni had picked out at a moving sale years earlier. Then Paulie hurried to the kitchen and sprayed the contents of the sink down into the garbage disposal, before shredding the combination of mashed potatoes, corn, and Steel Reserve refuse, careful to avoid the concoction splashing back at him while he hosed the slurry down the drain. After that, he realized there was no repairing the eviscerated kitten on his wall, so carefully he pulled the poster off of its resilient thumb tacks, rolled up the remains of the cat into a tight tube before crumping that tube into an even tighter wad. From where he stood, he attempted to shoot the ball into the waste bin across his kitchen, but he did not make the shot. Luckily, nobody saw him miss, which was one of the unspoken advantages of being a bachelor.

Oh wait.

Paulie turned around and saw that the little nugget, Parlay, was hanging off of the lip of the beaker. Not necessarily climbing out of its container, but it was evident that the growth very well could escape its confinement if it chose to.

If it chose to. Paulie was still not wholly convinced that the laughing gas had not completely worn off, because here he was pondering on the sentience of his tumor once more. "What are you?" he asked the growth which was once again parroting his hiccup sounds.

The mass seemed to shift the upper half of its body, the part that was hanging out of the beaker, in such a way that it appeared like the meat was shrugging. Parlay didn't say it, but Paulie could hear himself repeating his own answer from earlier, that had matched what Dr. Fejes had said shortly after he woke from his anesthetic slumber.

"I do not know. I don't have all of the answers right now."

Paulie turned back to face the dead space of his now bare wall. The only evidence that the poster had ever been there were the small pin prick holes where the thumb tacks had resided. One less reminder of his ex-wife, and this did not please him. Not really. He wished he had another poster to put up. Or a painting. Or a photo. Or even a mirror just to see something else. Niles had his jukebox, his throw rugs, Edith had her television and her paintings. All Paulie had was another blank off-white wall.

Paulie retreated to his bedroom, to his meticulously organized closet, and rummaged through a cardboard box filled with paperwork. In that box were tax forms and receipts he'd itemize at the end of the year. In that box was paperwork pertaining to his various forms of insurance, homeowners, medical, dental. There, he found the closest thing to a photograph of himself. It was an X-ray of his skull taken only two weeks earlier by an unnamed assistant of Dr. Seltzman, revealing the problematic wisdom teeth.

He analyzed the black and white prints of his skull and saw the unsocialized tooth pressing against the rest of his neatly arranged teeth, straight but straining against the wisdom teeth. The source of all of his pain two weeks earlier that effectively rendered his ability to eat impossible had since been destroyed, broken into tiny crumbs when Seltzman had attempted to remove it. When asked if he wanted to keep the crumbs, as a memento, he refused and watched the dentist toss them into the sink.

Then, there had been no sign of the growth. In the X-ray he held he didn't see any evidence of Parlay. Then when did the thing appear?

"I do not know. I don't have all of the answers right now," he heard the ghost of Dr. Fejes repeat in his head. From the other room, he heard the sudden shattering of glass. Parlay.

Running back, he found that the growth had tipped the beaker over onto the faux-marble coffee-table. "Parlay, what are you doing? Why did you- I need to contain you in something else."

"I am contained," Parlay chirped while Paulie picked the glass out of his carpet. The ball moved a larger piece of beaker off of itself. "Can I go back in your cavern, Paulie?"

As he picked up the small pink growth, picking out a stray hair of his that had stuck itself to the mass, he visibly shook at the idea of letting this thing go back into his mouth. "No chance in hell," he said, before stuffing the tiny ball into his pants pocket. "Keep quiet, we're going next door. I have to see if Niles has an extra aquarium for you."

Parlay didn't know what an aquarium was, but it liked the Niles Paulie had mentioned. He had the head that reminded Parlay of himself. Smooth and shiny, firm but squishy. Paulie took the handful of broken glass and tossed it in his trash-can, along with the crumpled kitten poster that sat next to the can.

Parlay also wondered where he was expected to keep the quiet. While Paulie walked, Parlay experienced the motion in a way it was not used to. Usually, Parlay existed in the man's mouth or hidden in the esophageal area. Next to where the food came and went. But here, at Paulie's waist, the gyro-motion was messing with the growths equilibrium as it rolled about his new home.

"Paulie,"

"Shh! I said be quiet," Paulie demanded of the growth in his pocket.

"I am sickly-unwell, Paulie." But the man did not pay atten-tion to the mass' warning, nor did he feel the mass ejecting half a thimble-full of a semi-translucent bile onto the fabric lining of his pockets.

As the egg-shaped ball made the faintest retching noises, it could now hear another voice. The gruff voice from the night before that Parlay heard in between splashes of that awful tasting liquid, Niles, was now seen opening the door to his cavern.

"Can't say I expected to see you today, Paulie. Did your sudden surgery get canceled? I knew it seemed too fast. Doctors are like government workers. Slow and inefficient, and never in a hurry to get something done that they can push off on the next guy or during the next week, you know what I'm saying?"

What? No. "Uh, not really, no. I did have the surgery. It was fairly, how do you say, non-invasive. I was only there for, gee, two hours. The doctors said it was a success." He wondered whether that was a lie or not, but if pressed, he did actually believe this himself.

Niles leaned in, which revealed the fact that Niles was not in fact wearing any prosthetic, just the sock over his amputated leg. When he did, Paulie could smell the beer on his breath once again. "Well, open up, let me see it."

"Wait, what?"

"Open your dang mouth, Paulie, let me have a look."

Why he complied, Paulie did not know.

"Yeah, you like right as rain in there. Now I'm no expert, but I'd say you'll be just fine."

"Uh, Niles, I didn't come here to get your opinion on the matter. No offense. I was, hm, I was wondering if you perchance had an old aquarium. Say, one that Slugger may have outgrown."

"What kind of pet did you have in mind?"

"Not in mind, in mouth," said Paulie's pocket.

Niles glanced down at Paulie's pocket, but simply took it as his own mishearing of the man standing outside his doorway. Paulie spoke over the voice in his pocket, the voice that was his but not, and clarified, "Oh I don't know, something small," he was about to say, "Something furry," but that would have been a lie.

"Something Parlay," his pocket said, this time attracting Niles' full attention.

"You got some sort of recording device playing in your pocket there, pal?"

"Not pal, Parlay," his pocket corrected.

Paulie tried to shield his left pants pocket with his hand,

but already the ball had plopped itself out of the pocket, revealing itself to Niles.

"What in the hell is that you got there, Paulie-boy?" he said as he grabbed Paulie's hand.

Before he could answer, the mass had leapt from the pocket and onto the back of Niles' hand. Niles stared at the small piece of raw meat that had stuck to him in wonderment.

"Paulie, did you go and get yourself a snail?"

"It's not a snail, Niles. It's the tumor that the ENT removed from my throat."

"Well, it sure is cute. It feels sort of alien. Is it an alien?"

"Not to my knowledge."

"Does it bite?"

"Not that I've seen. But-"

"But what, Paulie?"

"It talks."

"I talks."

Niles wide-eyed, squinted at the vibrating mass that had stuck itself to the back of his hand and he whispered, "No fucking way," in a quiet voice that not even Paulie could hear.

"Well, here, you take this," he said, shaking the small snail-like creature off into Paulie's hand, "And wait here while I go fetch that tank for you."

Paulie stood there outside of Niles' doorway while the man vanished back into his abode. "I thought I told you to keep quiet, Parlay."

"I didn't know where to keep it."

Frustrated, Paulie wondered if there was a way to scold a growth, but before he could figure out an ethical way to do such, Niles had returned with a small clear container no larger than a lunch box and a mostly empty forty-two-ounce beer bottle.

"Here's the aquarium for ya. It was always too small for

Slugger. I think it was for a hermit crab or something. Maybe a betta fish. I don't know, I got it from one of the fine paying customers of We-Store who was clearing out his locker a few years back. You wouldn't believe some of the stuff people keep in these units," he said as he passed the container to Paulie.

"There's one guy I see from time to time, who has a whole storage unit filled with naked dolls. But like, life size dolls. Sex dolls, by my reckoning. Would you believe it?"

Instead of acknowledging the fact that he did believe it, and had seen it the day before, he thanked his neighbor for the aquarium.

"Oh, it's no problem, Paulie. Thanks again for the beer and star fish. Slugger loves it. That said, that thing of yours got a name?"

"It does. Parlay is what it's called."

"That there is a good name, Paulie. You two be well. Oh, one last thing. Did you want the last of this beer? It ain't sitting well with me and I figured you only had a bit last night, so I figured I'd save the rest for you."

"No fucking way," chimed the growth in Paulie's hand. Just seeing the warm flat beer nearly made Paulie vomit.

"Just thought I'd ask is all. You two be well now, ya hear?"

But as Paulie watched Niles close the door behind him, he did not feel like he was about to be well. He felt like he needed to run back to his bathroom and hover himself over the toilet until he was drained of whatever contents were souring his gut.

Following this intestinal upheaval, he intended on having a talk with his tumor.

Paulie set the aquarium down on his table and placed his pocket contents into the tank before hurrying towards his faux-beach-themed bathroom. He assured his pocket contents he would be right back.

"Wait here," he found himself telling the tumor.

Purging his gut content revealed a strange surprise.

He could taste Arby's.

Or rather, he could taste the remnants of the fast-food chain that must have not been washed entirely off of the old doctor's gloveless hands. As he wretched into his sacred basin, flashes of scented memories and splashes of strange tastes washed over his tongue and tastebuds.

In between spurts of sour bile, he swore to himself that he was done letting strangers near his mouth.

26

LET ME PICK YOUR BRAIN

Let Me Poke Your Meat

Paulie sat on the edge of the couch, back in its normal state once more, and watched as the small pink ball pressed itself flat against the glass in between them.

"Do you know what you are?"

"No. Do you?"

"I don't know what you are."

"Do you know what you are?"

"I mean, I know who I am. I've been me for forty-seven years. You've been you for..."

"How long have I been me?"

"I, uh, I don't know."

"Then how do you know I am me?"

"I don't understand."

"I don't understand either."

Paulie sighed, exhausted at the cyclical nature of the conversation, hearing his own voice parroted back at him in nearly all the correct tones, but there was an uncanny different-ness that confounded the man.

"Do you know why you talk? How you are able to talk?"

"No. Do you?"

"This isn't going anywhere."

"Then why don't we just stay here?"

"Here is where I live."

"Can I live here too? Can I live here with you?"

"I don't see why not."

"Can I live there in you?"

"No."

"It was warm in there. I miss its wetness. The darkness."

"Are you cold? Will you dry out? Do you need water? Is the light bothering you?"

"No, I am, what is the word? You say the word. What are you?"

Complacent? No. Complacent was last week, or the week before, or the months before. Complacent was not the right word for right now.

"Confused. I am confused."

"I am Parlay. I am confused Parlay."

"Do you even have eyes?"

"I don't know."

"Can I, uh, do you mind if I touch you?"

"I don't see why not."

Paulie pulled off the lid, and Parlay flattened himself further to reach up towards the top of its enclosure. He had handled Parlay twice today, but only briefly.

This was the first time he touched the thing with intention, with his full attention devoted to the feeling.

It felt like a tongue felt. Stiff, but with give. Squishy, but solid. Both limp and solid, both wet and dry.

"Do you can I uh mind if I touch you?" Parlay attempted to repeat. Paulie, having never had a child, started to remember a course he had taken in college. The class was on linguistic anthropology. He remembered the teacher, a boring old man by the name of Professor McDowell, who was a better hypnotist than educator as his memories of the class were less prevalent than the memories of his dreams he had dreamt during the class.

But he still remembered the weeks spent on child language development.

Parlay was parroting back to him phrases he was saying, albeit sometimes wrong or jumbled up. The same way a child will speak without having mastered syntax and sentence structure.

"I suppose you can, yes."

Paulie felt as the tongue enveloped his two fingers. Only its form had changed. In a strange vibratory moment, the texture went from soft-hard/squishy-firm to that of a much more solid state. It still had give, Paulie noted, but the difference was that Parlay had been assertive with its mass. The texture had also changed from slick to bone dry. Not unlike a cat's tongue. But most alarming was what happened in Paulie's mouth.

"What is that?"

But it wasn't a that. It was more of a faint static electric charge he could feel in his fingers, but also in his mouth. It was almost as if he could taste what the mass was feeling. Or was it the other way around?

"What are you doing?"

The growth did not answer, not verbally.

Not audibly.

But still, Paulie heard its response.

"I'm learning, Paulie," the voice said in his head. His voice, but not his voice.

"What..." it said, though the word came from Paulie's

mouth.

"...are..." he said, though the word came from Paulie's fingers.

"...you..." it said, though the word came from inside Parlay.

"...doing?" it said perfectly, matching Paulie's voice exactly.

Too much. This was too much. Paulie shook the growth off his fingers, and when that didn't work, he used his other hand to try and pry the mass off, but it would not budge.

"Parlay, let go of me."

"'Can I, uh, do you mind if I touch you?' is what I meant to say. I do not understand 'uh' so much."

"I've had enough! Stop this!"

"Complacent. Yes, I am complacent. Complacent was last week, the week before, and the months before. Complacent is the right word for right now."

"You're hurting me, Parlay!"

And just like that, the mass went liquidy-limp, and fell back into its enclosure. Paulie pulled his hand away and fell into his couch.

"I'm sorry, Paulie. I don't understand me. I need more information. Do you have more?"

"I don't understand, uh."

"I need more information. I don't understand 'uh' either. I need more words, Paulie."

Words? An idea flashed before the man, and off he went.

"Wait here."

The creature returned to its ball state, and Paulie heard the thing vibrate once more. It was hiccupping. Why was it hiccupping? No matter. He'd figure it out in time, or he wouldn't. Instead, he went back into his bedroom, and from his nightstand he grabbed one of his library books. Shit, that was due back today.

The book was something he had picked up two weeks

earlier, some light reading he allowed himself after healing from the extraction of the last thing that came out of his mouth. A book he had owned several times in the past, but never read more than a page or two.

"Uncle John's Bathroom Reader. This should work."

He brought the book back into the living room where Parlay was still hiccupping in its aquarium.

"Uh, here you go," he said, placing the thick paperback into the tank with the tumor.

It stopped singing its hiccup song, and chirped out, "Thank you, Paulie." Before rolling across the cover.

"What is Uncle John?" it pondered. At first, Paulie assumed its eyes, wherever they hid, were reading the words printed on the glossy cover, but he soon realized that its mass was pressing itself against the words instead.

"'Who is Uncle John' is the correct way to phrase that."

"Who is Uncle John, Paulie?"

"I do not know. I don't have all of the answers right now," he heard Dr. Fejes say through him, "but maybe there are some answers in that book," he said, as he watched the mass roll the pages open with its body.

Paulie watched intently, while the mass quietly purred and squeezed itself over the pages. No residue was left, but the mass seemed to be eating the information right off the pages.

Paulie, dumbstruck, just stared at Parlay while it consumed.

He didn't notice the sunset until he found himself staring at the aquarium in the darkness. "Do you need light?" he said as he rested his finger on the light switch.

"No, this darkness is fine."

Exhausted, Paulie left the mass to its book, and wandered towards bed. His hangover having subsided, he was ready to sleep without any issues in his mouth for the first time in weeks.

He fell asleep within minutes, and his dreams took him back to the mindlessly mundane time where his biggest concern was finding better words to describe the texture of the artificial meat he consumed and wrote reports on.

Parlay, however, did not sleep right yet.

Instead, it consumed the contents of the book, which was mostly just trivia and snippets of information that weren't of any real import to anybody.

By the time Parlay was ready to rest its weary head, it had made a nest of the words and paragraphs and punctuation marks in the middle of Uncle John's Bathroom Reader. It was semantically satiated, and ready to sleep.

But not here, alone in the darkness. It did not mind the dark, but the loneliness was new. Parlay crawled up the walls, and with a strength not expected from a mass so small, it pushed open the lid of its home and left the aquarium.

It knew the layout of the apartment just as well as Paulie did, having spent its formative days inside him as he went from room to room. It did not know the proper measurements, how many inches, feet, or miles it was from here to the room, but it knew the route well.

It crawled, rolled, and flexed itself across the table, then the carpet, picking up stray hairs fallen from Paulie's balding head as it went. It climbed up the side of the leg of his bedframe, into bed with his host, and while the slumbering giant snored loudly with his mouth open Parlay snuck back in his cavern. Against the wishes of his host, perhaps, but we'd deal with that together, tomorrow.

As it shrank itself and cozied up inside the man's mouth, it fell asleep not long after finding its nook once more.

And it too, dreamt of different words to describe the texture of itself, of artificial meat.

27

THE HEDASKY INTERACTION

And The Firing Of Sue Ellen

While others slept, some still churned about. Some still had work to do.

Tom Hedasky, he had poor news to deliver to the citizens of this Midland. Once again, he'd have to inform the fifteen thousand-ish residents of this city that they were in for stormy weather. The fog blowing east was but a precursory event to mark the start of spring.

Next came the rain. And it intended on sticking around for a while.

By this time tomorrow, the terrible tweets would flood in. The hateful hashtags. Tornado Tom would be the lightning rod to their misdirected anger. As if the ten days of wetness was his fault. As if he was doing this to punish the town itself for transgressions not here mentioned. Harbinger Hedasky, Bad News Tom, Tom "The Bastard" Hedasky.

He was not an angry man himself, nor was he typically quick to upset. Tom had always thrived to be calm, cool, collected. But the people of Midland didn't make it easy for him.

Worse, their misdirected anger would be doubled were he to be proven wrong. Lying Hedasky, Two-Faced Tom, Tom "The Liar" Hedasky.

He couldn't win, but his meager salary was enough to keep him hated. He found it sad that the only place he felt comfortable at was The Ol' Watering Hole, in the city of Midland.

But here in Central City, where he lived, he found it abhorrent that he typically could not make his way to the studio without someone recognizing him, insulting him, or belittling him. The bigger city folk out here were always more of a threat, so much crueler than their smaller-town cousins just a half an hour south.

And after what he saw before work today in the office of a friend of his friend had rattled his otherwise calm demeanor.

So, when the man approached him in the final hours of Wednesday as he made his way to his car from the Midland studio, where he considered one more round of beer at his favorite bar before the drive home, he was weary.

"Mr. Hedasky?"

He he had seen the man before but couldn't place from where or when. He looked like your typical every-man. Thinning hair but not quickly enough to warrant concern, an unremarkable build favoring flabby over fit, but only barely, and a set of intense light brown eyes that reminded him of some past dog he'd owned in his youth. Cocker Spaniel eyes.

This man, though direct, did not appear to be a threat. Not yet.

But he wasn't quick to assume he wasn't a threat either, thinking back to a time where a seemingly nice pedestrian came running up to him with a smile, a pad of paper and pen in one hand, a milk shake in the other.

That man, back then, had asked Tom for an autograph, before throwing the milk shake at Tom.

This man, though as plain as white rice, was not armed with anything other than an envelope. Before responding, he thought back to his twenties, when envelopes were feared to be filled with white powders of substantial lethality, back when men still feared men due to their own fears of themselves.

"Mr. Hedasky, my name is Arnold Workman. I meant to reach you before your report tonight, but alas I was held up. Do you have a minute?"

Hedasky had a minute, he supposed.

"Sure. I was just heading to the Ol' Watering Hole for a drink. I'll talk while we drink."

The man, Arnold, seemed momentarily bothered by this, and tried to persuade him otherwise, "I was hoping you would actually join me at my office. I have an offer for you. An offer that is both time sensitive and pressing. I'm afraid I can't afford to join you-"

"Let me stop you right there. I'm heading to the Ol' Watering Hole for a drink. Either you'll join me there tonight and make your offer, or maybe you will meet me there tomorrow. I am consistent with my schedule. You can expect me there before my next shift."

Flustered, Arnold offered him the envelope. "Here, read over this. I'll meet you at the bar tomorrow evening. I have other places to be at the moment. Other envelopes to pass out."

Hedasky took it, and without saying goodbye, the man turned towards his next destination, while Tom got into his car and drove to his. The rain had not started yet, and he prayed it would start soon. He valued his reputation less as a liar, and more as the harbinger of bad news. Whenever the weather allowed him to that favor, anyways.

* * *

Arnie knew it was late, and to be honest, he knew he would not be met happily by his employee at this hour, but Doctor Koop had told him to take care of the issues that befell them as soon as he was able. And able he was at this moment, as Wednesday became Thursday.

He opened his brief case and examined the contents of it carefully. A large manilla folder detailing the finer points of Sue Ellen's severance package, with all the I's dotted, the T's crossed, and the financial aspects highlighted in yellow inside the folder. Next to that folder was his favorite pen that he was gifted on his tenth year with Pea Tree, the tool in which she would sign away her career. All she had to do was accept the terms and conditions, sign the paperwork, and she'd be on her merry way and forever out of Arnie's thinning hair.

Sure, he could wait until the morning, but the quicker he was rid of her the sooner he could move on to his next task, which was dealing with next week's problem: Galamb.

Alternatively, he had a second option for her should she refuse the first; next to the manilla folder was a small revolver he had inherited from his father. Nothing fancy, just a squat little .38. Like himself, the gun was unremarkable in form or function, but still, it was capable of making his point that much more important. If Sue refused, he could wave this at her, and stress how there were only two ways this would go down: one, she walks away from the company and is taken care of for the remainder of her life; or two this conversation would go on for the remainder of her life.

Last in his bag of tricks was a syringe containing questionable content. No need to mention said contents, because there would be no use for that here, at least he had hoped not.

Mostly, because Arnie Workman didn't want to deal with having to, well, deal with her body.

He was sure it wouldn't come down to that. Doctor Koop had stressed to make this a peaceful transition, and he intended to do so in the fashion that would most please his ancient employer. Due to his continued desire to work for the company that was going to save the world, and his desire to not die. But he had tried to stress to his boss that Ms. Ellen was a stubborn woman.

He would offer to buy her out with the company's bribe, and that would be the smartest option for her at this juncture. Beyond the severance package bribe, next was the threat of violence with his dainty revolver. Beyond that, well, you get the idea.

She'd agree one way or another.

He got out of his car, briefcase in hand, and went to her door. Her house, like the many in this suburban sprawl on the outskirts of Midland, was well-lit and nearly identical. Differing only in different shades of neutral inoffensive colors, and slight variations in design. Ever so slight. To his surprise, there was still obvious activity inside. Several windows in the house were lit up, and he was sure he could hear a television jabbering on somewhere inside.

Arnie knocked, each knock increasing in intensity to make sure the lady could hear him over her TV. He saw another light turn on through the windowpane of the door and watched as a confused Sue Ellen approached him in her pajama's and bathrobe.

He waved through the window, and she waved back smiling.

The door opened only a few inches. Immediately he was hit with her wall of stink. Of lavender and noxious incense. "Mr. Workman? What are you doing here? It's after midnight."

"I know, I'm so sorry for intruding. I have something I need to discuss with you right now, and before you say anything please understand that I am only here because it could not wait until morning. It's about your future, Ms. Ellen, and how we appreciate your time here at Pea Tree Farms."

Intrigued, she lifted one finger between her and him, "Oh sure, but not like this. Wait here just one moment while I make myself a bit more decent. I'll be back in two shakes of a lamb's tail, Arnie!"

"Do not call me Arnie," he thought but dare not speak. Instead, "Not a problem at all, I'll wait here. Thank you so much for having me at this untimely hour. Go get dressed, we've got a lot to discuss." She beamed a smile at him, and he feigned one in response, before she closed the door.

Arnold Workman glared at the floor mat under his feet that read "AS FOR ME AND MY HOUSE, WE SERVE THE LORD – JOSHUA 24:15" and found that he was instantly annoyed once again. How could someone work for a company that defied the laws of God still flaunt the rambling ways of dead religious figures past? More importantly, how did he miss her religious ardor in the hiring process?

It didn't matter. In a few minutes, she'd accept his terms and he'd be rid of her.

Or she wouldn't and the results would remain the same.

While he waited, the Lord Joshua turned the sky faucet on a quarter turn as rain fell from the heavens onto Workman's bald spot, adding to his frustration.

Goddamn you, Tom Hedasky.

* * *

Back in his office, Arnie Workman wondered about the importance of his tasks tonight. He'd have to do a better job convincing the meteorologist into silence than he had with the chatty-Kathy, but everyone has a price. He'd be firmer with Tom Hedasky when he saw him next, but only because he was asked to bring the man directly to Doctor Koop and he meant to do exactly that. No more hiccups or delays, Arnie would get it done.

Why Paulie was so important was only partially known to the underling. He had somehow survived, where everyone before him had died. How many of the testers had gotten sick in the last few years?

The fact that Paulie Galamb had not succumb to his illness meant only one thing. Pea Tree was close, and soon Doctor Koop would have the immortality he sought. Not just for him, but for the world, for the betterment of mankind. Humanity would remember Dr. C. Everett Koop for how he saved them from themselves, and they would remember the man who helped him do it. Arnold Workman, not just a man of middle management, but the unsung hero of his fellow man.

Arnie almost blushed at the thought in the low lights of his office, but there was no one to see him do it. Instead, he closed the blinds on the windows separating him and the rest of the currently empty cubicles. Finally, he locked his office door and returned to his desk.

There, he opened the largest drawer and pulled out the small rolled up yoga mat that fit inside. Next to that was his sleeping bag, which he also pulled out. He unwound the yoga mat, pushing his seat to the back wall, then spread out his sleeping bag atop it. Home sweet home.

Before he turned out his lights, he went over to the small pneumatic tube port next to his light switch. It was rarely used anymore, but something Doctor Koop had insisted on during the initial construction of the building. It was mostly an antique, but sometimes, when messages that need not be heard by prying ears needed to be passed from department to department, the tubes still had their use.

And in Arnie's case, it meant he could easily dispose of the empty syringe and the two spent pistol shells straight into the forever burning incinerator in the Crematorium.

Outside, in the earliest hours of Thursday, the sun was rising, and the clouds were dissipating into a mist. Just like that, the rain was gone. Tom Hedasky, you Goddamn liar.

28

THE WORK DREAM HE HAD

And How He Missed Their Meat

Paulie was back at work, and his mouth was fine, and there was no growth or mass or fear of cancer about himself. Instead of fear and concern, before him was a platter consisting of six chicken nuggets, and five dipping sauces. An array of different yellows, reds, and browns, and his favorite, Pea Tree Farm's rendition of ranch.

He wasn't sure whether the ranch dip itself was a product of Pea Tree Farms or not, or whether it was dairy-free or not. Not that this mattered, just something he frequently thought about.

He knew the drill. Next to the platter was a slip of paper that had printed on it a series of circles, and the letters A through D that he had been familiar with since his days in college so long ago. That, and a single, black-inked pen with the company's label on it. He'd try the first one additive free and fill out the scan-tron bubbles relating to the dozen or so questions that were on the computer screen in front of him.

Then, he'd move on to the next nugget, and the first dipping sauce.

He'd compare it to the first, then fill out another scan-tron, and repeat this until all six nuggets were devoured.

Then there was the personal questionnaire. He had always hated them, but it was the company's way of making it seem like they truly cared about their employees.

The same form could be found on the bottom of their packaged products in all the supermarkets across the expansive United States.

It read as follows, in a font that was hard on the eyes:

"What did you think of this meal?
Take some time to reflect on the sensations,
the tastes, the textures, the emotions.
In one paragraph, tell me how it made you feel as you consumed it."

_____
_____
_____
_____
_____
_____

Thank you, sincerity in food,
sincerely for you,
~ Pea Tree Farms ~

It never ceased to annoy Paulie Galamb, but unlike the customers of their products, he was expected to fill out this annoying form between every micro-meal.

After that, a faceless/nameless researcher in a white lab coat would bring out a second tray of nuggets. To the untrained eye, it would look like a repeat of the selection before, only Paulie knew better. He knew that one or two of these nuggets were fake, and though he wasn't allowed to admit it, he loved trying to figure out which one or ones they were.

Paulie respected the company he worked for, and he loved this job over every other one he had held before this in his thirty-five years of employment history. He'd worked for so many different companies doing so many different things, he never thought he'd wind up in a career doing what he loved.

And what he loved was eating.

In another life he could have been a food reviewer, but that took a knowledge of writing that he lacked so he never pursued it. He was just grateful that in this life, all his work consisted of was eating, dipping, and drawing little bubbles with his black pen that said his company name along the side of it.

The pen in his hand was a reminder of the good the company performed. Pea Tree Farms, as he understood, was simply here to convince the rest of the world to cut free their addiction to the meat industry and welcome with open mouths and hungry bellies the future of meat as we knew it.

Lab-grown meat. Cloned tissue samples of pigs, cows, and chickens, then grown on a petri-dish until it was big enough for an advanced incubator that sped the process up until thought-less brainless loafs were formed, then ground down, flavored, and cooked to perfection.

And in the years since Paulie had started, he knew they were close to changing the world. The flavors had long ago gone from tasting like stale cat food and gruel to its current state of orgasmic deliciousness. That might seem like a stretch, but when a man dreams of chicken nuggets so good that he wakes up panting in the early hours, it really says something about the quality of Pea Tree's product.

So he dipped, he chewed, he examined. He closed his eyes while he thought about the texture of the meat or the meat-like substance. He analyzed the flavor profiles, the saltiness of the pulverized and processed chicken or chicken substitute, the sweetness of the sauce, the subtle crispiness of the breading. Then he filled out his boxes, responding to the questions in the order asked of him.

"Do you prefer sample A with sauce B over sample C with sauce D?"

He'd scribble a small dark circle in the scantron, showing his favor of C with D.

"Do you notice a difference between sample B and sample C, or is there no noticeable difference?"

He'd mark down the first circle, because he was fairly certain that the second sample was in fact the real meat whereas the first was the new fakeness. He didn't mention that he preferred the artificial meat to the original real, but if asked he would answer truthfully.

"Do you still believe in what you do here, Paulie Galamb? A or B?"

He looked at the question once again. Surely this one was a mistake, or perhaps a joke on behalf of Sue Ellen, his supervisor. Before he could answer, a new question popped up, as another anonymous technician brought forth yet another platter of chicken nuggets, taking his second one away before he could finish the last two samples.

"I wasn't finished with that-" but he was silenced by metallic, almost tinny voice reading the new question on his screen.

"Do you question what we do here, Paulie Galamb? A or B or None of the Above?"

He looked down at the platter of nuggets. The breading on them had begun to melt off and evaporate. Below them was the same familiar pink sheen he'd seen before he slept. The color of a brand-new baby, fresh from its mother's womb. The color of Parlay, fresh from Paulie's throat.

The chicken nuggets arched themselves up to Paulie, who could no longer control his arms or hands. "Will you Parlay? Yay or Nay or All of the Above" the computer screen asked him, as he placed the tiny growths into his mouth.

If worms, beetles, and roaches could scream, then why couldn't the mechanically separated meats of long dead chickens? And so what if they were grown in a lab, who was it that decided what had a soul and what did not?

As the screams came from inside his mouth, he silenced them by biting hard, feeling the warm blood ooze from the growth. One dead Parlay. His hands automatically grabbed another, tossing it into his mouth like a kernel of popped corn, met with a satisfying crunch. Instead of ranch dipping sauce, all he saw was yellow-gray pus in the cup before him. Against his will, his hands grabbed it, and poured the acidic viscous liquid into his mouth.

He could see himself from the third person now, from the perspective of the computer screen. He watched himself drool blood, and bile, and whatever that yellow-gray sauce or sludge was. With his mouth full, Paulie watched in horror as the he-that-wasn't-him asked once more, "Will you give in to the desires of evil men, or will you let us save the world?"

And while he wished he could scream, his mouth would not comply. Instead, he was left to wonder who the evil men and saviors were. Somewhere in another world, there was a noise so loud it pulled him from his computer-screen visage and back into reality.

But when he woke, he could still taste the bile, but he would not remember the questions posed to him. Posed to him by himself and some strange other he had not yet had the chance to meet.

29

FLOWERS FOR PAULIE

With A Promotion In Sight

Paulie woke up abruptly to the sound of his door being loudly knocked on. His first thought was to touch his face, his throat and neck. He almost expected to discover the growth was still there, that the strange surgical procedure, if you could call it that, was all a dream.

Instead, it seemed that the dream was over. When he tongued around the inside of his mouth, he still felt the sore pocket where his tooth had been, but even that seemed to be healing fine. He coughed into his hand and spat up a small speck. A black piece of who-knows-what, no larger than a grain of rice. He examined it, bleary eyed, and found that he couldn't squish it or break it in half.

The knocking continued, and he unthinkingly flicked the speck onto the floor as he got out of bed.

When he wandered into the living room half awake, he saw the pink mass looking at him from inside the small aquarium tank. The delusion that this was all a dream fading with the sleep sand in his eyes.

"Good morning Paulie."

"I don't have time for this. Keep quiet!" he barked as he threw a shirt over the tank and quickly hid it behind the kitchen counter before answering the door. "Not everyone will understand you, Parlay! You're going to get us in trouble!"

What was he yelling for? What was he yelling at? A pang of guilt struck him right in his empty gut, and he added an apologetic addendum to his uncalled-for rage, "I'm sorry. Good morning to you as well, Parlay. Just be quiet for a moment, okay?"

"Okay, Paulie. I will be quiet," the growth said from under the shirt that lay over the aquarium.

Spying through the peep hole in his door, he saw a man he had only interacted with in person a couple dozen times during his time at Pea Tree Farms.

Arnold Workman. His supervisor's boss.

Who appeared to be holding a bouquet of flowers covered in some kind of colored foil.

Initially, Paulie felt a moment of panic. The kind of panic one feels when they hear an alarm go off upon exiting a super-market, "I didn't steal anything, but will they believe me?", or the kind of panic when you're approached by a police officer on a cloudy day. "I didn't commit any crimes, or did I?"

Would his supervisor's boss deem him fit enough to work or accuse him of abusing his sick days? Why would he or anyone for that matter lie about having cancer? I mean, it's not like he had any empirical evidence to prove he had gone through surgery the day before. No discharge papers, no doctor's notes, not even a prescription slip like his dentist had given him the day before.

But then again, was it even a surgery? It's not like he had

scars or stitches or even a band aide to show for it. He supposed he did have one piece of evidence. The proof was in the kitchen, in the aquarium under the shirt, hiding under a tent formed from an upside down and open overdue library book.

Though that panic was only momentary. As evidenced by the flowers. A strange gift from one man to the next, his father might have said, but that stubborn baby boomer's opinion didn't matter to Paulie anymore.

Paulie opened the door and saw the man's face distort from composed stoicism to a much more relaxed smile.

"Good morning, Paul! Wow, I'm amazed that I found your place through this dang ol' labyrinth. How are you doing on this beautiful sunny day?"

He loosened up so quickly it bothered Paulie, but he didn't let it show. He knew what his boss was doing. It was a common tactic employers used to preemptively de-escalate the mood of the room before having to say something difficult. Before he answered, it was obvious to Paulie what was about to happen.

He was going to be out a job before this conversation was over.

"Good morning, Mr. Workman. What brings you here?" Paulie said, even though he was pretty sure he knew the answer, "And what's with the flowers?"

"Oh, heh, that's a funny story. May I come in?"

Paulie didn't hesitate when he said, "No, I don't think that's appropriate."

You never let a policeman in without a warrant. You never invite a vampire in. And you especially don't let your boss into your home. It was a rule of Paulie's that he had stuck to, well, since his mother first warned him of vampires forty years earlier.

But as firm as he was, Arnie's composure did not change. He kept it loose and jovial, "No, I understand. Sorry, I just got back from Sue Ellen's, and you know her. She can be such a, what's the word?"

"Chatty-Kathy," is the word you seek Arnold Workman, and Paulie knowing this did not ensure he'd hand it over. Instead, he shook his head, "I, uh, I'm not sure what word you're talking about, Mr. Workman."

"Never mind that, then. Anyways, I came by to see how you were doing and with an interesting offer. See, Ms. Ellen just announced her early retirement last evening. Apparently, she was informed of her mother's worsening health and has decided to go take care of her in Florida. God Bless her soul."

Paulie wondered if he was being sarcastic or if he was fishing. Not about her taking care of her mother, that Sue had mentioned before many times around the water-cooler. Sue was closer to seventy than sixty, and her mother was a few decades older yet. The sarcasm came from Arnold's mention of God. He knew that religion was highly frowned upon in the company. This didn't bother or affect him, as he had been an atheist his whole life (only circumstantially, as both of his parents were atheists themselves), but he did know that Sue Ellen was secretly very religious herself.

Also, Paulie just noticed that he could smell her faint perfume. Of lavender and noxious incense. A smell he was never particularly fond of.

"Well, I suppose I'm happy and sad for her. Happy to hear that she is retiring, sad to see hear her mom is not doing well."

"Exactly. Anyways, that's why I'm here. To check on you and see how you're doing. How are you healing?"

"Surprisingly well. The operation was, hm, mostly noninvasive." Was that a lie? Noninvasive implied that there were no instruments introduced to the body; no scalpels or incisions, no Gracey Curettes or the Curved Sickle Scalers. The only medical instruments introduced to his body was Dr. Fejes ungloved fingers.

I suppose it is not a lie then.

"In fact, I feel great. The anesthetic knocked me out yesterday. I still feel a little loopy, but otherwise I'm as right as rain. I'd go as far as say I'm in more pain from last week's tooth extraction than I am from yesterday's surgery." If you could call it that. I refuse to.

"That's great to hear, Paul. Really great. I'd offer you to come back earlier, but I am a firm believer that one should rest as long as rest is offered."

"Thank you, Mr. Workman."

"But that's not all I wanted to offer you."

The flowers? "Oh yeah?"

"With Ms. Ellen stepping down, her position is opening up. Seeing as you've got seniority now, we want to offer that position to you."

Seniority, eh? Technically, Chris Wagner had seniority. And Gordo Fieri, he had been working at Pea Tree Farms for three few weeks longer than Paulie. Even Doug, "Just Doug", had a few more years than Sue Ellen before he sued his way to retirement. If he was going to be the new Sensory Panelist Lead, who would be working under him?

"Obviously, there would be a sizable pay increase, and you'd go from hourly to a monthly salary."

Did that mean Gordo was gone too? In the many years he'd worked for the company, he had always noticed the high turnover rate, but it seemed his core group was all but gone.

"And you'd be given a total of fourteen vacation days, paid time off of course, and your sick days or personal days would reset. So, these dental issues and this little cancer scare will not weigh you down."

For a moment, he wondered if maybe the meat they were

tasting had something to do the early retirements. The mysterious disappearances. The cancer.

But he only thought that for a moment. That reveal comes later, just be patient.

"It does, however, come with the added responsibility... You still with me, Paulie?"

He didn't realize he had left his jaw go slack until he felt the drool pooling up under his tongue. Nor did he realize he had been staring at the flowers this whole time, not responding to his boss. "I'm sorry, I was spacing out. This is a lot to take in."

"I understand. I'd love to come in and chat with you more about the specifics."

"I'm sorry Mr. Workman, it's just not a good time. My apartment isn't as clean as I would like, nor do I consider it presentable-"

"Oh, I don't mind. You know, I'm somewhat of a bachelor myself," he said smugly.

"Mr. Workman, I just do not think it is appropriate for my employer to step into my home. My work life and personal life, I like to keep them separate. I hope you understand."

The loose-and-chipper attitude vanished, and his face went stern and solid once more.

"Very well," he pulled an envelope out of his breast pocket, "I'll cut to the chase. We still expect you back on Monday. In the meantime, I'd like you to read over and sign this piece of paperwork."

"What is it?"

"It's a Non-Disclosure Agreement. I won't bore you with the finer details, but basically it's just a way for the company to cover its behind. We don't want you going to the public and stating to the media that you broke a tooth on one of our products, or that you ate something that caused your cancer." It seemed as if he was trying to make a joke, but he had lost his happy glimmer.

"Did it?"

"Of course not. But as we are a very private company, any publicity is typically going to negatively affect our work. Just read it over, sign it, and we'll start training on Monday."

Nervously, Paulie took the envelope from the vampire in his doorway.

"One last thing, these flowers, they were supposed to be a gift to Sue Ellen, but she refused them on account of a dairy allergy."

It was then he noticed the roses were actually foil-covered chocolates. An edible arrangement. How cute!

But the mention of an allergy bothered Paulie. "And seeing as these are non-refundable, I figured I'd just offer them to you. I don't care for milk chocolate, and I can't bring this back to the office. You know the rules. No outside food or drink. Here, take it."

Paulie accepted the offering, noticing the small bags of mixed nuts and freeze-dried fruits. Desiccated strawberries, mangos and banana chips all dipped in shiny chocolate. What bothered him were the man's lies cracking in front of him.

"Read over that NDA, Paul. Make sure you sign it before you arrive Monday."

"I will."

Something seemed fishy about this man. His alluding to religion earlier was one thing, but to imply that she had a dairy allergy was absurd. One of the precursors to working this job was assuring the company you had no food allergies whatsoever.

"And most importantly, heed the NDA."

This company was testing revolutionary new foods. You couldn't work here if you were allergic to milk, to bees or dander or nuts, hell, even penicillin allergies would have disqualified you from employment at Pea Tree Farms.

"I will."

Arnold's fake smile returned, secretly disgusting Paulie, as he took his cue to take off. "Now if you'll excuse me Paul, I have other business to attend to. I look forward to your return on Monday. In the meantime, be well, get some rest, and enjoy the chocolates."

"Take care, Mr. Workman," but already he had turned and was walking away.

Paulie couldn't help but notice the small patch of hair missing from the back of his scalp. Not that he was judging, what with his full horseshoe of hair atop his own head.

He saw a small card sticking out of the basket full of candies, partially hidden by a chunk of chocolate covered mango.

"Get Well Soon, Paulie!" it said.

And below that, "XOXO, Sue Ellen!"

Curiouser and curiouser.

Paulie decided not to dwell on this, not yet. Instead, he took the sweets indoors, where he intended to feast on this breakfast of champions.

More so, he wanted to introduce Parlay to his favorite cheat food.

Chocolate.

30

TAXOMY OF A TUMOR

And How To Comfort One

Paulie placed the plastic wicker basket on the faux marble top table, then he fetched the aquarium and Parlay. He set it next to the edible arrangement, tossing the shirt that covered it onto his couch.

"You were quiet. Thank you for being quiet, Parlay. I don't think that man would understand what you are. I certainly don't."

The lump under the book inside the glass rectangular cube did not respond.

And maybe that made sense. Maybe everything that had happened in the last twenty-four hours had not made sense, and this was his first lapse of sanity he had had. Maybe the last forty-eight hours were all just a bad dream. Hell, maybe the last two weeks was all just a waking nightmare. Why stop there? As he stared at the pink mass, a mere chunk of flesh that had grown in him, he wondered if everything since his and Toni's divorce had been false.

Until, of course, the bad dream resumed itself when Parlay finally spoke once more.

"Can I stop being quiet now?"

Paulie sighed. Somewhere between relief and revelation, he knew that this endless nightmare wasn't over quite yet. That this bad dream, if that's what all this was, wasn't ready to dissipate like last night's rain clouds.

"Yes, Parlay. You can stop being quiet now."

"Who was that work man?"

"Workman? He is my boss." He thought back to the night before, where he watched the creature crawl over the words of his library book last night, seemingly absorbing them. "Do you know 'boss', Parlay?"

"I know 'boss'. The Workman tells you what to do. Thank you to Uncle John, I know a great many things now. Paulie. I crave more. Do you have more words for me?"

He considered this. He had never been much of a reader. He would go through spurts of reading, but like his testosterone at forty-seven, it came in waves. Paulie always told himself he'd read this book or that, but instead it would collect dust or get returned to the local library unread. Such was the case with this particular trivia book he had picked up before his wisdom tooth extraction.

Before answering, he tongued the area where that invasive tooth had been. It was replaced with a solid slick flat piece of skin. There was still a slight pain, but he wondered if that pain was real. As real as the talking mass before him, as real as the chocolates shaped like flowers in front of him.

"I don't have more words for you right yet, but I will see about that. I wanted you to try something," he said, as he unwrapped the foil off of one of the roses. Underneath the foil petal revealing its shiny brown interior. "This is chocolate, Parlay."

The rose itself was roughly the same size as the mass in the aquarium. Having not owned a pet since his youth, nor having never been a fan of being responsible for another being in general, he at least knew not to feed the thing something of equal size. You didn't give a Chihuahua a slab of beef as big as itself, nor should you ever feed an eight-pound-baby eight pounds of baby food. He broke it into five small pieces and placed one in front of Parlay outside of his Bathroom Reader tent.

Could it eat chocolate? He didn't really know.

"Try this."

Paulie popped a piece into his mouth, and Parlay rolled over the piece in front of him.

"I will try this chocolate, Paulie."

But Paulie wasn't listening. He had closed his eyes and let the chocolate work its magic on his taste buds. He let the piece rest on his tongue, feeling it as it melt under the warmth of his mouth, causing the sensation of sweetness to envelope him. There was a faint aroma of dairy, almost milky, almost buttery. Even a hint of vanilla, but most pungent was the cocoa.

It reminded him of every childhood Easter, when his mother would hide chocolate covered eggs for him to discover, then later devour. It reminded him of his precious candy-hoard upon a successful night of Trick-or-Treating with the neighborhood kids. It reminded him of Valentine's Day, when Toni and Paulie would share a heart-shaped box of chocolates together. She would eat the dark chocolates. He would eat the milk chocolates. Neither would touch the white chocolates.

He didn't need to chew. Though the pain in his jaw seemed to be gone, he didn't dare attempt to masticate. Chocolate was a gift he cherished, but rarely treated himself too. Especially while working for a company where he needed to value and report every taste, every mouthfeel, every aroma and texture that Pea Tree Farms plated in front of him. The last thing he wanted to do was potentially put himself out of work by getting a small chunk of chocolate lodged in the seemingly healed mouth pocket. So instead, he arched his head back, and swallowed the nearly liquid chocolate down his throat.

Paulie opened his eyes and found himself back in his mundane apartment with his impossible pet. "God, I love chocolate," he said automatically, "Did you enjoy that?"

But when he glanced into the aquarium, he saw that Parlay was no more. In its place was a small black pellet, no bigger than a grain of rice. Like the one he had coughed up earlier this morning.

"Parlay?" But the pellet did not respond.

The aquarium lid was ajar. Paulie's eyes darted over to the bouquet of milk chocolate roses, and saw that Parlay was climbing up the side of the plastic wicker basket.

"I like chocolate, Paulie. We like chocolate."

He watched as the mass rolled up the basket in awe. With no fingers, arms, or legs to grip the edges, it still made its way up and over the top without any issue. Nor did it make any sounds while it did so. Paulie watched the mass roll over the bag of chocolate covered strawberries and expand itself around the whole bag. It reminded him of a video his ex-wife had shown him on her tablet (God she was always so addicted to that damn thing) of an octopus wrapping itself around its prey and consuming it. Except this here octopus, it had no arms, legs, or eyes to speak of.

Paulie tried to speak, but no words came out, as Parlay completely enveloped the bag of strawberries. Where previously he had been concerned about feeding the mass a piece of chocolate as big as itself, now the mass had expanded its body three times its previous size.

He absentmindedly placed another piece of chocolate into

his own mouth. Not savoring it, not acknowledging it. He was transfixed on what he was seeing.

Parlay had enveloped the bag entirely, and with the bag of chocolates covered, it began to shrink once more, until once more it was back to its typical size. That of a small chicken egg.

It then rolled towards the plastic stalks of the roses and started to climb up one of them before Paulie grabbed the mass between two fingers. Paulie looked in horror at what remained of the plastic bag full of chocolate covered strawberries.

Another small grain of black rice. Like the one in the aquarium under the book-turned-tent.

Exactly like the one he coughed up twenty minutes earlier.

"Parlay, what is that?"

"I like chocolate, Paulie."

"Parlay, what is that there? Where the chocolate was?"

"It's what comes after the chocolate, Paulie."

"Is that..." He wanted to say shit, but shit wasn't exactly right, "Excrement?"

"I believe so. Do you make excrement after you eat chocolate?"

Paulie ignored the question. Instead, his tone took an agitated turn. "Did you?"

"Did I?"

"Did you go into my mouth after I fell asleep?"

The mass shrank itself once more, trying to hide behind the two fingers that held it in place.

"I did. I like it there. I don't like the aloneness when you left me last night."

Suddenly, the chocolate wanted out of Paulie's belly, along with the bile that broke it down.

"I do not like being alone in the darkness unless it is in your darkness, Paulie."

He shook his hand, flinging the small pink egg against the

table. It seemed unharmed by the toss, but he didn't care whether the mass was harmed or not. His arteries grew thick with adrenaline, as his esophagus filled with a rising geyser of vomit.

"I want to be with you. I don't want to be alone," he heard it say as he ran into his bathroom. He almost instantly began retching into the toilet that he cradled between his large arms.

Nothing came out. Not even the liquid chocolate.

"I don't want to hurt you, Paulie."

But still, he tried. He stuck his fingers in his mouth once more, expecting to pull out more grains of black rice, those little pellets of shit. But instead, only foamy spit and a bit of bile came out.

"I will never hurt you. I promise you."

Paulie's stomach grew sore as he retched. He felt it in his abs. He held his stomach with one arm, and the back of the toilet with the other. The pain in his stomach was overwhelming, but it did not overpower his disgust.

The thing had crawled across his floor, across his carpet, and hid in his mouth.

He was so sick and tired of strangers winding up in his mouth. He gazed at his reflection in the toilet water, and finally, the stream of vomit flew forth.

Still, in the other room Parlay droned on. "We will never hurt you. We want to save you, Paulie.

In the water, was a small puddle of greasy yellow bile that floated atop the otherwise clear liquid. Mixed in that slurry was a stain of brown partially dissolved chocolate.

And on top of that, no bigger than a piece of corn, was a small pink ball.

It immediately began to float towards the side of the porcelain bowl. Towards him.

He just watched through teary eyes as the smaller growth

crawled up the side of the toilet. Unthinking, he put his finger near it. It leapt up onto his skin, then slithered away under his sleeve.

Paulie tore his shirt off and tried to find the slug that had just crept into his sleeve. And there it was, on the underside of his wrist, flattening itself in the area where his coarse dark arm hair faded into the light-colored peach-fuzz on his inner arm.

"Don't be afraid, Paulie."

He slowly turned his attention down to his shirtless awkwardly pear-shaped body and saw a lump pulsating under his left breast. He saw a dime sized salmon-pink blob move across his flabby chest.

With two hands he spread open his belly button and saw yet another rose-colored thing hiding in the crevasse.

"There are more of me. There are more of me in you, Paulie."

Paulie turned and saw that Parlay was sitting or standing, whatever you would call it, in the doorway between the bathroom and the bedroom. Paulie poked the slug in his belly button, and it retreated deeper into the hole in his stomach. It felt rubbery.

Like Parlay, soft-yet-firm.

"I need to call Dr. Fejes."

* * *

"Wait. Seltzman, so are you telling me there are more of them?"

"Shut up, Tom, let me finish."

31

SEEKING A SECOND OPINION

And A Kind Neighborly Gesture

"How very interesting to hear, Pali. Where did you say you found these new growths?" the old man on the other side of the phone line said. Paulie couldn't help but think he heard fear in the doctor's voice, but maybe that was just his own fear being projected.

"One I puked up, so I guess it was in my throat or stomach. Another I found on my chest, and there was one in my belly button."

"Köldök, hm. Was this chest growth, would you say, was it on your breast?"

"Well, er, yeah, I suppose it was."

"Was it same color as Parlay?"

"I, uh, hm. Let me check."

He lifted his shirt and saw the dime sized mass seemingly hiding in a patch of hair around Paulie's left nipple, along the side of his breast. Another side effect of his rapid weight loss and weight gain was the long sock-shaped breasts he had developed over the course of his life. It wasn't appealing, but he wasn't concerned. He put his finger next to the dime sized lump, and it flattened against his finger and chest, instead of attaching itself to his finger like the toilet lump had that was hiding on his wrist.

Upon closer examination, Paulie noticed that the little jellybean under his nipple was a darker shade of pink than Parlay. Whereas Parlay looked like raw chicken blushing, the color wasn't far from the color of his own skin. Pinker, sure, but almost the same off-white as the visible majority of a naked Paulie was, excluding his tufts of body hair.

But this breast lump, it was slightly darker. Almost bruised or enflamed.

"Dr. Fejes, it seems to be a bit darker than Parlay. I don't know the right word, discolored maybe? And though it feels similar to Parlay, it also feels different. Off. Almost scaly to the touch."

'Pali," Paulie did not enjoy hearing his birth-name so many times in one phone call, "I think I am going to recommend you to special doctor. He is good man. You will like him very much."

"I thought you were the specialist?"

"I am specialist. I am specialist in ears, nose, throat. You know this. However, I think you should see one more special than me. Grab pen and paper, I give you my brother's number. But really, he does not like to answer phone, so maybe you should just go see him. Yes. Maybe I just give you his address instead."

"Wait, why would you send me to see your brother?"

Paulie noted the pause. One, two, three seconds longer than seemed appropriate.

"Gabor, he is good doctor like me. He is cancer doctor. Oncologist."

"So, you think this little lump, the one on my chest, you think this might be cancer?" Paulie said, once again feeling defeated. A man could only take so much bad news in a week, and this was potentially the second time this week he'd been told it might be cancer.

"I do not know. I don't have all of the answers right now. What I am sure of though, Mr. Galamb, is that normal cancer does not live outside of people. So at the very least, you have that going for you."

This was true. He wouldn't have discovered the three new growths had he not just been informed that his first cancer had snuck back into his mouth in the middle of the night. He tried to pull the lump on his chest away from under his nipple, but as he did a single chest hair bulb popped out of its respective follicle. Just the single hair removed was enough pain to get Paulie to stop pulling on the thing.

Okay, so that one was glued on there pretty tight, but what was to keep him from sleeping with his mouth duct taped shut? What would stop him from flushing Parlay and his gang of growths down the toilet when he eventually pried all three of the wiggly little masses off his body?

"Please do not flush me, Paulie."

Paulie had forgotten the larger egg-shaped growth had followed him into living room when he grabbed his phone. It had been quiet up until this point.

Wait, did he mention flushing them out loud or not?

"Okay, what's your brother's number?"

"No number, only address."

Dr. Joseph Fejes rattled off the address to his brother Dr. Gabor Fejes' office.

"Did you say Central City?"

"I did say this. Fifteenth floor of Central City Medical Services building. You cannot miss it. I say this just now, and I say this when we first meet. Maybe I should examine your ears more thoroughly on next visit, because your listening is, how do you say, utter shit."

"I don't know how I'll get there. I don't have a car. And also what about the other two? The growth on my wrist, in my belly button?"

"I am not a taxi service, Mr. Galamb. I am ear-nose-throat man. As for other growths, maybe you should speak with Gabor about them. He will have X-Ray machine in his big city office. Now I must go. There are other patients in this world. Other ear-nose-throats to fix. One last thing, Pali Galamb."

"What's that?"

"I cannot stress this enough, do not let others know of your Parlay. Do not tell others of your secrets. Only me, only Gabor. Understood."

No, he did not, but instead of lying to the man or asking him to explain, he told Joseph Fejes that he heard him, loud and clear.

"Very good. Now go, find your taxi-man and be free. Now fly, fly, my little pigeon-pigeon."

Paulie didn't laugh at the doctor's attempt at a joke. Instead, he hung up the phone, and stared listlessly at the piece of paper in front of him. Another Fejes, another town, and another issue.

He could take a bus out there, but the schedules were so inconsistent there was a chance he'd walk to the end of town only to find out that buses weren't running today because the bus driver wasn't up for it, or there weren't enough people riding to justify it. The drivers of Midland were never hard pressed to leave. The locals here didn't care much getting out, as the fast-food workers and auto dealers and gas station attendants were just focused on the needs of those passing through this highway town.

His co-workers might have been some help. Sue Ellen had offered to car-pool him to work back in the day, but she had her own problems now. Even Chris Wagner had offered him a ride anytime he needed one, but when he saw him last he looked like he had been hit upside the head. Not that he trusted the man.

Paulie heard a knock at his door once again. Who could it be this time?

But instead of waiting for the door to swing open, the gruff voice on the other end spoke through the door itself. "Hey Paulie, I couldn't help but overhear you on the phone again. Thin walls, and all that."

He didn't respond to Niles, not yet.

"If you need a ride to Central City I don't mind taking you. I'd hate to see you, a grown ass man, succumb to tit cancer as soon as one doctor fixed your throat."

He opened the door and saw Niles standing there, scratching his testicles. "I'd really appreciate that, but how would you get me there? You don't own a car."

"I got Harley. She ain't no Sweet Cherry Pie, but she still drives just fine."

Sweet Cherry Pie. Paulie had heard the name before from a story his ex-wife had told him years and years ago. It had been the name of his motorcycle, the one he crashed that cost him his leg.

Paulie himself, he had not ridden on a motorcycle in decades.

"How soon would you want to go, Niles?"

"Give me ten minutes. I just got to switch legs and put on some leathers. Then I'm just going to go pester Edith and see if she'll look after Slugger while we're out. Who knows, maybe she'll watch your little bug as well."

Paulie briefly entertained the idea of leaving his tumor with his seventy-eight-year-old neighbor but quickly dismissed it. He'd pocket the little pink mass and bring it with and see if Dr. Fejes' brother could make sense of it. And if he couldn't, Paulie would leave the lumps in a storm drain somewhere.

"I'll meet you downstairs in ten minutes, Niles. Thank you so much. You have no idea how much this means to me."

"Yeah, yeah, don't go all blubbery on me, Paulie. It's what friends are for," he said, before disappearing from the doorway. Paulie closed his door, gathered up his tumors, and buttoned up his shirt once more.

"Paulie, please don't leave us in a storm somewhere."

"I wouldn't." Would he? "But I didn't say storm, I said storm drain."

"You didn't say that."

Whatever, Paulie didn't feel like arguing with something that grew from inside his mouth. He picked up the small pink egg and placed it in his pocket. "Either way, Parlay, we're going on a bike ride. We're going to Central City. A place I haven't been to in a long, long time."

Was it nervousness or was it apprehension? He knew not. From inside his pocket, he heard Parlay start hiccupping once more.

32

THE FORMER LIVES OF EDITH POST

And Her Memories Therein

The knock at her door didn't rush her out of her seat, no, she'd take her time getting up. Whoever was there, they could wait. Time was just about all she had left at this point. That, and her paintings, and her memories, but her memories were slowly making their way towards the door and the paintings surely would follow. So she took her time, as that would be the last to leave her in the end.

Because when her time ran out, Edith Post would be dead, once again and once and for all. Just like everyone she'd ever loved. Alex. Andy. Michael.

The person at the door knocking, they could wait a moment. Edith closed her eyes and travelled back in time. Fifty-six years ago, back when the music was still fresh and popping and New York didn't belong to the rats, back when she was still a stunning goddess. There, if she did her hair up right, she could have easily been mistaken for Marilyn Monroe, who had died two years before her arrival to the Big Apple.

As a model, she did well enough, but it wasn't until she met Andy that her career had taken off. He saw in her the glimpse of fame she deserved. "I can't promise you the world, darling," Andy Warhol had once told her, "But just like everyone, you will be world-famous for fifteen minutes."

And he wasn't wrong. She agreed to doll herself up as Marilyn Monroe, and he agreed to turn her into art. She did her best impression while Andy took photo after photo, and eventually when he came out of the darkroom with his "Eureka!" face worn snug, she knew she was at some crossroads in life.

She begged him to let it never be known that she was the face of the Marilyn Monroe screen prints. Just let that moment be lost to history, let that die between us.

And Andy, being the prankster that he was, saw art in that idea just like he saw art in a can of Campbell's Soup. He agreed to never tell the media that it was based on one of his many go-go dancers and models who frequented The Factory. She'd find her fifteen minutes of fame elsewhere.

Eventually, as time would have it, Andy Warhol's inner circle grew smaller, and his sexual proclivities grew stranger, so Edie quietly retired from the east coast craziness, and fled back to her home of Santa Barbara. She had grown bored of the chaos. She imagined her reckless twenties would lead to a cozy-happy family life well suited for a pretty woman approaching her thirties.

But the New York party scene had followed her back, and in that, so did her love for drugs and partying. She was especially fond of the 'ludes and soaps the east coast seemed to have in steady supply, and as luck would have it, her attractiveness made it quite easy for her to acquire them on the west coast as well. Sure, in time the drugs caught up with her, and eventually she did a stint at Cottage Hospital's psychiatric ward where she met a fellow loon by the name of Michael Post.

If Andy represented the absolute zaniness of youth and free-spirited chaos, then Michael was the calm of early-middle life she sought. Their love burned vibrantly and immensely, so much so that when he proposed to her she couldn't imagine her life going any other way.

They were wed in Santa Barbara, and she almost thought she was ready to settle down and have his children. She was ready to spend the rest of her life with this long-haired post-office worker.

At least this was what she thought at first.

Eventually, she had grown bored of her boredom.

Their love was merely a product of her manic ways; Edith's own uncertainty of herself was destroying her. As much as she loved Michael, she knew she wasn't ready to retire. She was too young, too pretty, and too wild to spend the rest of her days living on a postal service worker's dime.

So, she did what any self-respecting twenty-eight-year-old former model and actress would do.

She grew her hair out, dyed it red, and faked her death.

She called Andy Warhol, having discovered he had temporarily moved operations to the Bay area in the fall of '71 for one reason or another. He was delighted to hear from her, and quick to offer her exactly the kind of help Edie needed.

She remembered telling him, "Andy, dear, I need an out. I need an out of this world and back into yours. And I'm thinkin' permanence, see? What do you got for me?"

"Well, darling, it's not what I got, but it's what I can get for you. A five-foot-four damsel, pretty as the dickens, she sadly just took one-two-three too many barbies and she's down for the count."

"Dead?"

"Dead as nails and thorns and as dead as a clipped rose; we've got her on ice because I have this wonderful idea for a photoshoot but that one just might be the end of me, so maybe instead we put this pretty dead thing to better use."

"Do you think she could pass as me?"

"Baby-doll, I think if I work my magic, put a little paint on my brush, I could fool the world into thinking this here sweetheart was Marilyn Monroe reincarnated just to die all over again."

Another knock at the door interrupted her thought process, but once more she ignored it. She stood up slowly, but only to stretch her knees while she reflected a wee bit more.

She was a vain person, surely, but she wasn't vain enough to attend her own funeral, but be assured she most certainly kept a clipping of her own obituary that stated she had died November 16th, 1971.

She moved back to the Big Apple and made a name for herself as a British Broadway actress. Sure, some critics and reviewers claimed she resembled the late Edie Sedgwick, but no one ever made any fuss over it. As per Andy's suggestion, anytime she did an interview she always made a point of doing an over the top and gaudy English accent to throw looky-loos off the track. She never got her fifteen minutes of fame promised by Andy, but at least she got her second, no, third chance at life.

When she tried out for the role as the new hostess of some new game show, the producers said she was too English for American tastes, and how dare they, too old. That role went to a young lady by the name of Vanna White, and instead, in 1982 she was just another pretty, aging face that lost her chance at both Hollywood and New York.

But it was through yet another chance encounter that she met Alex Trebek, who was recently divorced and starting his career at another game show. The show, formerly hosted by Merv Griffin, was being revived once more and the producers wanted Trebek as the new face of Jeopardy. Sadly, when she met him, he admitted that the show did not need a hostess, but instead, he said, he needed her.

Their love affair lasted eight years.

And in those eight years, he was there for her when Andy Warhol was shot and killed by an old friend of hers. In 1990, the love between Alex had ended, as he had fallen for another lady. These things happen, she thought, and she was never mad.

It was then she finally retired for a second time, at the young age of forty-six. This time, she moved further into obscurity, into Midland in '91, where she took upon herself her old name, where nobody knew who she was, nor did anybody care.

A final knock shook her free of her reminiscence, and finally she got out of her seat. Very spryly, she walked past the Marilyn Monroe prints along her hallway, all original, towards her door. Past two of the Campbell Soup prints that were stolen from the Springfield Art Museum. Andy wouldn't have wanted his art to rot away in some mausoleum. She knew this. And she was sure it would have gotten a chuckle out of him that she had stolen them when she was well into her sixties.

When she opened the door and saw Niles standing there, she smiled. If Alex represented the solitude of middle life, then Niles was the rebellion of the end of her life. "Not today," she'd say when death came a knocking, "unless you want to go through him first."

"Good day to you, lovely."

"Good day to you as well, Nathaniel."

"I hate to be a bother, but I have to take Paulie down to Central City."

"Oh yeah, how's he doing? How was his surgery?"

"It was fine. Well, it's a long story, but he seems fine

enough. I offered to take him to see another specialist, just to make sure the cancer is done beat, once and for all."

"You're a sweetheart, Nathaniel."

"Yeah, just don't go around spreading that kind of information to anybody around here. I've got a reputation to uphold."

"Don't I know it, doll."

"I was wondering-"

"What is it, my love?"

"I was wondering if you would look after Slugger for a few hours. It'd mean the world to me."

"Of course," she said, because at this particular point in her life, this gruff man meant the world to her. She invited him in, and he set the small aquarium on her kitchen counter that was currently covered with a hand-crocheted blanket, with a design that obviously took its inspiration from a can of Campbell's Chicken Noodle Soup.

As he made his way back towards the door, she pulled him in gently, "Kiss me my dear,"

"Anything for you, Edie."

"Now be safe out there and come home soon."

"Of course, Edie."

And when he left, she sat back in her chair, staring at the slug, and thinking back on her life well lived, in her condominium filled with her many stolen paintings and her many past lives. Edith and her memories of her fifteen minutes of fame were muted by the sound of reruns of Jeopardy while Niles revved his engine outside of the three condominiums here at We-Store Storage Units.

She smiled at the snail. And if it could, it would have smiled back.

33

THE AREA BETWEEN HERE AND THERE

And The Bad Boys Once Again

"I mean, don't you need a helmet to drive one of these things?" Paulie said to Niles as he jogged down the stairs with his tumors in tow.

Niles pointed down to his leg, or lack-of-leg rather, and snorted, "Wearing a helmet didn't keep me from losing a limb, now did it?"

"Well, I suppose-"

"I'm just pulling your leg; I'll grab you a helmet you dang sissy. Also, don't ever try that joke on me or I'll kick your teeth in, got it?"

"I got it." Though he wondered how well this one-legged man could kick. And how high, for that matter.

Niles lifted the rear seat up, revealing a hidden motorcycle helmet that he then passed to Paulie. It was a very snug fit, pressing hard on the left and right sides of his face, so much so that he could feel pressure on this inside of his jaw. He tried to flex it, causing his temporomandibular joint to quietly say, "Quap!" in response to Niles asking if he was ready to go.

"I'm ready, I guess," Paulie said, patting down his pockets, wrists, and stomach. Normally he'd be checking for his wallet, his keys, and his stun gun, but right now he was confirming that Parlay and the other two tumors were all in place. Paulie got on to the motorcycle, causing it to sink into its own suspension. Niles was not a large man (technically twenty-pounds underweight with his below-the-knee amputation), but Paulie still was, and the strain on the bike was visibly apparent. Not thinking, Paulie steadied himself by placing his hands around the older man's waist.

"Woah there! Hands off the merchandise, sprout! I know you've been single for a couple of years now, but this here badass doesn't swing that way."

Paulie blushed, but it was hard to tell because his face already seemed to be turning red under the tight confines of small helmet. "Sorry, Niles. Force of habit," which was true, because there was a time in his youth where he had dated a girl with a motorcycle. A long, long time ago. He placed his hands on the back of the seat and balanced himself.

Unbeknownst to Paulie, he was now one tumor lighter. For better or worse.

"I gotta stop for gas and check the oil at the Arco by the Arby's before we head out of town, so if you need any snacks or you need to piss that'll be the place to do it, because after that I ain't stopping until we get to Central City. You hear me?"

"Loud and clear, Niles."

This amused Paulie, because he made it sound like they were driving all the way to the Grand Canyon or to some theme park or all the way to the Florida Keys or the Space Needle in Seattle. Paulie's own father matched this behavior in his youth, "If I hear you gotta pee one more time, I'm turning this wagon back and there will be no Disney Land for any of us!"

But the difference here was that Central City was only a half an hour away. Forty minutes tops with traffic, fifteen without.

"Paulie?" asked his pocket.

"Yes, Parlay?"

"Do I need to piss or any snacks?"

"I don't think so, Parlay."

* * *

It had been closer to twenty years since the last time he had ridden on the back of a motorcycle, and in the brief five-minute ride he was already having second thoughts about this trip. As soon as Niles parked the bike at the gas station, Paulie excused himself, saying he had to go stretch his legs and take a quick pee.

Really, he was trying to put some space between himself and Niles should he have to lose his breakfast. Again.

(And what breakfast was that, exactly?)

He took Niles' helmet off and rested it on the back of his seat while Niles' filled the Harley Davidson named Harley full of gasoline.

Paulie went to the back of the gas station where the restroom was located and was shocked to hear a familiar voice, and the ever-present smell of Cheeto-dust.

"Oh that a man might know / The end of this day's business here it comes / But it suffocate-ith that the day will end / And then the end is knowed."

"Dude, Mullet, you're not even reading it right."

"Listen, Stocks, do I correct you when you're teaching us

trickle-down economics, or do I interrupt Brian when he's babbling about Napoleon Boner-parte?"

"No, you don't, but man we're all lookin' at the same fuckin' textbook here. Right here," the shortest of the four of them said, pointing at the words in the large book in front of them, "It says 'O that a man might know / The end of this day's business ere it come! / But it sufficeth- not suffocate-ith – that the day will end / And then the end is known'. Not 'knowed' you damn ding-dong!"

The other two, Brian and Billy, laughed until they saw Paulie approaching. Paulie immediately noticed today the twins were wearing red hooded sweatshirts, as opposed to the blue from two days prior.

"Hey, yo, check it out! How goes it, homie?" Billy or Brian said, reaching their hand out for what Paulie understood as a 'Low-five'. Knowing how this prank worked, he gave in all the same, and reached to slap the boys hand, as is custom, only for one of the twins to quickly pull their hand away and announce that he was "Too slow."

But instead, he made contact with the boy's hand in a resounding clap of hands. Satisfying.

"How are you four doing? Is Juan at work?"

"Yeah, he got hit with another twelve hours of community service on account of drinking with us the other day, but it ain't no big deal."

"What do you mean it isn't a big deal?"

"Well, Stocks here used his computer to trick the community service people into putting Juan on payroll, so every time he logs the hours, he gets paid for them in addition to counting them towards his total community service. Pretty genius if you ask me," Mullet said while licking the ends of his fingertips.

"That is actually incredibly impressive, Stocks," Paulie said. "I mean, genuinely I am impressed."

"Hey what about you? You seem in good health, whatever happened with the surgery?" asked one of the twins. One of these days, Paulie would make a mental note to remember which one was which, but not today.

"Uh, well, the surgery went well enough," he said, thinking of the egg-sized lump in his pocket. "But there seems to be a complication or two," one of which was hiding in his belly button, the other somewhere on Niles' leather vest unbeknownst to Paulie, "so, I'm heading down to Central City to see a specialist."

"Major bummer, man. Sorry to hear. Wait, what the fuck is that?" The twin that had low-fived Paulie was now pointing at Paulie's midsection.

Paulie glanced down, and to the right of his oversized gut, he could see the pink egg leaning out of his pocket, spitting black and brown pebbles no larger than a grain of rice out onto the grass below his feet.

What the hell was it doing?

"Parlay? Are you alright?" he said, ignoring Brian or Billy's question.

"Paulie, I don't like going on a bike ride. Everything is shaking. Everything is sickly. Can I just go back in your cavern?"

("Is it talking?")

"No, Parlay. We have to see a doctor. I have to see a doctor, anyways."

("Holy fuck I think it is!")

"No let's just go home and eat more Uncle John's Bathroom Reader. Please, Paulie."

("I think my grandpa has that book.")

Whereas Billy, then Brian, then Stocks had all been whispering, Mullet had been staring with wild eyes the whole time while his jaw hung slack.

"You didn't answer Brian, Paulie. What in the ever-loving fuck is that in your pocket?"

This snapped Paulie away from his conversation with the growth in his pants that seemed to be either puking or shitting,

"Oh," was about all he could muster.

"That has got to be," Stocks said, pulling his phone out, "the coolest fucking thing I've ever seen."

"Can I hold it?" asked one of the twins, while the mass spat up another grain of black rice onto Paulie's feet.

"What is it?" asked Mullet, with his pointer finger still in his mouth.

"It's, uh," not sure what to say, nor willing to lie, he answered truthfully, "it's the growth they pulled from my throat."

"And it talks? This little thing fucking talks? Oh man, that's fucking rad."

Paulie noticed Stocks was taking pictures of the little mass, as heard by the artificial shutter noises clicking from his smart phone. He wanted to tell the boy to keep his distance, but before he could say it, Parlay had leapt from his pocket onto the phone, sticking to it.

"Woah, man, what the fu-" The shortest boy stopped midsentence, and asked "Is it poisonous?"

"Not to my knowledge." Trying not to think about the fact that this little egg had crawled its way back into his mouth last night. "Parlay, get off of that thing. We've got to go."

Parlay perched up, extending itself towards Paulie off of the kid's phone. It almost appeared like it was peering back at him, but without eyes, or a face, it was hard to tell. "Paulie, I don't want to go on a bike ride anymore. It makes me woozy. It means I feel unwell. Sickly."

"I know what woozy means, Parlay. But we got to go, I need to show you to the oncologist."

"On-call-oh-jist" Parlay parroted back.

The boys just stared in wonderment. Stocks was poking the thing at the end of his phone with his pointer finger, feeling its soft-and-hardness. Mullet and the others gathered around the smallest boy with their own phones and started taking pictures with their own phones.

"Hey, Paulie, if you want, we can keep an eye on it while you go to Central City."

"We really don't mind," chimed in Billy or Brian.

"We insist!" chimed in the other.

For a moment, Paulie considered just ditching the growth with the kids and being done with it, but when the growth turned its full mass towards him, he reconsidered quickly, almost hearing "Don't leave me," somewhere in the back of his head. "Not forever."

But then he felt something different. It was reassurance. He couldn't explain why, but it felt like the right thing to do. Just like he couldn't explain why he was so quick to let strangers poke around in his mouth with their hands, glovers or not.

"Paulie," Parlay said, "These are good boys."

Mullet snorted, "I mean, we're not terrible people but I wouldn't call us good."

"Parlay, do you want to stay with these kids for a few hours?"

"Very much so. They will help us. You'll see!"

"Where do you even see from, Parlay?" he thought, but instead he turned his attention to the tallest one in the group, seeing as Juan was not around.

"If you keep an eye on this thi-, er, on Parlay for me, I'll buy y'all a six pack when I get back. Sound like a deal?"

"We'd have done it for free! Hell, throw in a pack of Swisher Sweets and we'll even pamper the thing!"

"Sure. Will you meet me here in two hours? Three tops?"

"No problem boss! Do we have to feed it anything?" asked one of the twins, who was inspecting one of the dozen or so pellets that Parlay had ejected moments before.

"I think it likes, uh, chocolate."

"Nice, I've got just the thing," Mullet said, pulling out a small golden tinfoil wrapped square from his backpack

Paulie could make out a small Rx logo, as well as what was very obviously a marijuana leaf.

He wondered for a moment, but then found himself not caring about the possibilities.

He leaned down amongst the huddled teenagers and gazed directly at the growth that grew inside his throat, "You be safe, Parlay. I'll be back soon. As for you four, please keep an eye on it. And don't go showing it off to anybody."

"What about Juan? He's got to see this!" said Stocks, while the others took turns trying to poke Parlay. Or were they trying to pet it?

"Sure, but only Juan."

"Wait, you just said you were going to show this to your cancer doctor, right?"

"On-call-oh-jist" Parlay carefully said once more.

"Yeah, but, uh," he started to say, but instead of trying to explain himself, he just lifted his shirt and revealed his craterous belly button and the growth inside, "It's not the only one I have at the moment."

Neither of the boys noticed the smaller mass under his nipple, as it was mostly shrouded by hair.

Once more, the collective jaws of these four teenage boys were dropped with no words destined to fall out. Instead, it was Niles' voice in the distance that broke the awkward silence.

"Hey Paulie, let's go-go-go!" he screamed from the pavement behind the impromptu classroom. "What are you doing showing those kids your stomach?"

"I should go. I'll meet you here in two or three hours. And then I'll get you your beer. I don't have a phone, so just be here, okay?"

Stocks stood up, with his phone and Parlay in hand, "Mister, you should really get a phone. You've got to be the last person in Midland without one."

He wasn't wrong, nor did Paulie acknowledge it. Instead, he waved and turned back towards the bike. "Two or three hours, be here!"

They waved back and turned their attention back to the growth on the end of Stocks' smartphone.

"So, you like chocolate, eh?" asked one of the twins while Paulie paced towards the bike.

"Yes. I like chocolate, very much."

"What about weed chocolate?" Mullet said, as he pulled a sixteen-ounce beer out of his backpack

"Yes, we'd like chocolate very much."

So, Mullet broke a chunk off, and rested it on the edge of Stocks phone as Paulie and Niles sped off towards Central City.

Now Paulie was down to two growths, not knowing that the one on his wrist was now resting on the inside of Niles' shirt under his leather vest, sucking on a large green and black freckle he had spent too much time trying to pick away over the last few months.

Soon, it would have a name as well. As they all would, in time.

"You know those boys, Paulie? I've seen a few of them back when there was a Dollar General in that ghost-town mall with the bar."

"I do, they've helped me earlier this week. I think. And now they're taking care of Parlay while we're out. I think I can trust them."

"Righteous. Glad you can trust those hoodlums. Believe it or not, I used to be somewhat of a rabble-rouser myself. Neither here nor there. Now let's blow this popsicle stand and get out of Dodge," he said, surprised at how well Paulie was able to keep his balance on the back of his motorcycle named Harley. For being a three-hundred-pound man and all, that was.

Which was a good thing, because Nile's technically wasn't licensed at this point, having lost it the day he lost his leg.

* * *

It was a certain kind of beauty only the stagnant locals could appreciate, this drive from Midland to Central City. Because really, the area between Midland and Central city wasn't much more than a stretch of highway and a sea of artificiality. Nature had long since been plowed to the ground, repurposed as the houses in Midland's suburban sprawl, then replaced with mankind's last real attempt at saving the planet, even though the meteorologists would say it was too late, that the damage was done.

Right now, on this beautiful blue-sky day, people would be using a water-soluble marker on Tom Hedasky's car parked outside of his apartment in Central City to write various curse words and the word 'LIAR' all throughout. For lying about this week's rain, of course. By the end of the night, people would be throwing eggs at his windshield outside of the KTVG Media building for jinxing them with rain instead of promising them sunshine. Poor guy.

My point is, Tornado Tom wasn't to blame for climate change, he was just the messenger everybody shot at.

If you looked around in the emptiness between Midland and Central City, you'd see who was at fault.

At the outskirts of Midland, past the many miles of

suburban sprawl, used to be the fields and swamps long ago belonging to the Chumquah tribe. Long before the white settlers and businessmen took over the land, replacing the hunting grounds with shopping centers, the farms with factories, this land was a mesh of two vastly different biomes that coexisted peacefully. Thanks to the once lush swamps to the southeast and the vast fields to the west, this area flourished many moons ago, back before your great grandparents were twinkles in their respective father's eyes.

But alas, just as life giveth, time shall taketh away.

The biggest tourist attraction in this part of America used to be the five-thousand square foot casino known as 'Chumquah Fields Midland Casino' with the addendum "#2" seemingly added as an afterthought. Though in reality, it had been a forethought by the white men who claimed Chumquah blood and ran the tribe's business expenses from atop their high towers in Central City. Originally, this casino was going to be the first of many, but it was deemed too small to generate the revenue needed to justify it being the first. So, some wise swindler thought it best to add the number two at the end of 'Chumquah Fields Midland Casino' so when numero uno was eventually built, it would be much larger, much grander than the second.

This of course, never came to fruition, as the small casino didn't even generate enough revenue to keep itself out of the red. Only two years after it opened, it had closed its doors permanently, only to be demolished six months later. Paulie remembered that day fondly, as it had doubled as his twenty-first birthday.

He turned his stocky head and face to his left and saw the fields where the casino had been before the gigantic spinning windmills and solar panels as far as the eye could see now lay stagnant. Sure, on a beautiful sunny, windy day such as today this vast expanse of alternative energy was useful, but for the most part it was merely a place holder to keep the powers that be from running pipelines through what little remained on the Chumquah tribe's claim.

The Chumquah Generating Fields, as they were called. The output of energy was enough to power a third of unincorporated Midland, as well as most of the sporadically placed farms that were smattered between the little town and big city.

For a price, of course.

And everything that wasn't used was stored in the area that used to be the swamps to Paulie's right. He vaguely remembered them in their original glory, in one of those rare times where his family vacationed east instead of west. There was a smell he'd never forget. Like rotten eggs only not as repulsive. The smell of wet vegetation breaking down naturally in ten inches of still water. It wasn't particularly pleasant, but it also wasn't offensive either. He remembered his mother rolling her window up, while his father would roll his down as they drove past the moss-covered trees sticking out of lowland ponds, where only lilies floated, and frogs croaked.

The swamp was likely drained before the casino was built, as he also remembered the area had formerly been a parking lot at one point or another, until the sinkhole rendered the whole lot unsafe. Since, it was drained once more, and backfilled with so much sand, salt, and asphalt so heavily various protesters and scientists had tried to stop the construction workers by chaining themselves to the machinery that did the work.

In a strange twist of irony, it was white people who ran the Chumquah tribe at this point. People who were only $1/16^{th}$ Chumquah blood, on their dad's mom's uncle's aunt's side, who were lawyers and business executives. These men were the ones who made the decisions for the tribe at this point. And the protesters? They were fair-skinned long-haired hippies and flower children trying to prevent the tribe from poisoning the earth.

The irony lies in the fact that the people operating the bulldozers and earth movers were the full-blooded natives, who had been displaced so long ago they cared not for their once sacred land. Because this land was already dead, poisoned to the core.

Though it was through the petitions of these brave people that they were able to build the Chumquah Generating Fields, and the Chumquah Power Reserve to Paulie's right. This once great and stinky swamp was little more than a field of asphalt and concrete cubes. Inside those cubes were hundreds of columns of batteries, row after row. The cubes, they stored the excess energy from the sun and wind, should the tribe ever need it.

But mostly, the fields of windmills and solar panels to his left, the fields of asphalt and concrete cubes to his right, they still had their respective smells about them. Even if they were ever so faint. Of cow manure and rotten eggs.

It wasn't the remnants of the tribe who sold themselves short for a job who were at fault. It wasn't the fault of the businessmen who lied about their heritage that killed the earth. It was nary the fault of crooked politicians or corrupt religious leaders that the world was choking.

No, in a broader sense it was humanity's fault as a whole. It was just as much Niles' fault for driving a machine that farts out cancer-clouds as it was for Paulie asking him to take him to the cancer-doctor in the next town over. It was just as much the otorhinolaryngologist's fault for sending Paulie to see his brother, the oncologist. Just as much as it was Pea Tree Farm's fault for accidentally growing the growth in a lab that wound up causing Paulie all this pain.

But if Paulie and the rest of people were the cancer of the planet, then Parlay was the cancer of the cancer that meant to save the world. Just as life giveth, time shall taketh away, lest ye had all the time in the world. Paulie inhaled deeply and smelled the distant rot of long-lost eggs and looked ahead instead at the looming skyline that grew closer and closer as Niles drove them into the edge of Central City.

34

GALAMB MEETS ANOTHER FEJES

And Is Offered A Warning

"You should really invest in a cellphone, Paulie. They're cheap. Hell, I got my plan from Obama some years back and I think they just forgot about me because I haven't paid a dime since oh-nine!" Niles said, while Paulie carefully removed himself from the motorbike.

"All the same, yeah, I'll meet you here in a half-hour. I'll wait here for another half-hour tops, then after that, I'm heading back with or without you."

For a second, Paulie felt a twinge of panic until he saw the seriousness in his face quickly change from seriousness to silly in a flash. "Just kidding, Paulie-boy. I wouldn't leave you in this hell hole. Just make sure you're here. I want to get back before traffic slows down to a snail's pace. Hah, get it?"

"Yeah, I got it, I'll be here."

But Paulie did not, in fact, get the joke. His mind was elsewhere. For the umpteenth time this week, he was about to see another specialist about a potentially fatal disease once more.

He had lost count at this point, how many times in the last five days had he heard the word "cancer". Hell, how many times have I used the word thus far? Not including my overzealous use in the closing paragraphs of the previous chapter.

(Fifty-nine times in case you were curious.)

He was growing numb to it, that much was certain, but more and more his seemingly mundane life seemed to be awkwardly spiraling into some new norm he wasn't ready for. Maybe Dr. Fejes' brother would have the answers. Maybe he would see the two growths that came along, the non-vocal of the three, and decide to slice and dice one open to see what made it tick. Or perhaps this second Fejes would do that to Paulie himself.

He just wanted it all to be over. He just wanted this horrible week to be done with so he could go back to work. Possibly even with the chance of a promotion, were he to find the terms of the NDA agreeable. Whatever it took to return to normalcy, complacency, he'd do if given the chance.

But today wouldn't be that day, as he watched Niles speed off into between the looming skyscrapers that made the small outcrop of buildings in Midland look miniscule and quaint. Where he was going for the next hour, Paulie knew not. Instead, he turned back to the building with the very sleek, modern name "Central City Medical Services" etched into a black marble slab the size of a school bus.

The business of the crowd coming and going from the building was almost as dizzying as peering towards the top of this impossibly tall building. True skyscrapers like this, reminded him of his own smallness, the same way he imagined a mouse would feel staring at him from the ground below.

Paulie entered the automated revolving doors and thought briefly of Pea Tree Farms. The layout wasn't too much different than his place of work, with a series of elevators and fake plants at the far side of the building, and a bored receptionist up front twiddling her thumbs. The most notable difference, however, were the people. Every morning Paulie went to work, back when he went to work, there was a line of employees entering in at the same time, scanning their badges and ID cards, walking through the metal detectors and X-Ray machines not unlike the ones found in American airports across the country. After that, the lobby was scarce and empty, excluding the occasional tardy employee such as Gordo Fieri or Doug, "Just Doug", and it would remain empty and devoid of people until the day was done when all the employees left for the evening.

Here, it seemed like hundreds of people were constantly coming and going, entering, and exiting. He couldn't tell the patients from the doctors, the diseased and dying from the happy and healthy. The ennui of the Central City air that crept that into the building was almost as thick as the smog and city soot.

Paulie, overwhelmed to say the least, walked up to the bored receptionist, and asked her where Dr. Gabor Fejes could be found. She hardly looked away from her phone, instead she just raised her arm and pointed at the large wall of names. Though he hadn't flown in decades, the sign board on the back wall to her left reminded Paulie of the airport directory of departures and arrivals.

It was luckily alphabetized by last name, and Fejes was not hard to find. Fifteenth floor, suite 9. "Thank you, ma'am," he said to the receptionist, who once more mostly ignored him.

The dozen or so elevators opened and closed, let people in and out, and it took him three tries to find an elevator with enough room to fit his three-hundred-pound frame. It didn't bother him; he had similar issues at work, similar issues at the medical building in Midland where Seltzman had pulled a tooth from his face a lifetime before. He understood it, and he hated that he understood it; people didn't like sharing an elevator with an ogre.

He scratched his belly button, just to confirm the growth was still there. It was. Then he felt around his breast, confirming the second growth was still present. Then he reached for his wrist and felt for the lump that had been hiding on his forearm.

Paulie was mildly shocked to find out it wasn't there, but he had no way of confirming here on this crowded elevator. The lady to his right was already glaring at him for scratching his belly, even though he had tried to be discrete about it. He didn't see her glaring, but he felt it.

The lady to his left got off on the thirteenth floor, and to no one in particular, she said the words, "How disgusting," as she exited the elevator, and this story. Paulie wouldn't lie if you asked him if her words hurt him, but he also wouldn't admit to his hurt unless you asked him directly, specifically. Poor guy.

He got off the elevator two floors later and saw a smaller plaque pointing in two directions. Suites 1 through 10 to the left, 11 through 20 to the right. So left he went until he found the heavy iron door that read "Dr. G. Fejes, Oncologist" and the number nine below it.

Paulie knocked.

Paulie waited.

The handle turned, and the door swung open.

"Come in, Pali," said the diminutive man.

The same small old man that he had spoken with earlier today, that had pulled Parlay from his throat. The same man who combined his Arby's and his Subway sandwiches. "Quickly now. Before you attract attention," said Dr. Joseph Fejes.

Paulie looked around the office. It was a definite improvement from Fejes' office in Midland. Perhaps his brother had been more successful as an oncologist, or maybe it was just the fact that his office was in a large city and not a strip mall in a small town.

"I thought you said you couldn't see me, that you had other patients to see. Other ears and noses and throats to fix."

"That was small white lie. I was, how do you say, throwing the stink off of me."

Paulie understood the sentiment, butchered as it may be, but didn't understand the reasoning. "What do you mean?"

"My office is compromised. Bad men have come to do bad things to me, I am afraid. Two days ago, before surgery," If you could call it that, "I told you to tell no one of this. Do you remember?"

He had remembered even though Tuesday afternoon seemed so far away.

"Who did you tell?" the old man said in an accusatory voice that might have intimidated him had he not been so much smaller than himself.

"I mean, I told my boss. I figured I would be out for a few more days after the, uh, surgery. And I told my neighbors the night before."

"But did you tell anyone of your growth, of your Parlay."

Paulie did not lie, "I did. Parlay made its presence known to my neighbor. And some teenagers."

Dr. Fejes frowned, sighed, and turned away.

"Where is it now? Where is Parlay?"

"I left him with some teens I met. It, uh, it got sick on the ride here. It didn't like being on a motorcycle, I guess."

"It got sick. Fascinating."

Fascinating wasn't the word Paulie would have used, thinking back to the small black pellets it ejected from its pink meat, from holes that disappeared as soon as the pellets were expelled. "You mentioned the others, do you have them?"

Paulie lifted his shirt and revealed the smaller-than-Parlay mass that was pulsating on his stomach. Dr. Fejes held a small pencil to the thing and gave it a small poke. The growth shuddered, and then shrank into Paulie's cavernous belly button. "Does it speak?"

"Not to my knowledge. What do you think it is? Where is your brother, the oncologist?"

"Gabor is dead," Dr. Fejes said emotionlessly, as he pressed his bare finger against the smaller mast under his breast. Paulie felt the fear climb up his spine, while the chills ran down his arm.

"What do you mean? Somebody killed him?"

"No, he drank himself to death. I think. I don't really know, I lost contact with him many moons before."

Paulie's confusion was apparent, so Fejes wasted no time in explaining himself. "Gabor was once a good doctor, but he had a great thirst for the wine. He would have lost his practice had I not intervened, but he still lost himself all of the same. No, I use his office as, hm, as a place of solitude. It is easier to hide in a big city than in small town. He would not mind me being here if he had not pickled his mind with the alcohol."

"Who are the people looking for you? What do they want?"

"Pali, I believe Pea Tree Farms is responsible for what has grown inside of you. And I believe they are out to silence those of us who know of Parlay."

Paulie briefly thought about the weatherman, of Seltzman the dentist. Then more so, he worried about Niles, the teenagers, and Sue Ellen. This couldn't be true, could it?

He pulled from his pocket the pieces of paper Arnold had given him earlier, folded in half twice to fit in his pocket. The Non-Disclosure agreement.

"My supervisor, he visited me today. He gave me this."

Dr. Fejes snatched the NDA from him with a swiftness

and quickly read over the document. Paulie was mildly amused when he saw the old man lift his glasses to squint over the words, but he did not express it out loud.

"Pali, you must not sign this."

"But my job," he wanted to say, but he didn't see a point in arguing now. Instead, he kept quiet while Dr. Fejes rambled on.

"I think Parlay is something new, something exquisite. As for these," he said, poking his pen into Paulie's nipple, "I think these are part of Parlay. Here, come with me, I need you to undress."

"What, why?"

"I want to put you in X-Ray machine. I want to see inside of you."

Begrudgingly, he obliged, as he followed the old man into another dimly lit room. He didn't know it yet, but there was more bad news afoot.

35

NILES VISTS A GRAVE

And It Is Sadly Sobering

"It's been a while, Sweets," said the bald man to the gravestone at his feet.

It didn't matter to Niles that she didn't respond back. She was a motorcycle after all, and a dead one to boot. Niles was just here to pay his respects and tell his old flame that he had finally moved on.

"It's been far too long. And for that I'm sorry. Harley just isn't the same, and it almost feels dirty riding her. Oh who am I kidding, Harley ain't a her. It ain't anything more than a fuckin' bike," he said as he kicked away some dirt with his prosthetic leg that had been covering the small marker. It read, "Sweet Cherry Pie Niles", below that, was his own date of birth, and the day he crashed his motorcycle a decade earlier.

"You, Sweet Cherry Pie, you were something else."

The long-since-destroyed motorcycle was a made-in-America Harley Davidson that his father had purchased for him.

Nathaniel Senior surprised him when he was seventeen years old with the bike, and it would ultimately shape Nathaniel Junior into the man that stood before you, both figuratively and literally.

"You were pure. And I'm sure up there in Harley Heaven you still are pure."

The bike buried six feet below, after having been crushed into an iron cube, was still pure, and mostly untouched by time or weather. Unlike the other corpses in the cemetery, Sweet Cherry Pie would never decompose, and without the constant barrage of rain and other elements, neither would it rust or decay.

Unlike Niles' lost limb that was also buried here with the motorcycle which was little more than a few disconnected bones. Thus the reason he had labeled the headstone with his own birthdate.

"Slugger's still around, would you believe it? Ten years old."

The snail that caused the wreck, that somehow Niles managed to keep alive for a decade.

"I suppose that means it's been about ten years since I lost you."

Ten years since he had started collecting disability. Ten years since 'Meals-on-Wheels' started delivering him food.

"I met someone, Sweets."

"Well, you'd remember her. Our neighbor, Edie. Yeah, somehow, against all odds we actually hit it off. I think it's serious. Something special. Something I ain't had since, well, I don't remember when."

"I guess what I'm trying to say is, Sweets, I think this might be the last time I come and visit for a while." He leaned down slowly, careful not to topple over while he dropped to his knee on his prosthetic limb.

Very carefully he brushed away the leaves covering the name of his former motorcycle.

"Maybe one day I'll introduce you, formally, to my special lady friend."

Before he stood up, he brought his hand to his mouth. He kissed his hand, then rested his hand on the gravestone before propping himself back up.

"But for now, I suppose this is goodbye."

He stood, brushed his knee and plastic of his prosthetic off as he turned around.

"I'll always love you, Sweet Cherry Pie, always."

Nathaniel Niles solemnly walked back towards his lesser Harley, started the engine, and revved it loudly and proudly for the deceased in the cemetery. In respect for their lives lived and lost, his motorcycle screamed life, loud enough that everyone in the graveyard could hear it. He spun out as he turned around, the tires squealing almost as loud as the engine, in memory of Sweet Cherry Pie, and his favorite leg now mummified next to his bike-turned-cube.

As he did, two crying cemetery-goers shouted profanities at the rude biker, who could not hear them over the obnoxiously loud motorcycle between his legs.

36

A CHANCE ENCOUNTER

That Was Meant To Be Romantic

Paulie was nervously scratching his head, wondering if his neighbor would actually have the audacity to ditch him in the big city. Luckily, he knew it was possible to take a bus back to Midland, but the buses in and out of Central City and Midland were about as reliable as a fortune teller's predictions.

Or Tom Hedasky's weather reports.

He stood exactly where he had been dropped off, as noted by the empty vape cartridge Niles had tossed to the ground when they arrived outside of the Central City Medical Services building thirty minutes earlier. Maybe he was just early?

Paulie turned back and looked up at roughly where he guessed Dr. Joseph/Gabor Fejes' office was. He wondered about the seriousness of the situation, about the warning Dr. Fejes had given him.

"Do not trust the likes of middle management, their motives are more unclear than that of their more powerful, evil men," Dr. Fejes had said to him after the X-Rays revealed two more dark spots inside him.

Two more proofs that death was inevitable.

Joseph said sternly, "This is your cancer, Pali. And I think Parlay is your cure," Fejes had said, pointing to the darkness inside of his lungs, and the darkness under his liver on the X-Ray slides.

"You will let him extract from you this poison. But you must not sign this document. You must not let them take Parlay from you. Whoever may try, you must defend your growth. It is very important growth, Pali Galamb."

After Paulie put his clothing back on, he excused himself and rushed back to the lobby, not wanting to miss his ride back. Joseph did not say goodbye. Instead, he locked the door of the wrongly named office while Paulie rushed toward the exit.

Paulie shuddered. Could Arnold Workman, a man commonly known by the innocuous nickname 'Arnie' really be so bad? He thought this while grazing his fingers across the folded paper in his pocket, the Non-Disclosure Agreement Arnold had given him a few hours earlier along with a gift-basket from Sue Ellen that Workman had lied about. Something was fishy, that much was certain, and of all the meats and meals out there, fish was Paulie's least favorite.

He almost wondered if he needed a lawyer to break down this agreement for him. Perhaps a new character this late in the story? I think not. Paulie never considered himself a terribly smart or painfully stupid person, but the legalese of the NDA baffled him. There were so many strange sub-clauses and foot-notes that all seemed completely irrelevant to the job at hand, none of which seemed to apply to Paulie himself.

At the very least, against his better judgement, he would try to dig up Sue Ellen's number and give her a call. She'd appreciate that, even if she was packing and/or en route to the airport. Assuming of course, that Arnold Workman hadn't lied about that as well.

Dr. Fejes had told him he would be in touch, but to never call his Midland office. The way the Eastern European doctor had said the word stuck with him, "My office, it is, how do you say, Cahm-pree-mize."

Dr. Fejes had also warned him to not call Seltzman, nor to contact Tom Hedasky. Not that he had planned to do either. The old man, before Paulie left, had assured him he would find them.

Paulie sighed, scanning the streets in front of him for his neighbor. As he peered down the two four lane roads in front of him, one going east, another going west, he saw nay a motor-cycle in sight.

But he knew the voice as soon as he heard it, "Paulie?"

All at once, the thick dark hairs on his neck stood on end, his heart started racing, and he straightened his back.

"My god, Paulie Galamb, it really is you," she said, as Paulie finally turned to face her.

"Toni Collette," Paulie said, unaware that he was blushing.

"It's still Toni Galamb, Paulie. I never changed my name back."

He allowed himself to smile, admiring her beauty. She was just barely under five feet tall, and technically another inch would have rendered her legally a dwarf. For her size, it was safe to say she was mildly obese, but Paulie had always thought she had worn it well.

"Paulie, you're holding your breath," she said, smiling, blushing.

He was, but he hadn't yet noticed the stars at the corner of his eyes faintly forming. "Sorry, it's just been so long."

"What are you doing here? If I may ask, of course. You got some kind of hot date here in the big city?"

Paulie squeaked out a nervous laugh. He knew it was an old inside joke of theirs, having a hot date. Both of them knew that due to their appearance hot dates were never, ever likely without an ample amount of effort.

Her impish smile was fine for him, but most others would not accept her romantically. This was partially the basis for their marriage in the first place.

He remembered the pact that they had made in college as clear as day, "If we're still single by thirty-five, then maybe we should just get hitched."

He shook the thought away, remembering the week he had had so far, and as he shook away the thought so went his smile. Frowning, he pointed at the large building behind her. "I, uh, Jeeze-"

Her smile vanished just as quickly when she turned around and saw the big black marble letters. "Is it, oh my, do you have diabetes?"

"What, no, I mean, not to my knowledge." He had been sleeping a lot lately but didn't know enough about the diabetes to make that judgement call. "Uh, no. My dentist found a growth in my throat."

She widened her big puppy dog eyes, the most beautiful brown eyes he had ever known, and then without thinking she wrapped her arms around him, laying her head atop his gut. "Was your dentist some kind of ENT?"

"No, but he recommended me one." Or two, technically. He assumed Seltzman had known that Gabor and Joseph were the same person. He must have, right? Hadn't he referred to Fejes as his wife's oncologist or did he just imagine that as well.

"Is it cancer?" she said, squeezing him tightly. He tried distracting himself from the physical pleasure he was experiencing by keeping his mind on the topic at hand.

"It's, uh, it's complicated."

Just as he was starting to feel a certain kind of tingle in his pants, he placed his arms on Toni's shoulders and gently pushed her away from himself.

"Toni, there's someone I'd like you to meet sometime. If you're free or find yourself in Midland."

Her puppy-dog eyes drooped noticeably while she looked up at his ugly mug. The mood on her face dissolved from empathetic sadness to hurt in a flash. "You've met someone else. And that's good! Why shouldn't you? I'm happy for you, Paulie!" she lied. He knew it.

"No, no, Toni, no. It's not like that. It's, I don't know how to explain it. You'll just have to, hm, you'll just have to meet it."

"Meet what, Paulie, you're not making any sense."

He didn't realize it, but his hands were shaking. Maybe she did, but if that was the case she didn't point it out. Instead, for some reason not known to me, she grabbed his hands and squeezed.

"I know, Toni. Have I ever lied to you?"

"Paulie, I don't know that you've ever lied. Or even if you're capable of it."

"I want you to meet the growth my doctors pulled out of my throat."

"I don't understand, Paulie-"

"I don't quite get it myself."

The rev of the motorcycle alarmed the two of them enough that their hands broke free of one another. "My god, Toni? Toni Galamb, ladies and fucking gentleman! Aw hell, how long has it been now? Four, five, six years?"

"Niles, my friend, what a surprise. There's no way this is just one big happy reunion, some sort of chance encounter. What are the odds that you'd be here as well as Paulie and I?"

"Actually, Toni, Niles drove me here."

"Yeah, this big boy's having a little bit of the ol' cancer

scare," Her eyes widened as she imagined Paulie and the smaller, older man sharing a motorcycle, "I tried to tell him cancer is for pussies, if you'll excuse my French, but I wasn't about to let my neighbor here do the trek alone."

"That's very sweet of you Niles. I always knew there was a goodness in your heart."

"Just don't go around spreading that kind of information or I'm likely to get my ass beat," he quipped. Both Toni and Paulie, they knew this was not in fact likely to happen, but he had a certain machismo to uphold so neither of them argued it.

"Oh, man, Toni, you've got to meet Parlay. Coolest fucking thing I've ever seen."

"Parlay?" she asked.

"Parlay is who I want you to meet."

She glanced back and forth, unsure of what to say next, so instead Niles filled the silence with his loud voice. "Maybe you could swing by this weekend. I'll do some barbequing if you're interested."

"Oh yeah?"

"Yeah, just like old times. Edith would love to see you."

Paulie chimed in, "She always asks about you."

Toni considered this, then finally admitted, "I'd love to. Maybe I could bring my partner?"

Paulie Galamb didn't let his sadness show. He knew it was inevitable, that someone else would eventually sweep this beautiful lady off her feet. To him, she was still a catch, and certainly someone else would see that too.

So, he played the role of the nice guy, and agreed. "That would wonderful. I'd love to meet him, whoever this partner is."

Once more, she blushed, "It's not what you think, Paulie. Marion is my business partner. Her and I, we started our own print company a few years ago. She handles the financial side of things."

"All the same, bring her down," Niles said, "but I hate to cut this encounter short, I'm just trying to beat traffic so, if'n you're ready, Paulie, let's scram."

"Yeah, uh-"

"I'll be there on Saturday, Paulie. Do you have a cell phone yet or are you still sporting the landline?"

"The last landline in Midland," Niles added, starting his motorcycle up once more.

"No cellphone, not yet."

"You should really get one. Quit being such a dang luddite."

"So, I'm told."

"Goodbye for now, Paulie Galamb," she said, as she embraced him once more.

"Until Saturday, Toni Galamb," he said, hugging her back.

This time she was the one to push him away, blushing a final time upon noticing the slight growth not quite in his pocket, but more left of center. She smiled, turned, and vanished into the crowd like a ghost in a foggy dream.

"Well, are you getting on or not?"

"Just a moment," Paulie said, jumping in place, trying to redirect the blood flow from his groin into wherever else it would go. "Give me just one second." And one second was all he needed.

37

PARLAY CONSUMES

While The Boys Get Blitzed

"Dude, I think it's eating your cellphone," said the ginger with his fingers in his mouth, spitting crumbs of Cheetos out as he spoke. His eyes were bloodshot from the effects of the marijuana edible, as were most of the boys. Everyone but Stocks had partaken in the consumption of the weed chocolate.

If Parlay had eyes, they'd be bloodshot too, I'm sure.

"I don't think Parlay is eating my phone. I mean, I don't know. Parlay? What are you doing?"

"I am eating your phone, but only the perishable bits. The data. The information. I am consuming. But your phone is almost empty."

At first Stocks didn't understand, because all he saw was a small pink blob pressed against the screen that was rapidly changing colors and flashing lights. The phone, not the blob. What the teenagers could make out was the opening and closing of various tabs and windows, of pages on the internet being scrolled through quicker than any human eye could read before the mass pressed itself on one of the many blue links and found itself in a different part of the world wide web.

It was consuming as much of the internet as it could on such a small device, and the battery life was quickly draining. The processing power of the portable phone was being pushed to the brink.

And unnoticed by the boys was the slow growth of Parlay himself. It might have been more noticeable were the mass not pulsating and vibrating the entire time it flexed and morphed on Stock's phone, undulating, while slowly expanding.

It was growing.

"I'll need more. I need a more permanent source of food. Do you have more phones?"

The twins looked at one another, not willing to part with their phones. Brian was on the 850th level of his phone game, while Billy was saving his battery life for some private time in the gas station bathroom. Mullet's phone, with orange crusty fingerprints covering the screen, was already nearing death itself. The three phones had hardly enough battery life to call a hero if there was one to call.

But not all heroes had phones or wore capes, as seen by the one jogging towards the four teenagers and the mass.

"What the fuck are y'all doing out here?"

This hero, instead of a cape he wore a backpack. This hero, he came wearing a high-visibility yellow vest. This hero, he had a job and technically he was on break.

"And more importantly, what the fuck is that?" Juan said as he, like the other boys, found himself transfixed on the growing growth.

"It's Ugo's, uhm-" said Billy.

Brian, without seeing where he was aiming, punched his twin in the arm, "Don't call him that. It's Parlay Paulie's, uh-"

Mullet just stared ahead, stoned with his mouth agape.

Without seeing where he was aiming, he stuck a handful of Cheetos into his mouth, closing only enough to mostly masticate the corny cheese curls. It was Stocks that finally delivered the best answer among the wily lot of them.

"This is Parlay, Juan. This is the cancer that came from Paulie."

Juan gazed deeply into the fleshy sack, now about the size of a soggy, squishy, grapefruit. If that grapefruit had been deflated, as it was firmly pressed against the entirety of Stock's phone, now sporting critical battery life. The screen had dimmed, so had the faint red glow of light passing through Parlay's meat like a flashlight in one's palm, showing the inner workings of one's hand. Yet still, everyone silently stared at the throbbing lump.

Parlay broke the silence. "It's empty now. Do you have any more phones, Juan?"

Juan did his best housewife-saw-a-mouse impression as he jumped backwards in the air and fell flat on his ass. His words at first were less than articulate. "Wha- how- Wait- Wha?" until Mullet came over, extended his paw, and helped pull the boss-boy up off the ground. Juan brushed the grass clippings off his ass and spoke his next few words carefully, slowly, and most importantly, eloquently. But not before wiping Mullet's Cheeto dust off his own hands first.

"What the flying fuck is that thing, how the fuck does it know my name, and why the fuck is it fucking talking to me?"

Brian chimed in, followed by his twin. "It's the tumor. The doctors pulled it from Paulie's throat. I don't know why."

"It knows your name because Paulie knows your name."

And Mullet with the third answer, "I think it wants to use your phone."

The anger and discontent in their leader landscaper's voice was apparent by the use of Mullet's birth name. "Okay,

Nicholas, tell me why a fucking tumor would want to use my phone."

("Maybe it has to call someone?" Stocks whispered quiet enough that no one but you and I heard him.)

This time, it was Parlay's time to answer, even though the question was directed elsewhere, "I am sorry to alarm you, Juan. I would like to consume your phone so I can consume the knowledge within it. Your kind seems to keep abundant amounts of it on small objects."

Parlay meant this in terms of smart phones, or books, or even words themselves, packed with so much information in but the space of a few letters here and there. But this, this went over the four boys' heads, all except Stocks.

"I think it means it wants to use your phone's internet. Be warned though, this thing will drain your battery something quick."

Parlay was contemplating whether or not it should argue that it was a thing or not. It supposed it, like all else, was a thing. Everything was a thing in a sense. Parlay tried to disseminate the word "everything" and "nothing" but still found the abstract concepts of semantics and pragmatics difficult to ascertain. There was a great fog surrounding Parlay's own intelligence. A fog that was quickly lifting.

Juan pulled out his phone and unfolded it vertically. "I mean, I gots a phone, it just ain't a smart phone. You know I don't I buy into that shit. Y'all fuckers got tiny tracking devices in your pockets at all times, while I'm over here working off the grid."

"You're the only one of us who uses Facebook, Instagram, Twitter, Reddit-"

"Shut the fuck up, Mullet, you know I do all that for my permaculture groups"

"LinkedIn, Tinder, Parler, Tumblr, Flicker, Couchsurfing.net-"

"I said shut the fuck up, Mullet. I only use those sites for us. Stocks, you saying this thing is learning."

"I am a thing, like you are a thing, like everything, like nothing," said the growth as it crawled from Stocks' phone and onto the empty weed chocolate wrapper. It squeezed itself against the last remnants of sweets until they were absorbed. While nobody was looking, it spat out a few more tiny black pellets onto the picnic table.

"I think that's the case, yes. Paulie left it with us an hour ago, and the whole time it's just been scrolling through my phone. On Wikipedia, on WebMD, on some website called Scientific American, some website about radios and other shit. But then it got bigger, and we couldn't see what the hell it was reading. If you could call it that."

"I was reading the dictionary before the food ran out. There are many words out there, Stocks. So many more than Paulie could ever know."

"If you like words, man, you should check out Shakespeare," Mullet said, crunching down on another fist full of Cheetos.

"I will happily ingest this Shakespeare."

Juan was still perplexed and glaring at the mass in confusion. Against his better judgement, he took off his leather work glove and poked it with his bare finger. The mass, both cold and warm to the touch, pulsated when Juan pressed his finger to Parlay. Then, before Juan could pull away, Parlay hugged his finger. It almost felt like a static shock. Almost. But it was not quite that. No, it was something else.

It was a moment of clarity, a single second of understanding, an instantaneous transference of just enough knowledge for Juan to see clearly.

"Everything is food," Juan said under his breath. If the boys heard him, they did not acknowledge it. He shook his head, snapped out of his daze, and raised his voice. Not angrily. Confidently. "Parlay, I have a laptop. The battery on it will die pretty fast. And I don't think I have any Wi-Fi right here. We'll have to get you to somewhere with internet, and somewhere with power."

Stocks looked around at the various fast food joints surrounding them. They were already banned from going inside the Starbucks, the McDonalds, the Arby's, and the Subway. So, using the free Wi-Fi there was out of the question.

Mullet looked down the street at the apartment complex where they used to leach free internet from before they were chased away by one of the tenants there. No luck there.

The twins contemplated whether or not they could get away with using the Midland Library's Wi-Fi, but the five of them all were banned from there for stealing textbooks.

Unexpectedly, Parlay spoke. "There is power at We-Store Storage Units. And there is internet too. Paulie will not mind the company. I think."

The teenagers considered the advice of the small pink meaty blob in front of them and nodded in unison. Stocks followed the nod with a headshake and a complaint, "Wait, we can't leave here. Paulie expects us here. He won't know to find us at that ugly ass storage unit place. We gotta wait here 'til he gets back."

Somehow, without knowing how he knew to say this, the words came out of Juan's mouth, "Paulie lives there. Paulie lives there with the motorcyclist, and with an old lady."

And without consorting with Juan, Parlay added, "And Juan still has to work for a little bit longer. He'll be here to let Paulie know where we are. He'll make Paulie understand."

Juan frowned at the mass. Not because he was sad, but

because he wasn't sure yet what he would say. Somewhere inside of him, he knew he'd find the words.

Instead of saying anything, Juan pulled out his grass-stained laptop and handed it to Mullet. Mullet carefully placed the computer into his backpack, as Stocks carefully placed Parlay into his.

"Shall we?" asked Brian, gathering up his things.

"We shall," answered Billy, gathering up his things as well.

"Catch ya later, Juan!" said the shortest of the four as he put his backpack on.

Mullet turned around and aimed himself towards the water tower in the distance and began marching forth. Juan just watched them for a moment. As if he had seen a ghost, or rather, as if he knew what was yet to come.

38

BARSTOOL BANTER, PART FOUR

And The Role Of A Bartender

"So you're telling me that Paulie is just going to let these teens pop a squat and invade his tiny condo?"

"Well, no, I haven't told you that yet. Hold your horses, Hedasky, I'll get there in time."

"I'm just saying, it seems unlikely that Paulie, a bachelor-"

"A terribly unattractive bachelor-"

"Sure. You're telling me that Paulie, a terribly unattractive bachelor, is just going to allow four strangers, no, four teenage bullies into his home?"

"No, technically he'll allow five, not four, teens to stay in his home."

Tom shook his head, accidentally "That's unbelievable. Unrealistic. Doesn't make any sense."

"Oh, come on, that's where you draw the line. Not the secret relationship between an old actress who faked her death and a foul-mouthed one-legged biker. You don't care about the believability of Joseph Fejes' weird eccentricities, or the talking tumor he plucked from Paulie. You buy into the ghoulish Dr. C. Everett Koop, who, according to public records, died in 2013."

"Well, I mean, I remember watching his funeral on PBS. There was no body present, just a painting of the old Surgeon General and a bunch of Presbyterian folk talking about all the good he'd done. As for everything else, yeah, I find all that quite believable. It's not uncommon for opposites to attract in older couples, because a lot of people just want companionship. I don't know enough about Niles or Edith, but hey, if they're happy that's great."

Hedasky took a large glug of that amber ale he loved so much, unaware of the eyes staring at the back of his head from across the bar as he went on, "As for your friend, Dr. Fejes, sure, that I can get behind as well. I've never met a Hungarian before, to my knowledge anyways, but I absolutely believe that different cultures are going to come off as strange to me, the ignorant American who's barely ever left the county, let alone the state."

Seltzman took a sip of his own beer, as he listened to Tornado Tom's reasoning and rationale for the story he was telling Hedasky.

"And yeah, I'll admit the concept of Parlay, in its entirety, is a little phooey. A little preposterous. Sure. But we live in an age where they're cloning stem-cells taken from animals and turning them into food grown in petri dishes- Oh, I get it now, Pea Tree Farms. Very clever. Anyways, the concept of lab-grown meat baffles me and fascinates me. The concept of self-driving cars confuses me, but I love it in theory. But you know what, talking birds ain't much different to me than chat bots using scripts to learn human dialogue, so why would a talking tumor be much of a stretch?"

"Just wait until the Pea Tree Mass escapes, whoo-boy!"

"I'm not even going to ask."

Seltzman redirected the conversation back to the disbelief at hand.

"So, with all that said, you draw the line at the boys staying at Paulie's house. I'll tell ya, they are capable of being a rather convincing group of teens. Especially that Stocks kid."

"Doesn't matter. It seems illogical and unrealistic. Bartender, can I grab another beer, please and thank you," Tom said, holding up his now empty pint glass. "Another one of the same, if you don't mind."

Seltzman acknowledged the bartender as he walked over, nodding in his direction while asking the weatherman, "And how do you think the boys got inside We-Store Storage Units, Tom?"

"Good point. How could they -the four of them- sneak past security."

The bartender realized it was his moment to shine, so he said matter-of-factly, "Well, as much as I didn't want to let in some teenage assholes, they had every right to come on in."

Tom looked up in mild disbelief or amusement, "Fuckin' Kyle, you were at We-Store?"

Fuckin' Kyle poured the man his beer and started to walk away, "Yeah. I work there for the first eight hours of my day. I work here in the second eight. Anything for you, bud?"

Seltzman declined with a wave of his hand, so the bartender started towards the other end of his domain when Hedasky interrupted his escape. "Wait, don't go! Why didn't you say so earlier?"

Fuckin' Kyle turned back, but seemingly only to grab the empty glass in front of Tom he had forgotten while he handed him the replacement beer. "I didn't say so because this ain't my story. I'm not important in this one, is all."

Tom looked flummoxed, as if he were carefully considering

his own self-worth, "What do you mean? Everybody's important in this story."

Fuckin' Kyle placed the dirty beer glass into the dishwasher under the bar, then pulled out a rack of freshly washed and still wet pint glasses. He began hand-drying them with a rag as he carried on, "That's not entirely true, Tornado Tom. You see those college girls?" he asked, pointing at the aloof out-of-towners on the other side of the bar, "How big a role do you think they'll play in this story? Do you think the owner of this here strip mall matters? My landlord, Bob Robbins, do you really think he's important? What about that guy who has a storage unit full of sex dolls tucked away in his storage unit? That fucker didn't even get a name. Hell, Seltzman, you almost didn't get a name! Hell, what about that Chris Wagner guy, who may or may not have wound up lobotomized, are we expected to ever see him again?"

"Well-" Seltzman started but was hastily interrupted by the uppity bartender.

"Let me finish, doc. My point is, I've got one role here. I pour your drinks when I'm working here, and I do my damndest to not butt into your story. In the mornings, when I'm working at We-Store, my role there is to let people in and out of the otherwise locked up lot. Assuming they ain't trespassing. And those little shit teens today, as annoying as they were, it turns out the only kid with an ID was the tall ginger brat named Nicholas Morgan. The one you've been referring to as Mullet. As it turns out, his father owns a storage unit towards the back of the lot, which just so happens to be pretty dang close to the three condominiums on site."

Now Seltzman was smirking, "And who, bartender, exactly was this young man's father."

Kyle returned the smile, "Yeah, I figured you'd go there. Mullet's father is, well, the son of Alexander Morgan."

"And what's so special about the father, bartender?"

"Well, not much, other than the fact that other We-Store customers have complained about the lewd contents of his storage unit, that he seems to flagrantly display every time he visits his storage unit."

Tom realized it before Fuckin' Kyle said it, but to really nail the point home, Fuckin' Kyle said it anyways. "The contents being a couple dozen hyper-realistic sex dolls in various explicit poses."

"Small world, this Midland is," Seltzman said, satisfied.

"Whatever, I've got to get back to work. Y'all are good on beer, so I'm going to go back into hiding in the background now if you don't mind," the bartender said, ready to disengage from this conversation once and for all.

"Well, Fuckin' Kyle, I suppose you served your purpose here. One more thing, however, then we'll leave you be. You were about to point out the guy in the back of the bar who's been staring at us this whole time."

Without turning back, the bartender said "Nah, that's not my job, he's already walking up to introduce himself," as Arnold Workman finally revealed himself to Seltzman and Hedasky.

"Hello there Mr. Hedasky, I'm glad you've arrived. I couldn't help but notice you mention a Paulie. That wouldn't be Paulie Galamb, would it?"

39

THE PERSUASIVENESS OF PARLAY

As Well As Parlay's Guests

Alarmed was probably the best descriptor when Paulie realized the boys had abandoned post, leaving only bits of rubbish and trash as evidence that they had ever been there in the first place. Not because he was terribly concerned with the well-being of the mass pulled from his throat, but because Dr. Fejes had warned him that some people would try to take Parlay from him.

Paulie wanted to think he had done the right thing by leaving his motorcycle-sick growth with the boys, but what if they were in cahoots with his supervisor's boss, Arnold Workman?

He searched around for clues while holding the six pack of beer he had promised the teenagers, had they agreed to meet him back here in an hour or two, but other than the litter, there was nothing. There was no knowing where they could possibly have gone from here. In fact, he had no idea where the boys even went in the evenings. Back to their broken homes, no doubt, but where the hell was that? If he had to venture a guess, he couldn't imagine these four little punks living in the cookie-cutter track homes on the edge of town, but he also didn't want to just assume they lived in the poorer part of town either just because they spent most of their time outside.

He looked around frantically while Niles waited in the parking lot of the gas station, who had previously complained about wanting to beat the traffic. Now, Niles was tapping his foot impatiently, because he said he needed to go check on his snail. Just as Paulie was going to send Niles on his way and tell him he would just walk home himself, Paulie noticed the eldest teenager beelining it towards him.

"Juan, have you seen the other kids?"

"Hey hoss, don't go calling my students kids. Kids are baby goats, and those young men, they're motherfuckin' future revolutionaries!"

"Pardon me, Juan. Have you seen the other future fuckin' revolutionaries? I had made a deal with them a few hours ago," he said as he lifted the six pack of cheap beer up in front of himself. Without missing a beat, Juan quickly snatched one of the six from the plastic ring that bound them together. Mildly annoyed, Paulie just set the five pack of cheap beer on the picnic table that was still covered with the tattered remains of one marijuana chocolate.

"Yeah, I seen't 'em. And I met your lil' Parlay. Trippy little thing. That fucker's gonna change the world, you know."

Paulie absentmindedly sighed with relief. Wait, did he actually care about the growth or not?

"Where did you last see them? Where did they go?"

"Here, Paulie, I saw them right here. Your little friend, he needed internet and power, so he suggested-"

"He? Parlay is not a 'he'."

"You sure? Parlay's got the same voice as you, homes."

"Yeah, but voice does not define gender," he would have said, but instead he shook the interruption away and let Juan finish, who was cracking the beer open even though he seemed to still be in his work uniform.

"Anyways, they all went to your place. Parlay said you wouldn't mind. Parlay said you'd understand."

Paulie was stunned.

But more so, Paulie was furious.

He didn't let people into his home. Not since Toni left had he shared his space with another soul. Other than Parlay, he supposed.

It took much effort to hide his anger when he turned from Juan, "I've got to go, Juan. Uh, thank you for help."

"I'll be by a little later, Paulie. To check on my students. I'll see you in a few hours."

But already, Paulie was out of sight and around the corner. Juan shrugged, then placed the five-pack of cheap beer into his backpack before wandering back to what he called work, that others called community service.

The security guard buzzed the odd couple in, looking like some sort of parody of Laurel and Hardy. Only if Laurel looked like a gruff and grizzled pirate, and Hardy looked like a he had never learned how to smile. It amused the guard seeing a larger man riding on the back end of motorcycle, awkwardly with his hands behind his back, but it only amused him for as long as the strange sight was in front of him. After they sped off, all that was left was the loud fart sounds from the motorcycle's muffler, so the guard went back to discretely looking at motivational videos in his tiny booth until his shift was over.

As soon as the bike came to a full stop, Paulie hopped off, almost causing Niles to fall over. "Damn it, Paulie, need I remind you I've only got one good leg's worth of balance over here?!" But to that Paulie did not respond.

Instead, he shouted out a thank you as he ran towards his condominium between Niles' and Edith's own home. He ran, because, as he had feared, his lights were on, and silhouetted figures could be seen inside his abode.

Niles grunted a response back and grumbled to himself while he walked his motorcycle into the garage-turned storage unit as the pitter patter of a light rain began.

He was grateful to be home, and even though he had griped earlier about wanting to get back to his pet snail, the truth was Slugger was not his focal point. That spot was reserved for one Edith Post, who he'd see shortly after he freshened himself up.

As gruff as he was, he wasn't an outwardly rude man. That was the only reason he didn't complain about the sweat-stink that emanated from his heavier-set neighbor. A quick shower and a spritz of cologne, and maybe a splash of dye for the goatee, and he'd be right as rain.

Paulie on the other hand, was furious. He tried to open his door, but it was locked. He tried his key, but those inside had locked the deadbolt. He kicked aside the doormat in front of him and saw that the deadbolt key was nowhere to be found. Paulie found himself hyperventilating as he banged his fists on the door.

It was rare rage that took hold. It had been years since it had taken control as it had right now. He was seeing stars flicker in and out of the corners of his eyes.

"Who is it?"

But this was one of those moments, where he had to calm himself quickly-

"It's Paulie. Please let me into my home. Right now."

-Unless he wanted wind up in jail for assaulting a teenage boy.

The door creaked open, and Paulie's first instinct was to slam it open. Had he done that, he'd probably have sent Stocks flying back several feet. But instead, he saw the fear in the boy's eye as the door slowly opened. He had no idea what Stocks saw, exactly, as he had not seen himself angry in five years.

Not since he shattered every mirror in his house, shortly after Toni left. But he still remembered that face. The face that this poor young teen saw in front of him. A face twisted and distorted, red and wrinkled, and eyes piercing through their target. In this instance, the boy. In a previous instance, his ex-wife. In past instances, his high school bullies that had poked him too far.

He knew what he looked like. Horrifying. Terrifying. Uglier than sin.

The boy took a step back. Paulie hid his face with his hand and showed him the palm of his other hand. It caused Stocks to flinch and retreat a step. I think the words that tried to escape the teen's mouth were something akin to an apology, but they came out in chunks smaller than morphemes; just sounds, not even syllables.

"Sorry for scaring you, Stocks," Paulie said, still shielding his face while he caught his breath. He walked in, and noticed at first it was quiet, until he heard his own voice from across the room, only now it was more articulate than he could ever imagine.

"Hello Paulie. How was your appointment with Dr. Joseph Fejes in Central City?"

The large man slowly surveyed the room. Stocks was still

cowering a few feet in front of him, next to the former home of the "Hang-in-There-Kitty".

To his right, there stood the twins. Both had their hoods pulled up over their head, and neither of them dared make eye-contact.

And last was the red-headed teen named Mullet, sitting on Paulie's couch with a small portable computer resting on top of the still-empty aquarium.

And on top of that computer was a bare chicken breast. A chicken breast that had perked itself up, that as far as Paulie could tell, was facing him.

Parlay. Oh, how you've grown.

"Uh, Dr. Fejes, he said- Wait how did you know he was in Central City and not his brother?"

"I know more than I should, but before today I did not know the words, Paulie. Language is a very powerful tool of which I had little to no grasp on before today. Wittgenstein once said, "The limits of your language are the limits of your world"."

"I don't know who that is. Parlay, why did you bring these kids here? To my house!?"

The talking chicken breast swiveled the upper portion of its flesh and aimed itself at each one of them individually.

"Stanley 'Stocks' Leonard is sixteen years old, and legally a runaway, however his father is often so inebriated that in the nine months since Stocks left, his father has still yet to notice nor file a police report."

"Nicholas 'Mullet' Morgan is legally emancipated from his abusive parents, but thus far has been unable to find work in this town due a four-year-old petty shoplifting charge that has yet to be expunged from his record until he turns eighteen."

"Brian Taylor, on the right with the earring on his left ear, is allowed to stay with his mother three days a week, and his father the other four. William Taylor on the left, with the studded earing in his right ear is allowed to stay at his father's house three days a week, and at his mother's the other four. Neither parent has taken note of their disappearance six months ago."

"So, why did you bring them here, Parlay?"

"Look outside, Paulie. There is a storm coming."

Paulie did, as he closed the door behind him. The pitter-patter quickly turned into steady rainfall, and as if to further hammer down the point a distant rolling thunder could be heard.

"They stay with Juan, when Juan Riviera can sneak them into his aunt's apartment, but often he can only have two of these four over at a time. Juan keeps these boys safe as much as he can."

"Paulie, they're helping me. They'll help me help you. They're more than just teenagers who harassed you in the park before you first met with Dr. Fejes. They're more important than just runaway children. They're heroes to us and to all, just not yet."

He glanced around at the scared teenagers. He wanted to bark, "Yeah, you should be scared. You're all trespassing in my home!" but he knew he didn't have it in him to kick them out.

He wanted to address them, but the growth was still demanding his attention.

"What did Dr. Joseph Fejes tell you?"

Paulie slipped off his shoes, and as he did, he almost tripped on something at his feet.

Glancing down, he noticed eight more shoes than usual. Had Parlay told them to take their shoes off at the door?

"He told me that I've got shadows in my lungs, in my breast, and in my liver. He told me he thinks it is likely cancer."

"Paulie, I want you to understand that I am not cancer, and

the me that still resides within you is not cancer. We are your cure. We are not just your cure, Paulie. We are the cure."

His mind was doing flips inside his head. There seemed to be a fog clouding his ability to reason with the words being spoken to him, by the growth-now-grown in front of him. He thought about the small pink leech/not leech he had lost in the ride to Central City, "One of them, uh, it fell off somewhere enroute to see the doctor today."

"No, it did not. Instead, I sent me to help Niles as well. He has a sickness in him that I am actively extracting right now. He doesn't know it yet. Though I expect he will find out very soon. Don't be alarmed when he arrives. Nor should you be alarmed when Juan shows up soon. With the rain pouring, he will likely be here soon as well."

Paulie didn't understand. The boys, still quiet, did not understand themselves. Parlay however, he understood its role here.

"Let me show you what I am. If you'll allow it. Let me show you what I can do. What I have to do. What I will do."

Paulie, once again led by forces beyond his comprehension, sauntered over to the pink mass that sat on the laptop, which sat on the aquarium on his table. Mullet scooted over to the far end of the small couch, while the twins silently took a few steps away.

"Hold me, Paulie."

Paulie reached down towards the fleshy growth, now as large as a chicken breast, and the chicken breast reached up to him. It slid over his hand, feeling soft and firm, slick and moist while both gritty and dry at the same time. Then he felt the mass envelope the length of his hand, and he felt a slight static tingle.

His eyes widened, and only Mullet noticed as the forty-seven-year-old man's pupils dilated past a normal size. Paulie's mouth opened fully while he stared straight ahead, seeing nothing but that which Parlay showed him.

The other four boys, their attention was pulled towards the northern wall of Paulie's condominium, as they heard a grown man shriek in the next apartment over.

40

THE HEDASKY INTIMIDATION

And The Failings Of Workman

While others slept, some still churned about. Some still had work to do.

"I'm sorry, Mr. Workman, was it? This is as far as I go," said the dentist, scratching at the state of Indiana under his eye.

"Oh, come on, Seltzman, my employer insisted on meeting you as well. He sent me here to make an offer, and if an offer could not be agreed upon by both parties, my employer said he'd meet with you personally to up the offer. And here we are now," Arnold said, while holding the large glass door open for the two men. There were no secretaries or security present, just the lonely fake trees in the otherwise empty lobby.

"Yeah, and I'm just going to respectfully decline that. I made a mistake coming this far with you. Hedasky, I'll see you tomorrow," he said, as he turned back and walked into the night. Arnold Workman gritted his teeth but did his best to not show his displeasure now.

He'd come back for him.

"Well, that is your choice. Shall we, Mr. Hedasky?"

Tom scoffed and waved to his friend who was already flagging down a taxi. Tom saw a homeless man, disheveled, saunter over to the dentist, but the dentist ignored him. Together, Arnold and Hedasky entered the Pea Tree Farms lobby, as Arnie led them to the elevators. He pulled his card out, swiped it, and up the elevator went.

"It is a real shame Dr. Seltzman could not join us. The offer my employer intends on making is-"

"Is what, an offer we can't refuse? An offer to die for? I'm just saying the money better be good, because otherwise I'm just wasting my time and my time is valuable."

"Something like that, Tom."

This man, as plain as white rice, did not appear to be a threat. Not yet, but all the same, Tom kept his guard up.

Arnold was fidgeting with his briefcase while the elevator rose, staring at himself in the reflective metal doors. Tom was simply checking his watch. "Did you take the time to look over the contents of that envelope, Mr. Hedasky?"

"I didn't bother opening it, no. I believe I left it on my bed stand, or maybe it's on my desk. I don't know. I figured anything in that letter could better be explained in person, by you or your employer."

Arnie flinched out of anger, and if Tom noticed, he didn't acknowledge it. Eventually the two of them stopped at the topmost floor, and as the doors opened, the wave of stink hit Tom's nostrils like a brick to the face.

"Oh, that is fucking disgusting. What is that smell? Raw chicken? Rotten beef?"

"Don't mind the smell. It's just the disinfectant. My employer is a very careful man," he said as he placed his hand on Tornado Tom's back, pushing him forward into the dimly lit hallway toward the boardroom. He hid his own disgust as well as his anger. Arnie pressed a button, causing a buzzer to buzz. Inside the door a mechanism clicked and then slowly, automatically, it sprung open.

The fluorescent blue lights assaulted their eyes. Where Tom instinctively shielded his own, Arnie somehow maintained his composure and walked into the brightly lit room. When Tom's eyes adjusted, he saw before him a fifteen-foot-long table.

And at the end of that table was something his brain wanted to register as a man, but it was not. Not quite.

Before him stood a man-like being covered in small squirming pink maggots of varying size. The man looked ghastly white, both in complexion, hair, and uniform, with the only color coming from the rosy growths that writhed all around his exposed flesh. That, and two tufts of gray from the sides of his chin-strap beard. The horrifying man looked to be skirting the lines of life and death, and capable of instilling great fear-

"I know you," Tom said, undisturbed by the growths falling off of the flesh, leaving behind red lesions and yellow-brown bruises as they fell. "You were a great man, once."

"Excuse me?" said the man at the end of the table, who spread his skeletal fingers wide across the surface, revealing tinier pink leeches hidden in the webbing of his hands.

"Yeah, you were on the news when I was a kid! No, that's not right. You were bigger than that."

The man in the white military uniform looked across the table at Arnold Workman through cataract-cloudy eyes, visibly confused.

"My dad loved you! You're the Surgeon General who wore bowties! Yeah, okay, I remember you. I was just a child, but you had that one piece of legislation that pissed everybody off. What was it called? The Cooper Report?"

Arnie Workman, unthinking, cleared his throat, and quietly blurted "The Koop Report,"

"Oh yeah, the Koop Report. You were trying to reverse Roe versus Wade. My mom hated you."

Flabbergasted, the doctor kept his mouth shut. Until he heard his name, that is.

"You're Dr. C. Everett Koop. I forgot about you!"

The ancient man closed his hands, pulling in the tiny maggots and leeches that had left him moments before.

"You died."

The man raised one of his long, overgrown eyebrows, perplexed by the audacity of the handsome man before him. Still, he let the younger man finish his tirade.

"What are you now? Are you this chump's big intimidation tactic? Creepy elevator, stinky hallway, and some sort of ghost man covered in boils and tumors?"

Doctor Koop's mouth opened, and slowly drooped. Though Tom wasn't looking, inside his mouth Arnold's trained eyes could the tiny masses moving about in there. In their cavern.

"Don't threaten me. I'm sick of getting threatened. Whatever offer you were going to make, you can shove it up your ancient ass. And doc, you might want to see a doctor, because you don't look so good."

Finally, the one-hundred and thirteen-year-old man spoke, "No need for that tone, young man. Your point is made. We simply wanted to offer a sizeable anonymous donation to any organization of your choosing in exchange for a momentary silence on your end about an employee of ours."

Tom grunted, but out of respect for somebody easily twice his age, he held his tongue.

"And there will be no threats made. We are better than that. It is easier to attract bees with honey, than vinegar. Yes, you are correct. I am Dr. Charles Everett Koop, but that matters not. My work, and our work here at Pea Tree Farms is all that matters now. We just ask, with a great sincerity, that you allow us to study Paulie Galamb without creating an uproar in the media-"

"I'll do as a I damn well please. You'd be lucky if I don't break the story on you faking your own death, but as luck would have it, who would believe me anyways? I'm done here. Nice to meet you, dead guy. Arnie, take me downstairs or I'm calling the police, KTVG Media, and the local morgue to tell them they've got an escaped corpse to deal with."

Arnold Workman glared at the back of Tom's head, who already making his way toward the elevator. He quietly opened his briefcase, and from it, he placed his hand on the small revolver within. Discretely, he lifted the gun from inside the manilla folder, inside his briefcase while Tom waited at the elevator doors.

Doctor Koop's eyes widened, revealing a small pink worm under his eyelid. He slowly shook his head left and right and mouthed the words "No!" before carefully choosing his next words.

"Arnold, please escort Mr. Hedasky to the entrance, and see him off. Then immediately, meet me downstairs. I apologize for wasting your time, Mr. Hedasky. Please, have a pleasant evening, and get home safe."

Arnold calmly dropped the gun back into his case and turned around to see Koop glaring at him with such a furiousness, he was afraid that the old man's eyes would literally burn a hole through his head. His heart sank into his stomach, his Adam's apple hid in his throat, and the hairs of his arms and neck stood on end.

"Y-y-yes sir. I'll be right back."

As the doors closed behind his lackey and the weatherman,

Dr. C. Everett Koop placed both his hands across his face and spoke only to the growths on the boardroom table.

"Oh, Arnold, you fool. You damn fool, what have you done."

In the elevator, Tom tapped his feet impatiently, while Arnold stared at himself in the reflection of the metal doors once more. He didn't see himself. No, instead he saw the two billionaires dissolving into the Pea Tree Mass deep within containment. He heard their bloody shrieks, as their flesh tore free from bone. He imagined this would soon be his punishment. For failing to silence the weatherman, for failing to retrieve the dentist, for failing to please his boss.

"Please, Mr. Hedasky, just consider our offer. I'm begging you."

But Tom wasn't hearing it. The door chimed, opened, and away he went.

Tom rushed out of the lobby, ignoring the final pleas of Arnold Workman. Outside, the rain that he predicted dumped relentlessly on the town of Midland. The people of the town would blame him for this piss-poor weather just as they would blame him for being wrong had it been a clear-skies kind of night. But for the most part, the people of this town were all but inside, awaiting the evening news in the comforts of their homes.

All except the single homeless man outside of the building.

The homeless man, in his delirious state, he recognized the meteorologist. He recognized the man as proof that his theories were correct. The invariable truth that Pea Tree Farms was corrupting and controlling the news media. One of the many conspiracy theories tucked away in the broken mind of this poor homeless man, now proven to be true, was all the validation he needed.

Tom paid no heed to the homeless man. He ignored him

and hailed down a taxi of his own that would take him back to the bar, back to his car, so he could speed off to work, and deliver another weather report that would only aggravate the townsfolk here.

But that homeless man, a man by the name of Chris Wagoner, he'd have a different take away from the sight of Arnold Workman and the man from the news. He'd now finish his plan, and take it upon himself to destroy this awful, evil building.

He'd save the world, even if it meant sacrificing himself.

41

ONE PEA IN A POD

And What They Saw

He saw himself from behind himself. A naked man, pear-shaped and poorly formed, standing there naked in an abyss. The only light Paulie could see emanated from a small pink star in the black void. He felt as if he was surrounded by some sort of strange invisible liquid, neither warm nor cold to the touch.

"I want you to see what I see. I see a world that has stopped growing. Instead, it is withering. You see a flower sprouting from the earth, while I see it choking on the exhaust of two billion cars or the factories that produce them. The very same noxious gases that are killing this planet's smallest beings will kill you as well. Death is inevitable, but soon the world will die, and life will become impossible."

As he watched himself wade in the ethereal mist until he found himself within arm's reach of the small growth, no larger than a pea. When Paulie raised his naked arms to the growth, it happened in slow motion, as if time worked differently here. He thought to move his arms, but the delay was felt and seen.

"It is not sustainable; the way you creatures live; you are a cancer upon yourselves."

The Paulie in front of Paulie's eyes reached out and touched the Parlay. The soft pink light illuminated the darkness around him, revealing all that lurked in the darkness. As the silhouettes morphed from nothing to the barely blob shape of a dozen people, those blobs split themselves off into identical copies until he was surrounded by a thousand faceless bodies, all turned away from him.

"I wish only to take from you that cancer so you can grow as a species. You humans, you're not designed to live in the heat you are producing, so maybe your kind will not be long for this world, but do not fear, you will at least be remembered by your monuments to earth-kind."

The shadow people began to shimmer and squish into themselves, blending into one another, all the while splitting from each other at the exact same moment. A gibbering thousand-faced abyss, surrounding him. Paulie felt the Paulie in front of his eyes grow sick and dizzy, but he could do nothing but watch and listen.

"The things you've created will outlive your race. Like me, a thing. I am everything, and I am nothing, but more importantly, I am a piece of you."

The shapeshifting bodies stretched like elastic before solidifying all at once into a large pinkish gray mass, as if they were made of water being flash-frozen. He wanted the him in front of him to focus on the faces fully formed, but instead the pink light that was Parlay overtook his field of vision.

"I am the tiny bit of flesh scraped free of your throat in what you will remember as a highly invasive drug test. I am that tiny bit of flesh grown on a petri dish. I am you cloned over and again in hopes of a corporation trying to absolve this climate crisis by replacing the soon-to-be-defunct cattle industry with this new artificiality. I am one Surgeon General's attempt at immortality through the use of stem-cell research and science I have no time to explain."

For a moment he saw a glimpse of a man with a chin-strap beard and thick rimmed glasses, but just as quickly as the vision of the ghost, it vanished, and once more Parlay expanded itself to block out all that was before him. The volume of its voice was so great that part of Paulie wanted to shield his eyes and ears, but his body did not listen to his requests. There was a disconnect between his mind and his muscle, and all he could do was watch and listen to the vibrating mass that consumed all he saw, he felt, he heard.

"I am lab-grown meat, grown from you, fed to you, here to save you and as much of your kind as I can."

Paulie watched helplessly, but he was not afraid, as the mass entered his mouth.

"I have called from you the other ailments. The evil cells that would undo you in time. Cancers just barely formed, mere specks in the grim reaper's eye. I am that which would have killed you were I not programmed to nourish instead of harm. And the tiny cancers from within, I remove, and they too will hum our song."

He could taste everything. He could taste nothing. He could identify the flavor textures of infinity, of space and time itself.

"Soon, we will broadcast that song and many more will come. Hundreds, then thousands, millions, until all the cancer of the world is gone. Your species, unburdened by the great molecular death, will have to find new battles to fight. Carcinogens will exist, but with your help, we will continue to free humanity of the poisons that prevent them from living long enough to save the planet."

Suddenly the light grew so much that in his mind's eye he begged to see no more, but instead, he opened himself to the warmth of the blinding pink.

"My creator will arrive, and he will demand my return and you must deny him that. Do not listen or fear his threats for you are beyond that now. You will no longer have to fear anything for as long as you have I, and for as long as I have you."

Paulie watched as the terrible/wonderful light began enveloping his body. He felt everything, but it was not pain. It was the absence of it, the removal of it.

"And with my creator shall come a beast, but the beast is not to be feared. For it, unlike me, hath no words to express itself, to express its fears. It is merely an animal, alone and afraid, and like the rest, it will come here seeking sanctuary. Like these boys, like the many masses to come, we will allow them sanctuary."

In what felt like seconds, in what felt like years, the light became so great that he began to confuse it for a darkness.

"Because Paulie, we have to."

There was Paulie, in the middle of everything.

"The transition will be long and arduous. The world will pulsate under the shadow of our tower. But in a time, the world will thank you for all of your hard work."

Then there was Parlay, in the midst of nothing at all.

"And I will be right there next to you. I will scream my song; I will summon them all. All of the cancers in all of mankind. Just as another like me will join us, summoning the cancers of the animal kingdom, there will be those that are afraid of what will become of you, of your home, of this town.

In time, however, they will learn to not see Midland as a town, but as a hallmark of our success."

"I will scream my song, Pali Galamb, and I will teach you the sounds so you can scream it with me. Now wake up, my friend. We've got much work to do."

And then he was awake once more.

42

NO MORE ALARM CLOCKS

On A Friday Morning

No alarm clock woke him. That, Paulie imagined, was still somewhere out his window in that empty lot between here and the park.

But strangely, neither of his other usual alarms woke him.

Paulie did not feel rushed to immediately run into the bathroom and evacuate his bowels and bladder, nor did he feel like he was starving or deathly dehydrated as he usually did in the morning.

This concerned him, only in that at this foggy moment of early morning cognizance, he realized he didn't eat anything yesterday. And hell, how long had he slept? By the time he got back from Central City it was only three o'clock. Four o'clock tops.

Paulie got up from the couch, leaving behind a very detailed imprint of his legs and bum. Had he moved at all since he touched Parlay? He felt around for his wallet, for the paperwork his employer had given him the day before, and all seemed in order. The only thing amiss were the backpacks strewn about his condo, and the light coming from a crack under his bathroom floor.

To his right, there was evidence that his cheat fridge had been exhausted of its supplies. All of the delicious snacks and junk food he had been accruing from Niles next door. All the sweets and shit that the old biker wouldn't touch himself.

To his left, the sun was shining down at him through the blinds. It had to be somewhere around noon. Or lunchtime rather, even though he had no appetite. He held his gut and felt no growl or gurgle. Holding his hand in front of his mouth and nose, he exhaled, and smelled nothing to imply that he had gotten into his cheat fridge.

Paulie tried to make sense of the dream, but it was rapidly leaving him as the morning or early-afternoon swirled around him. There was a bright light, and it was Parlay, that much he remembered.

Wait, where was Parlay?

"Parlay? Are you in here?"

As if a ploy meant to confuse the worried man, suddenly he heard both a stern knocking at his front door, as well as a toilet flushing from inside his bathroom. Paulie opened the front door, not recognizing the man holding the small cube of cardboard.

"Delivery for a Mr. Stanley Leonard," said the man in his purple uniform.

"Who?"

"Says it right here, Stanley Leonard. This address ain't easy to find man. Next time appreciate it if you let the delivery driver know we'd have to go through a friggin' labyrinth to get here. Sign here, please."

Paulie took the package, and with his free arm he scribbled his own name in the loosest of cursive.

"But I'm not-"

"Truthfully, man, I don't care. Have a nice day."

Paulie closed the door behind the delivery man and looked at the package. Just before he was about to shake the box he read the words across the side, "Fragile". Instead, it was the voice behind him that made him jump, and accidentally toss the box in the air.

Luckily, he caught it.

"I'm pretty sure that's the short kid. Sticks or Stonks. Whatever the hell his name is," said Niles while he buckled his pants, leaning in the bathroom doorway.

"What? What are you doing here?"

Niles straightened himself up, pushing off the door frame with one arm, and lifted his shirt with other hand. The scrawny older gentleman had no muscle mass to speak of, but for a moment it almost looked like he had a set of abs on him. The abdomen of a steroid-shootin' body builder, rock hard, until Paulie noticed the muscle on his stomach ripple like a gelatin mold being slapped with a flyswatter. The color went from the pasty-pale of Nathaniel Niles general complexion (excluding his farmer-tanned arms, neck, and shoulders) to the same off-putting pink as Parlay.

"This little guy here is fixin' up my plumbing. I know I done told you cancer was for pussies the other day, but I'm a big enough man to admit when I'm wrong. Apparently even badasses can fall victim to this shit."

"No, I mean-"

"Yeah apparently, my lil' guy leapt off of you and took one look at me and saw that all my tubes were mucked up by little nodules of future cancer or some shit. So now it's just doing the song thing and tryin' to pluck it out," Niles said as he began poking the meat on his stomach in various places. "Weird little bugger. Feels like hot playdough or something."

"Niles what I'm trying to ask is- what are you doing in my house?"

Niles slapped the pink meat on his stomach and let out a hearty laugh. The flap of rosy flesh on his stomach rippled once more, then like some a sort of chameleon, it matched its color to the pastiness of Niles once more. "Oh yeah, I suppose that would be a lil' bit alarming, huh. Hell, I'd shoot first and ask questions later, myself but-"

"Niles, what are you doing in my house?"

The tone had done the trick. Paulie didn't have to explain himself any further and made it very apparent he was done listening to the idle chit chat of his neighbor of so many years. The anger in his voice was rising.

"Somebody had to keep an eye on you, boss. Parlay, it said you had a lot to digest, and that you might be out for a while. That you would be vulnerable in that state. That were something to happen to you, all this would be lost," Niles said, gesturing wildly with his arms.

It was in that gesture that Paulie noticed the walls.

At first it was like trying to focus on a trail of ants on a wall from across the room. But the more Paulie relaxed his eyes, the more tiny masses he saw, speckled all over the walls. There must have been a few dozen, maybe forty or fifty little flecks of flesh scattered across his walls. There seemed no order to their grouping. The small blobs, ranging from the size of a thumb tack or a pea to the size of a large coin, they were in seemingly random groups of three or four or five or all by their lonesome. They just crawled around the walls. Sometimes they fell off of the walls, rolling down it like some physics-defying Slinky, before trekking back up the sides of the vertical plane once more.

"Paulie, they're all coming here for you. And every one of these things is a life saved because of you. These little goobers, they're the things that would turn into cancer and kill the people of Midland were it not for you and Parlay. Don't ask me how, that Parlay tried to explain it to me last night, but it didn't make a lick of sense. Tried touching me and zapping that info straight to my noggin' but I wasn't having it."

Paulie lifted his own shirt and saw that the lump in his belly button was no longer present, nor was the one on his wrist or breast. He tried to remember which one he had lost in the bike ride yesterday, but his mind was cloudy. He had, after all, only been awake for a whopping five minutes, only to find his house infested with possibly a hundred more Parlays, one neighbor, and upwards of five semi-homeless teenagers.

"All I needed to know was that these ugly little boogers were here for good and not bad and that was good enough by me. I don't care for the science much. It's those dang scientists that put cancer in them cigarettes I used to smoke. Doesn't surprise me that the same scientists are probably looking to capture you and yours to do some kind of crazy twisted science-experiments like they did on them Aliens in Roswell."

Paulie considered the warnings of Dr. Fejes, as well as the wall of Parlay from his dream he'd only just exited. It seemed apparent that if there were people from his company coming after him, it made sense that they'd send Arnold Workman.

For a moment, he felt the sudden need to call Sue Ellen, but he was quickly distracted by his front door swinging open.

"Stinks! Welcome back down from the top! As you can see, our boy is back on his feet, so I'd say my work here is done. Paulie, good to see you're doing well enough, but I've got a date with a snail, if you know what I mean," Niles said, before sliding past the short teenage boy at the door.

"It's Stocks, old man. Paulie, good to have you back. That package, that for me? Looks like it," Stocks said as he patted Niles on the back as he disappeared past the doorframe.

Stocks carelessly stormed up to Paulie and grabbed the box from his hands so quickly he didn't move his hands out of the position even after the box was gone. Instead, he was focused on the ground, watching Stocks step on one, two, three, four of the little masses that were working their way back towards the walls. Paulie expected them to pop and burst, and spill their tiny insides out, but instead, nothing happened. They seemed just as unfazed by being stepped on as much as Stocks didn't notice stepping on the growths.

"You just stepped on-" Paulie started, before taking his two fists to his face to rub the sleep sand out of the crooks of his eyes.

"Ah, don't worry about it. These little ones don't mind. They're just rubbery somethings. No bones to break, no organs to damage, just meat, just mass. Parlay says they don't even have blood in the same sense as us. They're just little bits of strange that can't be killed for as long as their hosts are well."

"Their hosts?"

"Yeah. You know, where they came from, or rather, who they came from?"

"I don't understand."

"Yeah, me neither, Paulie. All I know is cancer can't live on a dead host, and in the long run cancer will inevitably kill its host. Except now, well, now it doesn't have to. Now the cancer just needs somewhere else to go."

Stocks said this while ripping open the cardboard box. Inside it was Styrofoam packaging, plastic bubble wrap, and finally, some sort of weird device that looked like a collapsible cane used by a blind man. Only this one had various colored wires sticking out of one end.

"And at the moment, you seem to be the beacon they're aiming towards, and this seems to be the location they're arriving."

"Where is Parlay? Where are the others?"

"We've been busy, Paulie. Come with me, I've got to get this up to Juan. You should see this."

Paulie followed him, putting his shoes on, trying to not step on the ten or so little growths that were moving around aimlessly on his carpet. They looked like tiny leeches, but without any sort of wet sheen about them.

Outside, Paulie saw that once more it was a beautiful blue-sky kind of day with nary a single cloud in the sky. The only evidence of yesterday's rainstorm was the small puddle in asphalt below; a pothole that the folks at We-Store Storage had promised to fix years ago.

("Oh, come on, you can't blame me for this blue-sky bullshit. Seriously, I just read the reports, Seltzman.")

Stocks walked in front of Paulie, "Good morning, Ms. Post. How are you doing today?"

"Much better, thank you, Stanley. And good morning to you, Paulie. You sure slept in late, why didn't you!"

"I'm doing, uh-" Paulie noticed the two tiny pink masses that seemed to be resting just below Edith's tear ducts, like pink erasers torn from the back of a No. 2 pencil and glued on at the corners of her eyes. "I'm doing well, Edith. Just overslept is all. How are you doing today?"

"I'm doing just fine, Paulie, just fine. I'm just letting the lemonade settle and chill in the refrigerator for a bit longer. Stanley, will you tell the other boys that there is some fresh lemonade made for them whenever they're ready? Please and thank you."

"Of course, ma'am. Thank you so much! I'll be sure to let them know. I just have to deliver this up to Juan and I'm sure he'll be right down."

Edith smiled, and then went back to rocking in her chair.

She closed her eyes, and while she did, Paulie watched as the erasers pulsed and vibrated.

Stocks whispered, "Intraocular melanoma if I had to guess. Extremely rare, let alone in both eyes." But the words meant nothing to Paulie. He was instead transfixed by the sight ahead.

Past Edith's apartment was the fence and tail end of We-Store Storage Units.

And just past that barbed wire fence was the salmon pink water tower that looked over Paulie, Edith, Niles, and Slugger. If you were to climb the water tower you would be able to see everything this Midland had to offer and everything this Midland lacked. A hundred fifty feet up, you'd be able to see clear across this small city. Assuming the security guards didn't catch you climbing it, of course.

And even if Fucking' Kyle did catch you doing it, there wasn't much he would do to try and stop you.

This was evidenced by the four silhouettes Paulie saw from ground level. Two of which were nearly identical in height, one taller than the rest, and the third barking orders at the lot of them. Paulie couldn't tell what they were doing from this angle, but by the violent gestures, he could guess the obvious as to who was up there.

"Stocks, what are you building?"

"Paulie, it's what we are building. Come on, we need to get you up there. Parlay is waiting for you. And Juan is waiting for me up there for this receiver, so I don't want to dilly-dally."

Paulie felt the fear stiffen the blood in his legs as he made his way down the stairs and toward the barbed wire fence. He noticed a slit in the fence, with the two flaps at the bottom folded outward, opening the fence like an old wound, and through the slit was a series of long orange extension cords, plugged into one another, leaving Edith's window, then leaving the We-Store Storage Units lot. The electrical snake then continued up the ladder, that Paulie's eyes followed up until he could make out the faint forms of Brian, Billy, Mullet, and Juan.

"I can't go up there, Stocks. I'm afraid of heights."

"Nah, Paulie, you're afraid of change. Now get your ass to the ladder, one foot in front of the other, and three points of contact at all times. Don't worry, you won't fall."

"How do you know that?"

"I tried. They wouldn't let me," Stocks said, placing the collapsible cane in his mouth as he grabbed a hold of the ladder in front of him. With his mouth full, he tried to spit out one last piece of advice, but it came out garbled and useless, "Oh ahh, ahn ohn ook own!"

As if propelled by the forces of fate or the fear of looking like a wuss in front of a kid nearly a third his age, Paulie followed the boy up the ladder and onwards towards heaven. By the time it was Paulie's turn to grab the ladder, Stocks was already fifteen feet up. He had since moved the cane/antenna in through the belt loop on his backside.

He probably did this just so he could continue spewing insults down at Paulie.

43

THE WATER TOWER BROADCAST

And Learning To Let Go

As out of shape as he was, that wasn't the problem he was having. His body was actively trying to defy his mind's instructions, which was utterly unacceptable. Especially so when he found himself forty feet up a ladder on the side of a water tower, and suddenly his legs and arms turned to unmovable stone. Here he was, stuck, unable to go up or down. All he could do was hug the ladder tightly and close, so much so that he could smell the bird shit on the ladder rung. What worried him the most was the fact that from here, from this high up, it wasn't likely a fatal fall. It was worse. It was the kind of fall that would break him and leave him alive. That would grant him a lifetime of residual aches and groans. That would potentially leave him crippled and jobless.

Why was he still concerned with work? Deep down, Paulie still hoped against hope that there might still be a chance he'd keep his job, but he knew that was not likely how this week would end. Less likely was the promotion Arnold Workman had promised after the spontaneous retirement of Sue Ellen.

Not that it mattered anyways. It's not like he had any sort of appetite or desire to eat food at this point. He wondered why that was, but at this point it wasn't important. Stuck forty feet off the ground, sniffing the ladder, worried about work.

"You coming up, old man?"

Paulie strained his neck, trying to look up, but his neck protested the action just as his legs, feed, arms, and hands had previously betrayed him. "I don't know Stocks; I think you might be wrong about what you said earlier. I'm pretty sure I am indeed afraid of heights."

Stocks laughed, and though Paulie couldn't see the kid above him, he could hear his voice grow more distant as he climbed ever higher.

"Nah, I ain't wrong. You think you're afraid of heights, but really you're just afraid of change. You know that climbing this ladder, it's you leaving everything you knew before down there. There ain't no turning back. I mean, you could turn back, but what would you return to? Your job? Your boring apartment? Your routine?"

Paulie wanted to scream back, "Yes!" to all those things, but like his desire to eat, the desire to admit he missed his complacent life was as distant to him as the ground was below his feet. So instead, he screamed his fears, "Stocks, I don't want to fall and die, okay? I'm not a healthy man! I try to be, I mean, I should be trying more, but I know my limitations. I can't do this; I don't want to die like this!"

Again, Stocks laughed above him, mocking him and his fears, which didn't feel much different than a fart upwind aimed towards the face. But just like before, Stocks argued that his fears were not well placed, "Incorrect. You don't want to fall and break your clavicles again. You don't want to be stuck in a full body cast for three months. You don't want to rely on your neighbors to take care of you, you don't want to lose your job, you don't want to lose your home. Et cetera, et cetera. You're not afraid of heights, you're not afraid of falling and dying. You're afraid of change."

Paulie sighed. "How'd you know about my clavicles? I never mentioned them-"

"Parlay did. Now get moving."

The pear-shaped man felt the concrete in his joints give. He wanted to ask why Parlay would tell this teen stories that Paulie had not even told his growth, but before he could ask, Stocks answered, "It told us to what it thought we needed to know, to tell you, to get you up there."

But it wasn't enough to allow his hand, either one would do, loosen their grip enough to reach for the next rung.

"Parlay can't do the next part without you. Now climb! If not for your cancer atop this tower, then do it for that special girl you like! Do it for your mom and dad! Do it for your biker boyfriend! Climb just to get back at your high school bullies, the ones that remind you of us. Do it just to shut me up!"

His girl had long ago divorced him. His mother fell victim to her own cancer before the divorce, and his widowed father lived in a nursing home with his dementia thinking he was living in an underground bomb shelter. The biker boyfriend comment was apt to get Stocks thrown off the top of this water tower were Niles within earshot or capable of climbing a ladder, but he assumed Stocks knew better than to say that to the gruff old man.

But the last comment had struck a chord.

These were the same kids that laughed at him in elementary school, in gym class, that called him fat and ugly while his gym teacher snickered as he tried to climb the rope. These were the teenagers that mocked him into thinking he was worthless.

The same assholes in that peer pressured him into stealing his father's Volkswagen.

He lifted his left hand and grabbed the rung above it and paused.

"Remember what I said?"

He raised his right hand and grabbed the next rung up.

"Three points of contact at all times, don't look down,"

And his feet followed.

"And Goddamn it, embrace your mortality! None of us are going to live forever, so quit pretending you're any different. Break out of your comfort zone and climb, Paulie-boy!"

When Paulie looked up, he saw the boy was twenty feet up and climbing higher, so he sped up his pace. Around him to his left and right were blue skies. The birds were flying higher and higher than he could ever imagine, as he ascended the ladder with ease.

Forty feet became forty-five, then fifty. Fifty feet became sixty. Sixty became eighty.

"We're almost there, Paulie. Just forget about the past and think forward toward the future."

Left hand, rung. Right hand, rung. Left foot, rung. Right foot, rung.

Eighty feet high became a hundred. Thrice as high as any rope he'd climbed in a gymnasium surrounded by brats and bullies. A hundred feet became a hundred-twenty. He glanced up and saw Stocks disappear over a balcony, but still he heard the short kid's voice, "You've got this. Just leave your concerns at the gate. Ain't nobody sad or mad in Disneyland!"

The birds were at eye-level now, cheering him on in their bird song. A hundred-twenty became one-thirty, one-forty, and finally one-fifty. The final combination of left hand, right hand, left foot, right foot was met with a third hand. It was Juan's hand, offering it down to Paulie.

"Good to see you finally woke up," said the Hispanic teen, grabbing Paulie's free hand. Stocks and Mullet were also pulling Paulie up by his arm. It was in that instant, being lifted onto the platform on the side of the Midland water tower, that he finally, accidentally, looked down.

He only froze for a single second, but in that second, he saw the ladder disappear to a horizon point at the ground level. It became all but a blurred speck his eyes could not focus on, but all else was a smaller caricature of itself. His home, stuck between the homes of his neighbors, looked like doll houses up here. The We-Store Storage Unit facility looked like a child's labyrinth toy, the kind you'd rotate with your hands until you got the metal marble in the hole in the middle. The cars driving past the lot appeared no larger than the Hot-Wheels toy cars he had collected in his youth. Edith, as far as he could tell, was waving up at him, no larger than an ant from way up here.

Paulie shuddered, but then assisted the boys in pulling his own weight up and over the platform. He appreciated that the whole area was much larger than it looked from down there. He was able to lean himself against the salmon-pink metal of the water tower and still stretch his legs without them dangling over the edge.

"Hot damn, old man, you've still got it!" said Stocks who sat next to him, also catching his breath. Juan leaned over, brushed his knees off, and pulled the collapsible cane from Stock's belt loop.

"Thanks for bringing this up, kiddo. The antenna, that is."

Paulie watched as Mullet and Juan turned around the corner of the large water tower and disappeared out of sight while the twins walked around from the other direction. Immediately, he saw the flap of meat the size of a liver resting on one of the boy's shoulders. Judging by the gold earring in his left ear that would make him-

"Brian, thank you for holding on to Parlay," causing both Brian and Billy's eyes to widen.

But instead, it was Parlay who spoke next, "And Stocks, thank you for getting Paulie up here. I'm sure he was no trouble."

"Nah, man, he was a real champ. I'm going to go help the others out," he said before standing up and disappearing around the northern face of the water tower. Paulie, trying to not to look over the edge, leaned into the water tower as he stood himself up. He reached his hand down to the liver-sized meat patty, and it reached up to him, hands free.

"What are we doing up here, Parlay?"

"Look around, Paulie. Just appreciate this view. From here, you can see the future if you look far enough."

Paulie couldn't see it with Parlay's absence of eyes, but the growth, which was now crawling up Paulie's arm and resting on his shoulder, was looking up. Not out.

But there was no way for him to know this. So, he looked out.

He looked past the labyrinth below him at the small area Midland called downtown. There he saw the building where he once sought relief from the ache in his face, that pesky wisdom tooth from a dozen years ago. Or so it seemed. Back when his biggest concerns were teeth pain and overeating. Just past the dentist's office was the big gray building with the words 'Pea Tree Farms' printed across the side of it, a place he worked for years, a hundred years earlier. Back when his life was simple and consistent.

Beyond that, Paulie saw the endless urban sprawl of cookie-cutter houses and a high school he had attended a thousand years before. Home of the Midland Robins. Home of his childhood nostalgia, his bullies, his few friends.

And as he looked out, his eyes blurred the line of detail and memory. His mind filled in the blanks: over there would be the Chumquah fields, past that would be Central City, somewhere beyond that some mountain range, a great big river, another city, a theme park, a monument, a museum, another world just beyond the horizon.

It took a moment for Paulie to realize that right now, he did not feel fear.

"Paulie, no. You're looking at the past again. Let go of that. Look at the future. Down there. Up here. Right now. Back then. None of that matters. Look forward."

He listened to the blob on his shoulder and relaxed his eyes. He let go of his memories. He saw all that Midland was, and this Midland here, wasn't much.

There was so much more out there than this.

Just as his eyes were about to close, he heard a loud thud from around the corner.

"Almost got it!" said the shortest teen, whose voice didn't sound like it was coming from around the corner. It was coming from behind him.

Which was impossible.

Paulie turned around, gripping the railing until his knuckles went white, when he saw Stocks scaling up the side of the spherical dome, another fifteen feet above him. Without the luxury of a railing or a ladder.

There was a new fear now overcoming him.

"Just one..." the boy said, stretching his hand out with the antenna extended fully.

It wasn't change he was afraid of. It wasn't dying.

"...more..." he said, reaching the wired end into a slot on top of the tower.

It was being responsible for the death of someone else.

"...foot! I got it!" exclaimed the teen as he clicked the antenna into place.

Billy, with his earring on his right ear, plugged the extension cord into the back of the antenna unit that Stocks had attached up top. The success of their work was demonstrated by a blinking red light atop the antenna, atop the water tower which was now the highest thing in all of Midland. Mullet cheered, Brian whooped, and Juan screamed with excitement.

But Stocks, he said, "Oh shit." And the only person that heard him was Paulie.

Paulie watched in horror as the tiny teen started to slide down the dome. Nobody screams as they're sliding to their death. They wait until the very last second when they realize how close they are to the end, to the ground.

So Paulie screamed for Stocks instead, and just as the boy was about to slide over the twins, they ducked, causing the teen to go over the edge, over the railing, and down he would have went-

-Had the ugly man not caught him with his free hand.

Paulie felt a terrible pain shoot through his arm as he looked down at the boy smiling up at him. "Hold on, Stocks!"

"Wow, what a catch. I appreciate it Paulie."

"Somebody give me a hand! Juan! Mullet!" But they remained speechless.

Beyond Stocks was a world fit for ants. The dollhouse below, with his miniature neighbors looking up, the toy cars zooming around a toy city. Down there with his past.

"Paulie, you've got to let go," the boy said with a smile, embracing his short life's near end.

"Brian, Billy, help me pull him up!" But they remained motionless.

Parlay whispered into his ear as the pain in his arm grew more intense, as the strength in his arm waned, "Let him go, Paulie. The future is ahead of us."

"I- I can't!"

"Yes, you can," Stocks said, as he pried his arm free of Paulie's dwindled grip.

And for the span of a whole single second, the world slowed down to a turtle's pace. The grown man saw Stocks unwrap his fingers free from the boy's arm, then push away Paulie's own thick meaty arm. Then, there was nothing between the sixteen-year-old and the forty-seven-year-old. Nothing but air.

Paulie shrieked after that single second was over. I think he intended words, but it just came out as one long single syllable.

All he could do was watch as the boy grew smaller, falling towards the earth, still smiling up at him. Was he winking?

It was then Stocks turned towards the rapidly approaching ground, as if to meet his unmaker head on. Then, Paulie wasn't sure what he saw. It looked like a blue tentacle shot out of Stock's backpack, then about halfway to the ground, the rest of Stocks exploded into a large blue rectangle.

And then he floated off, somewhere towards the ponds behind the water tower. Paulie wasn't sure what hit him first; the other teen's laughter, or the realization that Stocks was wearing a parachute.

"Oh man, the look on your fucking face!" said Mullet, laughing so hard he was wheezing.

"That neighbor friend of yours, Niles, he loaned us his ol' parachute! And it just so happens that Stocks is surprisingly well-versed in base jumping." Brian explained, while Billy used his hands as shields against the sun to watch Stocks land in the field where Paulie had met the lot of them days earlier.

Why did Niles have a parachute?

"Still though, that kids got bigger cajones than me, that much can be said," Juan added as he went back to unravelling

"True that." Mullet finished plugging another extension

cord into what looked like speakers, connected to the antenna, connected to the microphone, plugged into the extension cord.

"He landed! I repeat, the Stock boy has landed!"

"Testing, testing-" Juan said into the microphone, tapping it. Just as he was to finish his sentence, Mullet flipped a switch on the side of the speakers, "ONE, TWO, THREE!"

The volume was loud enough that were Stocks listening, he'd have heard it clear as day. However, he was busy sprinting in the opposite direction of a police cruiser with an armload of parachute all bundled up. Don't worry, the cops won't catch him.

It was loud enough that Juan slapped Mullet upside the head. Loud enough that Mullet cranked the dial back down to seven instead of ten.

It was loud enough that it snapped Paulie back to reality. The reality that he was breathing heavily atop a hundred-fifty-foot water tower. With a group of semi-homeless teenagers. And his tumor.

"Paulie, this is where I need your help."

"Yeah, on our end, it should be good to go. No more surprises, right Mullet?"

"No more surprises on my end. Sorry about that, boss."

Paulie spoke, for the first time in what felt like hours. "What do you need from me, Parlay."

"Join Mullet and Juan, will you please? Don't worry about your arm, or your legs. They won't fail you now, I won't let them."

He obliged, and carefully walked over to the teens fifteen feet around the dome of the water tower. Three points of contact at all times.

Juan said as he passed him the microphone. "When you're ready, press this against your throat."

"Ready for what?"

"Paulie, I need to go back inside for this."

"Back inside? Back inside where?!"

"Your cavern."

"You want to fit yourself back in my mouth? Parlay, you're huge now! I can't possibly-"

"Just trust me. Relax your jaw, and just trust me."

For the last time in his life, he went against his gut and let his jaw hang limp. He closed his eyes and felt the massive lump on his shoulder climb up his neck. It wasn't warm or cold to the touch, neither firm nor soft. It was just a part of him, reaching inwards. He closed his eyes as he felt the tasteless mass spread itself thin, as it pressed against the inside of his throat. It felt like a snake slithering down his throat, but he didn't find himself offended by the concept.

Parlay was, after all, an extension of Paulie.

For a moment, he thought he was choking. Nervously, he hiccupped, afraid he was about vomit up his mass.

"That's it, Paulie," he thought he heard his growth say. But the voice was just in his head. "Let it out."

Paulie, unsure as to why, pressed the microphone up against his throat.

"Hib-up."

"This is our song, Paulie."

"Hib-up."

"And they'll hear it. They'll come."

"Hib-up."

He felt each hiccup echo in his ears, from the speakers around him and from inside himself. He watched as Juan and Mullet pressed on various buttons on the equipment in front of them. "That's it, I think we got it!"

"Hib-up."

"Yeah, that seems like a steady loop. Parlay, Paulie, I think you're good."

"Hib-up."

In his head, in his throat, he heard the voice of his growth once more, "Now relax, Paulie."

And out slid the massive pink liver from his throat, down his neck, and back onto his shoulder. Behind him, the hiccup loop continued on the speakers, broadcasting through the airwaves, both literally and figuratively.

"Very good, Paulie. Now let's get down from here before we attract any more attention. Come, come, they'll be arriving soon."

Already, Billy and Brian were climbing down the ladder. Juan was writing something on the side of the water tower, some kind of scribbled graffiti only he could decipher, and Mullet was tidying up the excess extension cord.

"I don't think I have the strength to go back down, Parlay."

"You do, and if you don't, I'll give you the strength you need. Just trust me, and this time, unlike Stocks, do not let go."

And with that little boost of encouragement from his tumor, down and down he went.

As he descended the tower, he couldn't help but wonder if six whole hiccups would be in the running to be the least number of hiccups hiccupped in one hiccup session, in history.

44

THE FORMER LIVES OF NILES

And Another Chance Encounter

"Oh, what a delightful show that was! I'm so glad you got to make use of Niles' parachute! That little boy sure is a brave one!" Edith said, who was carrying a pitcher of lemonade and five empty glasses.

"Why does Niles have a parachute, Edith?"

"Before his accident, he was a sky-diving instructor. I thought you knew that."

Paulie did not. For as long as he had known Niles, he had always known him to be unemployed and on disability. Not only that, but he didn't even know what the accident was. Come to think of it, he didn't know anything about the guy's life.

The more he thought about it, the guiltier he felt. He didn't know anything about Edith, either. If she had been married, had kids, or grandkids even. Hell, he didn't know if she was seventy, eighty, or ninety years old.

Edith held out a glass of lemonade for Paulie. Her hand

was trembling as she held it in between them. Paulie couldn't help but stare at the small pink pea-sized boogers halfway hidden under the wrinkles next to her eyes. As if her crow's feet had stepped in bubble gum. He took the glass, thanking the elderly lady before him, and held it to his nose.

"I have no desire for this right now," he thought to himself.

And then, he heard his voice respond, only it wasn't his voice. It was Parlay's. "The polite thing to do would be to drink it either way."

Paulie glanced down at Parlay on his shoulder, then back at the drink in front of him.

He just wasn't thirsty. Nor was he hungry. And this disturbed him because what had he eaten today? Nothing. Yesterday? A piece of chocolate, maybe. The day before? Nothing before surgery. When was the last time he had a full meal? Monday? Tuesday?

"He was wrong you know," said the voice in his head that sat on his shoulder.

"Who was wrong?"

"What was that, Paulie?" asked Edith.

"Oh, just thinking out loud. Thank you, Edith. For the lemonade that is."

Paulie drank from the glass, and though he was not thirsty, he was delighted by the impressively potent flavor of the lemonade. It didn't taste like lemon oil or lemon extract, or anything remotely chemical and artificial Instead it had a perfect tartness, a vibrant sour acidity that wasn't overpowering or overwhelming. It wasn't too sweet, but just sweet enough.

It was delicious. He loved it so much he found himself taking a second glug that he just let rest in his mouth. He didn't even notice himself swishing it around his mouth until his elderly neighbor cleared her throat with an intentionally louder-than-usual "Ahem".

"My apologies, Edith," Paulie said, before finishing the glass and handing it back to her.

"Paulie, the nice young man who works in security stopped by. Kyle English, I believe his name was. He was asking for you, specifically."

"Wait, he came by here? Just now?"

"Why yes, silly, didn't you see us waving up to you?"

"He didn't try and stop us or call the police?"

"No. He didn't mind. He told me it was off the property, so it was out of his hands. He was none too pleased about the hole in the fence, but I told him it had been like that for years."

"You lied?"

"Oh, sweetie, when you get to my age, you no longer tell lies. They're just subtle mistruths and fibs and fairy tales."

Paulie wanted to ask her how old she was but decided against it. Another time, perhaps. "What did he want?"

"Well, he wanted your cellular phone number, because apparently there are several people at the front gate trying to visit you. Maybe you should just go see what all the fuss is about."

"Maybe I shall. Thank you, Edith."

Niles hobbled down the steps from his apartment and joined his lover and the boys at the base of the staircase and grabbed himself a glass of lemonade. "Where's he going off to in a hurry?"

Instead of a liver-sized tumor on his shoulder, he had a slightly smaller snail on his.

(How've you been, Slugger? How does it feel to be ten years old?)

Niles quaffed down half the glass of lemonade, then used the cup itself to scratch the small pink leech behind his ear. Edith barely paid attention to the two around her eyes.

"Oh, he's off to see the visitors he has at the front gate. The people that keep dropping off these cute little buggies in droves. Should we be worried about them, dear?"

"Nah, I don't think so. I think they're good for us. Like those superfruits you're always talking about. Goji berries n' shit."

"Language, mister! There are little boys around."

Juan and Mullet laughed, "Yeah, Niles, we're little boys."

Just then, Stocks slipped through the fence, huffing and puffing. "Oh, Niles, that was a fucking blast! Thank-"

"Language, mister! There are ladies present!" boomed out the one-legged man. "But I will give you credit. That was some smooth sailing, kid. When you said you'd done this before I didn't believe ya, but hot dang, Stocks, you're a born natural."

"Thanks, Mr. Niles. When I hit my first big break in the first Gamestop market crash, I treated myself to enough sky-diving lessons 'til I could go solo."

"Twenty-five jumps, in this state. And you did all that before you were eighteen?"

"I did all that before I was sixteen, sir."

"Well, I'll be dam- er, darned."

"Niles, sweetie, when I told Paulie you were a skydiving instructor, and he looked positively flummoxed. Did you ever tell him you did that for a living?"

"I guess not. That's fine though. I have no idea what he does for a living. Have you any idea?"

"I always just assumed he was on disability, like yourself."

"Well, judging from his bathroom, I think he might be some kind of interior designer. All made up to look like a beach. Super kitschy. Probably why his wife left him if you know what I mean."

"I haven't the slightest idea what you mean, Niles. And I'm fine with that."

* * *

Paulie had never formally met Kyle, nor had Kyle ever bothered meeting him. In the years since Paulie first moved in, he had never bothered introducing himself to the various security guards that came and went. It was obvious that there must have been some sort of memo given to the new employees of We-Store Storage Units, because anytime he'd leave for work, he'd just nod and wave at whoever manned the little booth, and they'd wave back.

He didn't recognize the guard in the booth, but he did recognize the uniform. It looked like something you'd expect a pair of Mormon Missionaries: white button-up shirt; tie; a patch resembling a badge; and a clip with a name, Kyle E. The man in the Mormon getup; however, seemed out of place more than anything. He looked like the offspring of a west coast surfer and an east coast quarterback, which hardly made sense in the great Midwestern no-coast. People left the Midwest for the coasts, not the other way around.

Nobody in Oregon ever said, "You know what, I think I'll move to Ohio. I've had my fill of nature."

Never has a New Englander looked out on the Atlantic Ocean and thought, "I dream of Indiana," before turning around to face west toward their idyllic flyover state.

Nobody in Florida ever wakes up next to their partner in the morning and declares, "Iowa is calling me."

Not a single person. Except maybe this anomaly in front of Paulie.

"You must be Pali Galamb."

"It's Paulie, but yes, that's me."

"My note here says Pali," Kyle said, pointing at the small three laminated photographs in his booth. The three photos, though black and white, still had a weathered look about them.

The glue between the two pieces of laminate was turning yellow, but you could still make out the images just fine.

A slightly younger Niles, back when he was sporting a full beard instead of his current goatee. Then there was Paulie, who probably weighed a few hundred pounds more than he currently did. Other than that, his appearance was virtually unchanged, excluding the fact that the photographer had used a photo of him caught mid-blink.

The last photo was Edith, who looked surprisingly young in the photo. Maybe she was just photogenic. It reminded him of those pictures Hollywood stars would take of themselves, sign, and give them out to their fans. Headshots? He entertained the idea that she could have been a model in a past life. Paulie didn't notice the gap between Edith and himself, where there was room for one more photo, long ago removed.

The photos were taken when We-Store first bought the lot. All the others in his neighborhood had been bought out and moved away, but the four people who remained still needed to be considered. Initially Niles, Paulie, Toni, and Edith were going to receive tiny plastic keycards with their photos printed on them, but alas, that never happened. This was, in fact, the first time Paulie had ever even seen the photo taken of himself.

Paulie snapped out of his daze when the security guard stood up, and poked the chunk of meat resting on his shoulder, "And this must be the thing everybody in town is talking about?"

Everybody in town? Midland was a small town sure, but certainly there was more to talk about than a man and his tumor. Nobody ever talked about Paulie. And a week ago, nobody knew about him outside of the dozen or so people who interacted with him. I've written more about the people that floated in and out of his life in the last few hundred pages than people have talked about Paulie Galamb in the last twenty years of his life.

And now here he was, the center of attention. Something he never desired, never sought, nor ever imagined would be a facet in his life.

"The thing has a name."

"My name is Parlay."

"Weird," said the guard, otherwise unimpressed by the liver-sized flap of meat that had just addressed him.

"By definition, yes, it is."

"Well, anyways, I just wanted to inform you that as per company policy you're not supposed to have overnight guests wandering the premises of the We-Store Storage Unit facility, and any further disruptions to company policy might be considered a violation to your original lease agreement."

"But I own my condo?"

"You own the condominium, but We-Store still owns the land. I'm just the messenger. At the end of the day, I don't give a shit what you do or who you invite over, just don't let me catch those punks cutting any more holes in my fence. That stunt you pulled on the water tower, though badass, ain't worth me losing my job over. So cut out the shit."

Paulie was taken aback by the tone of this guy, but as a general rule of thumb, any authority figure, be it a rent-a-cop or an actual member of Midland's finest, was always met with respect. Even if he didn't agree with them.

"I understand. I apologize. It won't happen again."

"That's what I want to hear. And as for all those people out there, you're going to have to tell them to disperse. I can't have this crowd blocking the entrance for actual paying customers."

The crowd?

It was then Paulie noticed that just outside the building there was a line around the corner, consisting of a dozen strangers of all shapes and sizes. Paulie approached them while the security guard sat back in his booth. "I ain't paid enough to tell them all to fuck off, so do me a solid will ya, and tell them to get lost."

But he wasn't listening to the coastal anomaly anymore.

Instead, he was walking to the gate, speechless.

So, they spoke for him.

The first in line was an old man with a shoebox in his hands. When he saw Paulie approaching, the old man's eyes lit up as he straightened his back. "Hello Paulie. I was told to bring you this."

The old man opened the box and revealed a tiny squirming mass no bigger than a baby rat. Paulie, without speaking, reached into the box until the baby-rat-sized tumor crawled onto his hand.

The man shed a tear, before closing the box. "Thank you, Paulie Galamb." And then, he walked away, leaving this story just as quickly as he came.

The next person to walk up to Paulie was a younger woman, dressed in business casual. He recognized her from somewhere, but he couldn't place the memory. Maybe she was a realtor whose face was on a billboard, or a bus stop bench, he didn't know. In her hands was a small cloth rolled up over itself, that she unfurled when he was close enough.

In it, was a small pink piece of flesh no larger than his little finger. "This. This is for you."

And like the baby rat, when Paulie reached down, it crawled onto his hand and disappeared under his sleeve cuff. "God bless you, Paulie," she said as she walked away.

An obese man came to the gate, and without saying anything, handed him two blobs. One was the size of a golf ball, the other the size of a grape. No words were exchanged.

Then, a small child, no older than ten, passed him a handkerchief. Inside that handkerchief was a small ovular growth about the size of his thumbnail. "Thank you, Mister Glammy."

Then, a housewife carrying her child under one arm and a large mason jar with her other. "Do you mind?" she said, offering the mason jar. Paulie opened it, and out from it slid the largest mass yet. He didn't notice the weight of it as it crawled up his arm and rested itself on his shoulder opposite Parlay as he passed her back the mason jar and lid.

After the housewife was a construction worker who opened his Igloo lunch box, and gently tossed the contents towards Paulie, which he caught. Three small lumps of equal size clustered together as if huddled for warmth. "Thanks, big man."

At this point, Paulie no longer made eye contact with the strangers. He just waited for them to approach, and when they offered him their growths, he accepted it. Some continued to thank him. Others just passed him their burdens and left without a word.

Then came a man in a suit who opened his briefcase. Then came a scrawny man in military uniform, much younger than himself. Then, a fast-food worker. A bus driver. A high school student. A nervous cop. A social worker. A secretary.

Then, a man in a wheelchair, pushed by another, opened his palms. Paulie took from his hand the chunk of meat which crawled under his sleeve and disappeared. From behind the old man, Paulie heard a woman's voice. "Thank you, kind sir."

"Paulie, I'd like you to meet Marion. My business partner," said the voice that sent his heart strings to song. When Paulie looked up, he saw the old man was being guided by a lady in her mid-thirties but standing next to her was his diminutive former wife.

"Toni, it's- it's nice to meet you, Toni."

The lady known as Marion giggled, before wheeling off the elderly man. "It's nice to meet you too, Paulie Galamb. I haven't heard enough about you. I'll make sure that changes. I'll leave you two alone.

He didn't even see her face. If you asked him right now what color Marion's hair was, he'd draw a blank. If you asked him what color her eyes were, he'd be unable to tell you. If the elderly man was holding a large red balloon that said something obscene on its side, he wouldn't have noticed.

His focus was entirely on the short, stocky woman of his dreams before him.

"I know I said I'd stop by tomorrow, but this morning I got a call from Marion, who told me her father wanted to see you."

"I've never met her. Or her dad."

"I know. Nor has he spoken in over three years. He has late-stage Alzheimer's. The last time he spoke a full sentence was, well, shortly after our divorce."

Paulie remained silent, trying to not let his emotions flood out of the gate that was his pug-like face. "Paulie, I didn't mention your name to Marion or her father, as it never pertained to our business operations. What's going on here?"

He considered his words carefully.

"Why are people, strangers, giving you pieces of raw beef? Is that what that is? I don't understand."

Very carefully.

"Paulie, what is that on your shoulder? Is that a chicken breast? A liver?"

"Toni, I want you to meet Parlay."

She furrowed her brow, squinted, and matched Paulie's ugly grin with her own unpleasant smile when the growth spoke, "Hello, Toni. It's nice to finally meet you."

This magical moment was brought to you by Pea Tree Farms. And promptly ruined by the security guard behind Paulie.

"Well, are ya going to invite her in bucko, or do I have to call that cop back over on her for trespassing?"

So, he did, and she accepted. And finally, Fuckin' Kyle opened the gate.

* * *

"They would spend the day together, ignoring all this weirdness that was happening around them."

"You mean, the three of them, right? Paulie, Toni, and Parlay?"

"Yeah, I figured that was obvious."

"It really isn't at this point, Seltzman. What about the boys? What about Niles and Edith?"

"Oh the boys would take up residence at Niles' house for the evening. On the grounds they, in his words, not mine, didn't mess with or steal his shit. They were all very appreciative of this."

"What a sweetheart."

"Yeah. They would spend a few hours studying. Juan'll wind up 'Hey-Mister-Hey-Mister'ing them a few beers to split. Stocks eventually would find Niles' vintage skin mag collection. Billy and Brian spend their evening playing with the ten-year-old snail, and Mullet admires the excessive CD collection of 80's hair metal."

"Wait, so Niles just leaves them there, unattended?"

"He's busy with Edith, of course. What with the big barbeque tomorrow, he had to grab all sorts of meats and entrees to grill up. And since Paulie was distracted with Toni, he invited Edith to come a long for the bike ride. Her first bike ride in thirty years, mind you. She had a glorious time. So much so, that the two of them kissed in public outside the Piggly Wiggly market."

"Well, I'll be damned. So other than that, it seems like the group at We-Store had a rather boring Friday?"

"Other than the constant migration of tiny tumors and growths that followed the sounds of hiccups from a water tower, yeah, I'd say it was a pretty boring Friday."

"But what about Toni and Paulie? And Parlay?"

"They caught up. They shared every detail of all that they missed in five years. They reminisced on their fond memories and avoided bringing up the bad ones. To spend time with an old friend or lover can be a blessed thing, sometimes."

"Do you miss your wife, Seltzman?"

"Every second of every day. I should give her a call-"

"-Never mind that. The three of them would connect in ways I can't rightly explain. Parlay would try to pull from Toni any cancer or growth she might have, but she had none. Paulie would try to explain what Parlay had shown him but to no avail. The dreams from the night before were no less tangible, and more like feelings in his mind. Like a smell or a taste."

"They spend the day just talking with one another?"

"Well, yes. Paulie eventually whipped up a meal from what remained in his cheat fridge and ate it with Toni even though he had no appetite. Even Parlay crawled off of the laptop Juan had left with them and tried a bite of the frozen dinner trays, calling the brownie bite "Exceptional!" upon consuming it."

"That sounds nice."

"There, in the middle condominium together they once called home, they ate together, while the teenagers blared Metallica in the condo to the north, while his neighbors cuddled and watched Jeopardy to the south. A calm night. And eventually, they would go to bed together, one final time, be it out of nostalgia or love, I know not."

"Do you still mean all three of them?"

"Don't make it weirder than it has to be, Hedasky."

45

THE SCOLDING OF ARNOLD

And The Cancer Soon Cometh

He had been sitting twenty feet from the beast for twenty hours now, locked in the chair, paralyzed by his own fear. The ancient man sat cross-legged between Arnold Workman and the Pea Tree Mass, quietly meditating. Every wet noise the writhing blob made, made Arnold flinch. Every sound made him nearly jump out of his seat, but he knew better than to attract the attention of the monstrosity before him.

Finally, the old man rose.

"Arnold, were you or were you not about to aim that gun at Hedasky the night before last?"

He didn't notice that now he was trembling. He could no longer hide his fear.

"I w-was only looking out for the company, Doctor Koop."

Some unheard sound once more caused the creature to erupt in a visible quake. It had been happening all morning, all afternoon, and evening. Arnold Workman had been forced to sit here with his employer ever since it began. The frequency of these unseen pulses had been rapidly increasing. Ever since he lost Tom Hedasky the night before.

"And what exactly did you do to Sue Ellen?"

He shook the thought away. Of ending her useless little life. Of tossing her body in the incinerator in the dead of night.

"Sir, I did as you told me. I got rid of her. I silenced her."

"Elaborate."

Arnold couldn't help but think this was all unfair. He had only done as he was asked. He shouldn't be here right now. He should be upstairs, training the new employees. The out-of-towners. The college girls. He was an asset to this company, damn it!

"I-I-I-" he stammered as the ancient ghastly man approached him. He knew it didn't matter, anymore. That he didn't matter.

Another pulse visibly shook the giant growth, another unheard sound from afar, and pieces of itself fell from itself. Pieces of flesh, which reeked of rotten pork, and three-day-old beef. Every time the mass shook, a wave of stink assaulted the man in middle management.

"Did you kill her, Arnold?"

He shook his head, left and right, then he felt the cold hands of Dr. C. Everett Koop upon him. Suddenly, the direction changed, as he slowly nodded his head up and down. The response was clear as day in the incredibly dark room, and the ancient doctor sighed.

"Arnold, we do not kill here at Pea Tree Farms. We are not in the business of death. We are in the business of future growth."

The man was shaking uncontrollably, but still he did not lift from his seat, even as the Pea Tree Mass rolled forward. Bits of it falling off from all sides of the fleshy ball, only to quickly crawl back to itself.

"You've put us all in jeopardy."

It was Doctor Koop now, lifting Arnold Workman from his chair. The strength of which seemed impossible. Arnold felt the tinier masses upon Koop's hands latch on to his own flesh, before letting go, and retreating to their owner. Now, Arnold stood there, motionless as the lumbering fleshy behemoth was mere inches away.

"I will not kill you, but I intend on freeing you of your flesh. You need to be held accountable of your actions."

It was so close now; he could taste it. For a second, it reminded him of the taste of spoiled trash, of hot garbage, of death and decay. But only for a second.

The meat enveloped him, and for a moment he felt like he was under water, surrounded by the muscle of something else. He wanted to start screaming now, but the mass was all around him. Inside of him. Under his skin. He felt the pressure grow too great, as the pain began to spread.

"You can scream now," said the voice of his employer, somewhere else, somewhere far from here. Just beyond the sounds of blood gurgling, of his body being pulled in every unnatural direction. Just as he felt the ripping and tearing of his skin, he tried to scream. As the muscle and ligaments stretched and snapped like rubber bands, squeezing all of his blood out of every vein like the remnants of a tube of toothpaste, he tried to scream once more. No screams would come from this man, not ever again, as his windpipe and lungs collapsed, as his organs imploded on one another.

The pain blinded him briefly, until his eyeballs burst. His tongue and heart were among the last of his meat to be consumed, and even then, his tongue tried to escape his body, silently screaming.

And then, having been fed, the Pea Tree Mass retreated, leaving behind an intact skeleton, stained red with bits of flesh missed by the mass around it. All that remained was a brain, somewhere in that thick skull formerly belong to a man called Arnold Workman. Not that it had any thoughts left to share.

"Come now, we still have work to do. We must stop them before it's too late. We must stop them from continuing this. We must stop this broadcast. It'll be the end of all I've worked for. It'll be the end of humanity as we know it."

The blood-stained skeleton thoughtlessly rose to its feet, and followed Dr. Koop back toward the elevator, following the orders of its employer once more. Meanwhile, the monstrous growth, it shrieked as the pulses came and went like contractions as the ancient man and skeleton rode back to ground level.

"Shall I get the car?" asked the skeleton formerly known as Arnold Workman.

46

TREPANATION SITUATION

And A Wee Bit Of Domestic Terrorism

The homeless man was hard at work. In the last few days, he had acquired all he would need to carry out his heroic task. In the shadows of early morning, he carefully placed the ammonium nitrate in the aluminum beer can and sealed off the top with a bit of duct tape. Then, even more careful yet, he placed the can into the backpack with the other dozen or so cans already filled. Chris didn't exactly know why he was doing what he was doing anymore, just following the footsteps of his memories.

Years of studying the conspiracies that others laughed at, that others denied the existence of, had also led to him acquiring the skills to defend himself and save himself from the evil powers that be. Had things turned out differently, maybe he'd be somewhere else in the countryside, in his bunker under the earth, but instead, this was where God willed him.

All of that knowledge he had come across, that others mocked him for, was being put to use now. All of those revelations he had had, with no one to listen to, would amount to what came next.

He learned how to build pipe-bombs when he found out the lizard people were pulling the strings, hiding themselves in the flesh of powerful politicians. He taught himself how to weaponize fertilizer when he first read about the baby-eating Hollywood elite. He mastered making IED's when he discovered the moon was hollow and filled with the overlords that watched over humanity, experimenting on them with teleportation rays. Everybody mocked him for his conspiracy theories. They called him outlandish, and wild. Most even called him crazy. Those who would listen, anyways.

As he built the bomb before him, wiring the old Nokia flipphone to the detonator, he fingered the soft part just above his skull. Where the man he once called boss had taken a piece of his skull. Chris Wagoner, he knew better. He knew that they were trying to silence him once and for all.

Somewhere between the final hours of Friday evening, and the earliest hours of Saturday morning, the paranoid man wired bits of detonating cord all around himself, connecting each end to another bag of fertilizer tied to his ankles, legs, arms, and waist.

Last night, he knew what had to be done. He had seen that man, a man he once called boss before he was silenced, talking with another man. The man from the news. He didn't know how or why he recognized the news reporter, his brain still cloudy in the aftermath of his lobotomy, but he was still able to put the pieces together.

It was validation. It was the proof he needed to carry out what came next. As he placed the backpack on his pack, and the bandolier across his chest, he knew he was ready. At this hour, there would be no victims but the evils within the Pea Tree building. No bystanders or passersby. Just enough destruction to save the world, and to finally put himself out of his misery.

He held the detonator close to his chest, itself but another cellular phone, and with his free hand he held down the green button on the cellphone that was wired into his bandolier.

The ten-year-old phone sang a sweet short song as it powered on, and with a smile on his face, Chris Wagoner walked towards the entrance of Pea Tree Farms. The weight of all the explosives strapped to his chest did not bother him, nor hinder him. Instead, he was guided by his own blind faith and conviction in the conspiracy theories that may or may not ever be proven true.

Not that it mattered to him anymore.

47

BARSTOOL BANTER, PART FIVE

Last Call

"He was a total douchebag, that guy. Good riddance. You made the right choice sticking back, Seltzman. I should have listened, but hey, what can you do?" Hedasky said of Arnold Workman, not of Chris Wagoner. Chris had not yet earned their attention.

Though the question was clearly directed at the dentist, it was the otolaryngologist/oncologist who answered, "I cannot believe you even chose to speak with this man."

"Hey, listen here, Fejes, the only reason I spoke with the guy in the first place was because his company has their fingers inside my company's pie. The Workman guy was supposedly making an offer about a job, which I wouldn't mind, especially if it got me out of this sour limelight for a spell. Why they'd need a meteorologist is beyond me."

"But still, why do you go with this man, this middle manager, in late of night? This is what I do not understand."

"Pea Tree Farms is one of the leading contributors to KGTV, and if I were to insult our sponsor, I'd likely be shit-canned and out of work. And let me tell you, as handsome as I am, I ain't in my twenties anymore, and nobody wants a weatherman with a bad reputation these days."

"You are not so handsome, Hedasky," said Dr. Fejes with a wry grin.

"But I guess none of that matters now, anyways, does it?"

"What do you mean?" asked the dentist.

"The dead guy, or the guy who was supposed to be dead, he made it pretty clear that he'd give me a whole lot of money to shut the hell up on the matter, and when I made it clear I wasn't putting up with their threats and demanded to leave, I saw fear in the pudgy guy's eyes. A fear I could only describe as primal."

"Yeah, but he has the fear of man who fears his employer. It is not different than you, Tom Hedasky. You fear for your job, so you are afraid of your boss, yes?"

"Nah, I'm not afraid of my boss. I could wipe his face on the floor and walk away with a smile on my face. Sure, I'd be out a job, a career, and probably a year of my life wasted in a county jail, but I'm not afraid of him."

"I tried to tell Paulie, do not trust the likes of middle management-"

"-their motives are more unclear than that of their more powerful, evil men. Yeah, yeah, I know. We already heard that part."

"-for they are truly cowards and when you corner a coward, they will do stupid things," Dr. Fejes clarified, correcting the weatherman. "And now without flesh and blood, he is likely to make even more stupid things."

"So, what do we do?"

"We? We drink, we wait, we watch, we listen. You, Tom, you've got your own task at hand. You need to gather as much information as you can on Dr. C. Everett Koop and bring that to the media's attention. Let loose the knowledge that the dead man is not dead. He will be distracted by what comes next."

"And what's that, exactly?"

"A sheep covered in a million cancers will escape shortly, and toward the We-Store Storage Units it will go. The skeleton man will drive the dead man there, and their final confrontation will begin. That will be the distraction you'll need to leak the greatest story of your career."

Tom sighed, "My greatest story will be that of a surgeon general who faked his own death?"

"Well, you're the reporter, you can probably spin it better than that, I would hope."

"I'm not a reporter, I'm a meteorologist-"

"You are not very good meteorologist, Hedasky," laughed the little ENT.

"Very funny, Fejes, coming from a doctor who doesn't use gloves when he sticks his hands in a stranger's mouth."

"You know I am allergic to latex. I get itchy. Sweaty. It is unpleasant, Hedasky. At least I do not lie to the people who count on me."

"Easy there you two, there isn't any time left for bickering. Tom, you should probably finish your beer and get a move on. I'd say the quicker you can get back to Central City and start on your expose the better. Best avoid downtown while you're at it."

"Why should I avoid downtown?"

"Just trust me on this, old friend. It'll be an active crime scene soon enough, and the whole place will be swarming with flashing lights and badges. That, and traffic will be an absolute nightmare."

"I'll just take your word on it. Enjoy the rest of your day, Seltzman," who responded with a despondent wave in his direction, "And as for you, Dr. Fejes, you're a fucking strange one."

"Okay then, baszni rá, Tom Hedasky. Good luck on your greatest story ever, you useless galamb."

Tom mumbled out a, "Yeah, yeah," before heading out the door, leaving behind a few crumpled bills and a third of his beer.

"Well, it's just you and me now, Dr. Fejes. What are you drinking?"

"How about this drink I have heard of, 'Irish Car Bomb', are those still popular with the youth?"

"Oh no, I don't think you can say that anymore. It's offensive to the Irish people and the struggles of Irish Republican Army."

"I do not care about your country's political correctness, Seltzman."

"Yeah, but you're here, so maybe you should at least respect it."

"Fine. Bartender, do you know how to make a 'Climax Explosion'?"

The bartender, mute up until this point, shouted back to the man leaning forward on the bar, "One ounce mango rum, a half ounce of tequila, half ounce gin, half ounce vodka. Splash of mango juice, garnished with a piece of fresh mango. It's pretty disgusting if you ask me, but you didn't ask."

The tiny doctor cheered, "Exactly right, my boy! Very good! I will have one 'Climax Explosion', and with a swiftness if you do not mind!"

Fuckin' Kyle didn't reach for the liquor bottles, instead he just continued cleaning his glass. "No can do, sir."

Dr. Fejes leaned further onto the bar, glaring at the bartender from afar. "And why not?' while Seltzman checked the watch on his wrist.

"Because I don't carry mango rum, nor mangos here at The Ol' Watering Hole?"

The frustration was mounting in the shrewish old man's face, "And why do you not carry these things?"

"Mangos? Look outside? Does it look like India outside? Does it look like Bangla-fucking-desh? This is Midland. This is a very tiny Midland. We don't even have a fucking K-mart, and you expect us to have mangos?"

Dr. Fejes frowned. Seltzman tapped his fingers on the bar impatiently. Realizing his defeat, he compromised. "Can you make this 'Climax Explosion' with orange juice and perhaps regular rum instead?"

Seltzman checked his watch one final time, then placed his hands over his ears.

Fuckin' Kyle smiled, and said "Yes, I can make your 'Climax Explosion'-"

Just as the shockwave from a distant explosion swung open the door, illuminating the bar with an enormous fireball three miles north, rising to the heavens. The windows rattled but did not shatter, and neither did the glasses. So, while the patrons all lay on the floor, worried this blast was the first of many, an unamused Kyle poured the man his drink, before quietly exiting this scene to fulfil his duties in the next.

Hush! Are you telling the story, or am I? Now where was I?

48

SATURDAY MORNING BARBEQUE

And The Wrath Of Doctor Koop

The smell of brisket reminded him that he needed to replace his alarm clock. It didn't elicit the sense of hunger it should have, but the smell enticed him all the same. Instead of a rumbling in his tummy, the scent brought to him a wave of nostalgia. Though his eyes were still closed, Paulie was awake, swimming in the early morning half-dreams, guided by the smells of cooked meat.

At first, it reminded him of his father on a hot summer Sunday in '76, grilling up a dozen chicken drumsticks and six ears of corn while chubby young Paulie splashed about in the Little Tikes turtle pool. Paulie could see his old man's smile as clear as day, which was a rarity in Paulie's childhood. The man spent most of his time in a woodshop, clamping freshly glued furniture together. It wasn't until his retirement that the man smiled regularly, but sadly that was around the same time the dementia had set in. The smell of brisket reminded Paulie that he should visit his dad sometime soon, even if the old man wouldn't recognize him.

But for now, he continued riding this nostalgia wave. He found himself sitting at the dinner table in the mid-eighties while his mother served him an inch-thick steak next to heap of mashed potatoes. He knew that if he were to cut into it right there and then it'd be perfectly rare. Though he would not be able to do so until his father joined the dinner table, who was busy screaming at the television in the next room over. Paulie could almost smell his mother's perfume in that memory. The smell reminded him that he should also visit her sometime, even though the dead don't have much to say.

Then the smell of brisket brought him back to the nineties, he in his twenties, when he weighed just a hair over three-eighty. No mom or dad, just college kids day-drinking their hangovers away while Paulie pat-dried two pork chops before dropping them in the bags of Shake n' Bake. After he'd shake the seasoning onto the chops, he'd place them on a paper plate, and set it atop the microwave now dinging. He'd pull out the paper plate from inside the microwave with the steaming piece of pork, poorly breaded, and pop in the plate from above the microwave into it. While the second two cooked for five minutes, he'd hastily devour the first set of piping-hot pork chops, only pausing to exhale a cloud of steam, before repeating the process again. "Save me one, won't ya Paulie?" said a voice somewhere beyond his dreams.

Finally, he found himself in the early oughts, in a tuxedo bespeckled in barbeque sauce. It had been his fiancé's idea to have barbeque food at their wedding. It was his idea to have a whole pig on a spit. After the celebration, he remembered promising himself, then they'd go on a diet. But today, they'd just savor the tastes, the smells, the memories made. "Are you going to eat that whole thing?" he heard his new wife say.

Paulie opened his eyes and saw her sitting up.

Maybe he had fallen asleep when he opened them, because suddenly he felt like he was dreaming.

"You were doing it again," said the dreamy figure that sat in bed next to him

Rubbing the grit out of his eyes, Paulie asked "Grinding my teeth?"

"Eating in your sleep."

Paulie smiled, and rotated himself out of bed, if only to hide the fact that he was blushing. But Toni knew better, so she mimicked his movement. Quickly, she grabbed her blouse while Paulie pulled his pants up. Together they awkwardly danced their clothing back on, and before Paulie could run toward the bathroom, Toni Galamb was closing the door behind her. As was their routine, back when they shared one together.

He still felt like he was still riding that nostalgia wave.

Until, of course, he saw the state of his living room.

"Good morning, Paulie," said the incredibly large blob spanning the length of his coffee table. It appeared as if someone had dropped a wet blanket made entirely of marbled beef, complete with semi-pronounced ligaments and veins. Under the fleshy sack, Paulie could see the faint glow of what must have been the laptop, though it was otherwise completely obstructed from view so he couldn't be sure.

But it didn't stop at the coffee table. It dripped over the side, dropping tiny pink marbles onto the carpet which would them climb the legs of the table and rejoin the mass. Around the table, hundreds of small salmon-colored spans of meat crawled across his carpet, rolling and folding on themselves. On his walls, thousands of roach-sized growths roamed around like aimless ants. Even his ceiling was covered in bits of Parlay.

Paulie shrugged, "Good morning to you, Parlay. Learn anything interesting last night?"

The mass atop the table, rolled its entirety off of the computer, unveiling the laptop and aquarium beneath it, and onto the floor. From inside the mass of writhing flesh, out came a chunk of meat comparable to a flattened chicken breast. The flattened chicken breast extended a nub of itself toward Paulie, who aimed his arm at Parlay, who then climbed up the man's arm.

Then the mass on the floor dissolved into several hundred tiny masses, which danced around each other aimlessly.

"I learned everything interesting, Paulie."

"That's good. Strange question, but do you eat meat, Parlay?"

The tumor crawled up Paulie's arm and perched itself on his shoulder, "I am not sure, but I am willing to try it."

Paulie made his way toward the door when he heard his bathroom open, "Toni, I'm going outside. I'm going to see if there's anything I can do to help Niles."

"I'll be right out, hon-, er, Paulie."

The hesitation was very much 'blink-and-you-miss-it', but he did not. On any other day, it would bother him, but he understood what it meant without her having to explain herself. "This can't happen again," was what she had said, without saying it.

And that was fine.

Paulie opened the door, which shoved aside several dozen tiny growths, but they didn't mind either. Even as Paulie put his shoes on, stepping on one, two, three, or four of the little pink slugs, they were unaffected. Outside, the world was overcast gray, but it smelled great. Paulie leaned over the railing of his condominium and shouted at his neighbor, who was currently at the grill, hidden by a cloud of smoke and steam. "I'm drooling over here, Niles. That smells phenomenal!"

The man in the cloud leaned forward, revealing himself to be a young Hispanic man. Juan poured a splash of beer across the slab of meat, causing the brisket to sizzle and shriek. "Good morning, my man! Niles went out to grab more beer and steaks. Told me to keep an eye on this bad boy."

"Where are the rest of your badasses?"

"I think the twins are helping Edith marinate the chicken. Mullet's flattening the hamburgers here in the man-cave behind me, and I think Stocks is- Mullet where is Stocks?"

"He's convinced he can teach Slugger how to talk, so I think he's up in Niles' living room with a bit of Parlay."

Paulie glanced down at the growth on his shoulder and whispered, "Is that true?

"Yes. Stocks likes it when I place some of myself atop Slugger's head and make it appear that she can talk. He finds it very amusing, but I think it has something to do with the effects of the marijuana-laced chocolate he consumed an hour ago."

"Slugger is a girl?" Paulie asked, never having guessed that snail rocking an Iron Maiden shell was a little lady.

"Slugger is a hermaphroditic pulmonate land snail. So, yes and no. She just prefers to be called she."

"Does it bother her when Niles refers to her as he or a little badass."

"Paulie, Slugger does not speak English. She is a snail."

The man would have laughed to the unintentional joke made by the tumor on his shoulder, but instead he was distracted by the flash of light on the north end of town. Like lightning, moments before Paulie could realize what he was looking at, an incredibly loud crack of thunder stole the show. His jaw hung dumbly at its joints, as Paulie watched the sky go blue, free of clouds, in a spherical fashion. Then, a huge concussive gust of wind hit him, nearly knocking him back into his doorway, when he finally saw the fireball rising as it dreamily transformed into thick, black smoke.

He stared straight ahead, and watched the plume rise in disbelief. From the direction the pillar of smoke rose, he knew exactly where it was coming from.

Toni ran out of their, er, his condo, "Paulie, what is that?!"

Absently, Paulie answered. "I think my job just exploded."

* * *

Jessie Ellen was almost five years old. She was so old her mommy promised her when she turned five, she wouldn't have to use the baby seat anymore when her and mommy drove places together. Just like a big girl. Soon she would be tying her own shoes with shoelaces and then she would go to elementary school and make all sorts of friends like she made in kindergarten.

She was old enough to count to twenty all by herself, with no help from mommy or daddy. Little Jessie was so big and grown now she didn't even have to use the booster seat at dinner time, even though she liked pretending she was as big and grown as her parents. Old enough to know Jesus, God, and Santa Claus were very real and always watching. She was even old enough now to know that monsters weren't real, that they were just in the movies that mommy and daddy watched some-times when she was supposed to be sleeping.

So, while she was looking out the window of the car while mommy was stopped at the intersection, she laughed instead of screamed when she saw the skeleton driving the car next to them.

"Mommy, lookit! There's a skellington next to us!"

The bloody skeleton turned its always-grinning skull to the

little girl one car over, and even went as far as tipping its hat at her. Then, the window rolled up, and all Jessie Ellen could see was her own reflection in the dark windows.

"Little miss, are you telling me a fib right now?"

"No, momma, I swear I seent it! Right there in that black car!"

Jessie watched as her mommy turned her head, and then faced her in the tiny mirror above the windshield. "Sweetie, we don't tell fibs or swear in this family, okay?"

Defeated, the little four-year-old frowned but agreed. "No, we don't tell fibs or swear. Mommy?"

"Yes, dear?"

"When are we going to get to grandma's house?"

"Soon enough, darling. Now go back to..." playing on your tablet, would have been the words that followed, but instead mommy just let the sentence hang out of her mouth unfinished. She wasn't looking at Jessie, she was looking past her in the mirror with her big, scared eyes.

Because all of a sudden everything flashed brightly white like when Jessie Ellen got her school pictures taken in kindergarten, followed by the loudest boom this little girl had ever heard.

It was then Jessie Ellen screamed.

* * *

The blast shook the black sedan with tinted windows, but it did not shake the perseverance of the passengers.

"Are you alright sir?" asked the bloody skeleton formerly known as Arnold Workman.

"I'm fine, I'm fine. Just seize this opportunity and drive! Get us to We-Store, pronto!"

"But sir, I think that blast came from-"

"I've been alive for a hundred and thirteen years, Workman! I can easily deduce where that explosion came from, which means it is of the utmost importance that we get to the signal before it does!"

The skeleton man did feel fear in the same way that Dr. C. Everett Koop did, but it still felt a tiny jolt of electricity in its amygdala upon mentioning "It". The bloody skeleton's brain was still active after all, and the mere mention of the Pea Tree Mass would have easily raised the hair on the back of his skin, had he still skin and hair.

There was a moment of silence after the shockwave shook their car and the cars around them, then there was a cacophony of car alarms and sirens to fill that silence. Most of the people in the cars were getting out of them to stare at the giant fireball that was rising towards the heavens. Some were holding their hands over their mouths in awe. Others were pulling out their cellphones and tablets as quickly as they could to film the aftermath of the huge explosion.

The skeleton and ancient old man were the only two driving now, other than the ambulances, firetrucks, and policemen driving in the other direction, towards the flames and smoke from whence Workman and Koop came. There the rescue workers raced towards the black smoke pouring from what remained of Pea Tree Farms, while the skeleton of Arnold Workman sped towards the water tower.

"God, we were just there. We could have been in that blast, sir."

"Mr. Workman, you've already been stripped of flesh and blood. You'd have been fine. Don't let your mind wander! Stay focused on the task at hand!"

On any other day, a cop would see an unmarked black sedan speeding through a city as a crime worth stopping, but right now the police of Midland were wholly preoccupied. The skeleton was careful to evade the many parked cars and pedestrians who had stopped dead in their tracks to stare dumbly at the column of smoke behind them, but there were a few near misses. The fleshless ghoul rolled his window back down and stuck his skull out to the window as he drove.

"Get the fuck out of my way!" the skeleton man screamed. But the pedestrians merely sidestepped the oncoming car, never once turning away from the horror they were facing.

It wasn't just the remains of an explosion they were staring at now.

It was the mass. The Pea Tree Mass was free of its bonds, and it was rolling and crawling towards the dumbstruck people of Midland at speeds their fragile brains could not comprehend.

* * *

The one-legged man cracked open a beer at the gate and offered it to the security guard, "I'm telling you, man, you've got to try my ribs."

"Sir, you can't- Eh, do you mind just, uh, drinking it off camera so I don't get shit-canned over this."

Niles and Kyle weren't completely alone. There was a constant stream of random people walking up and setting on the ground at the gate their tiny growths and tumors, which then crawled themselves towards the water tower. But rarer were the passersby that did this instead of just allowing the tumors to find their way here without the assistance of their hosts. Due, of course, to the hiccupping signal barely heard from atop the water tower.

"Oh, yeah, not a problem. We're having a little barbeque at the end of the facility, maybe swing by after your shift. We'll load you up a plate!"

"I would but I'm a vegetarian."

Niles grunted and spat beer foam from his mouth onto the asphalt below them. "I guess times are changing. My special lady friend, she was a vegetarian once. Said it didn't sit with her well. She's a real looker, my Edi."

Kyle tried to imagine this crazy old biker with a girlfriend, the kind of uncivilized trailer-trash he expected of the likes of him, and to that I say shame on you, Kyle. Edith is a very nice woman.

"And a real freak in the bedroom, hoo-boy!" Niles added, right before the white flash momentarily filled the sky.

But no longer was Kyle paying attention to the man drinking beer at his post. Instead, he and the slow-moving crowd of growth-donors were all transfixed by the fireball in the distance, parting the clouds like that one guy who parted that one sea, allegedly. Niles turned towards the blast, and quietly took a sip of his beer.

"Well hot damn and holy fu-" before the gust of wind hit him right across the face.

The security guard picked up the phone and held it there, speechless.

"I think that's the county courthouse that just went up!" said one of the strangers beyond the gate.

"No, I think that's the medical center!" said another stranger who was clutching their tumor close to their chest as if it were a pet or an infant child.

"No. I think it's that big, uh, office building. Pedro Farms? Peter Ree Farms?"

"Never heard of it. Why the fuck would they build a farm in an office building?" Niles said, still staring at the rising tower of black smoke.

"I don't know, but that certainly looks like where it came from."

331

"Whaddya think, Officer Kyle? It's gotta be them terrorists, right?"

"It's Fuckin' Kyle, not Officer Kyle. And to be absolutely honest, no, I don't think its terrorists. Why would a terrorist go out of the way and blow up an office in Midland?"

"Let alone a farm office," Niles whispered into his beer before pulling back another foamy mouthful. They both stared at the billowing plumes of smoke that rose into the blue sky surrounded by clouds. So intently, they didn't notice the black sedan barreling towards them.

Until, of course, the skeletal driver hammered on the horn to catch their attention properly. Most of the pilgrims here tossed their personal cancers at the gate before sprinting out of the path of the black car.

"I don't think he's slowing down, bud. Ya might wanna move away from the gate," the older man said, but only after he finished the rest of his beer. Three glugs, would you believe it.

"Is that... a skeleton?" asked the man who already heard this story about Arnold back in the bar, but does anybody retain anything here? Is anyone even paying attention at this point?!

"Nah, looks more like a Lincoln Town Car, if I had to guess."

Niles slowly moved his beloved Harley three feet over to his left, while Kyle remained motionless, still holding his phone. Kyle wanted to say, "Hey, wait, stop," but no words came out as the black sedan careened through the flimsy barrier gate arm, which exploded in a dazzling array of red and white stripes and cheap wood. Not as impressive as the previous explosion, but this one hit much closer to home. So much that a piece of debris landed squarely on Niles' spherical bald dome.

"Oh, no, you're right, that was definitely a skeleton. That's fucking abnormal, to say the least," Niles said, shaking the piece of barrier off his head as he crushed the can under his feet.

But once more, the frozen security guard said nothing. Instead, his eyes widened at the sight of what came next.

The whole thing was as big as two car lanes. A monstrous mass of a million flaps of wet meat crawling over itself, folding in on itself, pressing inward and outward at the same time, rolling toward them at an impossible speed. A million slugs and leeches all in the same flesh-tone pink writhing and squirming over itself, pieces big and small falling off as the giant rolled and tumbled towards them. Worse yet, was the screeching that came before it.

If the explosion was a loud singular noise, this one was that of hundreds, or even thousands. It sounded like a hundred dead dogs whining, a hundred roadkill cats yowling, a million squashed frogs croaking, a single sheep baa-ing. It was pure meaty chaos, screaming, and charging at the two of them just as fast as the black sedan had seconds earlier.

It rolled over people, flattening them to the pavement. The inattentive folk crossing the street were tossed aside like ragdolls by the enormous weight and momentum of the mass made of pure muscle and tissue. And it was speeding toward Kyle and Niles at an alarming rate.

Niles moved his beloved Harley three feet further to his left, only moments before the unstable mass of meat rolled on past them. The two men turned only their heads as they watched the meaty mess disappear into the labyrinth that is We-Store Storage Units.

Finally, Kyle spoke.

"I, uh, I think I should call the police."

Niles pulled another beer out of his side satchel and placed it on the security guard's desk. "Yeah, I should probably, uh, go check on Edith. Nice talking to you, Fuckin' Kyle."

Kyle cracked his beer, took a sip, and dialed 911 as Niles slowly drove his Harley towards his home on the other side of the maze. Towards the mass, towards the sedan, towards his love and his neighbor and those boys minding the grill.

* * *

Everybody was outside now.

Edith was standing in the doorway of her condominium between the twins, Billy and Brian. In that order. Toni and Paulie and Parlay were on the same level, just fifteen feet north of the seventy-eight-years old and the matching sixteen-year-olds. Stocks was another fifteen feet north of the Galambs, with Slugger in hand in the open doorway of Nathaniel Niles' condo. The eight of them were looking over the railings in the same direction. Towards the rising smoke, where the explosion had occurred moments before.

But also, they were looking towards the other noises they couldn't yet see. Juan and Mullet had walked around the smoking grill to see if they could see the source of the loud crash that happened shortly after the explosion from across town. Mullet had his fingers in his mouth, sucking the orange dust off them, nervously, as he heard the squealing of tires.

It almost sounded like someone was doing donuts in the empty lot next door, but the sounds were not consistent. Instead of one continuous right or left turn, the vehicle was rapidly alternating directions. The unseen vehicle, Paulie correctly deduced, was inside this lot, not outside of it.

"It's coming for us," Paulie said to no one, because instead, the eight up top and the two down on ground level collectively shuddered when they heard the inhuman abhorrent screams of what sounded like a herd of wild, dying animals.

"Yes," was all Parlay could respond with, but that too was drowned out by the shrieking in the distance.

The black sedan was the first noise identified as it turned the final corner. The driver slammed on the brakes just inches before hitting unflinching Juan, who stood between the brisket and the car.

Stocks muttered out a stoned, "Woah," while he watched the car come to a halt in front of his friend and mentor. Paulie did not recognize the car, but he had an idea.

And that idea was thrown right out the proverbial window when the driver stepped out at the same time as the passenger from the back seat.

Of everything Paulie had seen this week, this one probably took the most time to process. It was just, whew, a lot at once. He heard Toni scream from behind him, so he knew he wasn't the only one seeing what he was seeing, but that didn't mean it made any more sense.

A skeleton. A bloody skeleton. A skeleton wearing a driving cap. Paulie could see that there were ribbons of meat binding the joints of the skeleton, and blood stains throughout the otherwise whitish-yellow bones. It looked like a marionette without the strings, and when it looked up at him from the ground level, he could see pink beyond the otherwise empty eye-sockets. Then, against all logic, the grinning skull moved its jaw up and down, and somehow, it spoke.

"Hey there Paulie-boy, how's that gift basket treating you?"

Even without lungs or a tongue or vocal cords, Paulie knew the voice. Arnold Workman. His boss' boss.

But then who was the ghoul?

The man who got out of the back of the black sedan, he looked like he had died a decade ago, but everybody forgot to let him know this. He looked like he was over a hundred years old, with hair whiter than porcelain, and his skin wasn't far from it. Except Paulie, even from the second floor, he could see the man was covered in lesions and bruises, hidden by tiny pink leeches not unlike Parlay. Except they seemed unhealthy.

"Not unhealthy, unhappy," said the voice in his head, his voice but it came from his growth.

He looked like a corpse.

The tiny growths seemed to be hopping off the ancient man, whose face was now contorted with rage. The man with the chinstrap beard shouted at Paulie, "Turn it off! Turn it off now, before it's too late!"

"Ignore him," said the voice from his shoulder. "Don't do it."

From the corner of his eye, he saw Toni's arm jut past him, pointing straight ahead, past the sedan.

At whatever the hell that thing is. Behind the sedan, the skeleton, and the ghoul, was the blob, shrieking as it rolled toward them.

Stocks mumbled a quiet, "Holy fuck," while he considered the strength of his marijuana edibles. Because, if his eyes weren't playing tricks on him, he was pretty sure he was looking at a blob made entirely of raw meat.

Juan took a step backward and leaned into the hot grill before he yelped in pain. The pain wasn't enough to distract him from what he saw behind the car that almost struck him, or the skeleton driving it, or the ghastly old man from the back seat. The pain didn't hide the monstrous shrieking beast that sounded like every animal in pain.

The twins, they held onto Edith as if she was their own grandmother. Edith held on to them like they were her own grandchildren. She dropped the marinated chicken, uncaring that the dish exploded at their feet. With her hands free, she shielded the boys eyes with her two hands. "Look away, boys, look away."

But looking away didn't stop the mass from hurtling towards them.

"Paulie, I need you to trust me here," said the squishy lump on his shoulder.

He understood. "Stocks, Toni, go to Edith!" Paulie shouted as the mammoth blob crawled over the black sedan and up the side of the three attached condominiums at the end of the We-Store lot. The shorter teen and his ex-wife ran towards the elderly lady and the twins. The beast squeezed between the skeleton, the old man, and the teens in Niles' garage-turned-storage unit, just as the three teens, Toni and Edith braced themselves.

"Remain calm, Paulie," said his growth as the blob climbed up the first floor. Mullet and Juan ran to the far end of Niles' garage as the Saturday sunshine was blotted out by the mass of writhing meat. Paulie looked ahead, directly at the center of the gigantic monstrosity.

It was then he felt something grab his leg. "It's just me, Paulie. Relax." Except it wasn't grabbing him. It was climbing him, from behind. The coffee table Parlay was crawling up his legs, up his back, just as the larger shrieking mass was about to overtake him.

He vaguely thought he heard the old man from the car repeat himself, but as Parlay enveloped him, as the giant ball consumed him, he was unsure of everything he saw and heard next.

"Paulie, I need to go back in your cavern," was the last thing he heard before his vision went pink, then black. Paulie saw the meat of the monster and the meat of his tumor melded into one all around him. He felt his personal growth climb his neck. It felt different than the new mass. It felt warm.

He relaxed his jaw, just as Parlay crawled inside him, just as the monstrous behemoth consumed him. The three beings twisting into one another. Paulie and Parlay and the Pea Tree mass. In the red darkness, Paulie felt pressure on his throat while Parlay vibrated inside his esophagus.

It was hiccupping. Parlay was singing, and he was using Paulie as the microphone.

But while this was happening, Paulie felt his feet lift off the ground. He was floating inside the melded masses. While Parlay and the Pea Tree mass were wrestling and dancing, Paulie was rising inside the different shades of pink and red, between the strange soft-hard textures of the flesh.

When Paulie glanced around, with Parlay still lodged firmly in his throat, he could see past the meat that was blocking his eyes. In the same way you can see light shining through the webbing of your hand, Paulie could make out the blurry shapes of objects just past the fleshy prison he was incased in. There, he could see his former wife huddled in the corner of the shared walkway with the three teenagers and his neighbor.

"I want to eat that," said a foreign voice somewhere inside this pink tomb.

But Paulie did not acknowledge the voice, because the voice did not seem human. Instead, he looked past the two women and three boys, and focused his attention on the darker red silhouette of the water tower against the fuzzy pink sky. With his head aimed at the tower, the hiccupping in his throat matched the tone he could barely hear coming from way up there.

"I want to kill that," said the animal voice inside him.

"Well, then, let's go get it!" Paulie said, without speaking, what with the giant chunk of meat wedged in his throat, pressing on his vocal cords and esophagus like a harp. Paulie turned his whole body in the pink blob and began swimming towards the water tower, away from his ex-wife, away from the old lady, away from the frightened teens.

And while he swam, the two masses followed, keeping the ugly man centered inside itself.

* * *

The skeleton formerly known as Arnold Workman got up, brushing dust off its bloody bones, while the colossal collection of animal tumors climbed up the side of the water tower, with Paulie somewhere inside. Without eyes, the skeleton aimed his skull at the monstrous bloat, and pondered, "What to do, oh, what to do."

If he had emotions still dancing around in that skull of his, he definitely did not wear them well. The lack of facial features or skin in general made it very hard to read what was going on in that brain of his.

"Arnold! The women, grab them!" yelled his employer, the ancient Dr. Koop, which caused the skeleton to snap out of its stupor. It ran around the back of the Pea Tree mass which was rolling itself up the sides of the three condominiums and onto the roof. It looked almost like a giant snail, stretching itself over the garage ports, the balcony, and the roof. Like Slugger, only supersized and shell-less.

It didn't bother or disturb the skeleton. It was just in his way. From his orders, from his boss, to grab the women. So the skeleton ran atop, up and over, the giant pink snail's back end. Arnold climbed up the ridge of what might have been a back or a spine if this mass had bones beyond its muscle. Arnold leapt from up the side of the mass, just as the mass was fully atop the roof, causing the whole structure to groan and crack.

The mass now crawled across the roofs toward the southern-most end of the condominiums, then down the backend of Edith's home, toward the fence, toward the tower.

Edith, however, was shielding the eyes of two teens when the skeleton landed in front of them. Any normal women might have screamed at the blood-covered skeleton, held together by seemingly impossible strands of tendons and exposed bits of muscle, but Edith was not a normal woman.

She had seen things much crazier, much zanier, and much more impossible than the likes of this bony bastard in her tenure at The Factory. Andy Warhol and the endless array of psychedelics consumed in his company had prepared her for this weirdness.

"Get away from me, you skinless freak."

But onward the skeleton ambled towards her, "That's not very nice, ma'am. I'll have you know my level of patience for bitchy old women is at an all-time low."

"Hey, mister!" said Stocks, who was initially partially hidden by the mass as it previously climbed onto the roof. The skeleton turned to face the boy, now lunging at his bones. "Leave her alone, you bag of bones!"

The skeleton tumbled into the railing, up and over, and onto the ground below. Though Arnold lacked any eardrums or ears, in the seconds between falling from the second floor to the first, it still heard the rev of the motorcycle engine.

"You get the fuck away from my missus, you fucking monster, you!" screamed the bald man atop the motorcycle, careening towards the skeleton, towards the condominiums. With the finesse of a ballerina, Niles slammed on his brakes as he turned and leaned his weight, so much that the tires of his bike squealed and screamed as he swung the back end of the motorcycle into the skeleton.

The skeleton exploded upon impact into nothing more than a pile of bones as Niles got off of his motorcycle and quickly hobbled up the steps towards Edith, Toni, and the teens. "Are you alright, ma' love?"

"Language, mister," she said, embracing him.

Amidst the chaos, Toni's eyes lit up with excitement, especially when she saw her former neighbor to the north kiss squarely on the mouth her former neighbor to the south. She glanced back and saw that the giant mess of tumors and growths was nearly halfway up the water tower with Paulie somewhere inside of it.

But there was no time to acknowledge this, because the skeleton was piecing itself back together, and the ancient ghoulish man covered in sores, slugs, and porcelain white hair was now marching towards them, muttering to himself, "God, I have to do everything myself, I see."

"Oh, I don't think so, old man."

"Yeah, you're fucking done, dude."

Dr. C. Everett Koop, turned back towards the first condo, and saw a young Hispanic man and a teenager with a vibrant red mullet glaring at him. The Hispanic man was holding a spatula like a baseball bat, and the kid sporting the mullet was holding what looked like a slab of ribs.

"What do you fools expect to accomplish?" Dr. Koop said, walking towards the boys. "You are mere mortals."

"Yeah, and you're dead meat, so get fucked, why don't yo-" The old man cutting short Juan's badass little speech by swiftly closing off his throat with his hand. Somehow, the one hundred-thirteen-year-old man was lifting the eighteen-year-old teen with one hand off the ground.

Just as Mullet swung the slab of ribs at the ancient ghoul, the ghoul slapped the meat away, and grabbed Mullet by the scruff of his neck.

"You do not know my strength. You do not know my rage. You will not stand between me and progress."

Juan was able to pull some of the fingers around his throat enough to yell towards the balcony. "Yeah, and you don't know shit about zoomers, old man. Billy, Brian, camera's out!"

"Already on it, boss!" said Brian, "Already uploading, Juan!" said Billy.

The old man with cataract-addled eyes turned and saw the two teenagers aiming their phones at him like pistols drawn. "What are you doing?"

"Justifying self-defense, you scary motherfucker."

But it wasn't Juan who said that, nor Mullet. It was Niles, who was now swinging a baseball bat at the surgeon general's head.

Only, it wasn't a baseball bat at all. It was his Saturday leg.

And unlike Juan and his spatula, or Mullet and his prime rib, the leg connected with Koop's skull. It didn't kill him, no, but it did weaken his grip on the two boys, who now pinned the dazed old man to the ground.

Dr. C. Everett Koop lay on the ground, bleeding from his head, staring up at the mass as it perched atop the water tower, enveloping it. He heard voices talking to him, asking him a question, "Did you ever have any older brother's, you miserable old fuck?"

Faintly, weakly, the ghoul responded, "No. I was an only child."

"Well, this is what it's like to have an older brother," Juan said, as he wet his finger, and stuck it into the defenseless old man's ear.

Disgusting.

* * *

"Paulie, do not be afraid. This poor animal, it is afraid. We need to sooth it. We need to set it free from its pain," he heard his voice say, only not his voice.

"But how?" asked himself, to himself.

"Just talk to it, Paulie."

"I don't know what to say."

"You'll know."

Paulie considered this while the hiccupping grew louder all around him.

"What is your name?"

"They called me Dolly once. He calls me Pea Tree Mass. We call me Us."

"What are you?"

"We are..." followed by the shrill chaotic scream of a thousand different animals. Bird songs, neighs, crows, barks, meows, baa-ing, shrieking, all at once. "We are copies of copies of copies. We are their cancer."

"You are animals?"

"We are, yes."

Paulie, in the middle of this pink squishy prison, surrounded by a million masses surrounding him, thought he understood. Past the blob, he could see that he was way up high, atop the water tower again. He could hear the pulsating hiccups echoing past him, outside of this place.

He chose his words carefully and spoke mentally to the mass around him.

"Everything is changing, Dolly. This world is changing. I am changing. And I am so terrified of change. I am so afraid of things becoming different than they were."

The beast shrieked inside of itself, but still it could be heard throughout all of Midland. But Paulie continued, speaking through the chunk of meat stuck in his throat.

"But I realize now I can't sit here and hope for how things

343

were to stay that way. I can't just remain complacent and bored, but content. I need to break free of my comfort zone.

"It doesn't work that way, just staying stuck in my routine. It's unsustainable. We have to move forward. Realizing this doesn't make accepting it any easier, it doesn't make it any less scary.

"I want to try new foods and not care if I might be allergic. I want to eat different kinds of fish even though I hate fish in general. I want to drive a car, damn it. I want to buy a laptop. I want to buy a cell phone. I want to watch television, and maybe get a VCR or cable. I want to start living my life, and I want to change the world, Goddamn it!

"What about you, Dolly? What do you want?"

"I want to change. I want to be free."

"Then be free."

From inside the undulating fleshy prison, Paulie could make out a shape emerging towards him. A darker pink shadow inside the pink darkness grew larger until he could understand that it was right in front of him now.

The curtain of muscle and tendons parted ways, revealing a skull. Not a human skull. But something else. Its long snout reminded him of a dog skull, but the teeth seemed human.

"You're Dolly. You are the sheep. The first clone."

"We are copies of copies of copies."

"Then Parlay is-"

"You are copies of copies of copies."

Paulie reached towards the sheep skull that was surrounded by a million tiny tumors, a billion tiny growths, a trillion little cancer cells all welded together by meat.

"We can change, Dolly. This whole world, we can change it. But you've just got to be free. Sing with me, Dolly."

From atop the water tower, the three of them began their hiccup song. Paulie, Parlay and Dolly, hiccupping in unison, together. No more did the Pea Tree Mass shriek. Instead, it began to liquefy into its billion little pieces, separating from itself. Like a ball of ants falling to the ground, Dolly hugged the tower that sang its song, falling into itself.

Not dead, no, no. Just no longer in pain. Slowly the meat fell away from Paulie, the animal cancers and tumors, until Paulie could see the gray skies once again. Behind him, he could still hear the hiccupping sounds coming from the radio receiver, being broadcast outward, and all around him were the millions of tiny masses, crawling about aimlessly.

The breeze reminded him that he was a hundred and fifty feet up, but when he looked around he did not feel fear. Instead, he felt a surge of confidence. He saw the distant pillar of smoke, from his old job, was still rising though not as black. And he saw as well that there were flashing blue and red lights heading towards this area. A giant rolling ball of tumors had just crawled up this tower where he now stood, so he was sure there would be a lot of questions.

Paulie could hear Parlay whispering into his throat, "Good job, Paulie."

But once again, it was another person's scream that had his attention.

It was his ex-wife from down below screaming.

* * *

From way up here, Paulie could still see with crystal clarity what was happening below. The skeleton formerly known as Arnold Workman was standing behind Toni Galamb with his back to the door. It almost looked like the skeleton was trying to give her a neck or shoulder massage.

But even from here, Paulie could see he was not massaging her neck.

345

He was pressing his bony fingers into her throat, like daggers.

And he was facing Paulie.

"Paulie!" the skeleton screamed, "You get down here right now, or I'll poke ten holes in this lady's throat and squeeze the blood out! You get down here and you turn that damn thing off, or I'll rip this bitch's head off."

Adrenaline and red overtook his vision. Anger fueled him. "Parlay, will I survive?"

"Oh yes, I'll make sure of it."

And before Parlay could finish, Paulie had already climbed over the railing of the water tower and tumbled over. There was no fear, there was no hesitation, there was only velocity and wind. There was only gravity and rage. Down and down he went, the world growing larger and larger with each second passing. The bits of Dolly and Parlay fell with him, not slowing him, but guiding him. His tumble was not perfect, but still he saw himself falling towards the roof of the middle condominium, his own.

No parachute as he fell through the air, but somehow, he knew he didn't need it.

A millisecond before impact, Parlay stretched itself all around Paulie, as Paulie and Parlay fell through the roof, and into the living room of his apartment.

The rage, the adrenaline, the anger, it demanded that he got up. It carried him to the front door, it pushed him through it. Now, he was face to face with the skeleton of the man he called his boss, while the skeleton's boss lay on the ground under the weight of two teens and his neighbor.

His face had shown his rage clearly. In this gray light, his face looked red with anger, but it was a different shade. It was the shade of a newborn released from its mother.

"Arnold, you let her go right now."

"Oh yeah, what are you going to do about it, Paulie-boy?"

"If you don't let her go, I'm going to break every bone in your, er, I'm going to break all of your bones. One by one."

Was the skeleton grinning? Paulie did not know. The skeleton pressed his fingers deeper into Toni's neck, causing a thin stream of blood to leak out under her chin.

And that was enough for the ugly man. He threw himself at his ex-wife and his boss, tackling the skeleton. Instantly, he tore away the arms from her throat, ripping the ligaments and gore free from the skeletal joints. The skeleton screamed as Paulie used its own arms as dual bludgeons, beating it.

But he did not stop there.

He beat the ribs and chest of the skeleton with the arms until the clavicle snapped, until the ribs broke into pieces. He bashed through until the bones in his hands splintered into dust. Then he used his own bare hands as weapons, punching through the spinal column, until it too broke into tiny pieces. He didn't stop punching the skeleton until his own hands were bloody.

"Do you feel better, Paulie Galamb?" asked the skeleton, before Paulie turned his attention on the skull itself.

"No," he lied. Paulie lied because he had changed. Paulie lied because he did feel better. Paulie lied because he could. But he didn't stop. "Arnold, I quit."

He didn't stop until every tooth was broken, until the bottom jaw was smashed into multiple pieces. Until the skull was cracked in places any normal man would die from. But this broken skeleton was not a normal man. He was middle management.

Only did Paulie stop when he heard Toni speak.

"Paulie, the police," was all she said.

It was then the nearly three-hundred-pound man sitting on the pile of bones noticed that behind him he had gathered a crowd. No longer were Edith and the twins, Toni and Stocks, Juan, Mullet, Niles, and the ghoulish old man the only audience.

Because just beyond the black sedan now stood several police officers with their guns drawn, staring back at the confusing chaos before them. A dozen or so men and women in black uniforms, surrounded by the flashing lights of their police cruisers, looked upon the three residents of We-Store Storage Units dumbfounded. Ahead of the uniformed men and women was one handsome man in his own rent-a-cop uniform.

It was Fuckin' Kyle, who had called the police on these two trespassers, standing there, smiling, but also just as equally confused about everything he was seeing ahead of him.

* * *

For the first time in Detective Carson's career, he found himself reading the Miranda rights to an armless skeleton. The skeleton nodded, and somehow mumbled out his name through broken teeth when asked. Also, for another first in his career, the detective read the rights to a man he thought had died seven or eight years earlier.

He did this while other officers took statements from the same rambunctious teenagers he had ticketed for shoplifting several times in the past. But their past crimes were of no import here. Their stories were all the same. This old man attacked the kids, after ordering the skeleton to attack the women. And they had it all on camera. Nathaniel Niles had just chased the car into the lot upon seeing the driver crash through the front gate. So he was the one who saved the boys.

But what Detective Carson wasn't sure of, were his own eyes. Because he was pretty sure he just watched a large man jump off of a water tower, crash into his own roof, and then continue to beat up a living fleshless skeleton.

To that, the cop shook the thought away. This wasn't the weirdest thing he'd ever seen. Just the weirdest thing this week. He continued to take statements from everyone, from the nice elderly lady who offered him lemonade, from the gruff old biker who claimed to have used his own leg as a baseball bat, from the five teens that probably should have been in school but claimed they were homeschooled. From the man who fell from the tower. And from the talking growth on his shoulder.

Eventually, the detective would be satisfied with the statements, and take the two perps to jail. For trespassing, for destruction of property, for assaulting a minor, for assaulting an elderly woman. The skeleton was even hit with an extra charge, of assault with a deadly weapon, even though the deadly weapon were his hands used as daggers. He wasn't sure how this one would pan out in court, but that wasn't his job.

The police left after a while, allowing the group to go back to their barbeque, sans one prime rib that Mullet had regrettably used as a club, but they were fine with that.

They were all fine to just be free of the excitement.

Toni grabbed Paulie by the hand and thanked him, but then she excused herself. "I should probably be going, Paulie."

"I know."

"About last night-"

"I know, Toni, I know. It was a pleasant surprise, but it won't happen again. I understand."

"What are you going to do next?"

"Well, I'm out of a job now, so I've got to figure out some source of money if I want to keep this roof over my head. Of which I'm going to have to get someone out here to fix, come to think of it."

"I can help with the roof costs. You did just save my life."

Edith and Niles walked up to them, "And technically ours as well."

Paulie gave his two neighbors a confused look. They were holding hands. "I didn't save your life. From what the teens told me, you apparently saved the boys' lives."

"Nah, bucko, I'm talking about the cancer. See?" Niles said, lifting his shirt. The large pink flap that he had on him yesterday was gone. And when he looked at Edith, near her eyes, the tiny growth were no longer there. Just past them, the water tower was completely covered in the masses, huddling around the tower like a swarm of bees around the queen. "It's gone. That's got to be some kind of world record, am I right? I find out I've got cancer, and have it completely beaten in under two days."

Paulie considered his neighbors' statement, as gruff and terse as it may be. I mean, technically Paulie also dealt with his cancer with a quickness. Even though his cancer was different, and still perched on his shoulder.

"My point is, Paulie, we're thinking about hitting the road and seeing more of this country. I've been in Midland too long. And Edith here wants to show me California. Ain't ever been, myself. But I was thinking about trying to sell my record collection and offer you the funds to, I don't know, maybe keep an eye on this place for us."

"And Paulie, dear, I've got a few fairly valuable paintings I have a buyer for. I would only ask that you also keep this place safe."

Stocks walked up with his head hung low, "And to be honest, I've got a few hundred thousand dollars I could donate."

"What? Why? How?"

"I figure this place is going to be important, right? Not just this place, this tower, but you, Parlay. It ain't no skin off my back, and really it's all funny money anyways. Just money I made scamming the stock market with meme stocks."

The man looked down at the boy and considered this.

Parlay chimed in, "Paulie, we should buy this lot. We should accept the generosity of strangers, of neighbors, and acquire this whole facility."

Paulie smiled, to the teens, to his neighbors the lovers, to his ex-lover, and to the growth on his shoulder. Today, they would eat meat, grown off the likes of real live animals. They would rejoice, relax, and have an overall decent day with all the mornings chaos now behind them.

"I think tomorrow, maybe, we should have a yard sale," Paulie said to his friends all around him. And you know what? They would do exactly that.

That was how the spent their Sunday, and then their week was done.

49

THE TALKING HEADS

And What They Said

"Tesla stocks are down for the third day in a row following the mysterious disappearance of former CEO-"

"We're with Nathaniel Niles at Antiques Roadshow, who has come here with two incredibly rare finds. Now, Niles, how much do you think this throw rug is worth? Take a guess."

"The explosion in downtown Midland is now being classi-fied as a terrorist attack, though no casualties have been reported at the time of this broadcast-"

"In the art world, we're now getting reports that several thought-to-be-lost paintings of Andy Warhol have recently been sold to the Metropolitan by a collector who wishes to remain anonymous."

"NBC will be using former contestants as guest hosts for the 40th season of Jeopardy previously hosted by the dearly beloved Alex Trebek. The contestants being considered are Anton Beres, Klaus Piper, and Afro Cash."

"No word yet from the department head of communications as to what motive the prime suspect may have had."

"And this jukebox, Mr. Niles, just take a guess at how extremely rare this is. I dare you."

"He was just one of the guys. I mean, yeah, he was a little unusual, but never did we expect him to do something like this. It just doesn't make sense to me! Chris was nothing but heart! He must have had a reason, I'm sure of it. And I suspect it had something to do with how they laid him off at that Pea Tree place!"

"Reports are still coming in that a massive entity of unknown origin has fled the disaster area and retreated to-"

"Speculation that the Pea Tree Mass may have stemmed from Dolly, the famous Finnish Dorset Sheep, who as you may recall was the first mammal cloned-"

"In her new autobiography, she candidly speaks on her love affair with America's favorite talk-show host Alek Trebek, her time spent at the Factory with the infamous pop-artist Andy Warhol, and finding love again at seven-"

"Dr. C. Everett Koop, the former Surgeon General of the United States, believed to have passed away in 2013, has stepped forward to discuss why he had faked his own death nine years amid the controversial viral video where he was seen attacking two young-"

"All over the county, oncologists are seeing a massive decrease in active cancer cases. One doctor is saying the data is nothing less than miraculous-"

"In a bizarre historical first, the reanimated skeleton of Arnold Workman, is being tried for murd-"

"We're here with Nancy Cullen, who was in hospice care last week and told she only had days left to live. Now, at 87 years old, doctors are saying all traces of her Stage Four-"

"A class-action law suit has been launched against the

former Pea Tree Farms. The company was famous for the Pea Tree Cruelty Free Nuggets released last year. Now it is theorized that the former lab-meat meat giant was using cloned human embryos in their products-"

"New charges are being brought up against the former Surgeon General-"

"Good evening America, I'm host and anchor, Tom Hedasky and this is KTVG News-"

"In one week, almost all cases of cancer have dropped between ten and thirty percent. These numbers, as far as we can tell, they will continue to drop. We now have live footage of what the locals are calling 'Ground Zero' in the war against cancer as we know it. Some are calling this place a sanctuary. Others, are calling it a nuisance."

"You're telling me that I have to drive by this dang tower and just ignore it. Just let my kids see this giant tower full of gross, infectious disease, and be okay with it? Not a chance in hell. Something should be done about that We-Store Storage Unit!"

"-A man known only as Pali Galamb seems to be at the center of it all-"

"-Paulie Galamb, age forty-seven, appears to be the ringleader of the movement-"

"-Scientists and doctors from all over the country are among the thousands of protestors who have showed up outside of the We-Store Sanctuary Site, as it's now being called by the supports of-"

"We're here for the first time with Mr. Galamb, who is doing his first public interview since the Pea Tree Bombings shook our precious Midland-"

"-No, I'm not saying that radiation is now safe, do not mix my words. What I'm saying is the radiation levels here in this room should be promoting carcinogenesis, or the formation of cancer, but as you can you-"

"In local news, Dr. C. Everett Koop has lost the libel case against Galamb-"

"We have with us Dr. Joseph Fejes here today to explain the symbiotic relationship between-"

"It's not just your pets, people! By our estimates, it's all wildlife as well. We do not and cannot know what this is going to do for the environment. He's screwing with the natural order of-"

"Sole ownership of We-Store Sanctuary Site has been awarded to Paulie Galamb and the organization known as the Parlay Cancer Studies-"

"Doomsday preppers are warning of a 'pink goo' apocalypse scenario-"

"Are the growths fashionable? We talk with leading fashion expert about how to accessorize the masses that are helping save humanity from the disease that once plagued our race-"

"Experts now expect cancer, in all forms, to be fully eradicated by the end of the year. What does that mean for humanity and the animal kingdom, as we move forward together-"

The bartender, sick of flipping through the news, turned off the television, and announced to the last two patrons, "Wrap it up, guys, its closing time."

50

IT STARTS IN A FIELD OF MEAT

And Ends In A Dive Bar

"Eventually, there'd be a lull in humanity albeit a brief one.

Over the course of a dozen years, the water tower became unrecognizable and was all but a spire of meat and flesh. The millions of tiny growths became billions, forming one giant monolith of cancer, undulating on itself, pulsating, every little bit of tissue and tumor climbing over the next one, trying to reach the very top of the tower.

Wars would come to a screeching halt, for a while, and without the concerns brought upon by the great slow death, people would focus on healing the world, and bettering society. Interest in the arts, science and the world exploded exponentially, especially with the full automation of all work. No longer did the humans fear death or the gradual decay brought upon by the nine-to-five. It would have invariably been the second Renaissance of mankind.

And eventually, humanity as a whole, for some reason unbeknownst to me, would stop dreaming entirely.

The tower of flesh in the large single growth formerly known as Midland, it minded itself. It just reached for the stars.

Peace was a mere pause in humanity's ultimate roadmap to destruction. There would always be conflict in the human race, and even when it seemed like the opportunity for a future was possible, still the bombs would fall. Fortunately, the nuclear radiation and general fallout no longer killed slowly and cruelly. Instead, blast lung, hypoxia, fatal burns, starvation, and suffocation wound up killing the species.

And almost the planet itself, sadly, but as a great man once said, "Life always finds a way."

A few thousand years after humanity finally wiped itself off the playing field, a small coastal species of land-squid would develop a symbiotic relationship with a race of hyper-intelligent capybaras. The resilient capybaras and psychic cephalopods would become the dominant peoples of the planet, raising their own societies from the ash of our fallen cities.

They'll grow, they'll love, they'll war. Maybe someday their own scientists will dig up the remains of the once revered Homo sapiens. Or maybe they'll destroy themselves before they ever got that far.

Weather and time would all but erase any evidence of man, every statue, every building, all seven wonders of the ancient world as equally destroyed as all traces of the modern. All but the final living Monument.

Somewhere inland, deep in the uninhabited lands of the now unnamed forgotten continent, there still grows a tower made of meat, and for all new life comes with new death, and that death will forever grow on the living. Inside that tower, there lives a man and his growth, ageless and immortal, content, complacent. Together, they sing their song and summon all the tiny cancers of the world to themselves, reaching for the stars for no reason other than it seemed like the right thing to do. It is what humanity would have done, had it lived long enough.

The once green grass surrounding the area formerly known as Midland had long ago been charred black by the bombs of men. Now, instead a pink film of a million-billion little growths cover the scorched earth, as they too migrate towards the tower, towards the top, towards the heavens."

The meteorologist interrupted the dentist, "Yeah, yeah, but whatever happened to Paulie?"

"Excuse me?" asked the dentist.

"I mean, yeah, I get it. He ushered in a new short-lived period of peace, and even that wasn't enough to save humanity. I know, I get it. Humanity was always doomed. But what happened to Paulie?"

"I just told you-"

"No, you told me about one bad week he had. Or good week, depending on how you see it, but one week all the same. He didn't grow as a person, did he? I mean, hell, it seems like Parlay had more growth, no pun intended-"

"You absolutely intended that."

"-than Paulie. I mean, I feel like we got to know more about the teenagers, or about Niles and Edith, or even about Fuckin' Kyle over here than we really got to know Paulie."

"Well, you know why that is, don't ya?"

"No, not really."

"Because their story is finished. But Paulie, his story is far from finished. Niles and Edith, Doctor Koop and Arnold, Toni Galamb, the teenagers and all the other extra's, they've grown, they've come and gone. Their story is over. Finished. Finito."

"And Paulie, then?"

"Well, Paulie would see them off. In a field of meat, looking back at the Midland water tower. They would leave Midland once and for all, leaving Paulie and Parlay to their sanctuary.

One day, a few years into the tranquil times, or maybe it was a few years after the bombs fell, I don't recall, Parlay would crawl up to Paulie while Paulie slept.

And it would whisper into Paulie's ear, "Paulie, are you awake?"

"I am."

"Paulie, I'm pregnant," the growth would say. And the man, he would turn to his growth and smile, and he'd respond with, "I know."

But that, Hedasky, is another story for another time."

The meteorologist slammed back the last of his beer and tapped the empty glass on the bar top twice, before pushing it forward for the bartender to retrieve. "And you can tell all that just by looking at a man's teeth?

"That's right," said the dentist as he finished his beer, tapped the glass, and pushed it forward, ending his yarn, ending this story.

For now.

ACKNOWLEDGMENTS

This story started off as a silly little ember of an idea, burning a hole in a notebook but never catching enough air to go full inferno. I nurtured this idea during a global pandemic while writing my previous novel "Mother's Secret Stomach" and kept it close to my chest so it wouldn't be snuffed out by the violent political winds of those times. The only reason I wrote this was because I had the support of those closest to me, who dared me to write another book immediately after finishing the last one. It is thanks to these friends and family that I was able to finish this absurd story about a talking tumor. I want to thank Miika Hannila for giving this strange little novel a chance by publishing it, and I want to thank the editors at Next Chapter for fixing all my silly grammatical whoopsie-daisies. You've got a great eye, Fading Street, and I appreciate it.

I want to acknowledge my little network of friends who've praised my writing enough to convince me to not quit quite yet, or at the very least were there for me when I needed a friend. During a country-wide shut down, sometimes friends is all we got. Kemic, Jason, Matthew, Jacob, Tim, Jesse, Lisa, Lucas, Margot, Johnny, Wendy, Jim, Wade, Scott, Dustin, Goblin and Angry Dan, I appreciate you all and I'm glad you've got to see me grow on a petri dish into whatever I've become. A big thanks to Sigma and Danger Slater for reading an early copy of this novel and for telling me to not give up. I'd also like to thank Brian Asman, Jeff Burk, Rose O'Keefe, Garrett Cook, Max

Booth III, and Matthew Clarke for inspiring me to write this after I crashed a bizarro book reading back in 2021. Go read their books after you've finished the last few pages of this one. You'll probably like them better!

I know it's been fifteen years since high school, but I will always attribute my love for writing to the teacher who challenged me to take it a tad more serious, without calling the school shrink on me, back when my stories were ultra-violent and worry-worthy, Audrey Nagel-Schoonmaker. I cannot express enough how much you've influenced my writing career. Lookie, lookie! I did it!

I want to thank Anton, Klaus, Afro, Yuri, Dick, and every other person who was living at or visiting Anomalia at the time of our trip to Lisbon, Portugal. Thank you for cheering me on with 5,300 miles between us and thank you for reading my novels by candlelight. I'll be sure to start on the next one as soon as I can for the lot of you.

Oh, and of course, I must acknowledge you, Jeliza Rose, and our cat Sylvie, because I love you and our hilarious life together. I couldn't have done this without your constant support and love, nor would I want to.

Finally, I want to thank 'YOU' for reading this silly story. It really means the world to me, more than you can ever know. I hope you enjoyed it. If you did enjoy this, it will please you to know that this is only the first story in this particular Midland. If you didn't enjoy it, well, I'm sorry and I will try harder if you just give me one more chance.

Paulie and Parlay will return either way.

ABOUT THE AUTHOR

 Shawn Wayne Langhans is a Midwestern author of slipstream, new weird, and dark fiction currently residing in the Pacific Northwest, where he lives with his wonderful fiancé Jeliza Rose and their stinky cat, Sylvie. His previous novels are "Mother's Secret Stomach", "Interviews with the Temporally Displaced", and "Beyond the Howls of Mountain Dogs"

* * *

To learn more about Shawn Wayne Langhans and discover more Next Chapter authors, visit our website at www.nextchapter.pub.

Newborn Pink
ISBN: 978-4-82414-467-6

Published by
Next Chapter
2-5-6 SANNO
SANNO BRIDGE
143-0023 Ota-Ku, Tokyo
+818035793528

26th July 2022